SHARPE'S STORM

Für Dr. Hanno Hock und Dr. Miriam Hock,
ihr habt die 'goldenen Beeren' gefunden,
die meiner Frau Judy das Leben gerettet haben.
Wir werden euch für immer dankbar sein!

SHARPE'S STORM

Bernard Cornwell was born in London, raised in Essex and worked for the BBC for eleven years before meeting Judy, his American wife. Denied an American work permit, he wrote a novel instead and has been writing ever since. He and Judy divide their time between Cape Cod and Charleston, South Carolina.

www.bernardcornwell.net
 /bernardcornwell

SHARPE'S STORM

Richard Sharpe and the Invasion of Southern France, 1813

BERNARD CORNWELL

HarperCollins*Publishers*

HarperCollins*Publishers* Ltd
1 London Bridge Street,
London SE1 9GF

www.harpercollins.co.uk

HarperCollins*Publishers*
Macken House,
39/40 Mayor Street Upper,
Dublin 1, D01 C9W8
Ireland

First published by HarperCollins*Publishers* Ltd 2025
1

A catalogue record for this book is available from the British Library.

HB ISBN: 978-0-00-849682-1
TPB ISBN: 978-0-00-849683-8

This novel is entirely a work of fiction.
The names, characters and incidents portrayed in it are
the work of the author's imagination. Any resemblance to
actual persons, living or dead, events or localities is
entirely coincidental.

Typeset in Minion Pro by Palimpsest Book Production Ltd, Falkirk, Stirlingshire

Printed and Bound in the UK using 100% Renewable Electricity
at CPI Group (UK) Ltd

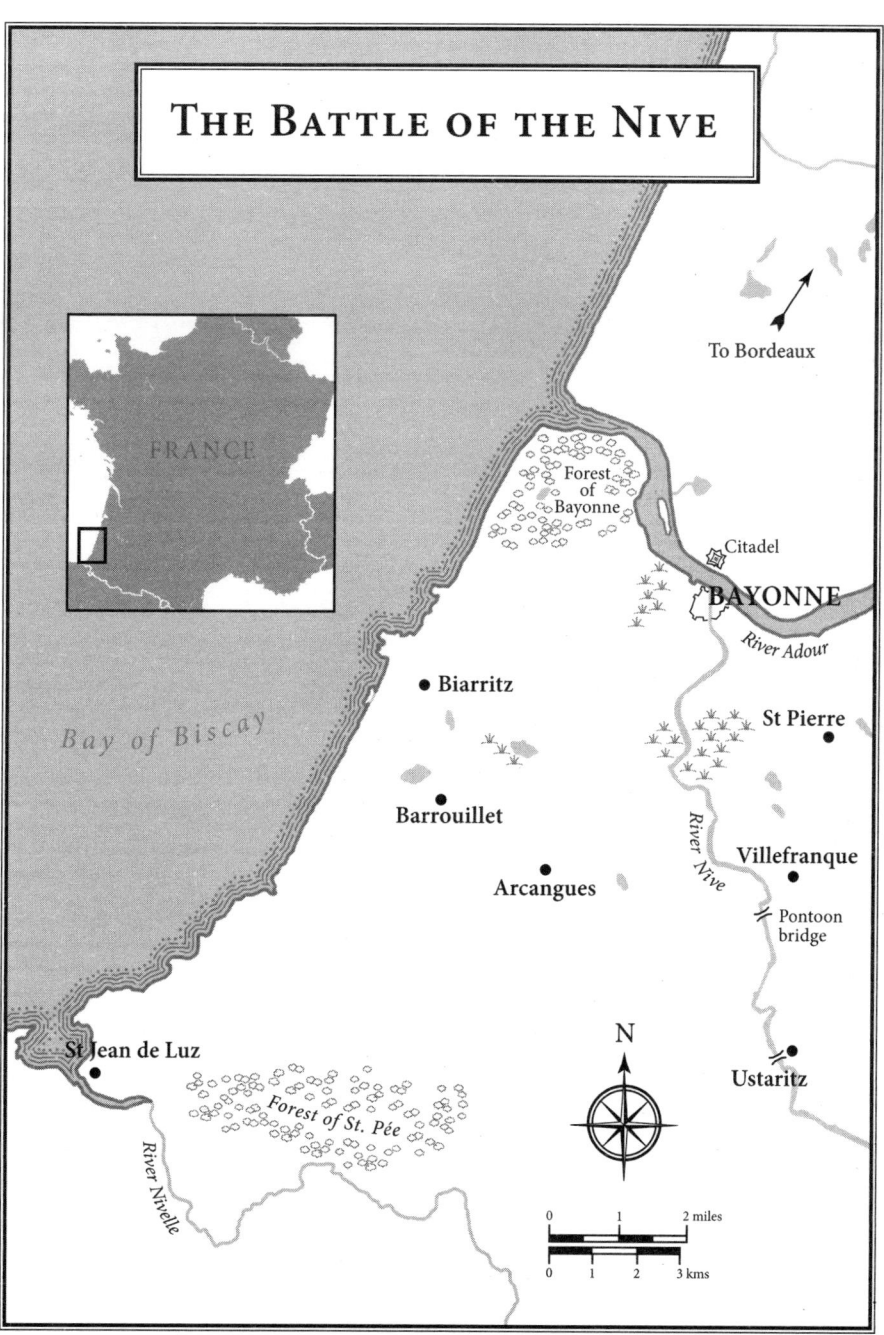

THE BATTLE OF THE NIVE

FRANCE

To Bordeaux

Forest
of
Bayonne

Citadel

BAYONNE

River Adour

Bay of Biscay

Biarritz

St Pierre

Barrouillet

River Nive

Villefranque

Arcangues

Pontoon
bridge

N

St Jean de Luz

Forest of St. Pée

Ustaritz

River Nivelle

0   1   2 miles

0   1   2   3 kms

CHAPTER ONE

Major General Edward Barnes stamped his feet irritably. 'New boots,' he explained, 'made for me in London, but they're too tight. Hurt like buggery.' He looked enviously at Sharpe's cavalry boots. 'Where do you have yours made, Sharpe?'

'France, sir,' Sharpe said, 'and delivered to me by a *cuirassier*.'

'And the overalls too, I see.'

'Those as well, sir.' The seat and inner faces of the cavalry overalls were reinforced with leather, while the cloth had been stained with blood and muck. He had taken them from an Imperial Guard Colonel, and both boots and breeches had served him well.

'You'd better kill me a *cuirassier*, Sharpe,' Barnes said.

'A pleasure, sir.' Sharpe did not take his eye from his telescope that was trained across a river at the countryside beyond. Behind him General Barnes and a pair of his aides were arguing about the river.

'It's the Nivelle, surely,' one of the aides remarked.

'It could be the bloody Mississippi, for all I care,' Barnes snarled, 'we still have to cross the bloody thing.'

The aide folded the map he had been consulting and pushed it into a saddlebag. 'I'm sure it's the Nivelle, sir.'

Barnes, normally a good-tempered man, grunted. Like the men under his command he was tired of the cold and of the endless rain. 'You see them, Sharpe?' he demanded.

'Yes, sir.'

'Train the glass east and say if you see any more of the scoundrels.'

Barnes, his two aides and Sharpe were on a hillside south of the river. The French were north of the river. Sharpe was certain that the enemy had spotted the small group of British officers watching them through telescopes, but that was none of his business. If Barnes wanted to be seen, then seen he would be. Sharpe obediently swung the glass east, seeing small wintry fields and, a half mile from the village, a big stretch of thickly wooded country. The trees were mostly leafless, but the wood was so dense that he could see nothing through the dark tangle of trunks and branches. 'Can't see any more, sir.'

'We've been watching for two days,' Barnes said, 'and we reckon the scoundrels have picquets in that big wood. We see the relief men march out two or three times a day. As far as we know there's nothing beyond that big wood, which means this village is the left flank of the river defences.'

Sharpe edged the telescope back to the village where he could see blue uniforms. It looked to him as though a battalion of French infantry was in the village, while on its southern edge, facing the river, he could see four of the powerful twelve-pounder cannons pointing south from the gaps of a makeshift emplacement made of earth-filled wicker gabions. 'Those cannon are covering a ford that leads to the village,' Barnes said, seeing where Sharpe's telescope was trained, 'they're hoping we'll cross it into their canister fire.'

Sharpe grunted, reckoning that Barnes intended the South Essex to be the battalion that would lead that crossing. Through the glass he could see the French gunners lounging near their cannons, and could even see a priming tube jutting from the vent of one of the guns that was obviously loaded and ready to fire. He edged the telescope left and saw that each of the guns had a priming tube. 'Unpleasant prospect, sir,' he said, lowering the telescope.

'Suicide!' Barnes said cheerfully, 'but not for your lads, Sharpe.'

Sharpe hid his relief. 'A few Riflemen up here could make life very unpleasant for those gunners, sir.'

'A thought which had already occurred to me,' Barnes said, 'but it won't be your Riflemen, Sharpe. Look east, see how the river bends?'

'Yes, sir.' About a mile to the east, the river's course made a sharp turn. It had been flowing north from the foothills of the Pyrenees and the bend let the river run west towards the distant sea.

'Just south of that bend, Sharpe,' Barnes went on, 'there's another ford. I want your lads to cross it at dawn tomorrow, then evict the picquets from the wood.'

'Yes, sir,' Sharpe said with neither enthusiasm nor reluctance. He raised the telescope again and trained it on the edge of the village that faced the thick woods. He saw small vegetable plots, dung heaps, a scatter of sheds, but no emplaced cannon. 'The French must know of the other ford, sir?'

'They damn well should, it's their bloody country. But we've seen no evidence of a picquet there. And they might consider it impassible. The recent rains have raised the water level. It'll be a damned uncomfortable crossing, I'm afraid.'

'You've seen the picquets being relieved, sir, how many are they?'

'John?' Barnes turned to one of his aides.

'Best part of a battalion, sir.'

'Why are they there, sir?' Sharpe asked.

'The bloody French aren't complete fools, Sharpe,' Barnes answered, 'they know there's a Spanish corps to our east and are guarding against an attack from that direction. They're not idiots, so there must be a picquet on that road, but we haven't spotted it.' A road left the village and ran due east, skirting the northern edge of the woods before snaking off into low hills.

The road led east, and the thick belt of woods had an eastern edge which Barnes seemed certain was guarded by enemy outposts looking east, which was the direction from which Sharpe was expected to evict the enemy outposts from the wood. He said nothing of that. 'So we're a diversionary attack, sir?' he asked instead.

'You are!' Barnes said with false cheerfulness. 'So you cross a deep river, Sharpe, get your men organised and turf hundreds of the rascals out of those woods.'

Sharpe nodded, but his mind was concentrating on the four formidable French twelve-pounders that guarded the river.

4

A French battery was six guns, so where were the other two? He suspected they were placed between the village's houses and pointing towards the east, the direction from which a Spanish assault might come. That meant that the French had two defence lines, one barring the river and the other at right angles to face an attack from the east, and Sharpe, once across the ford, would be to the east of the village which could well be guarded by a pair of the enemy's formidable twelve-pounder cannon.

'Sharpe?' Barnes interrupted Sharpe's thoughts.

'You want us to clear the woods, sir, and when we've done that, sir?' Sharpe asked.

'That's the spirit! You notice,' he had turned to his aides, 'that Major Sharpe doesn't say "if we do that", but "when"!'

Neither of the aides responded, but just looked at Sharpe. They saw a tall man with black unkempt hair and scars slashing across his grim, sunburned face. He wore the French overalls and boots and a Rifleman's green jacket that was scorched in places, deep-stained with blood and much patched. A heavy cavalry sword in a metal scabbard hung from slings suspended from his belt and on his right shoulder hung a Baker rifle. The sword and a faded red sash tied at his waist were the only items that marked him as an officer, while the rifle was the mark of a common soldier, but few soldiers, common or otherwise, wore the oak-leaf badge on his right sleeve which denoted that he had led and lived through an assault on a fortress breach, and the eagle on his shako's badge commemorated the capture of one of the enemy's prized battle standards. A most formidable-looking man, the aides both thought.

'If I were the enemy's commanding officer,' Barnes said, 'which thank the good Lord I'm not, I'd be most upset that my picquets had been routed and I'd try to reclaim the wood. So I'd attack you! Just hold them off, Sharpe, hold them off. I'll have a battery of howitzers up here and we'll rain holy hell on the bastards if they come for you, and once the 71st have crossed this nearer ford and captured the village you can join us for breakfast.'

'Very good, sir,' Sharpe said, collapsing the telescope. So, if Barnes was right, the French probably had at least two battalions in the sprawling village as well as a battery of twelve-pounders.

'I know what you're thinking, Sharpe,' Barnes said.

'You do, sir?'

'That the northern bank of the river is seething with heathen Frogs and you'll be stuck there while they assemble a demonic host to slaughter you.'

Sharpe nodded. 'That's more or less right, sir.'

'They won't,' Barnes said with blustery confidence, 'the scoundrels are spread along the northern bank from here to the Atlantic. Twenty miles, Sharpe! They know we have to cross the river to advance further into their fetid motherland, but they don't know where we'll cross, so they're spread out! We'll launch separate attacks in strength that will overwhelm the little darlings and panic them. Those scoundrels,' he gestured at the village, 'will call for help and be told there's none available because the nasty British are crossing further up the river and could they please send men west to help defeat them. So they'll call for help and the only answer will be "come

6

and help us!", and by midday tomorrow they'll realise that they're in danger from both east and west and they'll throw in the towel and bugger off northwards.'

'To find another river to defend,' one of the aides said quietly. Since advancing north from Spain the British had crossed the Bidassoa that had been strongly protected by fortified positions on its northern banks, and now they had to cross another river against an emplaced enemy.

'And we'll throw them off the banks of those rivers too,' Barnes said firmly. 'The Peer,' he meant Lord Wellington, 'wants us to capture Bayonne quickly and that's not some piss-poor village like that,' he gestured across the river, 'it's a bloody great fortress city! Then it's north to Bordeaux and Christmas in Paris!' That, Sharpe thought, was unlikely, it was already November and God only knew how many rivers would have to be crossed before the army reached Paris. 'I'd like your lads to be at the ford by nine tonight, Sharpe,' Barnes went on, returning to the more immediate problem. 'I'll send a man who knows the way to guide you, but don't start panicking the scoundrels until dawn. You'll hear four signal guns and that's when you cross the ford and put the fear of God into the heathens.'

'I thought,' a snide voice sounded behind Sharpe, 'that the four guns were my signal to advance.'

'Ah, Sir Nathaniel!' General Barnes did not sound welcoming. 'We have made a slight change to the attack. I was on my way to inform you.'

'So I do not advance at the signal?' the newcomer asked in a tone that suggested General Barnes did not know his own business.

'You wait, Sir Nathaniel, for my message. The guns provoke attacks along the whole river front, but you must wait until Major Sharpe provides a distraction.'

Lieutenant Colonel Sir Nathaniel Peacock, Sharpe knew of him but had not yet met him, gave a grunt that fully expressed his disapproval. 'I doubt my troops need a distraction,' he said pointedly, 'we can overrun that scum,' he gestured across the river, 'in minutes.'

'And you shall,' General Barnes said, 'when the right moment comes.'

'And what do I do if Major Sharpe fails?' Peacock asked.

'Major Sharpe never fails, Sir Nathaniel,' General Barnes said firmly.

Sir Nathaniel looked Sharpe up and down, noting the dirty ragged uniform, the frayed sash, the battered metal scabbard, and the rifle slung on his shoulder. He gave a sniff, evidently unimpressed. 'Your fellows are adequate to the task, Sharpe?'

Sharpe, in turn, and with deliberate disrespect, looked Sir Nathaniel up and down, noting the highly polished shoes, silk stockings and an elegantly tailored red coat with the 71st's yellow facings. Sir Nathaniel was the 71st's new commanding officer, freshly come out from Britain and, if rumour in the brigade was true, a vain, bombastic mountebank. 'My fellows are experts, Sir Nathaniel,' Sharpe said.

'Experts at what?'

'Slaughtering Crapauds,' Sharpe said curtly.

'And so they are,' General Barnes said heartily, evidently eager to end the obvious ill-feeling between Sir Nathaniel and Sharpe. 'You wait for the signal guns, Sharpe, then cross the river, assault the wood and drive their outposts away. Panic them! You're good at that.'

'Yes, sir,' Sharpe said, because what else could he say? He had his orders and would obey them because, at least once in a while, he was good at that too.

Thick clouds obscured the moon and, shortly after a Lieutenant Starkey had come to guide the Prince of Wales's Own Volunteers to the ford, it began to rain. Sharpe had inspected his men in the dusk, making certain that none had a loaded musket. Their approach to the ford was meant to be silent and he dared not risk a man tripping and accidentally discharging his weapon.

The South Essex, it was much easier to think of them by their old name rather than as the Prince of Wales's Own Volunteers, moved in single file, led by the Light Company. The first half mile was easy enough, they followed a hedge line that gradually dropped downhill. Sharpe carried his rifle in his right hand, the muzzle stoppered with a wine cork and the lock protected from the rain by a twist of rag. The wind and rain were bone-chilling cold, but at least they had left the Pyrenees, where, Sharpe had been told, the winter could bring deep snow.

Lieutenant Starkey, a thin young man as tall as Sharpe, suddenly spoke. 'Pause here, sir.'

'Halt and close up,' Sharpe grunted to Harper, who had insisted on keeping Sharpe company, 'and pass the order back. And order a count.'

'It's through thick woodland from here, sir,' Starkey said. 'There is a path and we marked a trail, but too damned easy to get lost.'

'You marked it?' Sharpe asked, wondering how anyone could follow marks in the night's darkness.

'Twine, sir, if I can find it.' Lieutenant Starkey had moved a few feet away and was evidently trampling undergrowth as he groped among the trees. 'We strung it this morning, sir,' he called back softly as he still searched. Sharpe stepped cautiously till he found a tree he could lean on and half shelter from the west wind. Behind him he could hear men muttering and shuffling as the long line settled.

'Found it!' Lieutenant Starkey called. 'Just edge towards me, sir.' He paused, then added, 'It's a bit steep, sir.'

'A bit . . .' Sharpe began, then stopped speaking as his feet shot out from beneath him and he landed on his arse with a thump and slid down a slippery slope. His rifle fell from his shoulder, his sword scabbard clanged against something wooden and he felt his jacket rip as it caught on a branch. He ended on his back amidst thorns. He fumbled for his rifle and used it to help him stand. Once on his feet he swore viciously.

'Sorry, sir,' Starkey said, 'I should have warned you. But easier going from here, sir.'

'And how the hell,' Sharpe said unhappily, 'do I get a battalion down that slope?'

'Sorry, sir,' Starkey said again, 'I should have brought a rope.'

'There was none available,' Sharpe said. He had thought a rope would be useful for crossing the river and had asked some Engineers who had denied having any such thing. 'Sergeant Major?' Sharpe called.

'Sir?' Harper called from above and behind.

10

'Musket slings! I reckon you'll need twenty. Tie them together and then lash one end around a tree where you are and toss the other end to me.'

That all took time, but after Sharpe had tied the loose end of the makeshift line to a tree trunk, the battalion slowly negotiated the treacherous slope and followed Sharpe to the river's edge.

It was daunting. For a start the river was as black as the clouded sky, the only evidence of its existence was the beat of rain on the river's surface and the heavy sound of water flowing, and Sharpe was irresistibly reminded of the River Styx. He had not learned of that river at school, for he had received no schooling, but when he was locked in the Tippoo Sultan's dungeons in Seringapatam, his fellow prisoner, Colonel McCandless, had talked of many things and, in one of his pessimistic moments, McCandless had spoken of the dark river which every dead man had to cross. 'The River Styx, Sharpe,' McCandless had said, 'is the way to hell! The Cauvery is like that!' Yet the army had crossed the Cauvery and captured the city, but there was something baleful about the river which now confronted Sharpe.

'You've crossed it?' he asked Starkey.

'Two times, sir.'

'And?'

'It's deep, sir, but has a firm bed, and it's no more than twenty yards wide. You can't cross now, but General Barnes wants you to try at dawn. It will be easier then.'

Sharpe grunted. 'How deep is it?'

'Came up to my chest, sir. Probably a touch deeper now

after all the rain, but there's a big tree on the other bank and if you head straight for it you'll be safe.'

'Dawn, eh?'

'Much safer then, sir.'

'And you're sure there's no enemy picquet on the other bank?'

'We've never seen one, sir. There are picquets at the river bend, but that's a fair way north.'

Sharpe grunted again. If there were picquets on the far bank they must have heard the commotion of his men clambering down the steep slope behind, but he reckoned he must accept Starkey's assurance that this ford was unguarded. 'The river runs straight from here to the bend?' he asked the Lieutenant.

'Straight as the Thames at Henley, sir,' Starkey said confidently.

'I've never been to Henley,' Sharpe growled.

'It's straight, sir,' Starkey said, chastened.

'So they don't need a picquet here, do they,' Sharpe pointed out, 'because the buggers at the bend can see anyone crossing here.'

'Not in this darkness, sir.'

'And they don't think anyone would be stupid enough to cross in the dark.'

'I'm sure that's true, sir.'

'So it's time for us to be stupid,' Sharpe said.

'But General Barnes . . .' Starkey began.

'General Barnes isn't here,' Sharpe interrupted the Lieutenant, 'and I am. We cross now. In the dark.'

And I wish we had a rope, Sharpe thought, and he briefly

considered making another line out of musket slings, but that would take time and he had no wish to wait till dawn when his men would be visible from the river's bend to the north. 'I'll go first,' he said.

'I'm with you, sir,' Harper muttered.

'Then the Light Company,' Sharpe went on, 'Grenadiers last.' He raised his voice slightly. 'You hold onto the man in front with one hand, and the other hand holds your musket and ammunition up high. You're coming with us, Lieutenant?' he asked Starkey.

'Of course, sir.'

'Then hold onto Pat Harper. He's a big bugger so you'll be safe enough, and hold his rifle out of the river. He'll have his toy gun to worry about.' Sharpe meant that Harper would be holding his volley gun. Sharpe took the ammunition pouch off his belt and, holding the pouch and rifle in his right hand, felt his way to the river's edge. 'Hold onto me, Pat.'

'Let me go first, sir.'

'I'm almost there,' Sharpe said and held onto a low branch with his left hand as he stepped down into the water. 'We go slowly,' he said, letting go of the branch and edging away from the bank.

'Slow and steady, sir,' Harper muttered, then, 'Jesus Christ, the water's cold!'

'Slow and silent,' Sharpe said harshly and stepped out. The water was cold and, worse, the current was powerful. It was only up to his knees and he could hear the river seething about his legs and trying to push him downstream. He took another step and the water came over his high cavalry boots.

The footing was firm enough, but he sensed the current was veering him to his right with every tentative step. 'We'll take five steps forward,' he said to Harper, 'then one to the left.'

'Five and one,' Harper said. He was gripping one of Sharpe's crossbelts while Sharpe held his rifle and pouch above the water.

The River Styx, he thought, death's frontier, then he tried to push that gloomy thought away and quicken his pace. His foot slid on a stone of the river's bed and he almost fell, but Harper's strong grip held him upright. He muttered a curse as the water came to his waist. He could hear his men muttering as they came behind him and he took a pace to the left and pushed on, the water still rising. 'The recruiting Sergeant didn't tell me about this,' Harper said, 'the bastard.'

Five more steps and one to the left and the water was now up to Sharpe's armpits and trying hard to sweep him downstream. It was Harper who was resisting the heavy current. 'It's all nonsense, Sharpe,' he could hear Colonel McCandless's strong Scottish accent in his head, 'we Christians know you cross the Jordan after death, not the Styx, but it's still good manners to put a coin in the grave to pay the ferryman.' And those words, conjured from a dungeon and spoken so many years ago, made Sharpe realise he had not taken an obvious precaution and he fumbled with his left hand in the pouch which held his spare flints and found a coin, which he flipped upstream. It was pure superstition, but he would pay the river for protection, and he hoped that protection would extend to his shortest men because the water was up to his neck.

He pushed on and sensed that the riverbed was rising. 'Not far now,' he muttered.

'Thank the good Lord for that,' Harper responded.

Sharpe's right arm was aching with the strain of holding the rifle above his head, and it was the rifle that first warned him of the ford's end when it tangled with the twigs of a low branch. The river was still above his waist, but another four paces brought him to a steep earthen bank. 'Hoist me up, Pat.'

Sharpe was almost thrown up the bank to sprawl in leaf mould. 'Stay there, Pat, and help the men up. Give me your volley gun.'

'The bugger's loaded, sir.'

'I won't fire it.' Sharpe took the volley gun and felt his way through a short line of trees to a pasture beyond, and it was there that his waterlogged battalion slowly assembled. The Light Company came first and Sharpe took Rifleman Hagman aside. 'You are all right, Dan?'

'Never better, Mister Sharpe,' Hagman answered, 'though I had to jump up and down a bit to keep breathing.'

'The enemy's that way.' Sharpe turned Hagman so he was facing downriver. 'Have a look for them, Dan. Don't let them see you, and for God's sake don't fire a shot unless you have to.'

Hagman was both Sharpe's best marksman and his best scout. Older than most men in the battalion, Hagman had been a poacher in his native Cheshire and had the skills of a countryman. He could move through the night like a ghost, had superb eyesight and common sense, and now he vanished northwards towards the trees that evidently hid the enemy picquets.

'There's a fire up there!' Patrick Harper muttered, sounding surprised.

'Up where?'

'That way, sir.' Harper steered Sharpe by his shoulders, pointing him downriver. 'Not a big fire, but it's there.'

'The bloody fools,' Sharpe said, because he could now see the dim, small glow of a fire burning deep in the far woods. The French picquets, evidently tired of the cold, rainy night, had lit a fire. 'Did all the men cross?' he asked Harper.

'Every one of them, sir. Some idiots fell in.'

'Company commanders to me, Pat, and tell them to be quiet about it.'

It took time in the wet darkness to assemble the officers and give orders, but at last Sharpe was able to array his men in a line with the Light Company furthest east and the Grenadiers at the riverbank. He thought about ordering them to fix bayonets and sword bayonets, but decided to wait. A fixed bayonet made a musket or rifle more awkward to carry through hedges or woodland and, even though the darkness was thick, there was always the small chance of a reflected gleam from metal betraying their presence. It was enough that the battalion's weapons were still without flints and would stay that way until Sharpe reckoned he could unleash his men.

'You are going to wait until dawn, sir?' Lieutenant Starkey was evidently worried that General Barnes's orders would not be followed to the letter.

'Near dawn, anyway,' Sharpe said, 'and the idiots have a fire in those woods.'

'They do?' Starkey sounded surprised.

'Their officers don't like being cold and wet, and I reckon that's the centre of their picquet line. Nice of them to tell me.'

And why, he worried, had the enemy not placed a picquet on the ford where the South Essex had just crossed? They must know of its existence; they were in their own country and the local people would know of the ford. So maybe they did know and this was a trap? Perhaps the far trees did not hide a line of outposts, but a whole battalion? Or maybe they had discounted the ford, reckoning the winter rain had made it too deep to be practicable. Or maybe, Sharpe thought, he should stop worrying about maybes and decide his next step.

Which was the sensible one of letting his men rest, though their waterlogged uniforms, the cold rain and bitter wind hardly allowed for sleep. Sharpe sat with his back to a tree, rifle across his knees, and felt himself sinking into a doze when a voice hissed nearby. 'Mister Sharpe?'

'Dan?'

'It's me, Mister Sharpe.' Hagman, silent as a snake, settled close by.

'What did you find?'

'Picquets, Mister Sharpe, a half-dozen of the buggers on the treeline.'

'Just six men?'

'Six squads of four or five men each, and a score or more near to a fire in the woods.'

'We saw the fire,' Sharpe said. 'Sounds like an understrength company.'

'Half a company,' Hagman suggested, 'with the other half relieving them at dawn?'

'That makes sense, Dan. How close did you get?'

'Near enough to hear them squabbling, Mister Sharpe.' Hagman sounded amused.

'Did you get a chance to reach the end of their line?'

'It stretches from the bend in the river to the road,' Hagman said, 'and there's a fair-sized hedge and a ditch at the road's edge. I didn't cross the road, but I reckon they're only guarding the wood's edge so the end of their picquet line is the road.'

Sharpe hesitated, thinking about what Hagman had said. If Dan was right then the enemy's picquets were lined north and south, presumably to warn of an approach by Spanish troops from the east. 'How certain are you that their picquet line doesn't go beyond the road?'

'Pretty sure, Mister Sharpe. They had an officer visiting the picquets and he stopped at the road, bitched to the lads there, then buggered off back into the woods.'

'You saw that?' Sharpe asked, incredulous.

'The silly bugger was smoking a pipe. I could smell it, see it sometimes, and off he went with it.'

'So no picquets beyond the road?'

'I reckon not, Mister Sharpe. Far as I could see the land north of the road is pasture, so the picquets in the wood can see across it.'

Odd, Sharpe thought. If the French truly feared the Spanish Corps that was advancing to the east then they would surely guard against it? Or perhaps they knew that the Spaniards were a good distance eastwards and thus no threat, which suggested they only feared an assault from the south which, in turn, suggested they knew of the ford and were confident their outposts could detect any attempt to cross it. But the ford was crossed and the enemy was none the wiser.

'So if we can cross the road and go north,' Sharpe spoke softly and slowly as an idea tempted him, 'we could get past their picquet line?'

'I reckon so, Mister Sharpe,' Hagman said.

'Well done, Dan, see if you can find Captain d'Alembord and bring him here.'

Hagman vanished as silently as he had arrived and Sharpe waited. Lieutenant Starkey had listened to Hagman's report and cleared his throat. 'Sir?'

'Lieutenant?'

'You're thinking of outflanking them, sir?'

'Maybe.' Sharpe was unwilling to discuss the idea with Starkey.

'General Barnes . . .' Starkey began.

'. . . wants me to clear the picquets from the wood, I know,' Sharpe growled, 'because he wants the French to think the attack comes from the east, not the south. And what, Lieutenant, is the purpose of that?'

Starkey thought for a moment. 'To capture the village, sir?'

'Exactly.'

'And that's the responsibility of the 71st, sir,' Starkey said firmly.

'Who are going to face a battery of twelve-pounders firing canister at point-blank range.'

'It won't be easy for them, sir,' Starkey allowed.

'And under a new commanding officer who has never experienced action,' Sharpe went on.

'I'm sure Sir Nathaniel will do his duty, sir,' Starkey said reprovingly.

'To die gloriously for his country?' Sharpe asked scathingly. His brief encounter with the 71st's new commanding officer had not impressed Sharpe. Lieutenant Colonel Sir Nathaniel Peacock had struck him as a pompous overbearing Englishman who had been given command of a tough Scottish regiment. He had never fought, his career having been spent in garrison duty, but rumour said he had arrived in France confident that he knew better than anyone how the French could be beaten. 'I'll tell you what Sir Nathaniel will do,' Sharpe went on to Starkey, 'he'll form his men in column of companies and march them straight at the ford by the village, and the Crapauds will open fire with canister and the 71st will die. It will be a massacre. The man's an idiot.'

'Oh, that's not fair, sir!' Starkey remonstrated. 'Maybe he's a little over-confident, but if we succeed, the French will be looking east, not across the river.'

'They could be gazing at the moon, but they can hardly miss a battalion forming up on the river's southern bank, and those twelve-pounders aren't there as decorations.' And the moment the French heard the signal guns which would trigger the British assault, they would realise that trouble loomed the whole length of the river and would double their attention on the southern bank.

'Sir Nathaniel's orders are to wait for your capture of the wood, sir, before crossing, and I'm sure our attack on the wood will keep the French distracted.'

'Distracted?' Sharpe sounded scornful. 'What will distract

them is a battalion assault across the river. Repel that and they'll have plenty of time and men to deal with us.' Footsteps sounded nearby and Sharpe turned towards the sound. 'Is that you, Dally?'

'It is, sir,' Peter d'Alembord answered.

'Dan Hagman's going to lead you through a hedge, across a road, and then through some pasture. It must be done in total silence, and the rest of the battalion will follow.'

'Total silence, sir?'

'If the buggers hear us, we'll fail. No flints, Dally.'

'No flints, sir,' d'Alembord acknowledged. Taking the flints from each musket and rifle's locks would ensure there was no accidental discharge.

'And Dan?'

'Mister Sharpe?'

'Go a ways eastward to stay out of their hearing.'

'I will, Mister Sharpe.'

'How long till dawn, Dan?'

There was a pause as the old poacher looked at the sky. 'Three hours, Mister Sharpe.'

'Long enough,' Sharpe said, hoping he was right.

The rain had become heavier and at least the sound of it would cover the inevitable noise a battalion must make as it trampled through the fields. It took time to give the battalion its orders, but at last the men were lined in the same formation that had crossed the river. Sharpe walked the length of the column, hissing that any man who accidentally discharged a musket would face his wrath, then took his place just behind Rifleman Hagman at the column's head. 'Let's go, Dan.'

Hagman led them away from the river, going eastwards until a thick hedge blocked the way. 'North now, Mister Sharpe,' the old poacher muttered. Sharpe guessed they were now some two or three hundred paces east of the French picquets who would be shivering at the wood's edge. Lieutenant Starkey had stayed with Sharpe, constantly trying to discover exactly what Sharpe planned, until Sharpe abruptly told the young man to be silent. Sharpe followed Hagman, and from behind him he could hear boots swishing in the long wet grass, muttered curses, and the occasional knock of a musket hitting a canteen, sounds that seemed abnormally loud to him, but no challenge shouted across the field and, besides, the wind in the leafless trees of the wood probably drowned the sounds of Sharpe's men. Then Hagman stopped.

'Dan?' Sharpe whispered.

'Another hedge, Mister Sharpe. It's the road.'

And Hagman had already discovered that the French picquets stretched as far north as the road, which made the idea of using the road to approach the village impossible. 'We have to cross the road into fields the other side,' Sharpe whispered to Hagman. 'We'll wait here.'

'I won't be long, Mister Sharpe,' Hagman said encouragingly and disappeared into the wet darkness.

'Sir?' Lieutenant Starkey said unhappily.

'Keep your voice down,' Sharpe retorted.

'Sorry, sir,' Starkey said in a hoarse whisper, 'but what are we doing here?'

'We're getting bloody wet and cold,' Sharpe snapped. He was tired of the Lieutenant's constant nagging. Starkey was frightened that by disobeying General Barnes's explicit instructions to wait until dawn, Sharpe was risking the success of the planned capture of the village. 'What are we supposed to be doing, Lieutenant?' Sharpe added in a kinder tone.

'We're supposed to clear the wood of their picquets, sir.'

'And what good will that do?'

'Distract the enemy, sir.'

'And do you think for a moment that the French won't notice eight hundred Scotsmen forming on the south bank?'

'They'll notice, sir, but they'll be alarmed by fighting on their left flank.' He paused. 'That's what General Barnes wants, sir.'

'What General Barnes wants,' Sharpe said firmly, 'is to capture the village.'

'But the 71st—' Starkey began.

'The 71st will still face a battery of twelve-pounders and God knows how many infantry. The poor bastards will be slaughtered.'

'But if the enemy has detached troops to face the wood, sir—'

Sharpe interrupted him again. 'What's the first thing the enemy picquets will do if we assault the wood?'

'Fight us?' Starkey suggested weakly.

'They'll withdraw, Lieutenant, just like ours would if it was the other way round. They'll retreat to the village and form line there, and as it would be dawn when we attacked, their relief will be ready to reinforce them. So we'll end up in a firefight. We'll win that firefight because we're better than they are, but the twelve-pounders will still be killing Scotsmen and there's bugger all we can do to help.'

'General Barnes has the 50th ready to help the 71st, sir,' Starkey said.

'And they're a good battalion too,' Sharpe said, 'but canister will shred them as easily as it shreds Scotsmen, and meanwhile we'll be advancing across an open field against infantry protected by the village buildings and, I suspect, a pair of twelve-pounders.'

Starkey hesitated, plainly unhappy by Sharpe's certainty. 'General Barnes knows what he's doing, sir,' he said plaintively.

'He does,' Sharpe said, 'and that's why he sent me.'

That was an arrogant claim, but it silenced Starkey who settled in the wet grass beside Sharpe. In truth Sharpe felt no certainty, and knew he was disobeying his orders and, worse, he had no confidence that his manoeuvre in the night would work. He remembered the disastrous night attack in India, how the troops had blundered around in the darkness and officers shouted contradictory orders as a well-positioned enemy rained musket and rocket fire on the attackers. Lieutenant Colonel Arthur Wellesley, not yet Lord Wellington, had been furious at the failure, vowing never to fight a night action again, and now Sharpe was planning just such a fight against a well-emplaced enemy of unknown strength.

'Going around the buggers, are we?' an amused Irish voice muttered from Sharpe's right.

'We are, Pat.'

'That'll wake them up, sir.'

'It will.' Sharpe paused. 'We'll go in with the Grenadiers first,' he whispered.

'Right up their arsehole, sir.'

'We have to make it quick and nasty,' Sharpe said, 'because I want to kill those gunners.'

A slight rustling to his right alerted Sharpe to Hagman's return. 'Mister Sharpe?' the old poacher called softly.

'Here, Dan.'

'Two gates, Mister Sharpe, not a hundred yards thataway.' From the sound of his voice Hagman was evidently pointing west, the direction from which he had approached. 'And once over the road it's open pasture. A few cows, all asleep.'

'Beef for breakfast!' Harper murmured happily.

'Well done, Dan.' Sharpe nudged Harper. 'Get everyone moving, Pat. Still no flints, tell them we're being forced to go nearer the enemy and I'll disembowel any man who makes a noise. Grenadiers first and meet me at the gate Dan just found. It's that way.' He found one of Harper's arms and pointed it westwards.

'Sir!' Lieutenant Starkey pleaded. 'We can't disobey General—'

'I'll disembowel you if you speak again, Lieutenant,' Sharpe growled before looking towards Hagman. 'Lead on, Dan.'

Quick and nasty, Sharpe thought, very quick and bloody nasty, but for whom?

CHAPTER TWO

It all took time, too much time, precious time. When the battalion reached the gate that Hagman had discovered, and where Sharpe reckoned he was safely out of earshot of the closest French picquet in the woodland, he had hissed to each company in turn the vital necessity for absolute silence. 'You'll die if you make a noise,' he had stressed, and naturally a joker in number two company had greeted that warning with a loud fart, which started them laughing. Miraculously neither sound reached the ears of any Frenchman.

'I'll have that bastard digging latrines for a month, sir,' Captain Carline promised.

'You know who it was?'

'Oh I know, sir,' Carline said menacingly.

'Just keep his arse quiet till it's over,' Sharpe said and moved on to the Light Company. He had been angered by the noise, but reflected he would rather have his men laughing than grumbling.

They had crossed the road quietly enough and, once in the

pasture beyond, turned back westwards. The rain persisted and its noise, along with the wind's gusts, helped hide the sound of boots in the grass. They went slowly, very slowly, and slowed even more when Hagman whispered to Sharpe, 'Crapaud picquet other side of the road, Mister Sharpe.'

'You're sure, Dan?'

'I can smell the buggers.'

They had reached the place where the thick woodland grew on the road's southern edge, and the evident limit of the French outposts. All Sharpe could smell was the rich reek of cow manure, but Hagman insisted he could smell burning tobacco and Sharpe trusted him. He ordered Sergeant Henderson to stay at the spot and warn each passing company of their proximity to the enemy, then crept on. After a while he became aware of small glows of light ahead and to his left, and realised it had to be fires or lanterns burning in the village. A dog barked there and immediately afterwards a challenge was shouted from across the road. '*Qui va là?*'

Sharpe froze, as did every other man. Lieutenant Starkey, close behind Sharpe, whispered, 'I speak French, sir.'

'Quiet!' Sharpe hissed back, then sensed that Pat Harper was moving again. There was a thump, then a cow moaning in protest, and French voices muttering across the road. One of the enemy picquets chuckled, evidently content that the alert sentry had merely heard a cow.

'Gave the bugger a good kicking,' Harper whispered as the cow lumbered away.

'Wait!' Sharpe hissed.

So there was a French picquet across the road? He sensed

it was about at the western limit of the woodland with nothing between it and the village except for the field which General Barnes had suggested Sharpe cross. Which meant he was not close enough and must move on past a picquet not a dozen yards away that had been alert enough to hear his men's steps.

'Lieutenant,' he whispered.

'Sir?' Starkey whispered back.

'Stay here and warn the men of this picquet. Total silence! Best to go back twenty or thirty paces to warn them before they get here.'

'Where will you be, sir?'

'Right opposite the village. Any place we can cross the road. Go.'

Starkey crept a few paces back the way they had come and Sharpe went on ahead. He guessed that the cow pasture would have another gate facing the village and so it proved. He stopped there and the small light from the village showed that the road's far side had no fence or hedge, but Hagman, whose eyesight at night was legendary in the battalion, whispered there was a ditch there. 'It'll be flooded, Mister Sharpe.'

'Then we jump, Dan.'

But he must wait first. Gradually the rest of the battalion gathered behind Sharpe who crouched in the pelting rain. His rifle was unloaded, but he reckoned it would be impossible to load in the soaking rain, not without dampening the powder, so he left the cork in the muzzle and eased his huge sword an inch or two out of the scabbard to make certain it would come free. It was only when he detected the smallest grey light in the east that he whispered the order for his men to replace their flints. There was a succession of clicks as men pulled their dogheads back to half cock, then rustling as men fitted flints into the folded leather pads and screwed the dogheads tight. There seemed to be no picquets at the village's edge, though more than once Sharpe saw the shadows of men passing in front of the small firelights glowing in the village street. Once the noise of the flints being replaced had subsided Sharpe whispered that his men must fix bayonets and he flinched at the metallic sound of bayonet sockets being pushed onto musket barrels and twisted to lock them in place. There were even louder noises as his Riflemen forced their sword-bayonets into place and the spring-loaded locking buttons clicked, but mercifully the sound appeared not to have alerted any enemy, the closest of whom had to be sleeping not forty yards away.

The light in the east grew slowly, dulled by the thick clouds, but just bright enough for Sharpe to see his men as dark shapes crouching in the pasture. The closest men were from Harry Price's Grenadier Company, supposedly the biggest and strongest men in the battalion. Sharpe crouched beside Captain Price. 'Your lads are coming with me, Harry.'

'Thought so, sir.'

'We go fast and nasty, straight down the street.' Peering through the gate, Sharpe had seen the main, indeed the only, street running from the road to the ford. It was not properly a street, but rather an elongated village green which divided the settlement into two halves, each with about a score of cottages. 'We go straight to the riverbank,' Sharpe went on, 'which means we'll leave some enemy behind us, but we'll let the rest of the battalion deal with them. Our job is to get to the twelve-pounders and slaughter the gunners. The Light Company and Number Three will be with us. Stress to your boys that they're to treat the civilians well; no murder, rape or theft.'

'I've got six Spaniards, sir, they won't like that.'

'Damn what they like! Tell them I'll put them in front of a firing squad if they disobey.'

'They won't believe you'd do that, sir.'

'Then convince them I mean it, Harry.'

Lord Wellington had made one thing absolutely clear, that French civilians were to be treated honourably. Food had to be paid for, not stolen, and any crimes against civilians were to be punished savagely and, ever since the troops had crossed the Bidassoa, that rule had been largely obeyed. It was not kindness, but sheer practicality. The French armies were notorious for their treatment of conquered territories, and their ravages and rapacity had made them hated, giving birth to the partisan bands which had sought revenge by plaguing the French in Spain and Portugal. Those partisans had fought the French with a cruel savagery that prompted an equally savage response, leaving thousands dead and whole communities destroyed. Wellington's fear was that the French peasantry, if treated badly, would form their own partisan bands to harass his army and, so far, that had not happened. The British troops were, on the whole, content to treat French civilians well, but the Spanish troops were understandably eager to revenge themselves on the homeland of the men who had tortured Spain and there were rumours that such units would be sent home, but that would not solve the problem of the hundreds of

Spaniards who had been allowed to volunteer into the British army. Sharpe had several such men and knew they needed watching in case they decided to revenge their country. 'Tell your men I'll have thieves flogged, and rapists and murderers hanged,' he finished.

'I'll tell them, sir,' Price said.

Sharpe moved on around the field, cursing the rain that still hammered down unmercifully. He would attack the guns at the river's edge with three companies, leaving five. A battalion should have ten companies, but even with the recruits he had brought back from Britain, Sharpe only led six hundred and forty-three men, so he had reorganised the battalion into eight companies. Two of those would clear the houses to the west of the street, and two others would deal with the eastern side, leaving the last company as a reserve to intervene if needed and to guard the prisoners he expected to take. The majority of the French infantry, he knew, would be billeted in the small cottages. 'You'll have to break the doors down and get in fast,' he told his men, 'disarm the buggers and get them into the open where we can guard them.'

'Won't breaking the doors down be seen as cruelty to the villagers, sir?' Captain Carline enquired.

'I'll pay them for each door,' Sharpe said. 'Once they know they'll be paid they'll be breaking down their own doors. Just don't harm any civilians. And Carline?'

'Sir?'

'I've a mind there might be two twelve-pounders between the houses on your side of the village. Make damn sure their crews are dead.'

He went back to the flimsy gate that stopped cattle straying onto the road. He crouched there, flanked by Pat Harper and a nervous Lieutenant Starkey. Sharpe could not blame Starkey, he was nervous himself. He was indeed disobeying General Barnes's explicit orders, but he had doubted the efficacy of those orders. Now, looking back, he reckoned the picquets that he had avoided in the woodland were no more than a company, certainly not the full battalion that Sir Edward had assumed were there. Which meant that the village was probably only occupied by a single battalion, reinforced by a battery of artillery. Sharpe could have routed the picquets easily and sent their survivors scurrying across the field to the village, but that would only have distracted the village's defenders for a brief minute. Sure, they would have sent men to the village's eastern edge to guard against an attack, but Sharpe would then have had to advance across an open field towards an enemy afforded plenty of cover, and the gunners would still be watching across the river for the expected assault. Now, poised to launch his men into the heart of the village, Sharpe began to have doubts. Maybe there was more than a single battalion hidden in the small houses? Maybe his desperate lunge southwards would be too late to save the 71st from a massacre that would turn the river red? And maybe his arrogance in disobeying Barnes would lead to disgrace and even punishment?

He fidgeted with the lock of his rifle, still wrapped in its cloth against the relentless rain. Pride, he recalled, preceded a fall. He knew his own abilities as a fighter and was proud of them. He even knew where that prowess sprang from. It came from his miserable childhood where as a boy he had learned

32

to fight off bullies and resist the workhouse rules. It sprang from his pure hatred of the officers who had despised him when, unexpectedly and surprisingly, he had been promoted from the ranks and given the King's commission; officers who reckoned Richard Sharpe was no gentleman, a man unfit to wear the red sash or to command troops. The memories of those slights gave him a fury in battle, but, he now wondered, did it give him the right to ignore orders and lead his men into a battle they could not win? He was even contemplating taking his men back to the woodland they had bypassed in the night and assaulting the few picquets, as he had been ordered. He resisted the temptation. God damn it, but he could capture the village before the leading ranks of Sir Nathaniel Peacock's battalion had even got their feet wet, and the thought of Sir Nathaniel with his elegant uniform and his sneer and his condescending voice just gave him a surge of the resentment that drove him in battle. 'We go fast, Pat. Don't worry about the enemy we leave behind us.'

'Just get to the guns, sir?'

'Get to the guns and butcher the bastards.'

'They'll likely have most of their infantry with the guns, sir,' Harper suggested.

'Those that are awake, yes, so we kill them too. It's going to be a brawl, Pat, but our boys are good at that.'

'The best, sir.'

Sharpe looked at Lieutenant Starkey. 'You don't have to come with us, Lieutenant. You want to join Number Four Company?'

'I think I should stay with you, sir.'

'Then enjoy yourself,' Sharpe said, happy that Starkey had

not complained about Sharpe's disobedience, but wishing the Lieutenant had chosen to stay further back. Now, he thought, he would have to keep an eye on the young man to ensure he was not killed. He glanced east and saw the sky lightening. He wished the signal guns would fire to release him to the madness, but the dawn stayed silent except for the birdsong and the grunts of cows waking to another day.

'They want to be milked, poor beasts,' Harper said.

And the first gun fired. Sharpe saw the bright flash from the hilltop across the river where he had been given his orders. Then he saw a flickering red trace and knew the gun had fired either a shell or a spherical caseshot. So it was an howitzer and the red trace fell fast towards the French gun battery facing the river. The sound of the shot punched Sharpe's eardrums, then the spherical case exploded above the nearer riverbank and Sharpe understood that General Barnes was trying to kill the gunners. Spherical case was a weapon exclusively used by the British army, a ball of iron packed with gunpowder and musket balls, ignited by a fuse that had left that faint red streak in the air. 'One,' Starkey counted aloud.

A second gun fired, another howitzer that sped its shot after the first, and in the sudden flash of its muzzle flame Sharpe saw the hillside across the river dark with men scrambling down the steep slope. The 71st, he thought, and the first French gun hammered the dawn with its opening blast of canister. Canister, which turned a cannon into a giant shotgun, was useless much above three hundred and fifty yards, but the far hillside was well within the range of the big twelve-pounders. 'Two,' Starkey said, as the second shot exploded over the nearer bank to rain down lead musket balls and shards of shattered casing.

Sharpe stood and drew his long sword. 'Follow me!' He kicked the gate, which splintered apart, and he charged across the road. A ditch, easily jumped, and he was running as fast as he could, his rifle banging against him as it hung from its sling, straight down the wide strip of grass that led to the river. The third shot sounded, the muzzle flash reddening the sky as it reflected from clouds. Dogs were barking, geese running across the grass. 'Come on!' Sharpe bellowed. The only enemy he could see were by the river and the first of them turned. 'Come on!' he shouted again and was dimly aware that his men were also shouting as they swarmed into the village. The fourth gun sheeted the air with lurid light and the fourth caseshot banged apart just above the river. A smaller flash ahead came from a musket and the ball whistled just over Sharpe's head. He could see other men with muskets at their shoulders, but the torrential rain must have reached the powder in their locks because no more shots sounded. A second French cannon sounded and its canister twitched the smoke cloud left by the first gun. The cannon did not load loose powder like a musket, but used a prepared bag of powder that offered protection against rain. The 71st was forming on the far bank, making themselves an easy target for the canister. Sir Nathaniel, Sharpe thought, should have just rushed the river and got his men with their long bayonets among the French gunners.

What looked like a half company of blue-coated French infantry was facing Sharpe. They were in three ranks, their muskets aimed at his men, but when their officer swept his sword down and gave the order to fire, only five or six muskets worked. The men just stood, apparently confused, and none had a bayonet fixed.

'Kill them!' Sharpe yelled. Pat Harper was also shouting, though in his native Gaelic, so Sharpe had no idea what he was saying.

The French facing them looked terrified. And no wonder! They had been rousted from their beds or from the emplacements facing the misted river to find a British force assaulting from their rear. The young officer, Sharpe reckoned, had done well. He had formed his ranks quickly, but now discovered the eternal truth that muskets and heavy rain did not mix, and was about to discover another truth, that bayonets did not care about the weather. And then the officer realised that only a handful of his men had bayonets fixed and he yelled at them, but it was already too late. Men fumbled with their long blades and instinctively began to back away, while others started reloading muskets. A Sergeant began hitting at men who scrabbled with damp cartridges. '*Baïonnettes! Baïonnettes!*' the Sergeant bellowed while his officer drew his sword, his eyes wide in the dawn's light.

'The officer's yours, Pat,' Sharpe called. It had worked! The French had been surprised and Sharpe felt the exhilaration of battle, a mixture of confidence and terror. The French Sergeant, who had been bellowing the correct order at his men, turned and drew one of the short swords many Frenchmen carried. He stepped towards Sharpe, intent on killing this impudent Briton who was threatening his men. He stepped a couple of paces ahead of his men and did not move, just held the sword low, planning to let Sharpe impale himself on the blade. There was confidence in his face, born from years of battlefield experience. He was shouting as he waited, doubtless telling the men behind him to stand firm and keep their bayonets steady.

Sharpe swerved to his left as he neared the Sergeant, which forced the Frenchman to move to his right. His sword was a full foot shorter than Sharpe's blade and he was wise enough to know that he could not win a slashing contest, but could allow his enemy to run onto the firmly held sword which had a curved blade. *Sabre briquet*, Sharpe suddenly remembered the name of the sword, which was about a foot longer than his men's sword-bayonets. The Frenchman did not take his eyes from Sharpe's face and held the *sabre briquet* so that its point curved upwards ready, to slice open an Englishman's belly. The rain, suddenly stronger and more malignant, pelted into Sharpe's face as he ran straight at the waiting man who had braced himself for the collision.

Then Sharpe suddenly dropped. Not three or four paces from the Sergeant he let himself fall onto the grass, feet first, and shot along the soaking wet ground so that he slid beneath the waiting blade, and his own sword, now gripped with both hands, pierced the Frenchman's belly and was diverted upwards into his chest. Sharpe was aware of blood brightening the day's gloom, of the Sergeant falling behind him and groaning as he died. The French officer, to Sharpe's right, was falling, his head misshapen from a blow of the butt of Harper's volley gun, while ahead of him the French front rank stood in apparent terror. Any one of them could have stepped forward and driven a bayonet into Sharpe, but none tried, then Sharpe's men were past him and were shouting as they used their own bayonets.

The French either died or broke. Men fled left and right, desperate to escape the long blades. A hand appeared above Sharpe to help him to his feet. It was Lieutenant Starkey. 'Are you all right, sir?'

'Never better. Go for the guns!' the last four words were shouted. 'Thank you, Lieutenant.'

Two more twelve-pounders fired. Smothering the river with powder smoke as the canister flayed the southern bank. Now all four cannon were being reloaded and Sharpe's men split into two, one half going left and the other right, each group assaulting a pair of the twelve-pounders.

It took Sharpe a moment to drag his sword from the Sergeant's corpse and he only managed it by bracing himself with his left foot on the dead man's chest.

'The guns!' Sharpe shouted, only to see that his men were already racing towards the horrified gunners. Peter d'Alembord was leading his Light Company westwards and Harry Price's Grenadiers were charging towards the brightening edge of the eastern sky. Sharpe followed them.

The half company that had been led by the broken-skulled young officer had died or fled, but that panic had not spread to the Artillerymen who stood to defend their guns. They were reinforced by more infantrymen who had lined the barriers raised between the guns along the river's bank and who now rallied with fixed bayonets. A gunner, braver than he deserved, ran towards Sharpe wielding a worm, a wooden shaft tipped with an iron corkscrew for extracting obstructions from the gun's barrel. There was no great weight to a worm, though if the lad pierced it into a man's belly it could do some horrid damage, but Sharpe merely knocked it aside with his heavy blade and then slammed the sword's iron guard into the youngster's face, breaking his nose, shattering teeth, and hurling him to the ground. 'Bloody fool,' he snarled at the youngster, 'doesn't know how lucky he is.'

'He'll have a pig of a headache,' Harper grunted, then pointed the volley gun at a French Sergeant, 'yours, sir,' he said.

The Sergeant, mesmerised by the seven half-inch barrels threatening to blow his head off, froze, and Sharpe chopped the blade down to half sever a wrist holding the musket. The Sergeant jerked into life, but lost his grip on the musket, and Harper used the seven-barrelled gun's heavy brass butt to stun him. 'Not even loaded,' he said scornfully.

'I thought you said it was.'

'In this bleeding rain? Powder would be porridge.'

Sharpe flicked the sword up to deflect a half-hearted bayonet thrust and the Frenchman, another youth, panicked and scrambled backwards to hide under the closest twelve-pounder. 'Bradley!' Sharpe called.

'Sir?' Private Bradley, close behind Sharpe, answered.

'Deal with that fellow under the gun.' Sharpe moved to his left to go behind the gun, leaving Bradley, who was about the same age as the youngster sheltering behind one of the gun's huge wheels, to either kill or capture the Frenchman.

Sharpe sensed, rather than saw, his men crowding in behind him. They were shouting crude insults as they carried their bayonets forward. The second gun, now some twenty yards ahead, was being reloaded and Sharpe saw the canister being thrust down the barrel. 'Kill them!' he bellowed, eager to reach the cannon before it could be fired. More French infantry were appearing, some came from his left behind the cottages and must have fled the rest of Sharpe's battalion who were clearing the buildings either side of the village's long green. He was outnumbered, but Sharpe had total confidence in his men, who were nearly all veterans of a lifetime's fighting. They had grown up in a brutal world, had survived countless tavern brawls or alley fights, and they could be viciously effective in this sort of wild melee.

As Sharpe himself was. He had learned to fight as a child and, like Patrick Harper beside him, had no fear of combat. The army had honed his skills, but his chief advantages were his rage and his belief that to fight fairly was to invite defeat. The object was to batter his enemies into swift submission, and to be pitiless. He swept another musket aside and speared his blade into an enemy's belly. A blue-coated gunner desperately lunged at him with the sponge-end of a rammer and Sharpe seized it with his left hand, pulled and so dragged the Artilleryman onto his sword. He heard Peter d'Alembord yelling at his men to follow and a rush of Light Company men rounded the muzzle of the cannon and slashed into the enemy while Harry Price led his Grenadiers to Sharpe's left to stab and hack their way forward.

Sharpe stood on the trail of the first cannon after plucking the firing tube from the vent. He could see that d'Alembord and Price were closing on the second gun, but the gun's Captain still managed to fire the canister and the riverbank was suddenly shrouded in noxious yellow-black smoke through which Sharpe's men fought like demons. He turned to look east and saw that his men had secured both guns on that side, while to the south the first redcoats were crossing the ford to complete a victory that was already won. To Sharpe's surprise the men crossing the river were in loose order, not the tightly packed columns he had expected from Sir Nathaniel Peacock, who was such a stickler for proper order. That loose order had saved many from the last desperate blasts of canister, though Sharpe could see too many redcoated bodies floating downstream, but nevertheless he decided he had been too harsh on Peacock who had at last demonstrated some common sense.

The companies that had been clearing the village street had caught up and now streamed behind the leading companies who were capturing the whole French battery, then Sharpe heard the ear-pounding roar of more cannon fire and turned back eastwards to see that the British howitzers on the far bank of the river were firing caseshot into the field between the village and the woodland. The picquets had been returning to the fight, meeting with fugitives fleeing the battle, and the British artillery was raining death on them. It was over.

Sharpe cleaned his sword blade on the skirt of his green jacket and thrust the blade back into its scabbard. He jumped down from the gun's trail and threaded the bodies of dead and dying Frenchmen. 'Well done, Harry,' he greeted Price.

'We did it, sir!'

'Of course we did. We're the South Essex.'

Price looked past Sharpe to where the first redcoats were

emerging from the ford. 'That's not the 71st!' he said in astonishment. 'It's the dirty half-hundred!'

Sharpe turned and saw Price was right. The men attacking across the river had black facings while the 71st, like the South Essex, had yellow. So the 50th was crossing the river instead of Sir Nathaniel's men? General Barnes must have changed his mind at the last moment, not that it mattered, Sharpe thought, because the village was taken and the enemy had either been killed, wounded, fled or taken prisoner.

Lieutenant Starkey, his sword still drawn, crossed to Sharpe and raised his sword in a formal salute. 'I apologise, sir.'

'Apologise?' Sharpe asked brusquely. 'What on earth for?'

'For doubting you, sir. General Barnes warned me you might do something unorthodox.'

'And you were ordered to stop me?' Sharpe guessed.

'I was told to keep a firm hand on the reins, sir.'

'And so you did, Lieutenant,' Sharpe said, 'but the horse ignored you.'

'And gained a signal victory, sir. I salute you.' Starkey again raised his blade.

'Did you manage to use the sword, Lieutenant?' Sharpe asked. He thought he could see a trace of rain-diluted blood on the slim blade.

'Indeed, sir!' Starkey said proudly.

'Well done, and now, perhaps, you could do me a favour?'

'Of course, sir,' Starkey said who, being one of General Barnes's aides, was not strictly under Sharpe's command.

'Ask my company commanders to meet me here.'

'Of course, sir,' Starkey said again and hurried off on the errand.

'He might make a useful officer one day,' Sharpe said to Harper once Starkey was gone.

'No,' Harper said dismissively, 'he ain't got the nerve for it.'

'You do, maybe I should make you a Lieutenant?'

'Christ no, sir!' Harper said in sudden panic. 'I can't read or write, sir, and an officer must have those skills.'

'You read just fine, and can write too.'

'I cannot!' Harper insisted. 'Besides I'm a Roman Catholic, and Catholics can't be officers.'

'Who said?'

'I don't know, I read it somewhere.'

Sharpe laughed. 'You're full of shit, Patrick. Don't worry, I won't promote you.'

'That was a grand fight, so it was,' Harper said, relieved.

'Till I get the butcher's bill,' Sharpe said. He had summoned his company commanders to discover how many of his men had fallen.

'It'll be light, sir,' Harper reassured him. 'I saw young Clark get run through, but no one else.'

'He was a good lad.'

'They all are, except for Bassett. He's an eejit.'

'Major Sharpe!' A loud voice hailed from the centre of the riverbank's defences and Sharpe turned to see Major James Lowe of the 50th beckoning.

'Company commanders are coming, Pat. Tell 'em I'll be back.' Sharpe walked to meet Lowe. 'Morning, Jimmy.'

'A good one! Your boys did well.'

'They did. Yours too, but why you and not the 71st?'

'Sweet Christ,' Lowe said, 'bloody Peacock fell off his horse,

43

got kicked by the beast and has a broken leg. That stopped them cold so Barnes sent us.'

'Why didn't they go without him?'

'Peacock insisted they stay with him.' Lowe shrugged as if Peacock's behaviour was beyond understanding.

'So Peacock's not going to win the war single-handed?' Sharpe asked.

'Seems not. I guess we won't be home by Christmas.'

'Was he suggesting we would be?'

'Two nights ago. He came to our mess to bitch about the way we deployed skirmishers.'

'He didn't!' Sharpe said, incredulous.

'Oh, he did indeed! And told us he confidently expected to be made a Major General before the war's end.'

Sharpe laughed. 'Before Christmas?'

'So he said. "Just let my men loose", Lowe was imitating Peacock's plummy voice, '"and the damned enemy will run all the way to Paris." He even dared suggest that we and your battalion would be part of his brigade.'

'God help us,' Sharpe said, then stepped to one side as Harper approached.

Harper threw a perfect salute, presumably to Major Lowe because the Irishman rarely saluted Sharpe. 'Fourteen dead and twenty-six wounded, sir,' he reported.

Sharpe grimaced. 'Not as many as I feared, Pat.'

'Lieutenant Swift was killed, sir.'

'Damn. He was shaping up well.'

'And Doc Hunter reckons we'll lose twelve of the twenty-six, sir.'

44

'Damn again,' Sharpe said. He had begun the day with six hundred and forty-three men, which was a small number for a battalion, but now it was being whittled down and there was small hope of any reinforcements coming from Britain. 'Ask Captain d'Alembord to muster the battalion in the field,' he pointed at the pasture leading to the woodland, 'and sort out some kind of breakfast. But if they take eggs or anything else from the villagers they're to pay for them.'

'Of course, sir.' Harper saluted again and strode back towards the carnage among the French guns.

'A capable fellow,' Lowe commented, looking at Harper.

'The best,' Sharpe said.

'And that bloody great gun on his shoulder?'

They stood for a few moments discussing the seven-barrelled gun, and Sharpe was doing some clumsy mathematics in his head and deduced that he would be lucky to have six hundred and twenty effectives for the next clash with the retreating enemy. But at least that enemy was retreating and the British would be advancing further into France.

'What's up north?' he asked Lowe.

'More bloody rivers,' Lowe said gloomily, then turned as a sharp voice called for men to make way. 'Oh my suffering God,' Lowe said, 'here the conquering hero comes.'

It was Sir Nathaniel Peacock, mounted on a sleek black stallion with his right leg sheathed in a splint, using a riding crop to split a knot of men from the 50th who were lingering around one of the captured twelve-pounders. 'Out of my damned way!' he bellowed and slashed the crop onto a Corporal's shoulder.

'Bloody man,' Lowe muttered and hurried off to calm his men who were jeering at the irate Colonel.

Peacock had swerved towards Lowe, but spurred past him. 'Sharpe!' he called, 'Sharpe!'

Sharpe pretended not to hear and walked towards the field where his men were gathering.

'Sharpe!' Peacock barked again, and Sharpe reluctantly stopped and waited for the Colonel's arrival.

Peacock curbed his horse and looked down from the saddle. He had a thin, bony face and his dark eyes looked angry. 'What the devil did you think you were doing?' he demanded.

'Doing, sir?'

'Your orders were specific! Capture the wood and drive the picquets in!'

'I got lost, Sir Nathaniel,' Sharpe lied calmly, 'so did the best I could.'

'And gave the bloody French time to loose canister over the river!'

'And if I'd driven the picquets from the wood,' Sharpe pointed out, 'the French would have had time to loose even more canister.'

'Don't quibble with me, Major.' Peacock rapped his wounded leg with the riding crop to emphasise his words and Sharpe wondered why the sharp blow prompted no reaction of pain. 'It is by meticulous obedience to orders that success is guaranteed.'

'And your orders, sir,' Sharpe countered, 'were to cross the river. It's fortunate that the dirty half-hundred were ready to replace you.'

'I was wounded!' Peacock shouted the words. 'I can't lead men if I have a broken leg! My horse was struck by canister and took fright.'

Sharpe glanced at the horse, which seemed remarkably calm and showed no sign of a wound. 'I'm sorry to hear it, sir,' he said.

Peacock seemed taken aback by Sharpe's mild tone. 'You're in temporary command of the South Essex, isn't that right?'

'Of the Prince of Wales's Volunteers, sir,' Sharpe gave his battalion its new title.

'And I'm sure the Prince Regent will make it his business to ensure that the regiment is given a competent Colonel soon,' Peacock said grandly.

Sharpe was of the opinion that the Prince Regent would not give a fart over the matter, but just nodded. 'I hope you're right, sir,' he said meekly, hoping that the competent Colonel would be himself.

The rain suddenly became harder, pounding the river and drenching Sharpe, who unslung his rifle and took a rag and cork from his cartridge pouch. The cork went into the muzzle, while the rag was tied around the gun's lock.

'I can't help noticing, Sharpe, that you carry a musket,' Peacock said, 'not becoming for an officer, surely?'

'It's a rifle,' Sharpe said, 'and I've carried a musket or rifle ever since I joined the army.'

'And you were allowed to carry one?' Peacock asked in a lofty tone.

'Oh, I was no officer, sir,' Sharpe said, 'I was a Private in the Oatcakes.'

'The Oatcakes?' Peacock asked, sounding incredulous, though Sharpe knew the incredulity was not about the regiment's nickname, but that Sharpe had risen from the ranks.

He also wondered how Peacock had become a Colonel without knowing which regiment had the nickname. 'The 33rd, sir. The recruiting Sergeants used to spit oatcakes on their bayonets. It was a promise you'd never go hungry.'

'And is that why you joined?'

'A magistrate gave me no choice.' Sharpe sounded amused.

'A magistrate!' Lieutenant Colonel Sir Nathaniel Peacock sounded anything but amused, but he did not pursue the topic. Sharpe had revealed a criminal past, which did not surprise Peacock. The man looked like a villain! From his battered uniform to his hard, scarred and suntanned face. If ever there was a scoundrel who deserved a prison sentence it was Sharpe and now the man held the King's commission! Even Peacock's horse took a nervous step away from Sharpe. 'You were in the ranks, Sharpe?' He seemed to find the very notion unbelievable.

'I was, sir, and so were a lot of other officers in this army.'

'One would have thought,' Peacock said snidely, 'that experience in the ranks would have at least taught you to obey orders.'

'It taught me a lot, sir,' Sharpe said in a firmer tone, 'and the most valuable lesson was which orders were best ignored.'

'Discipline, Sharpe, discipline! It's at the very root of victory!'

'Oh I don't disagree, Sir Nathaniel.'

'And discipline also means appearance.' Peacock looked at Sharpe's ragged, blood-stained uniform and seemed to shudder.

'Short hair and smart uniforms, Sharpe! Look at that man!' He pointed his riding crop at a tall Private of the South Essex who was wandering among the French dead looking for a body that had not been half stripped in a search for loot. 'He's a disgrace! Look at his hair! A mess!'

Sharpe beckoned the man, a good soldier. 'Rifleman Dromgoole!' he called. 'Here!'

Sean Dromgoole sauntered to Sharpe and touched a finger to the rim of his shako. 'Mister Sharpe?'

'Colonel Peacock thinks you need a haircut.'

Dromgoole looked up at the Colonel. 'And my hair's no longer than Mister Sharpe's, your honour,' he said. 'And it's as my ma said, it keeps me neck warm, so it does.'

'You call Major Sharpe "sir", not mister,' Peacock snarled.

'He's a rifle officer, your honour, so he's mister, so he is.'

'He's right,' Sharpe said, 'it's a custom in the rifles.'

'Damned stupid custom,' Peacock muttered, then louder, to Dromgoole, 'you're Irish?'

'Guilty, your honour. From County Monaghan. God's own county.'

'You're dismissed,' Peacock said and seemed to shudder as a bemused Dromgoole wandered away. 'The 71st,' he said, 'is supposedly a Scots regiment, but I've over fifty Irishmen. Can't trust them, Sharpe.'

'If you don't want them, sir, I'll take them. They're the best fighters in the army.'

'Damned rebels and Papists,' Peacock said, loud enough for the retreating Dromgoole to hear.

'Rebels and Papists?' a new voice said happily, and both

49

Sharpe and Peacock turned to see General Barnes approaching on a river-soaked horse. 'If you're talking about the Irish I wish I had ten thousand more rebels and Papists! Morning, Sharpe! Morning, Sir Nathaniel. And well done, Sharpe! You came straight up the enemy's arse! Bloody fine soldiering! How's the leg, Sir Nathaniel?'

'Painful, Sir Edward.' Peacock bent in his saddle, as if fighting off agony. 'Very painful, but my surgeon says it will repair itself quickly. More a fracture than a break.'

'Splendid news,' Barnes said, making it sound anything but, 'and you, Sharpe? What's your damage?'

'Fourteen dead, sir, and a dozen badly wounded.'

'Better than I feared,' Barnes said, 'and I have more good news for you, Sharpe.'

Sharpe's hopes soared, though he took care to show nothing on his face. He was hoping against hope that he would be gazetted as a Lieutenant Colonel and thus given official command of the South Essex. 'For me, sir?' he asked, taking care to show no excitement.

'This fine fellow,' Barnes indicated a Dragoon Sergeant who was leading a spare horse, 'is here to guide you to the Peer's headquarters! It seems Lord Wellington wants you to have dinner with him tonight if I can spare you. Can I spare you, Major?'

It took a heartbeat or two for Sharpe to recover from the news that Lord Wellington had summoned him, but he gathered himself and gestured northwards. 'The enemy seems to have fled, sir, and it'll take us time to find them again.'

'My thoughts too,' Barnes said happily, 'you concur,

Sir Nathaniel? I can permit Major Sharpe to dine with Lord Wellington?'

'I doubt the French will dare to make any move against us,' Peacock, utterly misunderstanding Barnes's mocking tone in asking the question, answered surlily, not troubling to hide his astonishment that Wellington would invite the ragged-looking Major to his dinner table.

'There, Sharpe,' Barnes said happily, 'you can go and have dinner with the Peer. Who'll look after your rogues while you're being wined and dined?'

'Captain d'Alembord, sir.'

'A good fellow?'

'Very good, sir.'

'Excellent, but as Sir Nathaniel assures us the French are too frightened to face us, I dare say I have no need to be concerned. Besides, his lordship assures me you'll be returning in a few days. You need time to change your uniform?'

'This is my only uniform, sir,' Sharpe said. He wore the tall boots and leather reinforced overalls of a Colonel of France's Imperial Guard over which was a Rifleman's green jacket that was ripped, patched and stained dark with blood, as was his red officer's sash tied around his waist. Instead of the light sabre issued to Light Infantry officers he had a British heavy cavalry sword hanging from the slings attached to his belt.

Barnes laughed. 'You look like a brigand, Sharpe!'

'Nosey's seen worse, I dare say,' Sharpe answered.

'Not at his dinner table,' Barnes suggested light-heartedly.

'I'll give it a brush-up, sir. Now, if you'll excuse me, I should talk to Captain d'Alembord.'

51

'Of course, Sharpe. Sergeant Williams will take you to head-quarters.' Barnes indicated the Dragoon Sergeant who spurred after Sharpe.

Lieutenant Colonel Peacock watched the Rifleman walk away. 'What the devil does Wellington want with that man?'

'Lord Wellington,' Barnes said pointedly, 'began his soldiering in Flanders, then fought across India, and has now thrown the French out of Portugal and Spain. That man, Sir Nathaniel,' he glanced towards Sharpe, 'fought with him all the way.'

Sir Nathaniel gave a snort. He resented that he had not been invited to dine with Wellington, and was also acutely aware of his own lack of combat experience, but was determined to conceal it. 'I just spoke with Sharpe,' he went on, 'and told him to be more particular in obeying orders.'

'Major Sharpe's great talent is in disobeying orders,' Barnes said, 'as he demonstrated this morning.'

'Just look at the man!' Peacock shuddered. 'He's a disgrace to the army!'

'You're referring to his uniform, Sir Nathaniel?'

'Filthy rags? And he needs a haircut! What kind of example is he to his men?'

'The oak leaf wreath on his sleeve, Sir Nathaniel, denotes that he led and survived a forlorn hope. And the eagle of his regiment's badge commemorates the French standard he captured at Talavera. His back is deeply scarred, Sir Nathaniel, because he was flogged as a Private,' Barnes enjoyed seeing the shock on Sir Nathaniel's face, 'and I've no doubt he deserved the flogging, but it didn't prevent him from becoming probably the most savage fighter in this whole army, and his men will follow him to hell. I trust you will raise the same devotion in the 71st.'

Sir Nathaniel glowered at the back of Major Sharpe who was rejoining his battalion. This army, he decided, needed reform. It needed discipline! It needed Sir Nathaniel!

CHAPTER THREE

There was a small delay before Sharpe could leave. General Barnes wanted Sharpe to deliver a message to Lord Wellington, a message that took the General an hour to write. Sharpe spent most of the hour talking with Peter d'Alembord and Pat Harper, confident that he was leaving the South Essex in competent hands. Then, just a moment after Lieutenant Starkey brought Sharpe the General's missive, Sir Nathaniel Peacock arrived on his unwounded stallion. 'You will do me a favour, Major Sharpe,' he demanded from horseback.

'If it's possible, I will, sir,' Sharpe answered cautiously.

'Lord Wellington is a personal friend,' Peacock said loftily, 'and I would be obliged if you would give him this,' he handed down a sealed letter, 'it is purely personal and, of course, private.'

'My pleasure, sir,' Sharpe had said, putting the letter into a pouch besides Barnes's missive.

'And I am sure you can bring back his lordship's reply,' Peacock said, turning his horse away.

Sergeant Williams, a handsome man in his short red jacket and wearing the new brass and black helmet, watched critically as Sharpe clumsily mounted the spare horse. Sharpe owned his own horse, a gift from his wife, but the mare from Wellington's own stable was plainly a better mount. 'She's a forgiving beast, sir,' Williams said in a strong Welsh accent. 'She'll take care of you.'

'She better had,' Sharpe said cautiously. 'I'm an infantryman, Sergeant. I don't much like horses.' He settled his right boot into the stirrup. 'Any idea why the Peer wants to see me?' he asked.

'No idea at all, sir.' Williams spoke respectfully, but stiffly, as though he somehow disapproved of Sharpe.

'I'll doubtless find out,' Sharpe said, then fell silent as he followed the Welshman through the ford, up the hill beyond and so through the brigade's ammunition park where Portuguese soldiers sheltered from the rain beneath wagons. They were riding south into the teeth of a chill wind that brought a heavy driving rain which made Sharpe regret he had left his greatcoat in his billet. Sergeant Williams had pulled out an oilskin cloak and kicked his horse into a trot as if eager to finish the journey.

Sharpe followed gingerly, gripping the saddle's pommel to keep his seat. They trotted through a dense wood and the drips from the trees seemed even more intense than the rain, then emerged into a stretch of rich farmland at the end of which lay earthen forts through which the muzzles of cannon showed. The wind had grown stronger, whipping the rain into Sharpe's face, but through the downpour he could see the blue-coated

Artillerymen manning the guns. 'The River Nive, sir,' Sergeant Williams said as they neared the forts, 'and we'd best walk the horses across the bridge.'

The army had fought its way across the Nivelle a few days before, a battle that had cost Sharpe's battalion thirty good men. Rumour in the army claimed that there were even more rivers to cross if the army was to pierce deep into the French homeland, but the presence of the earthen forts with their artillery suggested that Lord Wellington was wary of a French counter-stroke aimed to evict the British from precious French soil.

Williams saluted a redcoated Lieutenant who commanded the nearest fort's guards. The Lieutenant must have spotted the rain-soaked red sash at Sharpe's waist for he sullenly ordered his men to shoulder arms. Sharpe returned the salute, then followed Williams through the shoulders of the big earthen walls. In front of him was a pontoon bridge that spanned the River Nive. The bridge was a line of riverboats, each anchored against the Nive's northwards flow, and across the boats were five huge cables on which were mounted planks.

'It looks solid enough,' Sergeant Williams said, 'but the roadway still quivers and the horses don't like it.' He swung himself out of his saddle and waited as Sharpe clumsily dismounted. 'I'll lead both horses, sir.' Williams reached for the mare's bridle. 'She knows me.'

Sharpe relinquished the mare to Williams's more experienced hands, then walked behind the horses across the bridge which, he thought, more than quivered. It shuddered under the force of the swollen river. The rain, heavier now, pocked the Nive's surface that was wind whipped into small waves that broke white against the prows of the anchored boats. The anchor cables strained and creaked, shaking the boats beneath the roadway's planks that quivered on the tensioned cables. 'If I was a praying man,' he said to Williams, 'I'd pray that this bridge holds.'

'You're not a praying man, sir?' The question reeked of disapproval.

'Never had time for it, Sergeant.'

'A pity, sir.' Williams paused, as if pondering whether to say more. 'The bridge will hold, sir. I trust the Engineers who built it, and the good Lord who will protect us.'

The good Lord, Sharpe thought sourly, had better protect the bridge. The River Nive ran north to Bayonne parallel to the Atlantic coast, and that meant that the British army, south of Bayonne, was split into two parts by the river and was faced by a large French army guarding the city. That French army was at least of equal size to Lord Wellington's forces, and even a child could work out that if Marshal Soult, the French commander, attacked either side of the Nive he could overwhelm the half of Wellington's forces that faced him. Reinforcements would have to be sent from one side of the river to the other, and the bridge was one of only two crossing the river. There were places where the river was fordable, but the incessant winter rain had swollen the river, making the fords virtually impassable and bridges even more important. That explained the heavy guns in their formidable earthworks placed to protect the bridge from a sudden overwhelming French assault. More guns were emplaced on the river's banks, facing north to defend against an assault by river boats. 'I'm sure you're right, Sergeant,' Sharpe said, though the bridge's trembling made him wonder just how much strain the pontoons could survive. The second pontoon bridge was far to the south, which meant a much longer march for any reinforcing battalions to cross the Nive in support of their embattled comrades.

Once across the bridge Sharpe remounted the mare and followed Williams onto a road leading westwards. 'Lord Wellington is still at Saint-Jean-de-Luz?' he asked the Sergeant.

'He is, sir,' Williams replied.

Sharpe felt a pang of excitement. Saint-Jean-de-Luz was the French port on the border of Spain and had been Wellington's headquarters ever since the army had crossed that frontier, and where many of the army's followers now had quarters, and among them was Jane, Sharpe's wife. He had not seen her in a few weeks and her letters had become scarce and he had looked forward to surprising her, though a dark corner of his thoughts had wondered if she would even welcome the surprise. He could find little evidence to support that fear and, in the wet nights, he had even wondered whether he wanted to surprise her or not. There was a realisation that he had married Jane too quickly, prompted by her undoubted beauty and by the temptation to offend her uncle, Sir Henry Simmerson, and as Sharpe rode into the farmlands south and west of the pontoon bridge he realised that he was not so much excited at seeing Jane, but apprehensive. Jane's infrequent letters contained little affection, as his letters to her did, indeed her messages did little more than bemoan the 'lack of society' in

Saint-Jean-de-Luz, and the paucity of the town's shops. 'Are you married, Sergeant?' he asked, mainly to divert his confused thoughts.

'I am, sir.' The reply was stiff, hardly inviting any more conversation, so Sharpe fell silent. He was trying to imagine any reason why Wellington had summoned him, and the only reason he could devise was because his lordship was formally giving him command of the South Essex, thus promoting Sharpe to Lieutenant Colonel. That thought excited him, but why summon Sharpe all the way to the Atlantic? A simple message would achieve the same thing and be more economical, and Wellington was an economical man. But as Williams led him onto a farm track going westwards, he could not lose the hope that he was at last being given official command of the South Essex.

'The roads here, sir, mostly run north and south,' the Welshman said, explaining why he had left the road, 'so we'll be following cattle paths a good part of the way.'

'I'm impressed you know the way,' Sharpe said.

'The good Lord guides me, sir.'

Sharpe grunted, wondering now what Sir Nathaniel Peacock's letter to Wellington contained. He was even tempted to unseal it; a hot knife could unstick a wax seal with no evidence of interference, but he dismissed the thought, reckoning that whatever was in the letter would be annoying. And was Sir Nathaniel truly a friend of Lord Wellington? It seemed possible, but to Sharpe unlikely. He had known Wellington for almost half his life and the one thing he was certain of was that his lordship did not suffer fools gladly.

Sergeant Williams turned off the cattle path a few miles past the pontoon bridge to follow a cart-rutted track that led across small hills and wooded valleys. 'Not far to go from here, sir,' the Welshman said. 'Maybe a dozen miles?'

'No French patrols this far south?'

'All gone, sir, thanks to the good Lord.'

'Lord Wellington, you mean?' Sharpe enquired.

'Him too, sir.'

'Our forces must be well north of Saint-Jean-de-Luz by now?'

'We've patrolled a fair way north, sir, and encountered French cavalry who chased us away.'

'And you out-galloped the pursuit?'

'Always, sir.'

'Which doubtless you ascribe to the good Lord,' Sharpe said snidely.

'It was more likely, sir, that the French cavalry lost all their good horses in Russia, and the remounts haven't got the speed or stamina to keep up with us.' The Sergeant pulled his horse aside and Sharpe followed to let a farm wagon pass by. There were four labourers in the wagon, all armed with spades, and one wished them *bonjour* and the rest all grinned happily at the two British horsemen. 'They're friendly enough, sir,' Williams remarked as they resumed their progress.

'Because we're paying for all the food and fodder we take from them. They complain that their own army never paid.'

'So the good book is right, sir, do unto others as you'd have them do unto you.'

'Not if you're an infantryman, Sergeant. Then it's slaughter the bastards before they've had a chance to prime their muskets.'

Sergeant Williams treated that remark with an offended silence. They had been climbing a long hill and now reached its crest and Sharpe paused there to take in the view. It was magnificent, a rainswept rolling landscape of deep woods and fallow fields leading to the Atlantic, which looked surprisingly close. He fancied he could even smell the sea, the scent brought on the brisk wet wind.

'Not far now, sir,' Williams said, and spurred his horse onwards.

Once off the high ground the tracks became thick with mud, and still the rain fell, pelting down with wind-driven venom. The horses struggled for another hour, passing through small villages, crossing swollen streams until at last Williams led Sharpe into the small town of Saint-Jean-de-Luz.

It was indeed a small town, but by far the largest that Sharpe had seen so far in France. The streets were narrow and crowded with folk moving from shop to shop. There was no sign he could detect of hostility. A few people looked hurriedly away from him, but most were openly curious of the two horsemen. They were checked at a crossroads because a priest was solemnly passing. The priest was carrying a tray on which Sharpe could see a goblet and a small box, and was followed by two acolytes, one of whom lofted a silver cross. Sharpe noted how the watching men removed their hats and the women bowed their heads. He took off his own battered shako in polite imitation, a gesture that provoked a frown from Sergeant Williams who had left his elaborate helmet in place. 'Popish superstition, sir,' he remonstrated Sharpe.

'Courtesy, Sergeant,' Sharpe said curtly, replacing his shako.

The priest, he knew, was carrying the wine and bread to give a dying person the last rites. The ritual meant nothing to Sharpe, but Wellington's insistence that the occupying army did nothing to offend French civilians had prompted his respect. He kicked the mare on, threading the dispersing crowd only to be halted again by a succession of vast tumbrils, some hauled by oxen, the great carts loaded with ammunition and all heading north. He suspected they were the last supplies to be brought north from Spain because from now the British cargo ships could dock in Saint-Jean-de-Luz to feed the British army's endless hunger for roundshot, powder, canister, caseshot and musket cartridges.

And how long, he wondered, would the war last now? The French were yet to be defeated, and rumour in the army suggested that Marshal Soult, who was opposing Wellington's advance, had been reinforced heavily, which in turn suggested there was grim fighting ahead, but Sharpe reckoned the French could do nothing to withstand Wellington's onslaught. A month? Two months? And then what? He dreaded the prospect of peace, for what could he do to support himself and an expensive wife? He could muster men, he could throw out chains of skirmishers, he could reduce enemy lines to bloody ruin and, as he was increasingly becoming aware, he could sense an enemy's weakness and exploit it ruthlessly. His skills were the skills of war and, though he acknowledged that the purpose of war was to bring peace, he feared it would bring him nothing but ruin.

'What will you do when the war ends, Sergeant?' he asked Williams as they came in view of Saint-Jean-de-Luz's harbour.

'Return to my father's farm, sir, if the good Lord spares me.'

Sharpe grunted at that. He had been searching the people he passed for a glimpse of Jane's bright hair, but did not see her, and now he gazed at an inner harbour crowded with ships. Men were unloading fish, and women haggling prices. Beyond the inner harbour was another, larger harbour dominated by a moored ship of the line flying the white ensign. Her serried gunports were closed, but the sight of her flashed Sharpe's thoughts back nine years to his voyage onboard the *Pucelle* that had carried him into the carnage of Trafalgar, and that, in turn, revived the agony of Lady Grace. Was she the one woman he had truly loved? His eyes blurred as Williams led him north along a street bounded on the left by a beach being pounded by Biscay's waves and on the right by massive houses aspiring to be seafront palaces. 'Almost there, sir,' Williams said.

The Sergeant led him into an alley that ran alongside a great yellow-painted mansion, then turned into the mansion's stable-yard where men ran to take the horses. Sharpe dismounted clumsily and staggered slightly on the cobblestones. He waited for Williams to guide him into the huge mansion, but the Sergeant merely indicated a door, 'I daresay you can use the back door, sir, someone will tell you where to go.'

'Thank you for bringing me here, Sergeant.'

'My duty, sir,' Williams said, evidently relieved to be rid of responsibility, then led his own mud-caked horse towards the stables.

Sharpe, soaked to the skin and aching from the relentless hours in the saddle, pushed through a sturdy door into the blessed warmth of a big kitchen. The room was dim, lit only by a small open fire in the huge hearth and by sputtering candles on a vast table.

'And who are you?' a woman demanded in accented English, making Sharpe step back in surprise.

'Major Sharpe,' he said from the open doorway.

'Ah! A dinner guest!' She sounded surprised, perhaps because his uniform was so ragged, and it had not been helped by the rain and mud of the journey. Sharpe, saddle-sore, was limping towards the blazing fire and now saw a handsome black-haired woman grinning at him. 'You can't go to dinner like that,' she said sternly, 'take off the jacket. Quick now! And shut that door behind you!'

Sharpe sensed he could not win an argument with this confident, attractive woman and so he returned to close the door and tugged off the green jacket.

'And take off those boots and the overalls,' she said, 'and wait there.' She strode to a closet and brought out a big dark blue cloak, richly lined with scarlet cloth. 'Put that on,' she commanded, 'and sit down.'

Sharpe obeyed again. His shirt was damp, but he was allowed to leave that on as he draped the thick cloak about his shoulders and sank gratefully into a chair close to the hearth. The woman, meanwhile, hung his overalls and jacket to dry. 'No time to wash and dry them,' she said brusquely, 'but once they're dry they'll brush well.' She fed wood onto the fire, and then started cleaning the mud from his boots.

'I can do that,' he protested.

'Glory to God in the highest,' she said, 'a man who can clean his own boots! You just sit there, Major, and get warm. We have a little time before dinner. You want tea?'

'Please, ma'am,' he said.

'I am Candelaria,' she announced. 'Milk? Sugar?'

'Both, please ma'am.'

'I told you,' she reprimanded him, 'I am Candelaria.'

'Pleased to meet you, Candelaria.' He stumbled over the unfamiliar name. 'You're Spanish?'

She spat onto the tiled floor. 'I am Portuguese,' she said proudly, taking a kettle from a hob by the fire. 'From Vimeiro. And you are Richard Sharpe from London.'

'How did you know that?' Sharpe asked in amazement.

'His lordship has talked of you. You, I think, amuse him.' She smiled at that and spooned tea leaves into a pot.

'Ah,' Sharpe said, and then was struck dumb as he realised who Candelaria must be. There had long been rumours rippling through the army that Lord Wellington had a woman to warm his bed and Sharpe suspected he had found her, and that it was this woman who had accompanied his lordship through the whole campaign. She had a strong face that suggested humour and resolve, and Lord Wellington, Sharpe decided, had good taste. 'Are you cooking dinner, Candelaria?' he asked.

'I am only trusted with making his lordship's breakfast and tea,' she said, smiling again. 'He has his own cooks for dinner, and your dinner,' she gestured at a huge iron range across the kitchen, 'is already in the oven.'

'Mutton, I suppose?'

'You know him! Ha! He eats so much mutton that I am surprised he does not say "baa"!'

She dropped one of Sharpe's boots and poured boiling water into a teapot. 'One for you,' she said happily, 'and one for his lordship. Shall I tell him you are here?'

'Not till I'm dressed.'

She laughed at that and a moment later gave him a sturdy sensible china mug of tea, and Sharpe, reflecting on his comfort as he sipped tea in a padded chair before a now blazing fire, wondered how his battalion was faring as they advanced further north in the seething rain. He drank his tea and watched Candelaria arrange a tray with a teapot, strainer, milk jug and sugar bowl, all of which she carried further into the house, and, by the time she returned, Sharpe was asleep.

Candelaria woke him as the setting sun dimmed the kitchen that was now lit by lanterns. Sharpe felt confused, 'How long have I slept?'

'Long enough,' Candelaria said, 'and you must dress, Major.' She gave him what appeared to be a new jacket and overalls. Even the metal scabbard of his heavy cavalry sword had been polished, while the stock of his Baker rifle appeared to have been oiled so it shone.

'You washed these?' Sharpe held up the jacket and overalls.

'I just brushed them,' she said.

'*Muito obrigado*,' Sharpe said fervently. The French cavalry boots actually gleamed in the candlelight, while his red officer's sash, that had been greasy and stained by both blood and mud, now looked red again.

'The sash is still damp,' Candelaria said, 'because I had to wash it. It was greasy! You wipe your hands on it, yes?' she accused him sternly.

'I do,' Sharpe confessed, and he used it to wipe oil from his rifle's lock or grease from his sword blade.

'Then stop it. It is an honour to wear it, Major.'

'Yes ma'am,' Sharpe said, making her laugh.

She watched as he dressed. 'Those overalls,' she said, 'are French?'

'Yes.'

'What happened to the Frenchman?'

'I killed him.'

'His boots too?'

'Same Frenchman.'

'Yes.'

'Well done, Major.'

Sharpe buckled the belt, the heavy sword hanging from its slings, then glanced at the rifle which he always carried. Candelaria saw the glance. 'You cannot take that to dinner, Major.'

'I suppose not,' he said, reluctant to leave the rifle out of his sight.

'I will look after it for you. You will find it in the room where you will sleep tonight.'

'I sleep here tonight?' he asked in astonishment. Major-General Barnes had warned him that he would be away for a few days, but Sharpe had confidently anticipated sharing his wife's bed.

'You are surprised?' Candelaria asked.

'I am,' he said and realised, to his chagrin, that he was mildly relieved too.

'His lordship ordered it,' she said, then picked up his rifle,

'I didn't have time to polish the brass,' she said, indicating the trigger guard and patch-box cover, 'you would like me to do it?'

'Best not,' Sharpe said.

'No?'

'The sun reflects off bright metal, and if the sun ever does shine again, some Frenchmen have good enough eyesight to see it.'

'Ah!' she said. 'You know your business.'

'I hope so.'

'Then you are ready. Let me take you to his lordship.'

Sharpe followed Candelaria into a wide hallway hung with dripping cloaks and greatcoats where she knocked on a door and responded to the sharp answering bark of 'Enter!'

'Major Sharpe, your lordship,' Candelaria said, then backed out of the doorway, leaving Sharpe alone with Field Marshal the Lord Wellington.

'My lord,' Sharpe said, coming to attention.

'Ah, Sharpe! Come in, sit down. I see you smartened your uniform!'

'Miss Candelaria did, sir,' Sharpe said.

Wellington gave a grunt to that and waved towards a chair at the far side of his desk. 'How are things on the east bank of the Nive?'

'Quiet, my lord.'

Another grunt. 'I doubt they'll stay that way. Marshal Soult has an opportunity and he'd be a damned fool not to take it. On the other hand I'm not over-impressed by Soult, so perhaps he'll leave us in peace.' Wellington looked uncomfortable. He was holding a pencil in his right hand that he was irritably tapping on a document he had apparently been reading. The tapping suddenly stopped. 'You're effectively commanding the South Essex, yes?'

'Indeed, my lord,' Sharpe said, trying not to show the sudden excitement he felt.

'While you're here, Sharpe, I wanted to explain something to you,' Wellington paused, throwing down the pencil. 'You would think I know best who should be commanding the troops in this army, but there are gentlemen back in London who apparently think otherwise, and I cannot overrule their decisions.'

So, Sharpe thought, he was not about to be promoted and he felt his heart sink. He already commanded the battalion, and believed he had led it well in battle, but that counted for nothing. Some popinjay like Sir bloody Nathaniel would be promoted over Sharpe's head because he was a gentleman and Sharpe was not. He suppressed his fury and managed to respond calmly. 'I understand, my lord.'

'Do you?' The question was almost belligerent. 'I don't! They send me fools to command the finest troops in Europe!' Was Wellington thinking of Sir Nathaniel, Sharpe wondered, but said nothing. 'Those troops, and you, Sharpe, deserve better. How long have we known each other?'

'Almost twenty years, my lord.'

'Since you were Private Sharpe of the 33rd's Light Company.'

'Indeed, my lord.'

'If I could give you the South Essex, Sharpe, I would, but I can't. I did ask, even recommended, but the answer has been no.'

'Thank you for asking, my lord.'

Wellington reached for some papers on his desk and extracted one which he glanced at. 'It seems you've made enemies in the Horse Guards, Sharpe. Not a clever thing to do.'

For a moment Sharpe was confused, uncertain how to respond. It was true that on his recent visit to Britain he had indeed upset the officials in the Horse Guards, the commanding office of the British army, but he believed he had escaped unharmed from that harsh encounter. 'If I had not, my lord,' he said awkwardly, 'I could never have brought the replacement men from Britain.'

Wellington grunted again, then tossed the paper aside. 'What you did, Sharpe, was praiseworthy, brave, and damned stupid. Don't do it again.'

'I won't, sir.'

Wellington looked suddenly embarrassed. 'I owe you much, Sharpe.'

'I doubt that, my lord.'

'You doubt it! You remember Assaye?'

'Indeed, my lord.' It was Sharpe's turn to feel embarrassed.

'Stories spread through armies like fleas on a hound, Sharpe, but I've never heard that tale, which I suspect means you've never told it.'

'I haven't, my lord.'

'I'm grateful for that too.'

'I'm not sure I remember exactly what happened, my lord.'

'I do! I've never heard cursing like you cursed that day, and I've never seen a man fight as Sergeant Sharpe fought that day! You think I've forgotten?'

Sharpe said nothing at first. In truth he did not remember

all that had happened, only that Wellington had been thrown from his dying horse and fallen among the enemy, and Sharpe was the closest man to help him, and that opportunity had ended in a welter of killing which resulted in Sergeant Sharpe being made an officer. 'It was a confusing day, my lord.'

'A confusion which left me in your debt, Sharpe.'

Sharpe waved that comment away. 'We were both doing our duty that day, my lord.'

'Don't give me glib answers,' Wellington snarled, 'just know I have not forgotten, nor will I forget.'

'Thank you, my lord,' Sharpe said.

There was a sudden knock on the door which startled Sharpe.

'Enter!' Wellington called.

An aide appeared. 'They're back, my lord,' he said.

'Thank you, Todd. None of them drowned?'

'Not one, my lord.'

'Thank the risen Christ for that,' Wellington said fervently. 'Did they see what they wanted to see?'

'They say so, my lord.'

'No doubt we'll hear their report at dinner. Thank you, Major.' He looked back to Sharpe and waited till the door closed. 'We have visitors from the navy, Sharpe, and they wanted to examine some boats in the harbour here and it sounds as if they were successful.'

'The navy?'

'With all this rain we need the navy. We'll all be afloat soon.' Sharpe dutifully smiled at the thin jest. 'And the Admiral,' Wellington continued, 'particularly wanted to meet you.'

71

'Me, sir?'

'So he said, which is why you'll dine with us and take care of our visitors for a few days. Take them north. They particularly need to see our pontoon bridges, so show them the bridge at Villefranque. That's the one they need to see and that's all your job, except to keep them alive!' He glanced at a clock on the mantelpiece that wheezed loudly before laboriously striking five. 'We dine in one hour, Sharpe.'

'Very good, my lord,' Sharpe said, standing.

'There's a room directly across the hallway that serves as a mess,' Wellington said. 'I'm sure you can ring for tea or something stronger.'

'Thank you, my lord,' Sharpe said and turned to the door, then remembered he had an errand to perform and fished in his pouch for the two letters. 'Sir Edward Barnes particularly asked me to give you this, my lord.'

Wellington almost snatched the letter from Sharpe, tore it off at the seal and leaned back in his chair to read. 'Wait,' he said, 'sit. You're mentioned.' He went back to the letter.

Sharpe sat again. He gazed past Wellington, looking through a wide window at a restless grey sea. So he was to nursemaid some naval officers? It sounded a strange duty, but not too challenging, and it might even give him time in Saint-Jean-de-Luz and an opportunity to see Jane. He was imagining that reunion when Wellington interrupted his thoughts.

'So,' Wellington said brusquely. He was evidently reading from Major-General Barnes's letter, '"Major Sharpe, disregarding my orders, succeeded in encircling the enemy and in mounting a surprise assault on their rear which precipitated

72

the collapse of the enemy and the capture of the village, of over two hundred prisoners, six twelve-pounder guns and a good deal of useful material. All for the loss of fewer than thirty men." So, you're still disregarding orders, Sharpe?'

'Rarely, my lord.'

'Well done, anyway.' Wellington lay the letter on his desk and smoothed out its folds. 'What's that?' he demanded as Sharpe dropped the second letter onto the desk.

'A personal letter for your lordship from Sir Nathaniel Peacock.'

Wellington took the letter up and ripped it open. He muttered something under his breath as he read and Sharpe thought he heard the word idiot, but could not be sure. Then Wellington screwed the letter into a ball and hurled it towards the fire in its small grate. The letter fell short. 'Help it on its way, Sharpe.'

Sharpe stood, dutifully retrieved the letter and tossed it into the fire and watched the flames burn bright as the paper was consumed. 'Sir Nathaniel tells me you're a disgrace to the army, Sharpe.'

'I'm sorry to hear that, my lord.'

'And he also begs permission to return home on leave to give his broken leg time to mend. He says that might take two months. You saw him, I assume, so how badly is he wounded?'

'He assured me it was a mild fracture, my lord. It was splinted and he was walking without difficulty.'

'Then he can damn well stay.' Wellington pulled a piece of paper towards him, pointed at the chair indicating that Sharpe could sit again, then raised the lid of an inkwell and scribbled hastily. 'Your request for leave,' he said aloud as he wrote, 'is denied.' He scrawled his signature, sanded the paper, blew the sand away and folded the letter. 'I'll send the reply with the regimental mail,' Wellington said. 'He was given the 71st, yes?'

'He was, my lord.'

'A damn fine regiment. Cadogan was a real loss.'

'Indeed,' Sharpe agreed. Lieutenant Colonel Cadogan had been a fierce, tough Scottish warrior who had led the 71st with distinction, and then been killed at the battle of Vitoria.

'I lose good men,' Wellington said, 'and the Horse Guards send me idiots whose soldiering is mere prattle, not practice! You know why they're so eager to come, Sharpe?'

'Promotion, my lord?'

'That, of course, but London thinks the war is almost done. The Prussians and Austrians are on France's northern frontiers, we're advancing from the south and London reckons victory is imminent. It isn't! But that's what they think and every poltroon in the army wants to share in the victory! They want to boast that they helped defeat Bonaparte! And we will, Sharpe, but victory won't belong to prattling newcomers, it will be won by men who have fought and fought and learned how to win. Men like you, Sharpe.'

'Thank you, my lord.'

'I've said too much,' Wellington said, then stood and Sharpe followed his example. 'You deserve better, Sharpe,' he said in a low voice, 'and I know it. But I fancy you'll get your chance, one day.'

'Thank you, my lord.'

'Madame Silva will arrange your quarters. I've told Sir Edward he can expect you back within a couple of weeks.'

Sharpe thanked his lordship again, and supposed that Madame Silva was the tall, attractive Candelaria. He let himself out of the room and crossed the hall to find a comfortable parlour with a scatter of leather-upholstered chairs and a welcoming row of decanters on a sideboard. The room was empty, though warmed by a fire, and Sharpe helped himself to a glass of red wine and dropped into an armchair beside the hearth. So he was not to be promoted to command the South Essex, and that was a bitter pill to swallow. He was disappointed, but when he remembered that he had begun as a Private he could not feel surprised. Then he wondered why he was to 'take care' of the naval visitors. It sounded like a task any half-witted officer could undertake and Sharpe, if he had any choice in the matter, would rather spend this one night with Jane and ride back to the South Essex next morning. Then a sudden rattle of hard rain on the parlour windows made the thought of the return journey less inviting.

He heard voices in the hallway and, wanting to discourage conversation with Wellington's upper-class aides, he snatched a newspaper from a basket by the hearth and pretended to read it. It was an English newspaper and, as the door opened, he held it high to conceal his face.

'Anything in the news?' a confident voice demanded.

Sharpe was about to say there was nothing, but his eye had been caught by an article. 'A man claims to have seen mermaids in Exmouth Bay,' he said in a deliberately surly voice.

'By the good Lord!' a second voice exclaimed, 'we must sail there immediately! Is that you, Major Sharpe?'

Sharpe reluctantly lowered the newspaper to see two navy officers. One, who had black hair and a cautious, saturnine expression, he had never seen before, but the other, burly, fair-haired and grinning, was Joel Chase.

Sharpe dropped the paper and stood. 'Captain Chase!' he exclaimed, his surliness turning to pleasure.

'Rear Admiral Sir Joel Chase now, Sharpe!'

'My congratulations, sir,' Sharpe said.

'Stay alive long enough and we all get shoved up the ladder,' Chase said, then offered Sharpe his hand. 'By God, it's good to see you!'

'And you, sir,' Sharpe said. Joel Chase had been the Captain of HMS *Pucelle*, a ship that had carried Sharpe into the thick of the battle of Trafalgar. He was also one of the most decent men Sharpe had met and he now took hold of Sharpe's hand and tugged him into an embrace.

'Still alive, Sharpe! Well done!'

'You too, sir!'

'Allow me to name Captain Crittenden, my flag Captain.' Sharpe vaguely remembered that a flag Captain was the Captain of whatever ship the Admiral sailed in, a position of some privilege. 'And this,' Chase continued, gesturing at Sharpe, 'is the rogue I told you of. Led my Marines in the capture of your ship!'

'As I recall, sir,' Sharpe said, 'I followed you aboard that ship.'

'And the *Revenant* is my flagship now,' Chase said happily, ignoring the compliment. 'Is that monkey blood drinkable?' He looked at the sideboard.

Sharpe recalled from his time onboard Sir Joel's ship that the navy referred to red wine as monkey's blood. 'It's red and wet, sir, and hasn't killed me yet.'

'Then let's be about it. And what's this about mermaids in Exmouth Bay?'

'Just a newspaper report,' Sharpe said.

Chase stooped and plucked up the paper. 'In the *Observer*, eh? Then it must be true, though I'm surprised Florence didn't write and tell me! We live on the shore of the bay.' He scanned the page. 'The silly bugger fed them boiled fish! What a fool! Everyone knows you feed champagne and sweets to mermaids! No wonder he lost them!' He threw the paper down. 'It is good to see you,' he said again, 'and I'm told you're to be our preserver!'

'So I'm told, sir.'

'I've been fighting the damned French for twenty years, Sharpe, but I've never observed the army in action, and Lord Wellington is allowing Captain Crittenden and me a glimpse of the festivities.'

'I'm told you need to examine our pontoon bridge at Villefranque, sir?'

'Oh, we do and doubtless we will, but I'm hoping you'll show us some real fighting as well?'

'I can't think Lord Wellington would be happy about that, sir.'

'Oh he'd hate the very idea! He fears having to tell their lordships in London that he lost an Admiral to the French! Which is why I think he insisted on having you as our guide and protector.'

'So I can be blamed,' Sharpe said.

'First rule of the military,' Chase said happily, 'always have someone you can blame for disaster! Thank you, Crittenden.' He took a glass of wine. 'Mind you, Sharpe, don't blame Lord Wellington. I particularly asked if you were with the army so it's entirely my fault if you get blamed for my sad death.' He raised the glass in a toast. 'To happy memories, eh?'

'Happy memories, sir.'

Chase downed the glass and held it out for more. 'You remember young Harry Collier, Sharpe? A little sprog of a Midshipman?'

'I do indeed, sir.'

'First Lieutenant and commander of a damned good ship now! And taller than you or me!'

'Do remember me to him, sir.'

'Oh, I will! And Clouter? You must remember him?'

'I'll never forget him, sir, he saved my life.'

'He did? He never mentioned it. He's Petty Officer Clouter now, and you'll meet him. He wouldn't permit me ashore without coming to protect me. He's a good man.'

'The best,' Sharpe said feelingly, remembering the enormous black man who fought like a devil. Clouter had been freed from a slave ship and carried to the island of Saint Helena where all freed slaves were kept until there was a sufficient number to justify ships carrying them home to Africa. Joel Chase's ship, the *Pucelle*, had put into Saint Helena and, ever short of seamen, Chase had asked for volunteers among the freed slaves, and Clouter had been among those that stepped forward. And when the crew of the *Pucelle* had boarded the enemy ship Sharpe had slipped on a patch of fresh blood as a huge Frenchman, wielding a boarding axe, had hacked at him. Sharpe had been helpless. He had tried to fend off the axe with his sword, then seen the Frenchman taking care to aim a last killing stroke when Clouter had run him through with a pike. Clouter had then plucked up the axe and led a maniacal charge into the French boarders, killing left and right, but losing two or three fingers from his right hand which had done nothing to stem his fighting ability. 'He's a bloody good man, sir,' Sharpe said.

'He'll be pleased to see you again,' Chase said, then paused because Sharpe had raised a hand. 'What is it?'

'Not sure, sir,' Sharpe said. He opened one of the parlour windows and heard a faint rumble of thunder. 'Cannon fire, sir.'

'It could be thunder?' Captain Crittenden suggested.

'Nonsense!' Chase said, 'that's gunnery!' He cocked his head to listen and another distant boom sounded. 'Impossible to tell where it's coming from,' he said, 'could be one of ours?'

'Ours?' Sharpe asked.

'We have a pair of frigates in the bay,' Captain Crittenden answered instead of Chase, 'hunting down privateers.' He had none of Sir Joel's enthusiasm, but spoke with a cold reserve as if he disapproved of Sharpe.

'Whoever it is,' Chase said hungrily, 'let's hope they're giving Boney a bloody nose.'

'Amen to that,' Crittenden said.

The gun-thunder went on, rising in tempo, and Sharpe's instinct told him it did not come from the sea, but from the north where Marshal Soult's army defended their homeland. And somewhere out there was his battalion and he was at least twenty miles from them and feeling helpless.

He went to dinner.

CHAPTER FOUR

'Good news!' Lord Wellington said when his company was seated. 'Bonaparte's been well beaten!'

'Hallelujah!' Sir Joel Chase responded happily. 'Where, my lord?'

'Leipzig.' Wellington put a sheet of paper in front of the Admiral. 'The Prussians, Russians and Austrians beat him and he'll have to give up much of his German conquests.'

'Over five hundred thousand men involved!' Sir Joel was reading the dispatch.

Wellington gave a brief laugh. 'I never trust those numbers, Sir Joel. It's not like your battles, you can count the ships, but men seeing an enemy army can't count the men, but they can and do indulge in multiplication! But Bonaparte's been forced to retreat, and that's good.'

Sharpe remained mostly silent throughout the meal, concentrating on which knife, fork or spoon he was supposed to use, though as Wellington began passing the port he had looked at Sharpe and brusquely demanded what he intended to show Sir Joel the next morning.

'I thought we'd head straight for Villefranque, my lord,' Sharpe had replied.

'I'd suggest you stay on this side of the River Nive,' Wellington said, 'and take a brief look at Sir John Hope's positions, and that, Sir Joel, will give you an estimation of the amount of men and materials a pontoon bridge must carry. Then on to Villefranque, which might be of particular interest because it's not strictly a pontoon bridge.'

'It's not, my lord?'

'It's constructed with commandeered river boats. I'm sure the engineers there will be only too happy to explain how they made it.'

'I look forward to inspecting it, my lord,' Chase said, sawing at a piece of mutton.

'So pay your respects to Sir John,' Wellington said, 'but don't go farther north than his headquarters at Barrouillet. That's an order, Sharpe.'

'Understood, my lord,' Sharpe said. He knew that Sir John Hope commanded the forces west of the River Nive, while General Sir Rowland Hill commanded on the eastern bank, an arrangement that Lord Wellington was now explaining to Sir Joel.

'I have to advance troops on both banks of the River Nive,' Wellington was saying, 'if we're to trap Soult in Bayonne. My information tells me that Soult outnumbers us, which is inconvenient because I must divide the army into two halves, one east of the Nive and the other west, and Soult has more than enough men to overwhelm either half. He's not a fool and he will try. We have two pontoon bridges across the river, so one side can reinforce the other, but using the bridges takes time. If I know Soult he'll only attack down one bank, he's been beaten too often to take on my whole army by advancing against both halves at the same time, but if he takes out half my army we'll have no choice but to retreat back into Spain.'

'And your ambition, my lord,' Sir Joel asked, 'is to capture Bayonne?'

'Which is a formidable fortress city,' Wellington said sourly. 'No, Sir Joel, my ambition is to tempt Marshal Soult out of Bayonne and give him another thrashing.' Sharpe sensed that Wellington was extremely uncomfortable revealing his plans, and was only doing so as a courtesy to Sir Joel.

Sir Joel frowned. 'You say Marshal Soult outnumbers you, my lord?'

'He does.'

'But if the Prussians and their allies are threatening Bonaparte's northern frontier, might he not withdraw forces from Soult to counter the threat?'

'And thus ignoring the threat we pose?' Wellington said curtly. 'We are his only enemies on his territory—' He stopped abruptly because a scream had sounded elsewhere in the mansion. Wellington turned towards the dining room's door, frowning, as another louder scream sounded, followed by a rush of footsteps. He opened his mouth to speak, but just then the door opened and a black-haired girl rushed into the room, only to halt in astonishment when she saw the men sitting around the table.

Her astonishment lasted a heartbeat before she began shouting at Wellington. She spoke Spanish, but so quickly that Sharpe, who understood the language well enough, only caught some of what she said. 'I do not want to go home! You cannot make me! You must let me go!' She repeated the last phrase and dropped to her knees, holding her clasped hands towards his lordship, who looked furious.

'You will go home,' Wellington said firmly, and then Candelaria, who had plainly been pursuing the girl, came into the room and bowed her head towards Wellington.

'I am sorry, my lord,' Candelaria said, 'she ran past me.'

'Take her away, Madame Silva.'

'Of course, my lord.' Candelaria reached for the girl, but the younger woman snatched her hands away and squirmed to one side.

'Go!' Wellington roared in anger and the girl squealed in terror and froze in a crouch. Wellington's temper was rarely unleashed, but Sharpe knew how frightening it was.

Candelaria pounced on the girl, taking hold of her one garment, a long nightdress, and dragging her to her feet. The girl was heavy, but Candelaria hauled her upright and then, bending one of the girl's arms painfully behind her back, she pushed the girl, who was still crying, towards the door. 'I apologise, gentlemen,' Candelaria said, and then two more maids appeared at the door and helped take the girl out of the room. The door was shut, but the girl's sobs echoed from the hallway outside, only to fade as she was dragged upstairs.

'Bloody girl,' Wellington muttered, then looked around the table. 'That, gentlemen, is the Donna Alyssa, daughter to the Marquess of Cantarranas, who serves in Spain's ruling council and who, therefore, is vital to our alliance. The wretched girl ran away with a French cavalry officer who, as far as we can tell, abandoned her in this town as he retreated. We have undertaken to return her to her father in Cadiz, and she, as you could see, would prefer to be left to pursue her lover. Sir Joel has kindly agreed to convey her to Cadiz. The sooner the better.'

'A brig-sloop will be ready to sail in a week, my lord,' Sir Joel said, then grimaced, 'the girl's not what I expected.'

'And you expected?'

'A Spanish beauty, my lord, something to cheer up a weary crew. But she's a plump little piglet, isn't she?'

'An unattractive girl,' Wellington agreed, 'but evidently appealing enough to a French cavalryman. At least temporarily. Even so, you'll need to carry a pair of chaperones to satisfy her father.'

Sir Joel grimaced again. 'Extremely ill luck to have women aboard a ship, my lord.'

'Better that, Sir Joel, than deliver her after she's been rogered by half the crew.'

'There is that, my lord.'

'You say a ship will be ready in a week?'

'My swiftest ship was badly hit by a Biscay storm, my lord. Her sailing master assures me it will take at least a week to reeve new rigging and fly topmasts.'

'You have other ships?'

'We do, my lord.'

'Then why, pray, cannot the girl be removed at once?

The Spanish alliance is still vital! Major Todd,' Wellington indicated one of his aides sitting at the table, 'will have selected the chaperones. Two should be sufficient.'

'Of course, my lord.'

'The Spanish alliance,' Wellington said grimly, 'is still necessary, though their troops are a damned nuisance. They want revenge for the atrocities the French committed on Spain and the last thing I need is a hostile population. I've had reports of Spanish troops behaving like brigands! Plunder, murder and rape! I won't abide it! I may be outnumbered, but I'm tempted to send the Spanish troops back to Spain.' He stopped abruptly, as if realising his anger was ill-placed, and looked at Sharpe instead. 'I suggest, Sharpe, that you go north with Sir Joel, but for God's sake avoid the army's picquets.'

That provoked a brief laugh. 'I'll do my best to keep him safe, my lord.'

'See that you do. After that, Sharpe, look at the bridge and allow Sir Joel to pay his respects to General Hill. I expect you back here in ten days, by which time,' Wellington turned his gaze onto Sir Joel, 'the navy will have relieved me of that viperous girl. Above all, Sharpe,' Wellington looked at Sharpe again, 'keep Sir Joel alive! The Admiralty in London is uncooperative enough without me having an Admiral killed.'

'I'll do my best, my lord,' Sharpe promised again.

And next morning Sharpe did exactly that, though it was difficult to restrain Sir Joel Chase's natural enthusiasm. Sharpe, in a wet dawn and guided again by Sergeant Williams, followed the coast road north, then struck inland towards a group of small villages where, in a wide pasture, the ammunition wagons were parked. Each wagon had a white painted legend denoting what it carried, either musket or rifle cartridges, nine-pounder roundshot or canister, and shells and caseshot for the howitzers. Portuguese soldiers were camped around the wagons, ready to load their mules with the requested ammunition and carry it forward. 'The Artillery send their horse-drawn limbers, of course,' Sharpe said, 'the mules are for the infantry. But in an emergency all this lot,' he waved at the busy park, 'will have to cross the bridge.'

Captain Crittenden seemed to be counting the massed wagons and noting numbers in a small notebook, but Sir Joel appeared to have no interest in the sight. 'So how far away are the fellows who do the shooting?' he asked.

'Probably two miles,' Sharpe guessed the answer, 'preferably closer. This will be the main supply point, but most brigades will have another closer to the fighting.'

'Let's go see!' Sir Joel said eagerly.

A crackle of distant musket fire disturbed the morning. It continued for a few seconds, then died away. 'By the good Lord!' Sir Joel exclaimed happily, turning his horse towards the sound.

'Probably the picquets clearing their muskets,' Sharpe said to dampen Sir Joel's enthusiasm.

'Clearing muskets?' Sir Joel demanded.

'They've been in the rain all night with loaded muskets and they fire off the charged musket so the powder doesn't clog in the damp.'

'Our Marines do the same,' Petty Officer Clouter growled.

The huge man, bigger even than Sergeant Harper, was uncomfortably mounted on a sturdy horse and continually positioned himself to the north of Sir Joel because the French were in that direction. 'They'll hit me before they hit you, sir,' he had explained when the Admiral complained.

Sergeant Williams, going deliberately slowly and accompanied this morning by two Dragoon troopers, led them from the ammunition park onto a lane that rose steadily uphill. 'I'll take you to Sir John Hope's headquarters, sir,' he announced stolidly.

'I don't know, Sharpe,' Sir Joel now said as another burst of musketry sounded, 'there must be a hell of a lot of picquets! And that,' he said just after a much louder bang sounded from the north, 'sounds like a cannon!' He immediately kicked his horse's flanks and, pushing past the three Dragoons, hurried towards the crest of the low hill.

'Stop him!' Sharpe snarled at Sergeant Williams, who obediently spurred after the Admiral, closely followed by an anxious Clouter whose heavily laden horse lumbered uphill. 'Clouter!' Sharpe bellowed, 'get off the horse! Now!'

The big man half fell and half slid off the horse, then stood watching as Sharpe approached. 'I have to look after the Admiral!' Clouter complained.

Sharpe ignored him, sliding out of his own saddle and gazing at the hill crest. 'Sergeant Williams! Dismount! And the Admiral!'

A French shell came towards them, its fuse leaving a thin trace of swirling smoke in the winter air. The shot ploughed into the field to Sharpe's left where the rain-sodden soil extinguished the fuse.

'The Admiral shouldn't be up there,' Clouter complained.

'Damn right he shouldn't. Leave your horse.' Sharpe abandoned his own horse and started uphill. Ahead of him he could see that Sir Joel had obeyed Sergeant Williams's urgent instructions and dismounted. 'Stay there, sir!' Sharpe called, just as another French shell flew overhead to explode safely beyond Captain Crittenden who had accompanied his Admiral. Crittenden, hearing the urgency in Sharpe's voice, had already dismounted and now led his horse uphill. 'Leave your horse with ours,' Sharpe told him, 'from here on we're infantry.'

'Infantry?' Crittenden sounded understandably confused.

'The bloody French see horsemen on the ridge,' Sharpe explained, 'and one of them in a cocked hat. They'll think it's Lord Wellington.' Though that, Sharpe thought, may not be such a bad thing. If the French saw Lord Wellington they would be fearful because they had never beaten him, but from the continuous din of gunfire Sharpe suspected he was about to witness a rare French victory.

Two more shells screamed over the ridge, both leaving their smoke trails and both being extinguished in the mud. Sergeant Williams had succeeded in pulling Sir Joel back from the skyline, and the French cannon must have sought other targets for no more shells came. Captain Crittenden took off his own cocked hat and tucked it under his arm. Like the Admiral, he was swathed in a black oilskin cloak on which the rain pattered loud. 'Sergeant Williams! To me!' Sharpe called. 'Bring the horses!' He turned to Clouter. 'You can join the Admiral, but don't let him cross the skyline and tell him to take off his bloody hat.'

'Aye aye, sir,' Clouter growled and ran uphill.

The crackle of musketry was now loud, incessant and uncomfortably close. 'We're holding them,' Sharpe said. He could tell that from the rhythm of the British musketry. 'Sergeant! Well done, stay here with the horses. I'll find you when we're done.'

'Shouldn't we go back to the ammunition park, sir?' the Sergeant suggested. He knew, just as Sharpe did, that the sounds from the north indicated a fair-sized battle.

'Probably, but Sir Joel will want to meet Sir John.' In truth, Sharpe suspected, Sir Joel wanted to be in the thick of any fighting. 'I'll find Sir John,' Sharpe continued, 'and you just wait for us.'

'I'd best come with you, sir,' Sergeant Williams said obstinately. 'Bellock and Smythe can guard the horses.' Bellock and Smythe were the two Dragoons. 'I know where Sir John's headquarters are sir,' Williams finished, 'if we can reach them.'

Sharpe rather hoped they could not find Sir John who would not take kindly to an Admiral visiting in the middle of a battle, but he suspected Sir Joel would insist on pressing forward and, to be honest, Sharpe was as curious as Sir Joel to discover just what deafening chaos lay beyond the crest.

Sir Joel, urged by Clouter, had taken position in a ditch to the left of the road from where he could still gaze north. Clouter must have insisted on standing in front of the Admiral, who was now using the huge man's right shoulder as a rest for his telescope and, as Sharpe could hear as he came closer, continually expressing astonishment. 'Good Lord! Extraordinary! Good God!'

Sharpe indicated that Captain Crittenden and Sergeant Williams should shelter in the ditch, then walked to the crest.

'Good God,' he said quietly.

'This is magnificent, Sharpe!' Sir Joel called excitedly, climbing from the ditch to join Sharpe. 'But it can't last. Our fellows are doomed, surely?'

Sharpe said nothing at first, just stared at the extraordinary events to the north. Immediately in front of him, at the foot of the ridge where he stood, was a small village dominated by a large house closest to the advancing French. The house was built on a rise and was wreathed by musket smoke jetting from its upper windows and, even as he watched, a French roundshot tore through the roof, shattering tiles and splintering rafters. Beyond the house, in an orchard and pasture, a line of redcoats was firing platoon volleys at a monstrous French column that advanced on and either side of the road leading from Bayonne. Other French columns were to east and west, all faced by either British or Portuguese infantry arrayed in their fragile-looking two-deep lines. He looked east towards the distant River Nive and the whole countryside this side of the river was smeared with powder smoke and Sharpe reckoned Marshal Soult had sent almost his whole army to smash through Sir John Hope's forces. He used Sir Joel's telescope to look east beyond the Nive and saw no smoke on the far bank where, in the distant hills, the South Essex stood.

A roundshot crashed through the hedge to Sharpe's right. 'Take your hat off, sir.'

'My hat?' Sir Joel asked, surprised.

'They think you're a General, sir, and the next shot will be a shell.'

'Better they shoot at me than those poor fellows down there.' Sir Joel pointed at the redcoats defending the large house.

'And if they kill you, sir, Lord Wellington will break me down to corporal.'

Sir Joel reluctantly removed the cocked hat. 'And those scoundrels,' he meant the French, 'are trying to capture the village?'

'Apparently, sir, yes.'

'Then I insist we go down there.' He pointed at the big house. 'That must be Sir John's headquarters?'

'Probably,' Sharpe conceded, 'but I doubt he'll want to see us till this is over. We should really stay here, sir.'

'And leave the fighting to those poor fellows?' Sir Joel stared at the outnumbered redcoats. 'By God! I've already taken off my hat for you, Sharpe, isn't that enough?' The shell that Sharpe had promised struck the road some twenty paces ahead and bounded over their heads to explode behind them. 'Damn them,' Sir Joel said, 'they can't shoot straight!' He put his hat back on and started down the hill.

'Please, sir!' Sharpe hurried to catch him.

'No one will ever say a Chase turned away from the enemy, Sharpe!'

'I'll put that on your tombstone, sir,' Sharpe muttered as he followed.

'What was that, Sharpe?'

'I said that if we reach the village, sir, you stay with me.'

Sharpe, remembering Wellington's tart comment at dinner

on how men multiplied the number of troops opposing them, still reckoned there were at least five battalions of French infantry assaulting the village. They were advancing in column as the French almost always did and, for the moment, their advance was checked by the relentless musketry of the British battalion opposing them, but Sharpe could hear the French musket balls rattling on the big house's stone walls. More shots thudded into the redcoats, whose line was shrinking as Sergeants closed up the files.

The British line, despite its murderous volleys, was being pushed back towards the big house that was serving as a makeshift fortress.

'That's General Hope's headquarters, sir.' Sergeant Williams had caught up with Sharpe.

'Not for much longer,' Sharpe said grimly. Round shot was cracking into the house's stone walls and demolishing its roof. Musket balls were whipping over Sharpe's head, some lower shots striking the road and ricocheting upwards. Sharpe hurried and caught up with the Admiral. 'Do you want to die, sir?'

'Not particularly,' Sir Joel replied airily, 'it would upset Florence and the children. At least I hope it would.'

'Then we go back now, sir!'

'Let's get into the thick of it, Sharpe! God is on our side.'

'Amen,' Sergeant Williams echoed as he joined them.

'Then at least run, sir.' Sharpe plucked at Sir Joel's elbow. 'Run?'

'To get into cover, sir.' In another hundred yards the big house on its low rise would protect them from most of the musketry and from the French Artillery that lined a long low ridge north of the house. Clouter, catching up with them, obstinately took his place directly in front of the Admiral.

'Clouter! I can't see a thing!'

'I can, sir.'

'Cheeky bastard,' Sir Joel growled. He resolutely refused to run and Sharpe remembered how, back when he was a Captain, Chase had patiently, even slowly, paced his quarterdeck as the French marines had poured musket fire down from their masts and rigging. Chase had explained then that it was vital for a commanding officer to show no fear, but only to display a cool disdain for the enemy trying to kill him.

They reached the foot of the hill unscathed and passed an orchard where British surgeons were treating the wounded carried back from the house. Two Portuguese soldiers hurried past, their mules loaded with boxes of musket ammunition. An ear-splitting crack told of a cannon's roundshot hitting the north-facing wall of the house, and a moment later an howitzer shell exploded behind Sharpe as he reached the gateway to the short drive, which led to a yard at the house's southern side. To the left of the yard was a small stable block, opposite on the right was a substantial stone barn which was connected to the house by a short stone wall where a company of redcoats was firing their muskets over the coping at the approaching French infantry that was now only about a hundred paces away. The wall was on the same rise of ground as the house and barn and marked the last defensive line to protect the buildings. The redcoat battalion had retreated into the farm and was evidently determined to hold the position.

'Do we go into the house?' Sir Joel shouted over the cacophony of musket volleys and exploding shells.

'No!' Sharpe said. He had managed to guide the Admiral into the shelter of the house. 'You don't want to be inside, sir, if the French get in.'

'I'll bloody well help kick them out!' Sir Joel said indignantly.

'Best leave that to the defenders, sir,' Sharpe said, 'they know what they're doing.'

Sharpe hoped he was right. He was judging the fight purely by its sound and for the moment the house seemed strongly defended. At least two British artillery batteries were on the slope to the south of the house and their shells and round shot were striking the big French columns, ahead of which was a mass of skirmishers who had driven in the British Light Companies opposing them. The columns themselves were now in range of the British line of muskets which were pouring relentless volleys that had checked the enemy's advance, but the French were firing back and Sharpe could hear their musket balls rattling on the big house's stone walls.

Sir Joel had gone to stand behind the redcoats lining the low stone wall and was gazing at the nearest enemy column. 'I've heard about French infantry columns, but never seen one,' Sir Joel remarked, 'they're impressive!'

'And make easy targets,' Sharpe said, trying vainly to hurry the Admiral back to the dubious shelter of the big house.

'It's what Lord Nelson did at Trafalgar, isn't it?' Sir Joel said enthusiastically. 'He formed us into two columns and sailed us straight into the French line! What a man!'

And, Sharpe reflected, if French naval gunnery had been as

good as the British those two columns would have been pounded into helpless wrecks. He still shivered at the memory of a warship's gun deck in a fight; all noise, smoke, blood, splinters and death. An ear-splitting crack told of another roundshot hitting the north-facing wall of the house.

Sir Joel plucked at Sharpe's sleeve. 'Are you sure we shouldn't go into the house? I really must pay my respects to Sir John.'

'Not right now, sir.'

The defence was taking a heavy toll on the French columns, but the sheer disparity in numbers suggested that the French would soon overwhelm the defenders and, looking past the wall's defenders, Sharpe saw the eagerness with which the closest files of the nearest French column were running forward. The ground between them and the wall was already thick with bodies, too many in red jackets who must have been the skirmishers who did not retreat fast enough. He took the rifle off his shoulder and loaded it carefully, wrapping the bullet in the leather patch which would grip the barrel's rifling.

'Can I, Sharpe?' Sir Joel was beside him, reaching for the rifle. 'I'm a damn good shot!'

Sharpe primed the lock, shielding the pan from the rain as best he could, then handed the gun to the Admiral. Better, he thought, to let the Admiral join the infantry at the wall than blunder into the house and demand to see General Hope.

'Aim for an officer, sir,' Sharpe said, reckoning that shooting at pheasants in Devon was no guide to the accuracy of a man on a battlefield, but he could not resist Sir Joel's eagerness.

'Officer, eh?' Sir Joel had the rifle at his shoulder. 'The buggers with swords, yes?'

'Yes, sir.'

Sir Joel had advanced to the wall where he rested the rifle on the coping. 'Don't worry, lads,' he said to the men either side of him, 'the navy's here!' He fired. 'Ah ha!' he exclaimed. 'One Frog officer down! Cut the heathens down, boys!' he called to the redcoats and handed the rifle back to Sharpe. 'Another, if you please, Sharpe.'

Sharpe reloaded and handed the rifle back. Sir Joel, it seemed, was a crack shot or else a lucky one because Sharpe could see two men dragging an officer back from the front rank of the French column. That rank was being hit hard, not just by the muskets of the men at the wall, but by fire from the house windows and from a Portuguese battalion to Sharpe's right, just beyond the big stone barn, but every enemy that fell was immediately replaced and the column seemed to stretch back for ever.

'Did you bring the gun?' a young redcoat officer snatched at Sharpe's arm.

'Who are you?'

'Lieutenant Ellis.' Something about Sharpe's face made Ellis stand a little straighter. 'Sir,' he added.

'Is this your company?' Sharpe nodded at the men crowding the wall.

'Yes, sir, but the Captain's dead. He requested a gun.'

'Keep them firing, Lieutenant. Your captain asked for a gun?'

'He did, sir.'

'You keep them firing, I'll look for the gun.'

Sharpe doubted a cannon would arrive. Requests from mere Captains were usually ignored by gunners, and there were few

97

enough artillery pieces on the British side, and all of those were on the slope to the south firing over the roofs of the house, stable and barn.

'Sharpe! Another round, please!' The Admiral, his face alight with excitement, thrust the rifle at Sharpe who obediently wrapped another bullet, rammed it down the hot barrel and primed the pan again.

'There, sir.' He held out the weapon.

'This is good sport, Sharpe.'

'Just keep your head down, sir.'

Sir Joel ignored the advice, going back to the wall that was being repeatedly struck by French musket balls. Which meant, Sharpe knew, that the French were not firing high, the usual fault of raw troops, but these men were being forced to fire uphill which mitigated the usual sky-wasted shots. He feared for Sir Joel's life and knew he should somehow drag the Admiral back from his sport and remove him to a safer place, but just as he was about to pull Sir Joel backwards a roundshot struck the wall of the barn to Sharpe's right. The sound of the impact was huge and was followed by cheers from the French as a good section of the barn wall collapsed in a cascade of dust and shattered masonry. The head of the column rushed towards the damaged building, and the wild charge was fortuitously aimed into the gap between the defending redcoat battalion and the Portuguese infantry. Some Frenchmen fell to the defenders' musketry, but too many were clambering over the fallen stones to shelter inside the barn.

Sharpe swore. The big barn doors that opened onto the yard looked stout and were barred with a solid baulk of timber held by two brackets on the outside of the doors, but already the French were trying to open the huge doors from within, shaking them to rattle the locking bar in its iron brackets. Sharpe picked up the musket of a dead redcoat and snatched a handful of cartridges from the man's pouch. He loaded the musket and fired it at the door. The ball did not pierce the heavy wood and the sound of its strike coincided with a crash as an axeman on the other side began hacking at the doors. The bastards had a pioneer in there, Sharpe thought, with a big axe. He thought about ordering Lieutenant Ellis to detail men to face the doors, but the redcoats at the wall were already too few to check the oncoming French. The axe blows were shaking the left-hand door and a split appeared in the wood. Sharpe reloaded the musket and ran to the door, jammed the muzzle into the slit and pulled the trigger. A screech told him he had hit someone, but evidently not the axeman, who was still crashing his heavy blade into the timbers.

Then salvation arrived with a clatter of hooves, the jangle of trace chains and the rumble of heavy wheels as a nine-pounder cannon arrived. Two of the horses were immediately wounded by French musket balls, but the gunners managed to unhook the harnesses from the limber and lead the team away. 'That wall's too high!' a young Artillery officer shouted, pointing at the wall where the Admiral was looking for another target.

'Bugger the wall,' Sharpe called, 'do you have canister?'

'Of course, sir?' The last word was a question.

'Major Sharpe,' Sharpe named himself, then, 'train the gun on those doors,' he pointed at the barn doors, 'and fast.'

'Sir,' the Artilleryman said, 'just canister?'

'Just canister.' Sharpe turned. 'Clouter!'

The big man who, like Sharpe, had armed himself with a musket from a fallen redcoat, ran to him. 'Sir?'

'You can lift that locking bar?'

'Easily.'

'Wait for my word,' Sharpe said. He watched as the gunners handspiked the weapon so it faced the barn doors, and as they rammed a powder bag and canister down the barrel.

'Now, sir?' the young Artillery officer called.

Sharpe glanced at the gun's barrel and reckoned it was aimed dead centre on the barn doors. 'Wait,' he told the young Artilleryman, 'and thank you for coming.'

'My brother sent the message, sir, and it sounded desperate.' The gunner looked around the yard and Sharpe did not have the heart to tell him his brother was dead. 'Just wait, Lieutenant,' he said, and then to Clouter, 'now!'

Clouter ran to the doors and easily lifted the big beam from its brackets before running to one side. The next axe blow merely shoved the left-hand door outwards and the French infantry gave a cheer as they pushed both doors open.

'Now, Lieutenant,' Sharpe said.

The Frenchmen crowded in the barn's wide doorway had a heartbeat to see their death. They had been ready to charge out into the yard, now those at the front screamed at the men behind to back away. There were too many; the barn was crammed with men who had found temporary shelter inside the stone walls from the musketry outside.

Now those men were faced by a single cannon just ten paces

from the doorway, and the cannon was loaded with canister that was a tin can filled with musket balls. When the cannon was fired the tin can would be rent apart by the force of the explosion and the musket balls would spread from the gun's muzzle like duckshot from hell.

'Fire!' the Artillery Lieutenant shouted.

To Sharpe, his ears ringing from the gun's sound, it seemed as if the big open doorway to the barn was suddenly a mist of blood. The nearest Frenchmen had been shredded by the canister, their bodies torn apart, and Sharpe guessed that the fatal balls had whipped on to kill or wound most of the packed crowd behind. Some of the canister had struck a big iron plough that occupied the centre of the barn, the balls deflected upwards into more victims.

'Another, sir?' the Artillery officer asked as his crew swabbed the barrel.

'One more for luck,' Sharpe said, 'then load roundshot.' He pushed his way back to the wall and fired the musket at the enthusiastic French, then reloaded the rifle for an impatient Sir Joel. He heard the blast of the second canister round and turned back to gaze into the yellowish cloud of smoke. 'Lieutenant!'

'Sir?'

'Roundshot, and wait! New target!' He turned to Sir Joel, 'Admiral? When I give the command you're to clear men away from the wall. I need ten or fifteen feet clear.'

'Got it, Sharpe.' Sir Joel seemed to take no umbrage at being given a command by a mere Major. He fired the rifle. 'That's another bugger down.'

'Any minute, sir,' Sharpe said, 'and stay out of the way yourself.'

He went back to the artillery piece where a gunner was ramming the roundshot into the hot barrel. 'Turn the gun to face the wall,' Sharpe told the Lieutenant, pointing at the low stone wall that stretched from the house to the barn. Sharpe watched as the gunners handspiked the trail around so that the cannon was pointing at the wall.

'You told me the wall's too high to fire over,' Sharpe said to the Lieutenant.

'It is, sir.'

'So make an embrasure, then run the gun up loaded with canister.' Sharpe took a breath. 'Admiral! Now!'

'Admiral?' the Lieutenant asked.

'He wanted to see a land battle,' Sharpe said.

'Man must be mad, sir.'

The mad Sir Joel was now clearing redcoats from the wall by shouting and using the butt of Sharpe's rifle. 'Enough?' he asked when he had succeeded in making a space some ten feet wide.

'Enough! Out of the way, sir!' Sharpe waited as Sir Joel ran to one side. 'Now, Lieutenant.'

The cannon fired, the roundshot striking the wall with a resounding crash and knocking down a space some four feet wide. The crew was already sponging out the barrel and readying the canister.

'Load canister over ball!' the Lieutenant shouted and watched as his men obeyed. 'Canister and roundshot together do more damage, sir,' he explained to Sharpe. A gunner

Sergeant pierced the powder bag in the gun's breech with a wire pricker, then the crew ran the gun up to the wall and the Lieutenant gave the order to fire. More smoke as the gun leaped backwards, but through the smoke Sharpe could see that the attacking French had been hard hit as the expanding cone of balls flensed through the leading ranks.

'Keep firing, Lieutenant, and thank you.'

The redcoats Sir Joel had bullied away from the wall were back now, firing at the attackers, while the gunners were working frantically to keep up their deadly blasts. Sharpe could hear regular volleys being fired to the east of the barn where a Portuguese battalion was holding their attackers at bay. A half company of the Portuguese, in their brown uniforms, had come to help defend the yard and they took their places at the wall, replacing redcoats who lay on the blood-slicked stones.

Sir Joel, sensing that the defence was now holding, had joined Sharpe. 'One through the hat, Sharpe!' he said, taking off his cocked hat and showing a ragged hole in the peak.

'I think you've done enough, sir,' Sharpe said. He had reloaded the musket and now reloaded the rifle, not because he wanted Sir Joel to rejoin the fight, but because an unloaded firearm was of precious little use in combat. 'We should get you back to Lord Wellington and another shoulder of mutton.'

'Sounds sensible,' Sir Joel said. 'You think these fellows have had enough?' He jerked his head towards the French.

'They'll keep trying,' Sharpe said, 'and we'll keep killing them.'

'I really should pay my respects to General Hope,' Sir Joel said.

'He's gone, sir,' Sergeant Williams said, having overheard the remark.

'Gone?' Sharpe asked.

'Up the hill, sir. Had a rare fight cutting through some enemy on the road.'

Sharpe turned to gaze at the gateway and saw blue-uniformed bodies lying between the stone gateposts. He had been entirely unaware that the enemy had managed to advance past the house on its western side and had presumably been readying to attack the yard's defenders from behind when Sir John and his staff had sliced through them on horseback. The redcoats had succeeded in pushing the survivors back, but Sharpe realised the enemy had been on the brink of capturing the big house and slaughtering its defenders.

'We'll go back up the hill and join Sir John,' he said, but just then Clouter ran from the barn's doorway.

'The buggers are getting in again,' he said.

'Sweet Christ.' Sharpe turned and ran to the barn where, sure enough, half a dozen men were struggling through the charnel house mess of dead bodies that covered the floor. 'Sergeant Williams, go to the Portuguese,' Sharpe pointed east, 'and ask if they can block that entrance.' He meant the huge gap collapsed in the barn's wall by a French roundshot. He levelled the musket and fired at the men, while Sir Joel took the loaded rifle and added its bullet. 'We have to block that bloody hole,' Sharpe said, seeing more men peering through.

'Leave it to me,' Clouter said.

The living Frenchmen already in the barn apparently had unloaded muskets, because one of them stopped to take out

104

a cartridge. His musket had a bayonet fitted and Sharpe knew it would slow the man down. He reloaded his own musket with blinding speed, a talent he had learned in twenty years of soldiering and, unencumbered by a bayonet, he finished when the Frenchman was still priming his lock. He fired and the man was hurled backwards just as Clouter pushed past Sharpe. The big man leaped onto the bodies, a few of which still twitched or moaned, then leaned down and, with astonishing strength, hauled the whole plough off the floor. He had to kick a couple of bodies off the monstrous implement, then he pushed forward towards the gap. The men still living in the barn retreated in front of him, too amazed or scared to even use their bayonets, instead ducking out into the rain beyond the broken wall. Clouter rammed the huge plough into the gap and Sharpe heard bullets clanging off the plough's blade and frame as Clouter jammed it into place.

'Get out, man!' Sir Joel called.

'Coming, sir,' Clouter growled and, satisfied that the plough would prove an adequate obstacle, he retreated to the doorway.

'Well done,' Sharpe said.

A Lieutenant in Portuguese brown appeared beside Sharpe. 'Where do you need us, sir?' Like most officers in the Portuguese army he was British, though to Sharpe's eyes he looked scarcely more than sixteen years old.

'Keep the bastards from coming through this barn,' Sharpe said. 'How many men do you have?'

'Seven, sir.'

'That's enough,' Sharpe said, 'just watch that gap and if any of the bastards try to clamber inside, kill them. If they even show themselves in that gap, kill them.'

More cannon had evidently been brought to support the infantry defending the house because Sharpe could hear their reports from east and west, and the canister flailing at the attackers had slowed them. The French return fire was diminishing. The attackers were tired, they had marched from Bayonne and slogged though damp fields and had been biting cartridges all morning. They had succeeded in driving back the British outposts, but the big house and its outbuildings had proven to be a fortress which anchored the defending battalions, and the swift deadly volleys of the Portuguese and British troops had blunted the attacking columns.

'I reckon we've won here, sir,' Sharpe said to Sir Joel.

'Really?'

'Unless the Crapauds have more troops to throw at us, yes, sir, and I reckon I should get you somewhere safe before a Frenchman gets lucky.' It was well past midday, Sharpe was surprised to realise, because the time had flown by so fast. 'Back to the horses, sir.' He turned. 'Sergeant Williams!'

'Sir?' Williams was standing by the barn where the soldiers he had fetched were kneeling in the doorway with their muskets trained on the plough-impeded gap.

'Back to the horses, Sergeant!'

'Very good, sir,' Williams said, took one pace and then a musket ball cracked on his helmet, punctured through and the Welshman dropped. Sharpe ran to him, knelt, but saw the Dragoon was dead, killed instantly.

'Poor man,' Sharpe said, 'a good man too.'

'He's dead?' Sir Joel asked. 'Despite that helmet?'

'It only looks like iron, sir. It's boiled and painted leather.' He unbuckled Williams's belt, then tugged it out from beneath his body, 'Clouter!'

'Sir?'

'A gift for you.' He tossed the belt with its sword slings from which hung a heavy metal scabbard in which was a straight-bladed cavalry sword, the twin of the one Sharpe wore. 'It's an ugly bloody sword,' he said, 'but you can do immense damage with it.'

Clouter grinned. 'Thank you, sir.'

Sir Joel was finally persuaded to leave and they retreated back up the hill. On reaching the low crest Sharpe could see a long column of redcoats coming from the south. 'Marshal Soult has left it too late,' he said.

'Late?'

'Our reinforcements have arrived, sir. They'll push the buggers back to Bayonne now.'

'So we'll win!' Sir Joel said happily.

'We already won, sir,' Sharpe said.

'We did?'

'Here, at least.' Sharpe turned and looked north where the massive French column had been brought to a bloody standstill. The front ranks were still shooting, but every blast of canister from the nine-pounder gouged more men from the column and the survivors, surrounded by their own dead and wounded, had lost the will to keep going.

'By God, those men serve that gun well!' Sir Joel said, complimenting the gun-crew who had arrived in the yard and who now poured canister round after canister round at the discouraged enemy.

Sharpe turned away, thinking of the enthusiastic young artillery lieutenant who was about to learn that all his skill and courage had not been enough to save his brother. He touched the Admiral's elbow. 'Come, sir, we have a bridge to find.'

They walked south to find their horses and Sir Joel talked enthusiastically of what he had just seen. He had been energised by the combat, exulting in the defeat of what had at first appeared to be an indomitable enemy column, but gradually he sensed Sharpe's reluctance to share in his pleasure. 'You're not happy, Sharpe?'

'We don't know what's happening elsewhere, sir,' Sharpe said. 'We're holding the attack here, but Marshal Soult sent more men than we saw. If he had any sense he'll have sent men down the riverbank to capture the Villefranque bridge.' He looked east, but saw no cloud of gunsmoke in that direction, and none at all in the far distance where his own battalion was stationed. 'These lads did well,' he jerked a thumb towards the British and Portuguese who were defending the big house, 'but I'd be astonished if that was Marshal Soult's only attack. Still, we probably live to fight another day.'

'As do we,' Sir Joel said, 'on the Adour.'

'The Adour, sir?'

'A river flowing into the sea through Bayonne, Sharpe. The Nive flows north into the Adour which must be the next big obstacle to Wellington's advance. The only practicable bridges are deep in Bayonne itself and that's a bloody great fortress, so it'll be a busy day in hell if he attacks those walls. So he has to go round Bayonne.'

Captain Crittenden cleared his throat very deliberately, doubtless hinting that his Admiral was giving away secrets. 'Go round, sir?' Sharpe prompted Sir Joel.

'He doesn't have much choice. He can't go through Bayonne so he must go round! But inland of Bayonne it's a damn wide river and fast flowing, not easily bridged, especially if the bloody frogs are peppering you with artillery. But there is an alternative.'

Captain Crittenden cleared his throat again, but Sir Joel was in high spirits. 'The French won't expect a bridge on the seaward side of the city. The estuary there is too bloody wide and has massive tides. It would be much like trying to bridge the Thames downstream of Gravesend, and the bloody Frogs probably consider it impassable. Why do you think I'm here, Sharpe?' Sir Joel said happily. 'Wellington wants the navy to make a bridge across the estuary on the ocean side of Bayonne.'

'Sir Joel, please!' Crittenden said pointedly.

'Worry not, David, Sharpe won't run to the French and give away our plans, will you, Sharpe?'

'I won't sir.'

'So we'll round up a host of French fishing boats and throw a road across the estuary, all covered by my ships' cannons. Damned French won't know whether to piss upwind or shit downstream. But Wellington reckons the estuary is much too wide for your small pontoons so he needs the navy because we understand big boats. Or I hope we do. Do we, David?'

Captain Crittenden looked sour. 'We do understand the need to keep the project secret, Sir Joel.'

'Oh, nonsense, I trust Sharpe. So where do we go now, Major?'

'I propose heading for the Nive, sir, to join my battalion. But I think you should go back to Saint-Jean-de-Luz.'

'Why in God's holy name should we do that?'

'Because Lord Wellington would believe it prudent, sir.'

'He would? But why would it be prudent? If I recall rightly Lord Wellington ordered you to show us the pontoon bridge at Villa-wherever and you haven't done that!'

Sharpe paused, trying to gather his thoughts. 'The bridge may no longer exist, sir.'

'Why do you say that?"

'The French were repulsed here, sir, but for all we know they may have sent a column down the riverbank to capture the bridge and so stop General Hill sending reinforcements,'

'But we don't know they did that,' Sir Joel insisted.

'It would make sense, sir.'

'You're ascribing sense to the damned Frogs, Sharpe?'

'Capturing the bridge divides our army into two, sir, and the French would dearly like that.'

'Well, damn them to the lowest circle of hell,' Sir Joel exclaimed. 'I need to see this pontoon bridge!' They had at last reached their horses and the two Dragoons left to guard the beasts looked considerably relieved. 'You two lads!' Sir Joel was talking to the two Dragoons. 'You can find your way back to Lord Wellington?'

'Yes, sir,' one said uncertainly.

'Then tell Lord Wellington I'm accompanying Major Sharpe to see his battalion, and I'll return by,' he hesitated, 'Wednesday evening. Today is Sunday, yes?'

'Think so, sir,' one of the Dragoons answered uneasily.

'And tell his lordship it was not my idea,' Sharpe added forcefully.

'Yes, sir.'

Sharpe climbed awkwardly into the saddle of his horse, then turned to watch the stream of redcoats and artillery that was pouring down the road towards the big house. The French attackers had seen those approaching forces too and were already pulling back, realising that they were about to be overwhelmed by new, fresh troops. So that battle, if it could even be dignified by the name battle, was won, and Sharpe had the sudden hope that the repulse would dissuade Marshal Soult from trying again.

The two dragoons spurred southwards and Sir Joel kicked his horse to Sharpe's side. 'So which way do we go, Sharpe?'

'Damned if I know, sir.'

'We have to reach the River Nive, yes? To explore the mysteries of a pontoon bridge?'

'We do, sir.'

'And that lies eastwards?'

'It does, sir.'

'Which way is east?' Sir Joel glanced at the sky as if searching for the sun which was thoroughly hidden by the dense rain clouds.

'Don't know, sir,' Sharpe lied. He well knew in which direction the east lay, but he was worried that French forces might have launched an assault on the Villefranque bridge and that he would be taking Sir Joel straight into the enemy's arms.

'There must be a road leading to the bridge!'

'I'm sure there is, sir, but I'm unfamiliar with this country.'

'So it's simple navigation! Ride east till we find the river, then go north or south to find the bloody bridge. You have a compass?'

'No, sir.'

'Then you're damned lucky the navy's here.' Sir Joel fished in a pocket of his uniform and brought out a small object wrapped in leather. It proved to be a compass. 'A present from Florence,' he said, settling the compass on an outstretched hand, 'she has a horror of my being lost at sea and captured by corsairs. Ah, that way!' He pointed across the road. 'Let's be at it!'

They rode east, Sir Joel delighting in finding his way by using farm tracks where possible or following hedgerows. 'Good farmland, this,' he commented at one point, 'and damned fine hunting country. Do they have foxes?'

'They do, sir,' Sharpe replied. He often saw foxes when he toured his battalion's picquet line.

'Heaven on earth!' Sir Joel said. 'You know it all belonged to us once?'

'It did, sir?' Sharpe responded as neither Captain Crittenden nor Clouter seemed to be taking any interest in the Admiral's enthusiasm.

'It's all Gascony, Sharpe, and Gascony belonged to us in the good old days. We should bloody well take it back, then we could grow our own monkey's blood instead of buying it from the heathen French. I'm sure the people here would welcome us. Just think of it, Sharpe! In my lifetime they've had a monarchy, a republic, a consulate, a directory, and now they're an empire! Poor creatures probably don't know whether to salute or fart! Ah! And there's the river!' They had reached the summit of a low hill and in the far distance was a sliver of grey water that Sharpe supposed was the Nive. 'Don't see a bloody bridge, though,' Sir Joel grumbled.

'It's surrounded by earthworks, sir,' Sharpe said.

'And in this bloody rain I'm surprised we can see our horses' ears, let alone some bloody earthworks.' Sir Joel went on, 'I hope you've got dry quarters at your battalion, Sharpe?'

'Not nearly as comfortable as Lord Wellington's quarters, sir.'

'True,' Captain Crittenden murmured in support of Sharpe's hint.

'We've come this far,' Sir Joel said, 'we might as well keep going. Besides, it's essential that we examine a pontoon bridge. We're going to be asked to make one! So how is it done? I can't believe you just lash a few bloody boats together and expect people to merrily skip across their decks. There must be more to it than that!'

'There is, sir,' Sharpe said, thinking of the vast cables tensioned above the pontoons and the plank roadway laid on top.

'So I need to see one! And remember we'll be making one in the mouth of the Adour where it will be subject to fifteen-foot tides, Atlantic storms and killer waves.'

Crittenden sighed, but said nothing in response to the Admiral's irritated words. 'We'll find the bridge soon,' Sharpe said, hoping he was right and that no French attack had reached and destroyed the bridge.

Sharpe guessed they had travelled four or five miles since leaving Barrouillet and the sound of battle was fading behind them, though he could still hear the distant crackle of musketry and the louder reports of artillery, but the intensity of the fighting had lessened and Sharpe suspected the British reinforcements were pushing the French back towards Bayonne. He was fairly confident that Soult's lunge south-wards had failed to destroy a large portion of Wellington's army and, Sharpe reckoned, must have cost Soult a grievous number of casualties, but at least there was no powder smoke showing above the far rainswept hills on the Nive's eastern bank, which suggested Soult had only attacked on this one side of the river.

They had been following a muddy farm track that brought them to another hill crest from which they could see a consid-erable stretch of the Nive, but no sign of a bridge. 'So that's the bloody Nive,' Sir Joel said, still sounding irritated. 'Which means we just have to go north or south! Which?'

'South,' Sharpe said firmly.

'And your reasons?' Sir Joel asked suspiciously, plainly suspecting Sharpe wanted to travel away from the enemy.

'Marshal Soult attacked from the north, sir, and I don't think he got as far as the bridge. If he had, we'd see troops in front of us, and almost certainly a fight going on with the bridge's defenders, which suggests to me that the French never reached the bridge.'

'Or else they reached the bridge, captured it, and the bloody

Frogs are cooking a meal and sheltering from this bloody rain!'

'I hope not, sir,' Sharpe said.

'We've come pretty far south, Sharpe,' Sir Joel persisted. 'We followed that farm track and it went south-east rather than east. I think we should head north-east now.'

'Smoke over there, sir,' Clouter spoke up from behind the officers.

'Smoke?' Sir Joel barked.

'Over there, sir.' Clouter pointed south-east where a shimmer of smoke showed above a low wooded hill.

'It's not battle-smoke.' Sir Joel had trained a telescope on the distant smear. 'Probably a farmhouse cooking dinner.'

'Big farmhouse,' Captain Crittenden remarked. He held his telescope out to Sharpe who had left his own telescope with Peter d'Alembord, and now accepted Crittenden's and trained it at the far smoke. 'That's the bridge,' he said.

'I see no bloody bridge!' Sir Joel, thoroughly disgruntled by the seething rain, objected.

'It's hidden by those trees, but there's too much smoke. I'd guess it's the bridge's garrison cooking their dinners. Looks to me like at least half a dozen fires.'

'In this rain?' Sir Joel asked.

'The garrison built themselves huts, sir, with chimneys.'

'Oh give me a hut with a chimney,' Sir Joel exclaimed and kicked his horse on a few paces, then stopped abruptly. 'Dear Christ!' he exclaimed. 'What's that?'

Sir Joel's alarm had been caused by a sudden eruption of cannon fire to the north, and beneath those huge sounds was the crackle of musketry. Sir Joel turned to see a sudden veil of gunsmoke showing above the skyline. The smoke was far too close to be coming from the river bank which still lay to the east. 'The French are damned close!' Sir Joel said excitedly.

'Sounds like it,' Sharpe said.

'So to hell with the bridge, let's look at it!'

'Sir . . .' Sharpe began, eager to take Sir Joel far from the fighting, but the Admiral was already kicking his horse northwards towards the deafening sounds.

'We'll find the bridge tomorrow, Sharpe!' Sir Joel shouted back. 'These fellows might need our help!'

Sharpe doubted the four of them could offer much help. 'The bridge might be in French hands by tomorrow, sir.'

'Then by God we'll take it back! Besides, this noise might be their damned effort to reach it! And that's Artillery, by God!' The battle noise was dominated by the ear-punching sounds of big guns at work. 'I want to see French Artillery in action, Sharpe. I've no doubt the rascals will be dug in all round Bayonne and probably up the river too!'

Sharpe did not believe Sir Joel's explanation of wanting to see artillery in action for one moment. Sir Joel, he knew, was attracted to a fight like a dog to meat, but if he did want to see gunners at work he was in the right place. The sound betrayed that it was not one or two batteries in action, but maybe up to a dozen. The fire was incessant and suggested to Sharpe a determined French assault. Lord Wellington preferred to spread his batteries along a defensive front, while the French were far more likely to concentrate their artillery and use the guns to punch a bloody gash through the defenders that the infantry could assault. He had thought that the attack on the big house at Barrouillet had been the major French effort to pierce the British lines, but this new cannonade sounded much bigger.

'You can never go wrong by travelling towards the sound of the guns, ain't that right, Sharpe?'

'You can get killed doing that, sir.'

'Tally ho!' was Sir Joel's only retort as he spurred his horse uphill towards a crest thick with wintry trees.

Sharpe kicked his horse faster. 'Let me look first, sir.'

'Let Major Sharpe look, sir!' Captain Crittenden insisted and snatched to grasp the Admiral's bridle. 'He knows what he's doing, sir.'

Sir Joel reluctantly allowed his horse to be slowed and stopped. 'Don't take long, Sharpe!'

Sharpe ignored the command. Instead he dismounted at the edge of the trees and gave the horse's reins to Clouter. 'Wait here,' he said, then went on foot through the wood. Once in a while an errant musket ball flicked through the high bare branches and more than once a cannon ball crashed into the trees, either striking a trunk with a hammer blow, or burying itself in the soaking leaf mould and earth.

The sound was now immense, an unending pounding of artillery, punctuated by roundshot striking stone and the explosion of shells, and beneath it all the splintering crack of muskets and rifles. The fight sounded as fierce as any Sharpe had ever known, yet some sounds were lacking. He could not hear the French drums beating the *pas de charge*, nor thousands of voices chanting '*Vive l'Empereur*' when the drums paused.

He could hear bugle calls and piercing whistles which he recognised as British Light Infantry signals, and he hurried towards the far side of the hill's crest to make sense of the noise.

To find himself gazing down at a substantial village built in the steep valley immediately beneath him. The cottages were built either side of a road which ran east to west at the valley's foot, but at the valley's farther side was another ridge that was crowned by a church and a massive stone house, much larger than the beleaguered house at Barrouillet. That ridge to the north of the village was crowded with British infantry who were firing across a second, shallower valley towards a wide hill where the French had lined their cannon. Sharpe reckoned the great line of cannon was about four hundred paces from the two big stone buildings on the British-held ridge. In front of the cannon, carpeting the long slope that led towards the church and the château, were blue-coated bodies, suggesting that a French infantry assault had already been repulsed by the British infantry and now the French commander was trying to break his stubborn enemy with roundshot and shell. There was more French infantry in the fields behind the massive battery, ready to march forward when the defenders had been pounded into carnage by the cannon.

'Dear sweet God,' Sir Joel appeared beside Sharpe.

'You shouldn't be here, sir.'

'You and I had no business being at the battle of Trafalgar either, Sharpe, yet here we are.'

Captain Crittenden and Clouter had also come, on foot like the Admiral.

'And the horses, sir?' Sharpe asked.

'Tethered to a tree behind us,' Captain Crittenden said, 'so what's happening?'

Sharpe described the battle as well as he could, saying how a French assault on the ridge had been repulsed and that now the enemy commander had massed his cannon and was using it to pulverise the defending British. 'If he can kill enough of them,' Sharpe said, 'his infantry will march straight through them.'

'Damned if we can allow that to happen,' Sir Joel said. He had taken a small telescope from a pouch and now trained it on the French guns. 'Those guns are served damn well,' he said bitterly.

'The French were always good gunners, sir. May I?'

Sir Joel handed Sharpe the telescope and Sharpe used it to gaze at the French guns. It was difficult to count the guns because of the mass of smoke that lingered in front of the muzzles after each shot, but by counting the long lances of flame that gave the smoke a lurid glow he reckoned there were at least twenty artillery pieces lined on the far hilltop and, when the wind cleared a patch of smoke, he could see that most were the formidable twelve-pounders. None of that was a surprise.

The British-held ridge, centred on the two massive stone buildings, was equally shrouded in smoke, but none of it from cannon. Instead Sharpe could see the continuous gouts of powder smoke blasted from muskets and, he knew from their distinct sound, from rifles. The noise of that fusillade was unending.

'Bloody hell,' Sharpe said.

'What?' Sir Joel demanded, reaching for the telescope.

'I'm not sure I believe it!' Sharpe said.

'What!'

'We're bloody winning, sir!'

'Funny way of winning,' Sir Joel said dourly, 'they're beating God's own shit out of us!'

Another roundshot went high enough to crash through the trees near them, splintering branches and startling birds. More roundshot skimmed the British-held ridge to thump into the hillside beneath Sharpe who handed the telescope back to the admiral. 'What's the distance between the French guns and the church?' he asked.

Sir Joel looked. 'About five hundred paces?' he estimated.

'Less, sir,' Captain Crittenden said confidently. 'I'd reckon two cables.'

'And if your gunners were firing this high at two cables' distance,' Sharpe asked, 'what would you think?'

'That they'd need a bloody good spanking,' Sir Joel said.

'And too many shots are going high,' Sharpe said. And as if to confirm his words a shell thumped into the slope not far beneath them, smoked for a heartbeat and then exploded. Scraps of its casing tore through the bare branches above.

'So the Frogs are bad shots,' Sir Joel said, 'but that doesn't mean we're winning. If this was a battle at sea the buggers would be shredding our rigging.'

'Oh, we're winning,' Sharpe said, 'for now.' He paused, suspecting his next words would inspire the Admiral into action. 'I plan to go down to the village, sir, because someone down there will know the way to the bridge. I'll come back and we'll follow their directions.'

'If you're going down,' Sir Joel said, 'I'm coming with you!'

'Sir . . .' Captain Crittenden started.

'You should wait here, sir,' Sharpe said forcibly at the same time, 'and preferably back among the trees.'

'No one will ever accuse a Chase of avoiding battle,' Sir Joel said grandly, 'and besides, you claim we're winning! So shall we go?'

'Then run like hell,' Sharpe said, knowing he could never dissuade Sir Joel but worried that the French guns were doing more damage to the slope they needed to descend than to the redcoats and Riflemen on the village's further side. 'I mean it, sir, run like hell.'

They ran like hell.

CHAPTER FIVE

The village was called Arcangues, as Sharpe learned from a redcoat at the foot of the hill.

Sharpe had led his companions down the slope at a break-neck pace, worried that so many French artillery shots were going high, some skimming the church roof to shatter through the high branches behind him, while canister blasts were creating a metal rain that gouged the turf of the hill. Once at the foot of the hill he had gone into a small paddock where wounded redcoats and Riflemen were being tended by surgeons. The paddock, being in the heart of the valley, was sheltered from the enemy cannonade, though some howitzer shells fell to gouge small craters in paddocks and gardens. 'We wait here a moment,' he told Sir Joel.

'We should . . .'

'We wait, sir,' Sharpe insisted and Sir Joel reluctantly agreed.

Sharpe knelt beside the redcoat who had a bloody bandage around his thigh. The white facings of his red coat and the

Sergeant's stripes on his sleeve were splashed with blood. 'You know what this village is called?'

'Arcangues, sir.'

'And what regiment are you?'

'43rd, sir.'

'The Ox and Bucks?' Sharpe translated for Sir Joel's benefit.

'We're the Monmouthshire now, sir,' the Sergeant said resentfully. 'They changed us, God knows why.'

'London has nothing better to do,' Sharpe said, then patted the man's shoulder. 'You'll be back in line soon. So the 43rd is alone?'

'Some of your green fellows are here, sir. Not many.'

'We're winning, so you'll be fine.'

'Hurts like hell, sir.'

Sharpe had uncorked his canteen. 'That's Crapaud brandy, Sergeant. Drink it. It'll help the pain.'

He let the man drink as much as he wanted, then crossed to a wagon that stood beside the surgeons' tent. Weapons and ammunition pouches that had belonged to dead or wounded soldiers had been tossed into the wagon and Sharpe rooted through them to discover a pair of rifles and a musket. He suspected that both naval officers would prefer rifles, while he was certain Clouter was more than proficient with a musket.

'Hey you!' a voice bellowed, and Sharpe turned to see a stout Sergeant pacing towards him. 'Put those back!'

'If anyone asks, Sergeant,' Sharpe retorted, 'you say that

Major Richard Sharpe of the Prince of Wales's Own stole the weapons.'

'Yes, sir!' The Sergeant stiffened to attention and saluted. 'Didn't recognise you, sir.'

'No reason you should, Sergeant. And you can tell the wounded the French have no chance of capturing Arcangues today. Now I need to steal some cartridges.'

'Of course, sir.'

Sharpe found three cartridge pouches, added a fourth for himself, then rejoined Sir Joel. 'We're going up to the church,' he said over the din of battle, 'and you have a rifle each. They work just like muskets, except you wrap the bullet in a leather patch first.' He showed them the small, brass-covered cavity in the rifle's stock which held the patches. 'It makes it harder to ram the bullet down, but it makes it a hell of a lot more accurate. I brought you a musket, Clouter, unless you'd prefer a rifle?'

'I'm happy with a musket, sir.'

'Then let's go.'

'Why in God's name do you say we're winning, Sharpe?' Sir Joel demanded as they climbed the path to the big church.

'Listen to the artillery fire, sir, what do you notice?'

Sir Joel climbed a few paces in silence. 'It's slackened some,' he said, 'but that's only natural. It's a beastly hard business serving cannon.'

'It's slackened a lot,' Sharpe said, 'getting slower and slower, and too many are firing high.'

'So?' Sir Joel asked.

Sharpe turned to Crittenden. 'You said the distance between the ridges was two cables. How far is that?'

'One cable is a tenth of a nautical mile,' Sir Joel provided the answer, 'so one fifth of a nautical mile.'

'A cable is six hundred and eight feet,' Captain Crittenden answered more helpfully.

'So two cables is a little more than four hundred yards,' Sharpe said, after working the sum in his head.

'Four hundred and five yards,' Crittenden said.

'Which is a ridiculous range for a musket,' Sharpe pointed out. 'I won't let my muskets open fire at any range more than a hundred yards, and even at that range most shots will miss. They start to be deadly at sixty paces.' They had reached the door of the church and Sharpe paused. 'But the muskets here are cutting down their gun crews, and that's what's slowing the buggers down. Four hundred yards is an impossible distance, but put enough musket balls in the air and some will hit. That's what's happening.'

'And also why they're firing high?'

'It helps,' Sharpe said. 'The gun crews must hate being pelted with so many musket balls and they're not concentrating on their aim, but the real reason is recoil. Every cannon shot drives the gun back and the trail digs into the ground, and after all this rain the soil will be soft. Their guns are digging in and the muzzles go up as the trails go down and we've killed enough gun commanders for the crews not to care or notice,' he pushed open the door, 'and we can help that process.'

It felt good to be out of the driving rain, though the church's interior looked chaotic. Enough roundshot had struck the long northern wall to smash holes, and at every hole and window in that wall groups of redcoats were taking turns to shoot at the far ridgeline.

'Up!' Sir Joel said, and Sharpe noticed there was an ornate wooden gallery running around the whole nave where more windows and newly made holes were lined with men. He followed an eager Sir Joel up the stairs, then down the gallery to a gaping ragged hole in the masonry which looked north towards the French guns. Sir Joel unclasped and dropped his heavy oilcloth cloak. A nearby redcoat gaped at the sight of a man in full naval uniform, his cuffs gleaming with gold. Sir Joel grinned at the man. 'Don't worry, lad, the navy's here.' He looked at Sharpe. 'How do I know if this thing isn't already loaded?'

'Give it to me, sir.' Sharpe took the rifle, drew out the ramrod and let it fall down the barrel. The metal rod hit the breech with a dull clang. 'It isn't, sir.'

'The navy to the rescue!' Sir Joel said happily as he extracted a leather patch.

Sharpe, who knew his own rifle was loaded, knelt at the ragged hole and gazed down into the churchyard where scores of redcoats and a handful of Riflemen were sheltering behind the graves and firing blindly though the smoke towards the far ridge. Or perhaps not entirely blindly because the French fire had slackened enough to slightly thin their own powder smoke and Sharpe could dimly see gunners crouching behind their guns. He knew that a French twelve-pounder had a crew of eight gunners who were assisted by a handful of infantrymen responsible for replenishing ammunition and heaving the guns' trails with handspikes to realign them, but he could

126

only see six men by the nearest cannon and not one of them was holding the portfire which would actually ignite the charge in the barrel. He saw another cannon fire and saw how it bucked back to dig its trail deeper into the wet soil. That violent recoil inevitably raised the cannon's muzzle by a small amount, and each shot added to that elevation, yet not a single man tried to adjust the barrel's angle. He aimed his rifle at that gun, elevated his own barrel slightly, and fired.

'Are these sights any damn good?' Sir Joel had just primed his rifle and discovered the hinged sight just forward of the lock.

'Not really,' Sharpe said, standing to one side of the hole to reload, 'folded down it's good for a hundred yards and folded up, two to three hundred.'

'Up it is,' Sir Joel said wolfishly, then stepped so he could gaze through the hole in the wall, raised the rifle to his shoulder, waited a few heartbeats and then fired. 'Damn smoke,' he grumbled as he stepped aside.

A violent clattering sounded on the church walls and Sharpe saw the veil of smoke filling the space beneath the church's beamed ceiling twitch. 'They're firing canister,' he said, 'which is sensible, but they're still firing too high.' He knelt at the hole again and marvelled at the volume of musketry that was being poured across the small valley. The churchyard and its adjacent fields and gardens were thick with redcoats and Riflemen, all, like the well-trained Light Infantry they were, taking what shelter they could in ditches or behind graves or trees, and all firing across the valley. Their rate of fire was slow because each man had to protect the powder in the cartridge from the rain, but slow or not it was effective. The area about the French guns was hissing with musket balls, most of them inaccurate, but the fusillade was dense enough that a few balls had to hit their targets, and those targets were the gunners who were being mauled so badly that some cannons appeared to have ceased firing altogether. A gust of rain-drenched wind blew the cannon smoke southwards and he saw a short-barrelled howitzer being rammed. A shell, he thought, because howitzers almost always fired shell. He aimed without thinking at a man stooping behind the howitzer's breech. He fired, but the Baker rifle's own smoke obscured his view, then Captain Crittenden fired and the smoke thickened.

Coulter fired, Sharpe fired, Sir Joel fired, then Captain Crittenden again, and more and more French guns went silent and the smoke cleared enough to show the far ridge littered with bodies, and every French gun that persisted was immediately a target for the hundreds of muskets.

'You're watching a miracle,' Sharpe said, 'a battery of artillery defeated by infantry.'

That infantry was now standing and shouting insults towards the helpless gunners, who, instead of serving their guns, had either retreated beyond the crest or huddled behind their silent cannon.

'That'll teach the scoundrels to fight the navy!' Sir Joel said happily.

Sharpe half expected to see a French column of infantry appear over the crest, but none showed and he could not hear the drums that always accompanied such an attack. 'We should find the bridge,' he said.

'You mean the game's over?' Sir Joel asked, disappointed.

'It's over, sir, and won.' Sharpe hid his distaste for the word 'game', but at the same time he felt an immense pride for the work that the redcoats and their supporting Riflemen had done, and who had paid a price in so doing. Four hundred yards was about the effective limit of canister, even for the powerful French twelve-pounders, but just as the wild cloud of musketry had ripped through the Artillerymen, so had their canister taken its toll of the defenders. He could see too many wounded and dead men being carried back towards the village. 'We should join our horses,' he said.

'Clouter,' Sir Joel turned on the huge man, 'you can fetch the horses?'

'Aye aye, sir.'

'We'll be in the village.'

'I'll find you, sir.'

'Good man,' Sir Joel said then turned to Sharpe, 'there must be a tavern here?'

'Bound to be, sir.'

'Then anchors aweigh!'

The tavern, deep in the valley behind the church, had wine, bread and a hot mess of sausages in beans. A dozen British officers were already eating and all looked astonished as an admiral appeared among them. 'You don't suppose the Frogs will poison us?' Sir Joel suggested.

'Not if they want to go on being paid, sir.'

'Ah! Greed before patriotism! *Vive la France!* Damn, this tastes good!'

Captain Crittenden flinched as he ladled a helping onto his own plate.

'Bruised shoulder?' Sharpe asked.

Crittenden nodded. 'It'll mend.'

'Which is more than you can say for the scoundrels you shot!' Sir Joel exclaimed, then raised his glass. 'By God, Sharpe, you showed us some fighting today! Haven't seen anything as brutal since Trafalgar!' He stopped as a tall redcoated officer came to the table.

'I heard a rumour that the navy muscled in on our fight,' the newcomer said, then held out his hand, 'Colonel Mitchell.'

'You gave us damn fine sport, Colonel!' Sir Joel said before introducing himself.

The Colonel cocked his head to listen to the sound of marching feet on the road outside the tavern. 'Reinforcements,' he said, 'late, but very welcome. You'll forgive me, gentlemen, but I should welcome them.'

'You can tell us the way to the pontoon bridge, sir?' Sharpe asked.

'At Villefranque?' Mitchell paused. 'As one of my Irish rogues would say, you'd be better off not starting from here. You follow this road,' he gestured through a window to where new troops were pouring into the village, 'it turns north until you come to the first crossroads, where you turn right. The trouble is that the French hold those crossroads.'

Sharpe could see that the ebullient Sir Joel was about to dismiss that as a negligible problem. 'So you'd suggest, sir?'

'Ride east cross-country,' the Colonel said, 'and you'll come to a road leading south. Follow it. It's not far and you shouldn't encounter any damn French if you stay well south of the crossroads.'

'Pity,' Sir Joel said, 'but thank you, Colonel. Ah, Clouter! Saved you some fodder, sit down, man.'

The rain was still falling as they left the tavern and as Sharpe wearily climbed back into the saddle. He had been riding since dawn and guessed it might be dusk before they found the bridge and he could at last rest properly.

The rain did not slacken, indeed it seemed to increase as they rode into a freshening wind. Trees tossed wildly and when they crossed pastureland the horses' hooves threw up gobbets of wet soil. Sir Joel and Captain Crittenden again wore their oilskin cloaks, but Sharpe and Clouter were in uniforms that were now drenched. Sharpe wished he had borrowed, by which he meant stolen, the big scarlet-lined cloak that Candelaria had lent him. He suspected the cloak belonged to Lord Wellington, and he reckoned he deserved it in compensation for that maniacal moment on an Indian battlefield ten years ago, but in truth he allowed that Wellington had rewarded him amply for that service.

'Jesus Christ!' Sir Joel suddenly exclaimed, curbing his horse. They had been riding eastwards, guided by Sir Joel's small compass, and had crossed two roads leading southwards, both of which Sir Joel had dismissed as being nothing more than cattle tracks, but one of which had undoubtedly been the road Colonel Mitchell had advised them to follow because now, as they emerged from a thicket of trees, they found themselves on the bank of the river. 'By God, that's running high!' Sir Joel was staring at the water which had flooded the path ahead. 'Best go gently,' he said, 'don't want to frighten the horses.'

The river was indeed surging relentlessly northwards, the current swirling under a wind that was whipping small white-caps from the surface.

'Damned glad we're not at sea!' Sir Joel said, leading them southwards.

'I say that every day, sir,' Sharpe said grumpily.

'Nonsense, Sharpe, you had a fine voyage with me!'

'I did, sir.'

'Speaking of which,' Sir Joel said, then let his horse fall back so he rode alongside Sharpe, 'I've long been wanting to ask you, Sharpe, what happened to Lord William Hale?' Sir Joel had dropped his voice so that neither Crittenden nor Clouter could hear him.

'He died, sir, at Trafalgar.'

'I know that, Sharpe! I watched his corpse being thrown overboard, but how the hell did he die? I had him and his wife safe in the lady hole!'

'A splinter, sir? Or a fragment of shell casing? I don't think anywhere on board the ship was safe that day.'

Sir Joel gave a brief laugh. 'Sharpe, the lady hole is the safest place on board ship, it's well below the waterline, down close to the lower rudder pintle. How in God's name is a man killed there? As I recall he died of a head wound, yet the deck above him was unscarred.'

'Strange things happen in battle, sir.'

'Bloody strange!' Sir Joel hesitated, then dropped his voice just sufficiently to still be heard above the sound of the wind, rain and roiling river. 'I hate to say it, Sharpe, but there was a rumour on board that you might have gone down to the lady hole during the fight.'

'I didn't, sir,' Sharpe said firmly and truthfully.

'I don't care if you did, Sharpe! I just want to know the truth. He was an odious man.'

'He was, sir.'

'So no truth to the rumour?'

'I didn't go down to the lady hole till after the battle,' Sharpe said, 'and by that time Lord William was dead.' He paused. 'And why do you want to know the truth, sir?'

'It was my ship! If there was foul play I want to know, even if it's only to rest my mind.' Sir Joel looked at Sharpe keenly. 'If you remember Lord William's secretary also died in odd circumstances.'

'Oh I killed him,' Sharpe said, 'damn nearly screwed his head off.'

'Screwed his head off?' Sir Joel repeated.

'I was a captive in India for a time, sir, and there were men called *jetis* who specialised in killing a man by turning his head front to back. I wanted to know how difficult it was, and that bloody secretary was blackmailing me.'

'How difficult was it?'

'Much harder than I thought, but I did it.'

'The surgeon thought it was a mighty odd injury for a man falling down a companionway,' Sir Joel said, 'and blackmailing you?' He peered at Sharpe and lowered his voice still more, 'about you and Lady Grace?'

'Yes, sir.'

'Well, I suspected the two of you were,' he paused, 'mis-behaving. Not that I blame you! Christ, she was a beauty!' He paused again, thinking, then, 'Are you saying she killed him?'

'I gave her a pistol before she went into the lady hole,' Sharpe said tonelessly.

'Dear God,' Sir Joel said, 'so she killed her husband?'

'He was about to kill her, sir, so yes, she did.'

'You and Lady Grace,' Sir Joel said musingly, 'well I knew the two of you were too close for comfort on a crowded ship, and I saw she died a couple of years later. I was sad about that. She was a beautiful creature.'

'She was,' Sharpe said feelingly.

'*The Times* didn't say how she died, just something about sickness.'

'She died in childbirth,' Sharpe said bitterly. *The Times*, he remembered, had been tactful, not mentioning that she was an unmarried widow.

Sir Joel heard his tone and lowered his voice. 'Forgive me for asking, yours?'

'Mine, and the baby died too, a boy.' Sharpe looked away, hiding the tears in his eyes. He often reckoned that had been the happiest time in his life, living in a small house Lady Grace rented in Sandgate while he trained as a Rifleman in the nearby Shorncliffe barracks. He had thought then that the happiness would last for ever, while now he wondered if he would ever know such joy again.

'I'm so sorry, Sharpe,' Sir Joel said, 'I didn't mean to dredge up old tales.'

'You were very generous to me, sir. I suppose you had a right to know.'

'Well I had to account for Lord William's death to the directors of the East India Company, and I've long wondered how wildly I lied.'

'What did you say, sir?'

'That he died on deck trying to help with the fight.'

'A hero, then.'

'A fool, Sharpe, and a bloody unpleasant fool at that. I believe the East India Company has erected a marble monument to him in Leadenhall Street, which is more than you or I will ever get. Oh good Lord above! Destination in sight!'

They had turned inside a bend of the river and the bridge and its protective earthworks lay just a half-mile ahead. And the flag above the makeshift forts was still British.

Sharpe watched as the two naval officers scrambled over the pontoon bridge, not trying to cross it, but rather examining how it was constructed. 'Ingenious!' was Sir Joel's verdict, 'and I can see why Wellington wanted us to see it! No pontoons!'

The bridge, instead of being made of the usual flat-bottomed pontoons, had been constructed with river boats, normally used to carry farm produce to Bayonne. To Sharpe's eyes it looked much larger and sturdier than a bridge made with the smaller pontoons and, he supposed, much more like the kind of bridge Sir Joel must throw across the Adour's estuary. 'It's impressive,' Sir Joel continued, 'but it will be much harder for us.'

'Harder, sir?'

'The mouth of the Adour,' Sir Joel said, 'is a good deal wider, and of course it's tidal and exposed to the open ocean.' He stamped on the plank roadway as if testing its strength. 'Imagine building something three or four times as large as this, Sharpe, and tensioned to take a fifteen-foot rise and fall in the tide and to resist a gale out of the west. Should be exciting!'

'But you can do it, sir?'

'We're the Royal Navy, of course we can do it.' He turned to stare downriver. 'So the rascals didn't get this far?'

'They must have been stopped long before they could reach the bridge, sir,' Sharpe said.

'And that was without the First Division?'

'So it seems, sir.'

Lieutenant Colonel Aldridge, a gunner who commanded the troops guarding the bridge, had received news from Sir John Hope, who admitted that only the day before, believing the French to be quiescent, he had sent the whole First Division of the army the twenty miles south to Saint-Jean-de-Luz to find winter quarters.

'Poor buggers,' Sir Joel said, 'and they had to march all the way back today?'

'They did, sir.'

Those were the troops Sharpe had seen coming to the rescue of the embattled men around the large house and farmyard at Barrouillet, and the last message from Sir John had confirmed that the French had been driven back almost to Bayonne.

'So the excitement is over,' Sir Joel said, sounding disappointed.

'It is, sir.'

'But I must say I did enjoy it! Better than potting at pheasants, and tomorrow we'll see your men?'

'Unless you return to Lord Wellington, sir.'

'You want to get rid of me, Sharpe!'

'Not at all, sir,' Sharpe said dutifully. 'His Lordship will be concerned that you got tangled in today's battles, sir, and now that you've seen the bridge . . .'

'He didn't expect us back till ten days had passed!' Sir Joel interrupted. 'So I'm off the leash for at least another week! Besides . . .' he hesitated.

'Sir?' Sharpe prompted him.

'I admire Wellington, Sharpe, I do. But talking to him is damned hard work!'

Sharpe was forced to smile. 'It is, sir.'

'And frankly I'd rather have a look at the countryside. We fellows rarely see the places we visit. It's into harbour, a quick run ashore if you're lucky, and out again! And I won't be missed. My flotilla knows what they should be doing.'

'Then it might be wise to send a messenger to Lord Wellington, sir?'

'Covering your arse, Sharpe?'

'Yes, sir. I'm certain Colonel Aldridge can arrange a messenger.'

'Then I'll send one. I don't want you lined up in front of a firing squad for indulging my curiosity!'

'Thank you, sir.'

'You have to understand, Sharpe, that my orders were to come ashore and discover how best we could help you fellows. So the more I learn about the army and its practices, the better.'

Sharpe pretended to believe the explanation, though in truth Sir Joel was seeking even more excitement.

'So how far is it to your fellows?' Sir Joel asked.

'Colonel Aldridge reckons their new position is about three miles north-east, sir,'

'And you have decent quarters?'

'I hope so, sir. The battalion's moved north since I saw them, but my Sergeant Major will have found something decent.' Sharpe suspected that something decent might be nothing more than a cattle byre, but Sir Joel kept stressing his need to see the army.

'A fire and a hot meal?'

'I think I can guarantee both, sir.'

'Then let's go there!' Sir Joel turned. 'Seen enough, David?'

'Too much, sir,' Crittenden replied glumly. He was staring at the centre of the bridge where a fallen tree, presumably washed from the river's bank, was buffeting the pontoons. Men were trying to attach a rope that could haul the flotsam away. 'That's a right bugger's muddle,' the Captain said disparagingly.

'We'll weigh anchor in ten minutes,' Sir Joel announced, ignoring the chaos on the bridge, 'Clouter! Bring the horses!'

Sir Joel went to talk to Colonel Aldridge while Sharpe and Clouter led the horses across the bridge which seemed to be vibrating under the pressure of the rainwater that had swollen the river. The fallen tree was still obstinately lodged at the bridge's centre where its branches seemed to have entangled with the anchor rodes of at least two boats. It still rained and twice as they led the horses slowly and carefully towards the eastern bank there were rumbles of thunder and Sharpe saw jagged spikes of lightning slanting down above the distant Pyrenees.

'I hope that's not coming here,' Sharpe grumbled.

'It'll stay over the mountains, sir,' Clouter said authoritatively, 'but the water?' He nodded at the churning river. 'It comes hard.'

'We should build an ark,' Sharpe said.

'The Almighty will provide for us, sir.'

Sharpe wished the Almighty would kill the rain and wind, but kept quiet. He and Clouter had reached the eastern bank where Sharpe laid a hand on one of the three taut cables that supported the plank roadway. The thick rope trembled beneath his hand, but the three cables were still supporting the roadway and holding the serried river boats steady. He watched as Sir Joel and his flag Captain crossed the bridge, and waited as Clouter heaved them up into their saddles. 'Colonel Aldridge sent the message, Sharpe,' Sir Joel said. 'I told Lord Wellington that I'd ordered you to escort me to this side of the river, and he can't blame you now. I do rather outrank you!'

'You do indeed, sir.'

'Then lead on! Where are we going?'

'We'll follow the wagon tracks, sir,' Sharpe said, gesturing at the deep water-filled ruts that betrayed where ammunition wagons had laboured north-eastwards towards General Hill's troops.

'And you're taking us to a paradise of roaring fires, banquets, and fair women?'

'If it's anything like our usual billet? Yes, sir.'

'Good man, lead on to paradise!'

*

Paradise turned out to be a large farmhouse with ancient stone walls and big hearths that had blazing fires. There was a barn where the tired horses could rest, and a kitchen dominated by Madame Esquibel, the farmer's stout wife, who greeted the newcomers with a clumsy curtsey and a long, enthusiastic speech.

'I speak reasonable French,' Sir Joel said, 'but I don't understand a word she says!'

'She's speaking Basque,' Sharpe explained.

'She's very friendly,' Sir Joel said.

'They're all friendly, sir. Lord Wellington insists we pay for everything, and their own soldiers just robbed them blind.'

'Sensible,' Captain Crittenden said.

Sir Joel felt in a pouch at his belt and brought out a pair of gold five-franc coins that he slapped onto the kitchen table. 'Will that cover dinner?'

'Much too generous, sir,' Sharpe said.

'Best to have her on our side, Sharpe. Don't want her poisoning our forage!'

For a moment Sharpe thought that Madame Esquibel was about to kiss the Admiral, but instead the two coins vanished into a pocket of her apron and were replaced by bread, butter, cheese and wine. A smaller fire was lit in the front parlour and wet uniforms were draped over chairs to dry. The shutters rattled in the wind. A meal of roasted salt pork, bread and potatoes was served, after which Sharpe pulled on his still damp uniform and, leaving the three naval men in their warm sanctuary, walked north, pursued by the wind and driving rain.

Most of his men were in their bivouacs, small tents shuddering beneath the lash of wind and rain, but Captain Carline, officer of the day, greeted him with evident relief. 'Glad you're back, sir. That bloody man keeps trying to take our ground.'

'Peacock?'

'This morning, sir,' Carline said, 'he paraded his men on this side of the hill and ordered Peter to take the other.'

'And Captain d'Alembord did what?'

'Paraded us directly behind the 71st, sir, then ignored the bloody man's orders.'

'Good for Peter! Did they move?'

'He had to, sir, General Barnes came along and had a conniption.'

'Splendid! And no nonsense from the enemy?'

'Would that be the French?' Carline asked, 'or Sir Nathaniel.'

'The Crapauds.'

'Quiet as mice, sir.'

'Picquets?'

'Seven are out, sir, all on this side of a stream at the foot of the hill. I inspected them half an hour ago.'

'Who's in charge?'

'Sergeant Henderson, sir.'

'I'll do a walk around just before dawn,' Sharpe said, 'with an Admiral and two other sailors.'

Carline gaped at Sharpe. 'An Admiral, sir?'

'It's the rain, Carline. We'll all be in the navy soon.'

Sharpe and his sailor companions slept in the farm's parlour and some time before dawn, after a mug of stewed tea, he led them north again, this time on foot. By some miracle it had stopped raining, though the air still felt heavy and damp and dark clouds threatened.

'You wanted to see the picquets,' he said to Sir Joel, 'so we'll tour them, but for God's sake be careful and quiet! The enemy's picquets will be well within musket shot and usually they don't bother us, but seeing a group of us they might suspect we're planning mischief.'

Sharpe led them over the brow of the hill and down the long slope towards a tangle of hedges and thickets on the low ground. 'If the French come,' he said in a low voice to Sir Joel, 'they have to climb this hill, and they can't.'

'Can't?'

'Not with British infantry on top.'

'What if they advance that way?' Sir Joel gestured towards the valley which ran alongside the slope.

'It's evidently marshland, sir, and sodden.'

At the foot of the slope Sharpe pushed through a gap in a hedge and continued northwards across a rain-soaked field. Another thicker hedge lay ahead and when they were twenty yards from it a voice called from the shadows. 'Halt! Who goes there?'

'Sharpe,' Sharpe growled, then completed the counter challenge, 'is a right bastard.' He decided he would throttle Carline for devising that phrase.

'That's really you, sir?'

'Me,' Sharpe said, 'and good morning, Seamus.'

'Morning, sir.'

'All quiet?'

'Good and quiet, sir.' Corporal Rourke's picquet was three men, uncomfortably lodged in a flooded ditch that bordered the hedge.

'Where's the enemy picquet?'

'Other side of the next field, sir.' Rourke pointed north. 'There's a stream there, sir. And they're in a hedge just beyond it. We haven't heard a peep from them since they wished us goodnight, sir.'

'Wished you goodnight?' Sir Joel asked, surprised.

'They always do, sir,' Rourke answered.

'May I?' Sir Joel asked.

'May you what, sir?' Sharpe asked.

Sir Joel, instead of answering Sharpe, cupped his hands beside his mouth and bawled as loud as he could. *Bonjour, mes amis!*

There was a pause, then a grumpy voice called from the enemy picquet, 'Good morning!'

'So they're awake,' Sir Joel said, pleased with himself.

'They'd better be,' Sharpe snarled, 'that's the first job of a picquet. Well done, Seamus, your relief will be here soon.'

'Sir?' Corporal Rourke sounded nervous.

'What is it?'

'Were you looking for Sergeant Henderson, sir?'

'I was told he's at a bridge across the stream?' He pointed east. 'Thataway?'

'He was relieved, sir.'

'Why? Was he ill? Asleep?'

'Sergeant Major Harper relieved him sir.'

'I'm sure he had good reason,' Sharpe said, believing nothing of the sort, 'but thanks for telling me. Hope the rest of your watch stays quiet! G'night, lads!'

He followed the hedge eastwards, knowing that Sir Joel's cheerful greeting would have alerted every picquet within a quarter mile that something strange was happening, but at least no French sentry opened fire. Not that Sharpe really expected it. There was an unwritten rule that picquets left each other alone, and Sharpe knew the two sides often met under the cover of darkness to exchange food, tobacco or liquor. Better still, they almost always warned their opposites if an attack was coming, thus giving their enemy time to scramble back to their battalion. Lord Wellington even encouraged such warnings, reckoning they had value, while a major attack on an enemy position had no need to slaughter the scatter of men positioned ahead of the main enemy.

Sharpe had explained all that to Sir Joel, who still did not entirely grasp the idea of cooperating picquets. 'But if the enemy come tonight,' he asked in a slightly too loud voice, 'won't these fellows be doomed?'

'They'll run back once they're warned,' Sharpe said, 'but the French don't like attacking at night. Nor does Lord Wellington. It usually leads to chaos.'

'Yet you keep picquets out anyway?'

'You never know when an enemy General has a sudden bright idea,' Sharpe said, 'and decides a night attack will surprise us.'

'But he'll lose the surprise if his picquets warn your picquets!'

'He will, but the picquets make friends across the line and they'll warn the other side whatever the General orders.'

'Mighty rum way to fight a war,' Sir Joel growled. Sharpe said nothing, just greeted the next picquet who, like Corporal Rourke, reported that all was quiet. 'They're asleep, sir, the dozy bastards,' Corporal Liddell said, 'you can hear him!' And Sharpe could indeed hear a man snoring some distance north-wards. 'It's that fat Frog Sergeant.'

'Better that he's asleep than you, Tom.'

'I'm wide awake, sir!'

'Good man. Who has the next post?'

'Sammy Lee, sir.'

'Not long till you're relieved,' Sharpe said, and led his companions along the tree-shrouded path. Whatever noise they made was probably drowned by the sound of the quick-flowing stream that ran to their left, but Sharpe placed his feet with exquisite care and the three naval men did their best to imitate him. The night was black, any moonlight blocked by the thick rain clouds, though once in a while a vaporous gap allowed a small dim light.

A sudden metallic crack sounded behind them. Sir Joel gasped and stopped, but Sharpe gently pulled him on. 'Just a musket being dry-fired,' he whispered, 'it's Tommy Liddell warning the next picquet that we're coming.'

A moment later they were challenged again and Sharpe gave the ludicrous counter-challenge. This picquet, under Rifleman Lee's command, was beside a dilapidated hut that Sharpe supposed had once belonged to a forester. Lee seemed very nervous. 'All well, Sammy?' he asked.

'Nothing happening, Mister Sharpe, nothing.'

A slight scuffling noise sounded from the hut and Sharpe turned towards it. 'What the devil . . .'

'It's that bloody fox, Mister Sharpe,' Rifleman Lee said hurriedly, 'he's got a den in there. He probably heard you coming.'

'I expect he did. Well, keep listening and looking.'

'We will, Mister Sharpe,' Lee said, sounding relieved.

Sharpe led onwards for about twenty paces, then stopped. 'You heard that noise in the hut?'

'There was a hut? I didn't see it.'

'Just a tumbledown shack,' Sharpe spoke very softly, 'the only fox in that hut is either a local girl or one of the battalion wives. The lads take turns in there and pay her, of course.'

'You are not serious?' Sir Joel insisted.

'I'm not going back to show her to you,' Sharpe said, 'the men think I don't know, and it's best left that way. And her presence keeps them alert. If they fall asleep they'll miss their turn. You might see her just after dawn, making her way home.'

'Staggering home, I should think,' Captain Crittenden observed drily.

'More importantly,' Sharpe went on, his voice scarcely audible above the rushing sound of the swollen stream, 'the next post is our forward post. It's about ten paces from the French forward post, so I suggest real silence! We don't want to alarm the enemy.'

Sir Joel peered through the dripping foliage. 'Is that a lantern, Sharpe?'

'I fear it is, sir.'

'What the devil is a lantern doing at a picquet?'

'Signalling the enemy, sir.'

'Holy God!' Sir Joel said.

'Leave it to me, sir.'

Sharpe stepped forward again and a moment later was challenged, 'Who goes there?'

'It's me, Dan,' Sharpe said.

'Welcome back, Mister Sharpe.'

'Thanks, Dan, I'm bloody glad to be back. All quiet?'

'The Crapauds are behaving themselves, Mister Sharpe.'

'What about the Sergeant Major?'

The lantern was standing in the middle of a small wooden footbridge that crossed the stream, and its dim light silhouetted a vast man, easily the same size as Clouter and who now turned towards the sound of voices.

'Rifleman Hagman!' he said loudly. 'Did I hear the correct counter-challenge?'

'No, Pat,' Dan Hagman answered.

'Then why haven't you shot the right bastard?'

'I'm outnumbered,' Hagman answered.

'Mary, mother of Christ, you're a Rifleman aren't you? We're always outnumbered!'

'Sergeant Major,' Sharpe called, 'will you tell your friends across the bridge that we're harmless?'

'Right away, sir!' Patrick Harper turned and shouted into the darkness on the far bank, 'Hey, Jules! These men are *amis! Pas de* problem!'

'*Bien!*' a voice replied, 'thank you, Pat!'

'Come here, Pat,' Sharpe said, and Harper stalked off the bridge and in the very dim light saw the naval officers' cocked hats. He came to attention and saluted.

'Allow me to introduce Sergeant Major Patrick Harper, sir,' Sharpe said very formally, 'and Pat, this is Rear Admiral Sir Joel Chase, Captain Crittenden and Petty Officer Clouter.'

'God save Ireland,' Harper said, 'delighted to meet you.' He looked at Clouter. 'And you look useful.'

'He is,' Sharpe said, 'and perhaps you can explain to the Admiral why you have a rifle, a volley gun, and a musket hanging from your shoulders?'

'Of course, sir!' He looked Sir Joel in the eye. 'The rifle's mine, but this piece of crap, sir,' he indicated the musket hanging from his left shoulder, 'belongs to a Frenchman, a little weasel called Guillaume Perrier, sir, and I'm minding it for him.'

'Truly?' Sir Joel asked.

'Truly a little weasel, sir.'

'Explain to Sir Joel why you are minding a French soldier's musket,' Sharpe said.

'I'd like to know that,' Sir Joel put in.

'Private Perrier, sir,' Harper continued, obviously relishing the story he told, 'has a friend in the Quartermaster's department, and he also has ten francs of mine which he's using to buy brandy. Now if he doesn't give me three bottles of brandy or my money back, the eejit loses his musket! Then he gets flogged, except the bloody Frogs don't flog their men, sir, on account that they're too delicate, but Monsewer Perrier will be on latrine duties for the next month.'

148

'That seems a most admirable arrangement,' Sir Joel said, 'does it work the other way?'

'We buy baccy for the bastards, sir,' Harper confessed, 'and they hold our rifles as surety.'

'And the lantern?' Sir Joel asked.

'Shows it's safe for the Crapauds to cross the bridge, sir.'

'Very admirable,' Sir Joel said, amused, 'and forgive me for asking, Sergeant Major, but isn't that a naval weapon on your shoulder?'

Harper patted the heavy butt of the volley gun. 'Is it naval, sir?' he asked innocently. 'I wouldn't know on account of it being a gift from Mister Sharpe.'

'And the navy can't get it back,' Sharpe said, 'on account of it having saved our lives more times than I can count.'

Sir Joel laughed. 'Is that one of the early rifled guns?'

'Smooth bore, sir,' Harper answered, 'all seven barrels.'

'The rifled ones were wicked,' Sir Joel remarked, 'they broke men's shoulders. Did you ever fire one, Clouter?'

'Once, sir, but those smooth bores? I like to double load them with ball.'

'Good idea!' Harper said enthusiastically.

'It kicks more!' Clouter said in warning.

'But it will kill even more Crapauds!' Harper sounded excited. 'A musket ball down first and a half-incher on top!' He unslung the volley gun, which had seven barrels, the outer six bunched around the inner barrel, all fired by a single flint-lock and designed to shoot seven half-inch bullets in a spreading pattern that might flense an enemy ship's rigging of sharpshooters. The only drawback to the weapon, other than the lengthy time needed to reload it, was its vicious kick and only the strongest men could be relied on to use it, but in Harper's huge hands it had proved a battle-winner, blasting bloody holes in ranks of the enemy. 'Now why didn't I ever think to double load it?' he asked.

'Because you're from Donegal?' Sharpe suggested.

'And maybe you're right, Mister Sharpe,' Harper said, unoffended.

Sir Joel looked puzzled. 'Your men call you Mister Sharpe, not "sir", is that your choice?'

'It's the normal practice in the Rifle regiment, sir,' Sharpe explained, 'but most of my redcoats have picked up on it.'

'Yes,' Sir Joel said, 'I've heard the Rifles are distinct.'

'Not just distinct, sir, but the best damned regiment in the army!' Harper said.

'Patreek!' a voice called from the northern bank.

'Jules?'

'He is here!'

'He can cross! *Pas de* problem, Jules!'

'Speaking Crapaud now, Pat?' Sharpe asked, amused.

'Fluent, sir.'

A clinking noise sounded from the deep shadows on the stream's far bank and then a small skinny soldier appeared on the bridge carrying a bulging sack. 'All there,' he said to Harper.

'Good man, Willie,' Harper said, and bent to the sack that had been placed on the bridge. He groped the contents, then stood. 'Five bottles!'

The Frenchman replied in rapid French, which left Harper confused.

'I'm not paying for five,' Harper protested.

'It's a gift!' Sir Joel explained. 'You owe him nothing.' Sir Joel switched to French and spoke to the diminutive soldier, who smiled, nodded, and replied.

'He says,' Sir Joel translated, 'that they conceive Sergeant Major Harper as a decent and honourable man, and want to pay their respects.'

'And quite right too,' Harper said, and unslung the French musket. 'Here you are, Willie! I put an Irish curse on it and the next time you fire it, it will blow up in your weaselish face.'

'*Merci.*' The small Frenchman took the musket and held out a hand that Harper shook.

Harper brought the bottles to the bank. 'They're not such bad fellows when you get to know them.'

'*Timeo Danaos et dona ferentes,*' Captain Crittenden said solemnly.

'Beware the Greeks bearing gifts, Sergeant Major,' Sir Joel translated.

Harper had already uncorked one bottle from which he took a deep swig. 'Tastes good to me, sir.'

'They could have something else in mind,' Sir Joel said. 'If they're contemplating an attack they would like our troops to be drunk?'

'We Irish fight as well drunk as we do sober, sir,' Harper reassured him, 'in fact we probably fight better!'

'That's true,' Sharpe put in.

'And if the eejits were planning an attack they'd warn us,' Harper insisted. 'Here, sir,' he handed the opened bottle to Sharpe, 'enjoy.'

'And I suspect Marshal Soult will have shot his bolt,' Sharpe said. 'He just mounted his big attack and got a painfully bloody nose. He won't want another.' He took a mouthful of the brandy and handed it to Sir Joel. 'Thanks, Pat.'

Harper watched as the two naval officers drank and as the bottle was passed on to Clouter. 'Keep the bottle, big fellow,' Harper said, 'it'll warm ye up on a chill night!'

'Which is a good reason to get into shelter,' Sharpe said. 'I'll see you as soon as you're relieved, Pat.'

'Aye, sir, you will.'

Sharpe led his three companions on a path that weaved south through the woods and so to the long slope on top of which his battalion would muster to face any French assault. The grass was slippery with rain and the slope steep enough to leave an ache in his legs. 'They'd be mad to attack up here,' he grunted as he climbed.

'But you think it unlikely?' Sir Joel asked.

'I think they'd be mad to try, and Soult isn't insane.'

'What are his choices?' Sir Joel asked.

'Stay where he is and invite us to attack him.'

'But Lord Wellington intends to pass by him with a bridge over the Adour's mouth.'

'Which you're not supposed to know,' Captain Crittenden interjected.

'I've forgotten already,' Sharpe said, 'but even if the bridge works we still have to lure him out of Bayonne, and from all accounts that place is a fortress. If we leave him there we leave a big force of Frenchmen in our rear, and that will tie up half the army just keeping them there.'

'So,' Sir Joel concluded, 'Marshal Soult frustrates you by simply doing nothing.'

'Exactly.'

'And you believe he'll choose that option?'

'I'm only a Major, sir, what do I know? If he's got an ounce of sense he'll do nothing, but I suspect the Emperor will be nagging the poor man to fight harder. As I understand it, we're the only allied army on French soil, and Bonaparte will want us gone.'

'No doubt he will,' Sir Joel said and then, after a pause, 'God forbid, Sharpe, this isn't criticism, but your fellows seem very informal?' He posed it as a question to draw any sting from his words. 'Another Rifle thing?'

'I suppose it is, sir. All Rifle officers have to go through training with the men in their ranks and doing what they do, and most of the men you just met are from my old Light Company. They know me well, and some, like Pat Harper, are close friends. The most important thing is that they fight like fiends. I wouldn't want to face them.'

'I'm sure they're effective,' Sir Joel said, 'I suppose I just had the notion that discipline in the army was harsh and imposed by strict officers.'

'It is,' Sharpe said, 'but I began in the ranks. Twenty years ago I was a Private.'

'And that gives you a sympathy with the ranks?'

'Probably, but trust me, sir, I can be a right bastard if they break the rules.'

'I'm sure,' Sir Joel said, 'so they fear you?'

Sharpe thought about it for a few paces. 'I think what they

fear, sir, is letting me and themselves down. I've convinced them they're the best in the army, and they want to be that. And, forgive me, sir, but when I was aboard your ship I noticed you weren't exactly a tyrant?'

'I wasn't,' Sir Joel agreed. 'I think you get more from your men by expecting them to be good than by enforcing goodness, though I'm sure there are many naval officers who consider me to be wrong.'

'But few who have your record, sir,' Captain Crittenden put in.

'That's just luck, David!'

'And my men call me Lucky Sharpe,' Sharpe said. He glanced eastwards to see the far horizon just lightening with the first grey wolf-light of a new day, then he half tripped and looked down to see a white painted peg lying flat on the short grass. 'What the . . .' he began, then stopped.

'What is it?' Sir Joel asked.

'A range peg, sir.' Sharpe lifted the peg and looked around to see that every other peg had been uprooted. 'When we're defending a position and have a chance to prepare the ground we set out pegs at a hundred, two hundred and three hundred paces, sir. But someone has lifted them all.'

'And the purpose of the pegs?'

'For my Riflemen, sir. They don't really need them, but in the chaos of battle they're helpful.'

'And they start firing at three hundred paces?' Captain Crittenden asked, sounding dubious.

'At much longer range, sir,' Sharpe said, 'but at three

hundred I want the *voltigeur* officers dead, and at two hundred the Sergeants.'

'And at one hundred?' Sir Joel asked.

'The redcoat skirmishers can start firing muskets, sir.'

'So who would have uprooted your markers?'

'I think I know,' Sharpe said curtly. He quickened his pace uphill just as the first bugles sounded the reveille beyond the crest. 'We must get you some breakfast, sir.'

As Sharpe reached the crest of the hill he saw Peter d'Alembord hurrying towards him. 'Morning, sir! And welcome back!' d'Alembord called, then stopped and uttered a curse. 'The bastard!'

'Let me guess,' Sharpe said, 'Sir Nathaniel?'

D'Alembord was gazing down the slope, obviously missing the range pegs. 'Who else, sir? He does it every night, he claims this is his ground.'

'Sir Nathaniel who?' Sir Joel was listening.

'Peacock,' Sharpe said.

'He claims he should defend this side of the hill and we should be over there.' d'Alembord pointed west. 'General Barnes disagrees, but bloody Peacock insists.'

Sir Joel smiled. 'Lord Wellington mentioned Colonel Peacock, said he was typical of the less than useful officers being sent from England.'

Sharpe hid a smile. 'Peter, this is Rear Admiral Sir Joel Chase and his flag Captain, Captain Crittenden, and the big fellow is Petty Officer Clouter. My second in command, Captain Peter d'Alembord.'

'You gentlemen are a little far from the sea?' d'Alembord ventured after saluting.

'Lord Wellington put us in Major Sharpe's care,' Sir Joel answered, 'and he has led us astray.'

'Mister Sharpe does that, sir,' d'Alembord responded with a smile.

'We are tourists,' Captain Crittenden offered.

'And most welcome, I'm sure,' d'Alembord said politely, then gave a small bow of his head towards Sir Joel. 'I believe Major Sharpe has talked of you, sir, and always with the highest regard.'

'Major Sharpe fought alongside me at Trafalgar,' Sir Joel said, 'and I invited him to stay on as Captain of my marines.'

'I prefer dry land,' Sharpe said.

'You realise it's not raining?' d'Alembord said brightly, 'and forgive me, sir, I need to have the pegs reset, or did Sir Nathaniel's men take them away and burn them?'

'I only found one,' Sharpe said.

'We'll have replacements in by midday, sir,' d'Alembord said, 'though no one's expecting trouble.' He gazed towards a dark smear on the northern horizon that was evidently distant Bayonne. 'They're cooking their breakfasts.' The land immediately to the south of the city was misted by the smoke of cooking fires. The French army was camped there, protected by a massive earthwork that made a new outer defence line to protect the city's own formidable ramparts.

'Breakfast! Good idea!' Sharpe said. 'Carry on, Peter!'

Madame Esquibel provided a breakfast of ham, toasted bread, eggs, and a pot of stewed tea that Sharpe was just finishing when Madame Esquibel hurried back into the kitchen and gabbled an urgent and incomprehensible message, but as she kept pointing at the farmyard Sharpe went out into a new drizzle to see Sir Rowland Hill, commander of all forces east of the Nive, on horseback.

'Sir!'

'You're back, Sharpe!'

'I am, sir.'

'Glad of it. Do you happen to have an Admiral with you? It seems he's escaped the navy.'

'He's here, sir.'

'Lord Wellington wants him back urgently! Claims it's your fault.'

'Don't blame Major Sharpe.' Sir Joel, insatiably curious, had followed Sharpe into the farmyard. 'I insisted on accompanying him.'

Sharpe made the necessary introduction. The half-dozen aides who had followed General Hill stared at the naval officer as though he were some strange beast, while Hill bent from the saddle to shake his hand. 'Lord Wellington was concerned less Major Sharpe led you into danger, Sir Joel.'

'Oh he did!'

'Well now he can lead you back to the bridge at Villefranque. You can do that, Sharpe?'

'I can certainly arrange an escort, sir.'

'Lord Wellington's orders say it must be you, isn't that so, Cooper?'

'Indeed, sir,' one of the aides answered and took a piece of paper from a pocket. '"Instruct Major Sharpe",' he read aloud, '"that he is personally responsible for conducting Sir Joel and his companions to the Villefranque bridge as soon as possible." He's arranged another escort to conduct the Admiral back to headquarters.'

'Wellington fears the French are feeling frisky,' Hill explained, 'and might capture you, Sir Joel, but I suspect he's worrying unnecessarily. I gather Sir John gave them a bloody nose yesterday and last night they lost three whole regiments to desertion!'

'Three French regiments deserted, sir?' Sharpe asked, astonished.

'No, no, not French! Germans! Poor bastards had been forced to fight for Boney, but they heard about the battle at Leipzig, so last night they marched across the lines with all their weapons and demanded to be sent home! Useful troops, the Germans, pity they didn't volunteer to fight for us, but we can't have everything. It's a privilege and a pleasure to meet you, Sir Joel, but Lord Wellington is eager for your immediate and safe return.' Hill touched his riding crop to his hat, then turned his horse.

And Sharpe, weary and aching from too much time on horse-back, ordered the horses saddled again. It was time to go.

CHAPTER SIX

The sun was barely showing in the eastern clouds as they left the farmyard, turning the horses south into a freshening wind that was bringing the first spatters of rain. 'Why the devil is Wellington so eager to have us back?' Sir Joel grumbled.

'He doesn't want the French to capture you,' Sharpe guessed, 'he doesn't even want them to know you're here, sir.'

'Why not?'

'Because they're not fools,' Captain Crittenden answered for Sharpe, 'if they see a senior naval officer they're quite capable of adding two and two.'

They cantered past a plump girl hurrying into the rain with a scarf over her hair. '*Bonjour!*' Sharpe called.

'*Il fait un temps vraiment sale!*' she snarled back.

'Was she your fox?' Sir Joel asked, amused, 'she doesn't seem very happy in her work.'

'None of us are in this weather. Except it will keep the French quiet.'

'Why?'

'Lousy weather for firearms, sir. Wet powder and water-logged ground doesn't make for easy attacks.'

'Didn't stop the buggers yesterday!'

'And that failure will restrain them, sir,' Sharpe opined. 'They got a bloody nose once, why risk another?'

'Then cheer up, David!' Sir Joel called to his flag Captain, 'we're not missing anything.'

'Our frigates won't be happy.'

'Nonsense, a good blow will do them good! They can head offshore and ride it out.'

'Frigates?' Sharpe asked.

'I keep two off the Biscay coast,' Sir Joel said loudly, 'just to keep the natives tame.'

'And your ship is in harbour?'

'Damn right she is! Safe in Saint-Jean-de-Luz being re-victualled and doubtless swarming with whores.'

'You allow that, sir?'

'No more than you do! But it happens anyway.'

More conversation became drowned by the rising wind and by seething rain that now thrashed at them. The road was slippery, the horses tired and, despite his greatcoat, Sharpe was drenched. Why in God's name had Wellington insisted he guide the three sailors to the pontoon bridge, a job any half-competent officer could do? But at least the bridge was not far and he should be back with the battalion before midday and no longer forced to deal with the Admiral's unquenchable enthusiasm. Sharpe liked Sir Joel, liked and admired him, but his proper place was with his men, working to make them the best in the army.

A splintered shaft of lightning dazzled the sky a mile or so ahead, followed by a deafening crack of thunder and a gust of wind so strong that the horses half shied. 'You think the bridge can survive this, sir?' Sharpe shouted.

'Colonel Aldridge seemed very confident!' Sir Joel bellowed back.

'Not far now!' Sharpe yelled.

'What?'

'Not far now, sir!'

Sir Joel tried to urge his horse into a canter, but the beast, tired of struggling with wind, rain and the slick road, obstinately stayed at its steady trot. 'You ever see French cavalry back here?' Sir Joel shouted.

'No, sir.'

'Isn't that their job? To reconnoitre behind your lines?'

'They're running out of horses!' Sharpe bellowed, 'they lost too many in Russia!'

'God's bollocks,' Sir Joel cursed loudly as they crested a low rise and saw the bridge ahead, 'we'll never cross that! Just look at it!'

The bridge was suffering from the howling wind which drove the heavy rain horizontally above the river, which was being whipped into turmoil.

'That's not healthy!' Sir Joel shouted.

The wind was pushing the bridge downstream so that the river boats were tugging frantically at their anchor rodes, each separate rode jerking up from the foam-flecked water in sudden spurts, while the plank bridge above heaved and bounced on the straining cables. Debris was being swept downstream, whole uprooted trees crashing into the bridge and adding their weight to the storm's maniacal power.

'Reckon we can cross that?' Sir Joel called out.

'You'll never get the horses across, sir!' Sharpe shouted.

'Damn the horses!'

One brave man, Sharpe reckoned he had to be an officer of the Royal Engineers, was trying to cross the bridge by crawling on his hands and knees, pausing to inspect the stanchions on each boat and, as he neared the centre, the motion grew worse, each heave forcing him to grip for dear life onto the plank road-way's edges. He finally gave up and crawled back towards the farther bank where a crowd of gunners and infantrymen watched. River water broke from the straining boats in great deluges of spray, soaking the poor man who finally made it to safety and to the cheers of the onlookers who lined both banks of the Nive.

'Christ!' Sir Joel slumped in his saddle, 'we'll never get over that! Is there another bridge?'

'Way south,' Sharpe said, 'place called Ustaritz.'

'Austerlitz?'

'Ustaritz, sir.'

'How far?'

'Three or four miles, sir?' Sharpe guessed.

'A proper bridge?'

'A pontoon, I think.'

'And how far from there to Saint-Jean-de-Luz?'

'Maybe twenty miles, sir?' Another guess.

'And if the bridge at Austerlitz is anything like this one then God help us.'

'She's going!' Captain Crittenden said with alarm. The bridge was bending, its centre straining downstream as the ends of the bridge stayed anchored to their enormous posts sunk in the banks. The river boats in the centre noticeably jerked, and then, suddenly, the bridge cracked apart and the boats dragged their anchors downstream as they fanned apart. In the maelstrom the huge cables supporting the roadway stayed in place, but, denied the support of the boats, they sagged and the flotsam that had built upriver struck the planks and the whole roadway shattered.

'Dear sweet God,' Sir Joel said, 'we have to build something like that, only far bigger, and able to withstand tidal surges, currents, gale-force winds, and God only know what flotsam coming down-river! Time to pray, David!'

Captain Crittenden was examining the wreckage with his telescope. 'At least the cable held firm, sir.'

'Bugger the cables! How long will it take to rebuild?' Sir Joel asked sourly.

'A few days,' Sharpe guessed, watching as planks and scraps of shattered boats were swept downriver, 'maybe they can rebuild it with pontoons?'

'And we're stuck here.'

'And how long before the French realise the bridge is gone?' Captain Crittenden asked.

'They'll know tonight,' Sharpe said.

'How?' Sir Joel snapped the word.

'A farmer will see it's gone, sir, walk a mile north and tell someone, and the word will spread,' Sharpe guessed.

'And if Marshal Soult attacks again then Wellington can't send reinforcements across the river,' Crittenden observed.

'Only by marching them down to Ustaritz and back up again,' Sharpe said.

'Presuming that bridge still stands,' Sir Joel said sourly, 'which is bloody doubtful. And if we go by Ustaritz, how long will it take us to reach Saint-Jean-de-bloody-Luz?' He paused, then answered his own question. 'It's going to take hours! And do you know the roads from Ustabloodyritz to Saint-Jean, Sharpe?'

'No, sir, but I'm certain there's someone in Ustaritz who will know the route. There has to be a British post there, sir.'

'You're not coming, Sharpe?'

'I'm going back to my battalion, sir. I'm not doing any good waiting here for the Engineers to rebuild the bridge.'

'Then, damn it, we'll come too!'

Captain Crittenden rolled his eyes, but Sharpe knew there was little point in arguing with Sir Joel. 'I think I'll just check with the Engineers on how long the bridge repair will take, sir.'

Sharpe kicked his horse downhill and Sir Joel kept him company. Every soldier in the riverside encampment was standing on the bank, gazing at the remnants of the bridge, and among them were a half-dozen men wearing the blue coats of the Engineers. One was a Captain and Sharpe beckoned to him. 'Can you give me an estimate on how long it will take to repair the bridge?'

The Engineer glanced at Sir Joel's cocked hat and stiffened. 'We'll have it up by tomorrow morning, sir,' he said.

'That quick?' Sir Joel asked dubiously.

'Easy, sir, most of the boats aren't lost,' he pointed to the far bank where a chain of the river boats was still lashed together and anchored to the bank, 'and we can probably commandeer a half-dozen replacement boats from upriver. We have more than enough extra planks, and the three cables are intact! By mid-morning tomorrow it will be as safe as London Bridge!'

'Can I assure General Hill of that?' Sharpe asked, ignoring Sir Joel who had begun singing 'London Bridge has fallen down' very softly.

'By midday at the very latest, sir,' the Captain said confidently and cheerfully.

'Five guineas says it will take longer,' Sir Joel said to Sharpe when they rejoined Captain Crittenden.

'Done, sir.' Sharpe thought the wager risky, but he had learned to have great faith in the army's Engineers.

'What about you, David? Want to thicken my purse?'

'I'll stay out of it, sir, though I can't see it taking less than three days.'

'Three days would be a bloody miracle,' Sir Joel said, 'so back to your farmhouse, Sharpe?'

'Back, sir,' Sharpe said. Not that he had any choice. He and the admiral were cut off from Wellington so they might as well go north, to where only the French still threatened. They turned north.

The sight of two men in cocked hats worked on Sir Nathaniel Peacock like a lantern to a moth, besides, he was also desperate to know what business had taken Sharpe to see Lord Wellington. And so, the sight of Sharpe standing on the hill's crest with the two naval officers brought him galloping.

'I heard you were back, Sharpe!'

'You heard right, sir.'

Sir Nathaniel fidgeted with his reins. 'Anything we should know from headquarters?' he asked.

'Only that Lord Wellington is entirely confident in our ability to defeat any French assault.'

'He summoned you just to tell you that?' Sir Nathaniel asked indignantly.

'Oh no, sir, there was much more.'

'And did he send a reply to my letter?' Sir Nathaniel demanded.

'He did read it,' Sharpe said unhelpfully. 'And how is your broken leg, sir?' he asked with fake sympathy.

Sir Nathaniel, who appeared to be in no discomfort, suddenly looked pained. 'It mends,' he said abruptly.

'I'm glad, sir.'

'There is something we need to talk about,' Peacock said brusquely, as if glad to change the subject. 'The 71st is senior to your battalion, isn't that so?'

'Is it, sir?'

'When were you formed, Major?'

Sharpe had an urge to lie, but decided to keep to the truth. '1801, sir.'

'Ha!' Peacock crowed. 'The 71st was established in 1777. We're by far the senior regiment, which means, does it not, that the 71st should occupy the place of honour?'

'The place of honour?' Sharpe asked, though he knew perfectly well what Peacock meant.

'The right of the line!' Peacock snarled. 'I should be on the right of this hill, and you on the left!'

'You want to change places, sir?' Sharpe asked disingenuously.

'It's not a matter of "want",' Peacock snarled, 'but of right!'

Sharpe gazed down the long slope which any French attack must climb. 'The right side,' he said, 'is an easier climb. Any fellows who attack your boys on the left, sir, will be tempted to fall off to the west.' The slope on Peacock's side of the hill was steeper and was bordered by an even steeper ravine. Sharpe reckoned that any French attackers on that left side of the hill would be tempted to shelter from volleys of musketry by dropping into the ravine's cover.

'Are you suggesting,' Peacock's voice was icy now, 'that we can't cope with this side of the hill?'

'I'm suggesting, sir, that if you stay where you are then your task will be easier than mine.'

'I did not join His Majesty's army to have easy tasks, Major,' Peacock said very stiffly, 'and I, like my battalion, am senior. I will insist that Major General Barnes changes the deployment.'

'Then I'll wait for Sir Edward's decision,' Sharpe said, utterly confident that Barnes would order Sharpe's men to stay exactly where they were.

Sir Joel, amused by the hostility in Sir Nathaniel's demands, had let his cloak fall open to reveal his uniform. The Admiral's cocked hat had drawn Sir Nathaniel irresistibly, but the glitter of his uniform almost made him gasp. Instead he just stiffened in his saddle. 'I don't have the advantage, sir,' he said awkwardly.

'Rear Admiral Sir Joel Chase,' Chase introduced himself.

'My fault, Sir Joel,' Sharpe said, 'allow me to name Sir Nathaniel Peacock, commanding officer of the battalion on my left flank, the 71st.'

The words 'left flank' made Sir Nathaniel snort, but he was too intrigued by the presence of an Admiral to make anything of it. 'You're rather far from the sea, sir?' he observed abruptly.

'Well, damn me, but I thought there was something wrong with the scenery,' Sir Joel said cheerfully. 'But that damned man Wellington sent us here.'

'To do what?' Sir Nathaniel could not resist asking.

'To see whether we could bring two ships of the line up the Adour,' Sir Joel said, pointing towards the distant river that marked the right flank of the British position, 'to take any French assault in the flank.'

Sir Nathaniel peered at the river, which, even at this distance, looked scarcely wide enough to float a hay barge, let alone a pair of battleships. 'But you'd have to sail them through Bayonne!' Sir Nathaniel observed, evidently believing Sir Joel's nonsense.

'A detail,' Sir Joel said grandly, 'we are the navy.'

'I won't deny your presence would prove invaluable,' Sir Nathaniel said, 'but General Hill reckons a French attack is most unlikely.'

'And I'm certain the presence of two 74's would deter them even more,' Sir Joel said.

The sound of mallets came up the hill and Sir Nathaniel looked indignantly to where three Riflemen were replacing the closest range markers. 'You approve of that nonsense, Sharpe?' he could not resist asking.

'I ordered the nonsense, Sir Nathaniel,' Sharpe said, 'but I have a problem.'

'A problem?'

'We mark the ranges, Sir Nathaniel,' Sharpe said, 'but it seems every night the markers are taken away.'

Sir Nathaniel grunted, but said nothing.

'I suspect it's the local people doing it,' Sharpe went on, 'but I'll stop them.'

'How?'

'I have a half-dozen Riflemen who were once poachers,' Sharpe said cheerfully, 'they're crack marksmen and have eyesight like cats. Tonight they'll wait here, and if they see so much as a shadow move they'll fire. That will stop the nuisance.'

'If they can even hit a man at that range,' Sir Nathaniel said dubiously.

Sharpe cupped his hands at his mouth and shouted, 'Dan! Here!'

Daniel Hagman, one of the three down the hill, came up and saluted. 'Mister Sharpe?'

'Reckon you can hit one of those pegs you just hammered in?'

'Which ones, Mister Sharpe?'

'The furthest away,' Sharpe said, meaning the small pegs three hundred paces down the hill.

Hagman gave a quick glance at the officers accompanying Sharpe. 'You know I can, sir.'

'Two guineas says he can't,' Sir Joel said, 'well, Sharpe?'

'Two guineas it is, sir,' Sharpe said.

'I'll join that,' Sir Nathaniel said hurriedly, 'three guineas with you, Sir Joel?'

'Three it is, Sir Nathaniel. You, David?'

'I'll hold the stake,' Crittenden replied, probably doubting

169

that any man could hit so small a target as a peg three inches wide, a foot tall and three hundred paces away. Sharpe knew himself to be incapable of an accurate shot at such a small and distant target, but Hagman's precision as a Rifleman was legendary.

Sir Nathaniel watched Hagman load his rifle. 'Were you one of Major Sharpe's poachers?' he demanded.

'I was, sir.'

'And joined the army rather than endure prison?' Sir Nathaniel asked.

'I did, sir.'

'Should have been hanged,' Sir Nathaniel said.

'Oh, that was me,' Sharpe said, 'a hanging or a red coat. Wasn't much of a choice.'

'You were to be hanged?' Sir Nathaniel asked in astonishment.

'It's the usual fate of murderers, Sir Nathaniel,' Sharpe said, enjoying himself.

'Who did you murder?' Sir Joel asked, also enjoying himself.

'An innkeeper,' Sharpe said.

'Good man! Buggers always overcharge us. Here, David,' Sir Joel said, and held out his three guineas to Captain Crittenden, then looked at Sir Nathaniel, 'your stake, Sir Nathaniel?'

Sir Nathaniel reluctantly took the coins from a pouch and handed them to Crittenden. Hagman had just plucked a blade of grass and tossed it to measure the wind, and now lay flat on his back and propped the rifle's muzzle between his boots.

'Hold on!' Sir Nathaniel said loudly, plainly wanting to

distract the Rifleman. 'You're holding our stakes, but not Major Sharpe's! You can't trust a murderer!'

'Is that an aspersion on Major Sharpe's honour?' Sir Joel asked dangerously.

'Of course not,' Sir Nathaniel saw a duel looming, 'merely an observation.'

'And Sir Nathaniel is right,' Sharpe said, and took coins from his own pouch and gave them to Crittenden. 'In your own time, Dan.'

Hagman looked somewhat awkward with the rifle lined down his prone body and having to bend his upper torso and head upright to look down the sights. Sharpe noted that he had not raised the hinged backsight, but was aiming purely by eye.

Sir Nathaniel touched his horse with a spur, causing the beast to step sideways, the hooves heavy on the wet grass.

'I'm aiming at the left-most marker,' Dan said, and flinched as Peacock nudged his horse again and a heavy iron-shod hoof thumped the turf a foot from Hagman's head just as he pulled the trigger. The doghead snapped forward, there was a spurt of sparks from the uncovered pan, and a heartbeat later the rifle fired to spew a cloud of powder smoke on the ridge top.

'Ha! My wager, I think!' Sir Nathaniel said happily.

'You think wrong.' Captain Crittenden, standing well to the right of the gun smoke, was gazing down the hill with a small telescope. 'He shattered it!'

'Impossible!' Sir Nathaniel insisted, but as the smoke drifted away on the wind he could see for himself that the

171

peg was indeed splintered. 'Poachers and murderers,' he grunted unhappily.

'That's us, sir!' Hagman said proudly as he stood. 'The poachers and murderers! Best battalion in the army!'

Sharpe smiled, reckoning he had just heard the new nickname of the Prince of Wales's Own Volunteers.

'And just how many men have you murdered, Sharpe?' Sir Joel asked mischievously.

'Not sure, to be honest, sir,' Sharpe said offhandedly, 'maybe half a dozen?'

'Disgraceful!' Sir Nathaniel barked.

'I imagine you'll be damned glad of England's murderers if the French come up this hill, Sir Nathaniel,' the Admiral said, watching as Sharpe accepted his winnings from Crittenden.

'I shall be damned glad of English pluck!' Sir Nathaniel was being forced to watch his gold being given away. 'We shall beat them, sir, with English discipline and unconquerable bravery!'

'Scottish discipline and bravery,' Sharpe said reprovingly as he accepted his coins. 'Sir Nathaniel's battalion,' he explained to Sir Joel, 'is from Scotland and there's few finer in the army.'

'None finer!' Sir Nathaniel insisted.

Sharpe clapped Hagman on the shoulder. 'Damn fine shooting, Dan, but how good is your night-shooting these days?'

'Good as ever, Mister Sharpe. I dropped a midnight doe at four hundred paces a week ago.'

'Good man, and thank you, Dan.' Sharpe handed Hagman half his winnings.

'Thank you, Mister Sharpe! Permission to return to duty?'

'Off you go, Dan.'

'Always a pleasure to help you, Mister Sharpe,' Hagman said and, with a gesture that could be charitably described as a salute, ran back down the hill.

'Damned insolence,' Sir Nathaniel said, then, sensing his presence was unwelcome, turned his horse and rode away.

'A very nasty man,' Captain Crittenden observed as Sir Nathaniel spurred into a canter.

'Newly arrived,' Sharpe said, 'God knows there are a score of men deserving of a battalion,' including himself, he thought grimly, 'but the Horse Guards keep sending new men who want to join in for a chance of glory before the war ends.' He looked at the retreating Sir Nathaniel. 'Luckily for Peacock his men will keep him safe. They know their business.'

'And will you really fire on local people removing your range pegs?' Captain Crittenden asked.

Sharpe laughed. 'If that really happened, sir, I'd just send men down to beat them up. But the local folk aren't the ones doing it.'

'They're not?'

'It's Colonel Peacock's men. It's his way of claiming this side of the hill, but I reckon I've frightened him off.'

'Peacock's men?' the Captain asked, shocked. 'But why?'

'Because he's a bloody idiot,' Sir Joel answered instead of Sharpe.

'My battalion,' Sharpe explained, 'is on the right of the brigade, and Sir Nathaniel believes that's the place of honour.'

'And therefore his,' Sir Joel finished for Sharpe.

'And between you and me,' Sharpe went on, 'he can have it. My boys will have a much easier job on the left of this hill.'

'How so?' Crittenden asked.

'Because in front of his Scotsmen,' Sharpe pointed down and across the slope, 'the ground falls ever more sharply away into a valley. Once his men start firing volleys, the French will be tempted down that slope to get into cover. On this side the fight will be a lot grimmer, but it won't happen. The Crapauds won't want a second fight like yesterday's.'

'But if they learn the bridge has broken,' Sir Joel said, 'and that Wellington can't send troops over the river to stiffen the defences here, isn't that a golden opportunity? If I was *Maréchal* Soult, I'd see it as a chance to break Wellington's army!'

Captain Crittenden had produced a telescope and was gazing northwards. 'From what I understand,' he said, 'Bayonne is a fortress city?'

'So we're told,' Sharpe said.

'And if anyone was mad enough to make a pontoon bridge across the mouth of the Adour, and I hasten to add that I know of no proposal to do anything so lunatic, they are going to be very close to a city crammed with enemy troops.'

'A pair of frigates will see them off,' Sir Joel said confidently. 'Think of the firepower on those gun decks!'

'I was thinking of the firepower of concentrated French artillery, sir.'

'Which was defeated by musketry! You saw that yesterday!'

'I suspect you already have the answer, sir,' Sharpe said to Crittenden.

'I do?'

'I reckon your imaginary bridge will have to put men ashore on the north bank to fix the cables and so on?'

Crittenden nodded, 'We'll need a considerable number of artificers,' he said, 'who might be frighteningly vulnerable to a French attack so close to the city.'

'Then I'd suggest the navy uses its boats to land a good battalion of British troops first, along with some artillery. You have the boats to do that.'

'I'd planned on doing that anyway,' Sir Joel said, 'I already have Lord Wellington's assurance that he can provide us with troops. Does that satisfy you, David?'

'If such madness was contemplated, sir,' Crittenden said, 'I think at least one battalion would be a necessity.'

'Consider it done,' Sir Joel said happily, then looked at Sharpe. 'Would you like your Poachers and Murderers for that job, Sharpe?'

'We're on the wrong side of the river, sir. Nosey will choose men from Sir John Hope's command.'

'Pity,' Sir Joel said. He gazed at the long stretch of peaceful countryside to the north, then shrugged. 'Time to get out of this bloody rain for one of your landlady's meals, I think!'

The meal was boiled ham, which they ate in the farmhouse kitchen as rising winds lashed the windows with tempestuous rain.

'It's shifted to the west,' Captain Crittenden remarked gloomily of the weather.

'Winter in France,' Sir Joel said happily, 'at least it's not snowing.'

A clatter of hooves in the farmyard made everyone look expectantly at the kitchen door which opened to reveal the rubicund, kindly face of Sir Rowland Hill.

'Ah, Sir Joel!' he said, 'I bring you good news!'

'Napoleon's surrendered?' Sir Joel asked.

'Alas, no, but I'm assured the bridge at Villefranque will be restored by tomorrow.'

'Tomorrow!'

'The boats are already in place and they're laying the road's planks now. His lordship sent a message assuring you that you can safely return to his headquarters.'

'That was damned fast!' Sir Joel said.

Sharpe flinched, knowing that Rowland Hill detested any foul language, even a mild 'damn', but Hill passed over the word with nothing but a slight frown. 'It was fast indeed, Sir Joel! But our Engineers can be magicians when the need is urgent.'

'I'll make a point of thanking them tomorrow,' Sir Joel said. 'Will you accompany us, Sharpe?'

'I need Sharpe here,' Hill said. He took off his cocked hat and shook water from it. 'Not that we're expecting trouble. This rain should keep Marshal Soult at home. The lower ground must be a morass by now! No land to march troops across, and horrible for artillery.'

'It will keep you at home too, Sir Rowland,' Sir Joel said.

'Oh we'll be on the move soon,' Hill said happily, 'his lordship will have a plan to break out of here.'

Sir Joel, who was a major part of that plan, managed to keep silent about it, instead politely offering the General a glass of wine.

'A little early for me,' Hill said, 'but I should reply to his lordship's enquiry about you, Sir Joel. Can I say you'll be with him by tomorrow night?'

'Of course, Sir Rowland.'

'In that case maybe you'll do me the honour of dining with me this evening? You and your flag Captain?'

'We'd be honoured,' Sir Joel said.

'The honour will be mine,' Hill said as he put his damp hat back on his head, then checked and listened for a moment before hurrying to open a window and listen again. 'You hear that?' he asked.

They listened and Sharpe thought he could hear a distant rumbling sound, like thunder a long way off. 'It's not gunfire,' he said uncertainly.

'Nor thunder,' Hill said with a frown. 'We heard it first a couple of days ago.'

'Too prolonged for thunder,' Sir Joel put in.

'There are a pair of bridges that span the Nive in Bayonne,' Hill said, 'and both are made of timber, and that sound is heavy wagons crossing the bridges. I scarcely credited that explanation, but the local priest, a good fellow, assures me that's the source of the noise. A big hay wagon, he says, sounds just like thunder.'

'That's a lot of hay,' Sir Joel said, still listening to the rumble.

'Twelve-pounders weigh a few tons each,' Sharpe put in.

'Precisely!' Hill said happily. 'They're moving their guns again. But where? They could be bringing them to this side of the Nive, but even so I can't credit Soult with planning an attack on us.'

'No?' Sir Joel asked mildly.

'He suffered a pounding on the west bank,' Hill said, pulling the window closed, 'so why would he come here to receive another? No, I think *Monsieur* Soult has learned his lesson. He's probably returning yesterday's guns to their positions in the outer defences. So! I'll welcome you to dinner tonight, Sir Joel. Major Sharpe knows where you can find me. Shall we say six o'clock?'

'Four bells it is,' Sir Joel said happily.

'Four bells?' Sir Rowland asked.

'The dog watch, sir,' Captain Crittenden murmured.

'One day I'll understand you watery fellows,' Hill said with a smile, then grimaced with anticipation of the rain. 'Till this evening, gentlemen,' he said, and ducked out into the wind and rain.

'There's one thing you should know about Daddy Hill,' Sharpe said.

'Daddy?' Sir Joel asked.

'Nickname,' Sharpe said, 'the men like him.'

'And what is it,' Sir Joel asked, 'that I should know?'

'He cannot abide swearing,' Sharpe said.

'Well, bugger me!' Sir Joel exclaimed. 'A soldier who doesn't swear?'

'He doesn't,' Sharpe said, 'though it's rumoured he said "damn" at the battle of Talavera.'

'Why?'

'He was surprised by an unexpected French attack.'

Captain Crittenden held up a hand. 'And maybe we'll be surprised too?' He cupped a hand to an ear and Sharpe heard the dim grumbling noise carrying over the sound of wind and rain. 'They're either moving a lot of hay, or that's more cannon on the move. How far away is the town?'

'Three, four miles?' Sharpe guessed.

'And the sound carries that far?' Crittenden asked in a dubious tone.

'Easily!' Sir Joel broke in. 'Remember that Frog merchantman we captured off the Azores? We heard the captain's wife screaming more than four miles away! Only thing that made us aware of him!'

'Sound carries further at sea, sir,' Crittenden pointed out.

'The bugger was giving his wife a right caning,' Sir Joel explained to Sharpe, 'so we thrashed him as punishment until the wife begged us to stop. I never can understand women. What was the bugger carrying? You remember, David?'

'Rice, indigo and rum,' Crittenden answered.

'Which gave us a pretty penny in prize money. So why are the buggers moving guns, Sharpe?'

'Probably General Hill is right, sir. They must have taken twelve-pounders away from the earthworks around the city to make that attack yesterday, and now they're returning them.'

'Makes sense, I suppose,' Sir Joel said grudgingly. He looked down at his uniform, its glory much reduced by mud. 'Do you suppose this good woman would spruce up my uniform,' he asked Sharpe, 'before supper with the clean-mouthed Sir Rowland?'

'I'll ask her,' Sharpe said, 'and if there's a coin for her? The answer will be yes.'

Sharpe asked, then went to visit his battalion's billets.

The rumbling to the north went on and the rain still fell.

Next morning Sir Joel declared that General Hill provided a much better table than Lord Wellington. 'Roast beef, Sharpe! Damned fine roast beef.'

'I hope you didn't tell General Hill it was damned fine, sir.'

'I behaved myself, Sharpe. Even Florence is kind enough to say that once in a while I can mind my manners in society.' Sir Joel had drawn his sword and was glowering at a hard-boiled egg. 'There was a strange fellow at dinner last night, a local landowner. Didn't like the fellow myself, he spoke not a word of English and cursed away in French.'

'What did he have to say for himself?' Sharpe asked.

'That this was the sacred soil of France and we had no business being here! Damned rude, I thought, since he was our guest. I asked the fellow what business the French had in marching all over Spain, and he had no answer! None!' Sir Joel swept the sword and succeeded in knocking egg and egg cup off the table. 'Damn! I saw a fellow behead an egg in London! Never works for me.' He sheathed the sword and retrieved the dented egg along with scraps of the broken cup. 'Damned rude fellow! Telling us we had no business being here! What was his name, David?'

'I don't recall, Sir Joel.'

'Not that it matters, we'll never see him again so we don't need to know his name!'

'He made the point,' Captain Crittenden went on in a reasonable tone, 'that we now control a part of France, and the Emperor would not permit it to continue.'

'Damn all Bonaparte can do!' Sir Joel said. 'He's got his hands full of bloody Russians!'

'He might insist Marshal Soult makes a more determined effort,' Sharpe pointed out.

'Which is why you're here,' Sir Joel responded, 'and damn it, we can't stay with you!' He peeled the egg and took a bite out of it. 'I suppose we should be on our way.'

'We should, sir,' Captain Crittenden said with obvious relief.

'You're worried about bloody Bampfylde, David?'

'I am, sir.'

'Bugger Bampfylde,' Sir Joel said, digging into his egg, 'he's commanding the squadron while I'm gallivanting with you, Sharpe,' he explained, 'and bloody Bampfylde doesn't believe we can construct a bridge over the Adour in a single day. Says it's not possible at all! And doubtless he's making Lord Wellington nervous. The truth is that bloody Bampfylde doesn't know his fat arse from his bloody elbow.' He paused, spoon halfway to his mouth. 'I suppose we should hurry back and calm everyone's nerves. D'you mind if we steal the rifles, Sharpe?' Sir Joel gestured at the two rifles Sharpe had provided at Arcangues. 'You stole a volley gun from the navy so it seems a fair exchange.'

'Very fair, sir.'

Sir Joel, his breakfast demolished, pulled his oilskin cloak over his newly cleaned uniform and led the way into the farmyard where Clouter held the horses. The rain was relentless, drumming on the farm roof and spreading puddles across the yard. Sir Joel insisted on embracing Sharpe with a brief hug before mounting. 'I hope you'll visit me in Devon when the war's over, Sharpe!'

'I should like that, sir.'

'Get yourself to Exeter and ask anyone. They all know where to find me!'

'I don't doubt it, sir.'

Sharpe had a brief sour moment wondering where he would be when the war was over, a question to which he had no answer. He brushed the thought away and shook Clouter's undamaged hand. 'Look after yourself, Clouter.'

'The good Lord does that, sir,' the huge man rumbled, then clambered onto his horse and Sharpe watched the three ride away. He felt a sense of relief. He liked Sir Joel, liked him a lot, but the man's enthusiasm and ebullience could be tiring, and ever since Sharpe had been appointed as the Admiral's protector he had been forced to ignore battalion business.

Now, it seemed, he was to be forced to ignore it again because, as Sir Joel left, a mounted Artillery officer clattered into the yard. 'Major Sharpe?'

'That's me.'

'Captain Anderson, sir,' the Artilleryman said. 'General Barnes said you'd be good enough to show me where we can place the guns.'

'What guns?' Sharpe asked.

'Nine-pounders, sir, and five-fives. Three of each.'

'Howitzers!' Sharpe said, pleased. He well knew what a five-five was, but the news that he might have three of them on the hillside was welcome indeed. He glanced north through the yard's gate and saw a full battery of guns, limbers and caissons waiting in the rain. It was an impressive and heart-ening sight. The prospect of any French attack might be minimal, but every Infantryman liked to think there were guns close by. 'Come with me, Captain,' he said.

Anderson called to a Sergeant to accompany him. 'Far to go?' he asked.

'Not far,' Sharpe said, 'what are your orders?'

'We have to enfilade the main road, sir,' Anderson said, 'and General Barnes didn't want us interfering with your men.'

'My men will be more than happy to see you, Captain. Is General Barnes expecting an attack?'

'He says not, sir. He reckons the Crapauds have shot their bolt and just want to lurk behind their defences, but he wants us to be ready in case they get itchy.'

Sharpe led Anderson and his Sergeant to the hilltop where he noted with satisfaction that all his range pegs were undisturbed. 'We'll be here, Captain,' he said, pacing along the brow of the hill. He took the two Artillerymen to the crest's eastern edge where the hill fell away into a sodden valley. Another hill formed the valley's farther side and Sharpe pointed to it. 'The main road climbs that hill, Captain, and if the buggers were to come then they'll probably attack straight up that road.'

'You don't think they'll attack you on this hill?'

'Oh, they will,' Sharpe said, 'they have enough men to attack the whole line of hills, but that road will be the centre of their attack. They'd expect the strongest defence will be on the road itself, so they'll want to push us off this hill to get behind it.'

Anderson peered westwards, looking at the road which led south-west from Bayonne, then climbed to the hill's summit where it turned southwards. 'We'll have more guns on that hill, sir,' he said, 'but this crest does give us a nasty chance to hit them from the flank.' He turned to his Sergeant. 'John? Bring the guns here.'

'Sir.' The Sergeant turned his horse and spurred back towards the farm.

'Place your guns,' Sharpe said, 'and we'll form to your left.'

'And I'm guessing,' Anderson said slowly, 'that a couple of my pieces can be turned to fire across this slope.' He pointed towards the ground where any French attack might assault the hill Sharpe's men would defend.

'We'd appreciate that,' Sharpe said, 'it almost makes me wish they would come.'

'I somehow doubt they'll oblige us,' Anderson said.

'You've got three nines and three five-fives?' Sharpe asked. 'Isn't that a bit unusual?' Almost all British batteries possessed one five-and-a-half-inch howitzer and five nine-pounders.

'Damned strange!' Anderson answered, 'but we had to scavenge guns from the defences at Villefranque, and their Colonel reckoned he could spare three of each. I like it! We can throw a lot of shells.'

'I like it too,' Sharpe said grimly. The short-barrelled howitzers fired explosive shells, while the longer nine-pounders were restricted to roundshot, canister and the lethal spherical caseshot.

'Nothing like a well-laid shrapnel round to ruin a Frenchman's day,' Anderson said, then turned, startled, as an imperious voice called from behind.

'Hey! You!'

Sharpe turned. 'Bloody man,' he said quietly when he saw Sir Nathaniel galloping towards them.

Sir Nathaniel dragged on the reins to bring his horse to a stop. 'Who are you?' he demanded of the Artilleryman.

'Captain Anderson, sir.'

'And I am Colonel Sir Nathaniel Peacock and I command on this hilltop. Why did you not report to me?'

Anderson stiffened. 'Because General Barnes ordered me to report to Major Sharpe, sir.'

'And since when did a Major outrank a Colonel?' Sir Nathaniel paused. 'Well, answer me, man!'

'It's a question best put to General Barnes, sir.'

'Damn your impudence!' Sir Nathaniel snapped. 'I assume you're placing artillery on this hill? Am I right?'

'You are, sir.'

'Then I will tell you where the guns are to be placed, and it will not be here!'

'Captain Anderson has his orders, sir,' Sharpe put in, 'and those orders come from General Hill.' Sharpe assumed he was right. 'And to obey those orders he will need to place his guns here.'

'Where they are no damned use if the French assault the left of this hill, where my men are! The army does not exist for your convenience, Sharpe!'

'It exists to defeat the enemy, sir.'

'Damn your insolence, Sharpe! Captain? You will spread the guns along the hilltop.'

'I will obey my orders, sir,' Anderson said.

'And I have just given you one. The whole hilltop will be defended, you understand me?'

'I do, sir.'

'Then make sure you obey.' Sir Nathaniel wrenched his reins, dug his spurs in and galloped back the way he had come.

'What do I do?' Anderson asked.

'Put the guns here, of course. What happens now is that Sir Nathaniel Pisscock will go and complain to General Barnes who will tell him to stop being a damned fool and to leave you alone, and that will be the end of it.'

Anderson looked towards the retreating figure of Peacock. 'I thought all the fools like that had been happily killed in the last few years.'

'I'm told London has an endless supply of them to plague us.'

'New, is he?'

'Wet behind the ears,' Sharpe said bitterly, 'never seen a battle, but keeps telling me how to fight.'

'And you're Sharpe of Talavera, sir?'

'I was at Talavera,' Sharpe said cautiously.

'Me too,' Anderson said, 'I was a Sergeant.'

'I was once too,' Sharpe said, thinking that Anderson must be a capable and efficient soldier if he had risen from Sergeant to Captain in just four years.

'So what do I do if that bugger gives me an order to move the guns?'

'Shoot him, of course.'

Anderson laughed. 'It might come to that.'

'And then we might win the war,' Sharpe said, 'that's what ex-Sergeants are good at.'

'What are those poor buggers doing?' Anderson asked. He was staring northwards and slightly east, where a long ridge

186

protruded from the extreme right of the British line. The ridge was slightly lower than the hilltops and constantly lost height so that it resembled a long ramp with the River Adour to its east and the flat farmlands to the west. Sharpe reckoned the ramp was a little more than a mile long, and a lone British redcoat battalion was advancing in column along its summit. Every step took them nearer and nearer the French lines.

'They're invading France, silly buggers,' Sharpe said. The advance of the single battalion made no sense to him, but General Hill must have ordered it, and Daddy Hill was no fool, and certainly no man to risk soldiers' lives unnecessarily. 'Maybe,' he said slowly, 'they're to stop the bloody French from using that ridge as an approach to our heights?'

'They could be cut off easily enough,' Anderson said. He had taken a telescope from his pouch and aimed it at the distant battalion. 'Looks like the Buffs,' he said.

'Colonel Bunbury's no fool,' Sharpe said. 'Maybe he's just provoking the bastards. Go out there, fire a volley or two and come back while they're still pissing their pants.'

'Still doesn't make much sense,' Anderson said, then turned as he heard the jingle of trace chains, the pounding of hooves and the crashes as tons of guns, limbers and caissons approached across the wide hilltop.

'What's your name?' Sharpe asked.

'My . . .' Anderson was momentarily confused by the question, then realised what Sharpe wanted. 'Samuel, sir.'

'I'm Dick,' Sharpe said. 'I fear we won't have a chance to fight side by side, Sam, but if we do we'll show those bastards what good Sergeants can do.'

He shook Anderson's hand then left him to do his job. If it came to a fight, and all the signs pointed the other way, he would have Sir Nathaniel on his left and Sam Anderson on his right. Which meant his right was safe.

Sharpe sat in the farmhouse with the battalion's papers spread on the kitchen table. The surgeon reported six hundred and thirty-six men fit for duty, which was better than Sharpe had expected, but there were still fifty-three on the injured and sick list. At least half the men wounded in the assault on the village by the river had returned to duty, which was good news. He signed off on the report and then, bored with the work, made himself a cup of tea. Rain made its way down the chimney to hiss in the hearth's fire and Sharpe wondered where he could find linseed oil. He was not even sure he knew what linseed oil was, but Sir Joel had assured him that any good cloak, if soaked in linseed oil and well rubbed with beeswax, would make an efficient rain-proof cape. He sipped his tea and felt a temptation to sleep in the heat of the fire.

'I thought I'd be finding you in here,' a voice said.

'Come in, Pat,' Sharpe said, 'there's tea in the pot.'

Harper poured himself a generous cup and sat opposite Sharpe. 'I liked your Admiral, so I did.'

'He's a fine man.' And by now, Sharpe thought, across the repaired bridge and on his way to Saint-Jean-de-Luz.

'And that black fellow! He looks as if he can do a wee bit of damage.'

'I fought alongside him at Trafalgar,' Sharpe said, 'and he's a right bloody demon in a fight. A bit like you, Pat.'

'Not me! I'm a gentle soul, so I am. Ask anyone.'

Sharpe grinned, sipped his tea and said nothing.

'So I see we've got guns now?'

'Nine-pounders and five-fives, three of each and under an excellent officer,' Sharpe said.

'Thank the saints for the five-fives,' Harper said. 'And you put them on our right?' Harper went on, 'not playing nice with Pisscock and putting them between us?'

'I didn't put them anywhere,' Sharpe said, 'General Hill, I assume it was Daddy, demanded they fire across to the road on the next hill, but their commander promised me he could support us if we needed it.'

'Nice of him.' Harper uncapped his canteen and added a slug of brandy to his tea. 'And they repaired the bridge?'

'Sounds as if they did, and bloody fast! Which means the Admiral owes me five guineas.' Sharpe glanced at the kitchen window as a gust of wind slapped rain hard on the glass. 'Any idea where we can get linseed oil, Pat?'

'Easy, sir. We find which battalion has some and we nick it.'

'Brilliant, Pat, why didn't I think of that?'

'Because you're an officer, sir?'

A sudden clangour of bells sounded from the distant city and Sharpe tried to count the separate tolling. 'Christ, is that only eleven o'clock? I thought it was mid afternoon.'

'Eleven o'clock and only two weeks to Christmas,' Harper said.

That thought depressed Sharpe. He knew Jane would be expecting a Christmas present from him, and he had no idea how he was to find one, let alone send it to Saint-Jean-de-Luz where most of the army's wives were billeted. Nor had he received a letter from her in a week, though that was not unusual, and even when she did write it was only to complain of the boredom of the small French port and how sour the shopkeepers were. Sharpe tried to write to her twice a week, but found it hard to find things to say that might interest her. He had decided to say nothing about having visited Saint-Jean-de-Luz, lest it prompted a squall.

'We'll have to think of something special for the lads,' he said, 'maybe roast beef for Christmas?'

'A day of sunshine would be nice,' Harper said, cocking his head to the relentless sound of the rain.

The kitchen door burst open to reveal a very wet Harry Price. 'Aren't you officer of the day, Harry?' Sharpe asked.

'I am, sir, and the Crapauds are coming.'

'What?'

'Thousands of the buggers, sir, bloody thousands! Straight at us! Picquets are already in.'

'Sweet Jesus,' Sharpe said. If the picquets had been warned and had already retreated then the French had to be close. He tossed the remains of his tea into the fire, strapped on his sword belt and picked up his rifle.

Because Marshal Soult was coming to break the British army.

CHAPTER SEVEN

'I never thought I'd hear myself saying this,' Patrick Harper spoke in a soft voice, 'but . . .' his voice faded away to a mutter.

'But what?' Sharpe asked.

Harper steeled himself by taking a deep breath. 'God save England, sir.' He was standing beside Sharpe and gazing northwards where the damp green countryside that lay between the British-held hills and the fortress city of Bayonne was being turned blue. 'Thousands of the buggers!' Harper said in wonderment.

'Enough of them,' Sharpe muttered. Blue-coated columns of French infantry were marching from their camps south of Bayonne and spreading across the landscape. As far as Sharpe could determine they were following three paths, one to the east, which would bring them up against the sole British battalion guarding the long ramp which led to the right of the British line, another following the road which Sam Anderson's guns would enfilade, and still more skirting the waterlogged ground beside the River Nive to assault the left of General

Hill's defenders. 'We'll be busy, right enough,' Sharpe said. It was impossible to count the massive force coming south, but one thing was certain, that it vastly outnumbered General Hill's fourteen thousand men who had to defend the line of hills. The only advantage Sharpe could see in General Hill's dispositions, other than that they held the high ground, was that the recent rains had made the approach so sodden that the enemy infantry had to be wearing themselves out as they struggled through the waterlogged farmland. Those infantry columns were staying close to the roads that had been left to the horse-drawn guns, which Sharpe knew must be the grim twelve-pounders. So the enemy, at least the infantry, would be tired from the long march, and the roads betrayed where the attacks on the British-held hills were most likely to be mounted, but those were small consolation because one of those places was the hill where Sharpe's battalion waited, and the size of the blow would be massive.

As it would be on the Buffs, the fine battalion from Kent, that was isolated in front of the British-held hills. Sharpe still did not understand the purpose of the deployment, and the Kentishmen, unlike his own troops, could not even retreat behind the crest to protect themselves from the artillery fire that would surely precede an infantry attack. He could see a large French column approaching the spur where the Buffs waited, and he supposed that column was intended to drive the Kentishmen back before hooking behind the right of the British line that lay about a mile ahead of the French attackers.

But that farther French column, sizeable as it was, was dwarfed by the massive numbers of the central assault approaching south along the major road, and already that huge mass of men was dividing as infantry slanted westwards towards the slope where Sharpe's men waited.

'Fetch me Tom Kelleher and Dan,' he told Harper, who broke away to find the two men.

Sharpe strolled to the right-hand end of his line and beckoned to Captain Anderson. 'You see what we're facing, Sam?'

'Hard to miss it, sir.' Anderson had a small telescope that he used to gaze at the enemy. 'And they're deploying guns to tickle us.'

Sharpe used his own glass to see that two short-barrelled howitzers and a half-dozen of the twelve-pounders had left the road and were being hauled through the soggy pasture to confront the slope where he waited. It was hard going for the enemy, the gunners were whipping the horses and infantrymen heaved at the wheels of the guns and limbers to keep the cannons moving in the mud.

'You reckon they'll bring the guns through the wood, sir?' Anderson asked.

'They'll not get those twelves across the stream,' Sharpe replied, 'but they might manage to get the howitzers over.'

'That'll bring them close.'

'I'll put some rifles down the slope. It will be horribly long range for them, but they'll discourage the bastards.'

'I'll ventilate the bastards with spherical case,' Anderson said wolfishly.

'And if you have a chance to put some canister across the slope,' Sharpe gestured to the long hill where the French must climb to face his men, 'make sure my skirmishers are in first.'

'We've yet to kill any of our own skirmishers, sir, and we'll not start today.'

'Sorry, Sam,' Sharpe said, 'I should have assumed you know your own trade.'

'It'll be an hour yet before they get here,' Anderson said, nodding north towards the approaching French.

'At least. And on that sodden ground? Their guns will be the devil to position.'

The rain still pelted down, and the lower ground beyond the trees, where the heavy French artillery would have to place themselves, would be soft. The massive recoil from each shot of their guns would dig the trails deeper into the soil, just as had happened at Arcangues, and necessitating a laborious realignment of the barrel before another shot could be fired. It was a small mercy, but on this rainswept day, Sharpe was glad of anything that could slow the enemy's assault. 'Aye,' Anderson agreed, 'it won't be a good day for their gunners. But the soil up here is firm enough.'

'Enjoy yourself, Sam.'

'You too, sir.'

Sharpe paused to look at Anderson's guns which were arrayed in a semicircle. Two of the nine-pounders were pointing towards the distant road, ready to hammer the attackers with shot and caseshot, while the final nine-pounder, along with the shorter-barrelled howitzers, was aimed north-wards. They could be swung to fire at the distant road, or handspiked around the other way to offer fire across the slope immediately to Sharpe's front. Sharpe was about to walk away when a thought occurred to him and he turned back. 'Captain Anderson!' he called.

'Sir?'

'You heard the bridge at Villefranque is repaired?'

'I hadn't heard that, sir.'

'Nosey will know what's happening here by now, so you can be sure reinforcements are already on the way.'

'Good!'

'Your lads might like to know they're not going to be alone.'

'Thank you, sir!'

Sharpe stared west across the Nive to see whether there was any sign of another French attack on that side of the river, but the land there looked encouragingly empty, which meant Wellington could indeed strip troops from that bank of the Nive to support General Hill.

And that, he thought, was a French mistake. Soult was surely no fool, and must have known Wellington's army was divided by the Nive, which meant any French attack on either bank would only face half an army. But if the other half of Wellington's force was unthreatened, then they could march to the help of the beleaguered half. Or perhaps Soult had not yet heard that the pontoon bridge had been rebuilt? And even if he did know that the bridge was again intact, it would have made sense for Soult to attack both sides of the Nive, thus preventing men from one bank crossing the river to support the men on the other.

So, if as it seemed, Soult was only attacking the eastern bank, then the western half of the army could send help, but it would take a long time for those men to be marched south to the bridge and then north to the battlefield, and so huge was the French force now coming straight towards Sharpe that possibly there would not be enough time for those reinforcements to arrive.

'You wanted us, sir?' Lieutenant Kelleher and Rifleman Hagman were waiting for him.

'Tom,' Sharpe said, 'your skirmishers are going to be a mite busy.'

'You think so, sir?'

'I'll send Captain Carline's company to thicken your line.'

Kelleher gazed at the vast mass of French infantry. 'Still won't be enough, sir.' Tom Kelleher was a redcoated Lieutenant who, officially, was second in command to Peter d'Alembord who led the Light Company, but who was equally busy serving as the battalion's only Major. That left young Tom Kelleher to lead the Light Company most of the time. He was as tall and lean as Sharpe, but lacked Sharpe's experience and confidence. He was nervous, plainly in awe of Sharpe and d'Alembord's long experience of skirmishing and, though he knew his business well enough, Kelleher was slow to make decisions even if, usually, those were the right decisions. Sharpe thought about asking d'Alembord to lead the skirmishers, but suspected d'Alembord would be more useful with the main line.

'Of course it won't be enough, Tom,' Sharpe answered Kelleher, 'but Number Two Company's men will thicken your fire, and don't forget we should be getting some of Ned Griggs's Riflemen to be skirmishers too. And Dan?'

'Mister Sharpe?'

'I want you and three chosen men to keep an eye on the French artillery. The buggers are bound to try and knock our battery out of the fight, but if you can kill a handful of gunners that might teach them manners.'

Hagman gazed north. 'It'll be a rare long shot, Mister Sharpe, if they unlimber beyond the trees.'

'Which they probably will, Dan,' Sharpe said, 'but do your best. Even a few near misses will slow them down.'

'And the rain will slow us down, Mister Sharpe.'

'True, Dan, but none of us like shooting in the rain and I'll guarantee you the Crapauds like it much less than we do.'

The 71st were forming up to the left. Sharpe had half expected Sir Nathaniel would attempt to array his men on the right of the crest, but either he had accepted that the argument was lost or else General Barnes had knocked the nonsense out of him. And someone there knew their business. Sharpe suspected it was one of the battalion's two Majors, because the Scotsmen were some twenty paces behind the crest where they would be hidden from the French at the foot of the long slope. Sharpe's Murderers were the same distance back, formed into two long ranks where Peter d'Alembord was inspecting them.

Sharpe beckoned to him. 'I have a mind, Dally, that the skirmishers will have to shoot and run.'

D'Alembord glanced at the distant French. 'Because that lot will send a horde of *voltigeurs*, sir.'

'They will,' Sharpe said grimly. The French had started to use more and more men as *voltigeurs*, the skirmishers who came in front to overwhelm the British skirmishers and to snipe at the waiting line in an effort to kill as many officers as possible. 'I'm detaching Carline's company to thicken our boys,' he hesitated, 'and Tom Kelleher knows enough to survive the onslaught?' He inflected the last few words as a question.

'Tommy knows his business,' d'Alembord said confidently, 'I'll have a word with him and tell him he has to retire quickly if he can't hold them. And tell him not to be a bloody hero.'

'You think he'll be tempted?'

'He has an exalted idea of our prowess,' d'Alembord said sourly. 'He's heard you say that light companies win battles and he believes it.'

'Then disabuse him, tell him this battle will come down to volley fire.'

D'Alembord gazed at the approaching horde. 'Do we have enough ammunition to kill that lot?' he asked.

'Send Joe Henderson back to fetch more,' Sharpe said, 'but even so it will probably come down to bayonet work.'

'Oh bliss.'

'And the gunners there will help with canister.' Sharpe pointed at Sam Anderson's battery.

'That'll be a blessing,' d'Alembord said.

'And the bridge is back up,' Sharpe said, 'so I'm sure reinforcements are on the way.'

'And how long will they take to reach us?'

'God knows,' Sharpe said, 'could be hours.'

'By which time we'll be dead,' d'Alembord said sourly. 'We've marched all the way from Portugal, beaten the buggers every time they tried to stop us, just to die on this miserable hill. Sorry, sir, I'm feeling a bit gloomy.'

'You are!' Sharpe unslung his rifle and, more out of habit than concern, made certain the flint was firmly held in the doghead. 'It's the waiting that's the worst, Dally.' He slung his rifle again. 'And think how those poor bastards are feeling.' He nodded towards the enemy. 'The veterans there know what's waiting for them, and the new conscripts? They've heard stories about us and they're terrified.'

'The 71st will advance!' A piercing voice startled Sharpe, who turned to see Sir Nathaniel marching his two ranks to the crest of the hill.

'Bugger wants to kill his own men,' Sharpe said angrily. He thought briefly of going to Sir Nathaniel and warning him that he was merely making his men convenient targets for the French artillery, then decided he might as well not waste his breath. Sir Nathaniel would certainly not welcome the advice which, anyway, was already being given to him by Major Mackenzie who Sharpe could see talking to the mounted Sir Nathaniel.

Mackenzie, a decent officer, was plainly speaking emphatically and gesturing back to where the 71st had been waiting, but Sir Nathaniel made an abrupt gesture with a riding crop that, for an instant, Sharpe thought had struck Mackenzie, and then the argument finished and Sir Nathaniel was riding behind his men shouting at them, and shouting loud enough for Sharpe to catch some of the harangue. 'You are British! The scum attacking you will run away! Stand firm and fight for King and country!'

'You think the poor buggers care a fart for the King?' Sharpe asked d'Alembord.

'Some of them might have heard of him,' d'Alembord said airily, then grinned. 'Here comes trouble.'

Trouble was Captain Griggs of the 95th Rifles whose company was attached to the brigade to add firepower to the skirmishers. He ran to Sharpe and d'Alembord. 'Greetings, mere infantrymen,' he said, 'I bring you good tidings of great joy.'

'You're resigning your commission?' Sharpe asked with a grin.

'Alas, no, Mister Sharpe. I merely wanted to tell you that we are here and by the look of that bloody lot,' he glanced at the French, 'you'll need us.'

'We will,' Sharpe said.

'But,' Griggs said acidly, 'Sir Nathaniel Peacock commands me that all my men must join his Light Company and ignore your skirmishers, on account of you having cannon and he doesn't.'

'Which order,' Sharpe said, 'you will ignore.'

'I will,' Griggs said. 'I intend to scatter my fellows along the front of both battalions, but please don't be alarmed if, at the commencement of the dance, I hold them all in front of Sir Nathaniel's heroes so that it appears I am being an obedient Rifleman. Once the music starts I'll send half to join your skirmishers. The fellows in front of you will be commanded by Lieutenant Charles Brooke, while I prance in front of Sir Nathaniel.'

'Brooke's a good man,' Sharpe said, 'and thank you, Ned.'

'The day I let Sir Nathaniel Pisspot tell me how to fight a battle will be a cold day in hell, Mister Sharpe.'

'And if he bitches about you, Ned, I'll back you up.'

'If we lose today,' Griggs said, 'it won't matter, and if we win, nobody will care.'

'I'm sending for extra ammunition,' d'Alembord said, 'you want me to fetch some extra rifle cartridges?'

'We'll need them, so thank you.'

D'Alembord strode away to arrange for the extra ammunition and Griggs moved a pace closer to Sharpe. 'You think we can stop them, Mister Sharpe?' he asked, glancing northwards at the dark mass of Frenchmen.

'Ten guineas says they'll attack in column,' Sharpe said.

'I won't wager against you.'

'If they come in column, we'll stop them. It won't be pretty, but we win.'

'One day,' Griggs said, 'they'll learn better.'

'We've been fighting them for twenty years,' Sharpe said, 'and they still haven't learned.'

A thudding of hooves made the two Riflemen turn to see Major General Barnes, accompanied by three aides, spurring towards them. Barnes curbed his horse close to Sharpe and gazed at the approaching enemy.

'Plenty of the scoundrels,' he said mildly. 'Morning, Sharpe! Morning,' he hesitated, 'Captain Griggs, isn't it?'

'Yes, sir.'

Barnes spent another minute or so simply inspecting the approaching enemy, then collapsed his telescope. 'Mister Soult is sending us all he's got, isn't he?' No one answered him, and he sighed. 'And we have to hold. If he pushes us off this ridge he can play merry hell with us. But the bridge is back and Lord Wellington is sending reinforcements. With God's help we'll give Mister Soult a bloody nose and a sore arse.'

'Amen,' Griggs said.

'Three to one, maybe four,' Barnes murmured, staring at the horde that was fast approaching the woods beneath the ridge. 'I reckon those are the numbers. Sharpe, you've been down in those woods, d'you reckon they can get artillery over the stream?'

'If they really want to, sir, yes, but it'll be damned difficult. The howitzers will be easier, but my guess is that they'll make their twelve-pounders shoot from beyond the wood.'

'Wherever they shoot from,' Barnes said acidly, 'Sir Nathaniel evidently plans to give them target practice.' He glanced to his left, then, in a low voice, 'Speak of the devil.'

Sir Nathaniel, becoming aware that a General was on the hilltop, could not resist galloping over to join the small group. 'They're retreating!' he said indignantly, pointing to the lone British battalion that had been positioned on the low ramp of hills far to the north of any other British troops.

'Sensible man,' Barnes said, 'I can't understand why he was placed there in the first place!' He used Sir Joel's telescope to watch the Buffs slowly back away, firing volleys against a large French column to their front. 'No point in committing suicide,' Barnes said, 'which, with respect, Sir Nathaniel, you seem intent on doing?'

'Me, sir?' Sir Nathaniel's voice was indignant.

'Your fellows make a brave sight on the skyline, Sir Nathaniel, but they'll soon be under fire from French twelve-pounders. You'll note that Major Sharpe's rogues are lying down back from the crest?'

'The 71st, Sir Edward, do not retreat and cower in front of the enemy!'

'Then they should!' Barnes said with asperity. 'When those scoundrels reach the top of this hill we'll need every musket we have to repel them.'

'And you'll have them!' Sir Nathaniel insisted.

'What's left of them. Pull your men back,' Barnes ordered, 'lay them flat, and don't stand till you see Sharpe's men get to their feet.'

For a heartbeat it seemed that Sir Nathaniel planned to protest the order, but then he made a sound like a horse snuffling and turned away. 'Major Mackenzie!' he bellowed. 'The 71st will go right about and retire!'

'Twenty paces!' Sharpe shouted, expecting an outraged protest from Sir Nathaniel which did not come.

'A bit cheeky, Sharpe?' Barnes said, sounding amused.

Sharpe had dared call out the impertinent command because he feared that once the 71st began retreating Sir Nathaniel might never stop them.

'Twenty paces it is!' a patently relieved Major Mackenzie called back.

'I sometimes forget I'm not still a Sergeant, sir,' Sharpe said apologetically to General Barnes.

Sir Nathaniel had wheeled his horse and stared angrily at Sharpe. 'My officers know their business!' he called.

'My fault, Sir Nathaniel!' Barnes called back. 'I suggested it.'

Sir Nathaniel gave another equine grunt, then turned and cantered away to make sure his men were laying down. He rode along the front of their formation, making Sharpe hope the French possessed an adequate sharpshooter.

'Sir Edward!' one of Barnes's aides called and pointed down the hill to where a French howitzer had appeared in front of the trees. A second was being manhandled from the trees where the two guns' limbers were parked.

'Ah,' Barnes said, 'the dance begins.'

Sharpe turned towards his battalion. 'Skirmishers out! Your men too, Captain,' he added to Griggs before looking back to Barnes. 'By your leave, sir?'

'Go, Major, and remember I have reserves and relief is coming.'

'Thank you, sir.'

Sharpe ran to his right, just as a massive ear-pounding bang sounded from the north and he saw a cloud of powder smoke blossom in a pasture beyond the trees where the French had arrayed a line of six twelve-pounders. The roundshot seared overhead to land God only knew where.

'Captain Carline!'

'Sir?'

'Your fellows will join the skirmish line. There's a pair of howitzers at the bottom of the hill and I want them discouraged. It's bloody long range for a musket, but two days ago I saw the 43rd kill French Artillerymen at the same range, so good luck!' Had it only been two days? He watched Carline's company scramble to their feet and scatter across the crest to join Tom Kelleher's skirmishers who were spread along the slope.

The Riflemen were already shooting at the howitzer crews and Sharpe saw two of the gunners carry a third away. The first howitzer fired, belching smoke and noise, and the shell thumped into the slope a dozen yards below the crest where it exploded harmlessly. Cold barrel, Sharpe thought, knowing the next shot would be higher and more deadly. He paused to stare at the enemy. The leading infantry were just passing the line of twelve-pounders and about to enter the wood. They would be hard-pressed to keep their formation among the trees, but from the look of them the troops approaching his position were in two columns of half company, which suited Sharpe just fine. If they had a mite of sense they would reform into wider columns or even form line once they were through the entangling trees, but Sharpe's experience suggested they would stay in their present formation and be ripe for slaughter.

A sudden succession of louder bangs alerted Sharpe to Sam Anderson's battery on the right flank opening fire. Most of his shots were sent eastwards to the foot of the next hill where caseshots exploded above the heads of a vast French column advancing along the main road, but one of Anderson's nine-pounders was firing at the French twelves in front of Sharpe, using caseshot, while the howitzers were shooting shell at the two French howitzers who now found themselves uncomfortably close to Sharpe's Riflemen, yet still the pair of howitzers fired up the hill, their shells now exploding either on or just beyond the crest. At least one of Sharpe's men was dead, killed by a shard from an exploding shell.

'Who is that?' Sharpe called.

'Horseface, sir,' a redcoat called back.

Kendall had been the man's name, Sharpe remembered, a slovenly and unreliable soldier, but still one of Sharpe's men. 'The rifles will take out their gun crews, lads,' he told the men as he walked along their line, 'not long now and the bastards will be coming up the hill and you're going to kill them! They're tired, they've slogged through mud and muck all the way from Bayonne and they'll have to come uphill into our fire. Half of them are new conscripts and frightened as hell!' He had no idea if any of that was true, but it was what his men needed to hear. 'They're tired and frightened and you are the Prince of Wales's Murderers!'

The French twelve-pounders had settled into a steady rhythm as they pounded the hill crest without doing much damage. In truth they had nothing to aim at; the only British troops they could see were the widely spread skirmishers and Sam Anderson's battery, but the French knew from experience that the hill crest concealed the redcoated infantry and so tried to lob their shots just over the skyline. Their fire, while accurate enough, was slow, and one of Sam Anderson's caseshots had already killed half a gun crew as the missile had exploded directly above the enemy cannon to drive a load of musket balls down in a vicious blast. More caseshots were exploding above the trees where the first French infantry had vanished. Sam had aimed one of his nine-pounders towards the men assaulting Sharpe's slope, while the rest rained iron hell on the big French column that was climbing the main road to the east. Beyond them the Buffs were still retreating along the spur towards the safety of the higher ridge where more redcoats waited. The Kentishmen were being pursued by a cloud of skirmishers and a big column of infantry, and again Sharpe wondered what madness had positioned the battalion so far from the rest of the defenders.

Peter d'Alembord joined Sharpe on the crest of the ridge. 'I hear drums,' he said.

'Me too.'

'We should have a band, sir,' d'Alembord said.

'We do have a band.'

'But it would help if they had instruments, sir. A trumpet or two, perhaps?'

'Bugger the trumpets,' Sharpe said, 'they'll be busy enough today.' Two of the bandsmen were carrying Kendall's body to the rear, while the rest waited to rescue casualties or remove the dead. Other British bands, supplied with instruments, were playing along the ridge, thumping out patriotic songs or popular ballads, while from the wood came the distinctive sound of the French drummers who would drive the infantry forward.

'What do you plan?' d'Alembord asked.

'I'm assuming they'll try to whittle us down with skirmishers,' Sharpe said, 'then hammer a column into us. Our skirmishers must do their best and we wait till we can smell the buggers in the column, then stand and fire away. Just the usual, really.'

D'Alembord nodded. He was gazing at those French infantry who had yet to reach the wood. 'We must be somewhat outnumbered, sir?' he enquired tentatively. 'Four to one, perhaps?'

'General Barnes reckoned three to one, and he has reserves.'

'Really, sir?'

'He just told me,' Sharpe said confidently, though he suspected the reserves were pitifully few. 'We'll give them a welcoming battalion volley, Dally, then go to company firing.' Sharpe thought for a second, reckoning that volley fire might not be enough, which only left the bayonet, but that thought, he decided, was best kept to himself. 'The lads are good,' he added instead, 'and they know what to do.' A roundshot thumped into the turf not a pace away and spattered both men with scraps of sodden turf and grass. 'Bastards,' Sharpe said, brushing off his jacket.

Down on the slope his skirmishers had gone far forward and their fire was galling the howitzer crews so fiercely that the French were trying to drag the two guns back among the trees. 'Well done, lads,' Sharpe muttered, then went silent as the first ranks of French infantry emerged raggedly from the trees and began forming. 'Half company columns,' Sharpe muttered, counting the men in the first rank.

'Two columns,' d'Alembord said.

'Sir Nathaniel will get the bastards on the left, we'll take the other.'

'Oh, my God,' d'Alembord said under his breath, because the French skirmishers now ran forward and must have outnumbered the British skirmishers by at least five to one. Sharpe heard Tom Kelleher's whistle sound to order his men to retreat.

'Not too far, Tommy, not too far,' Sharpe said softly and nodded approval as his skirmishers, now mixed with Captain Griggs's Riflemen, took their positions halfway up the slope.

The day became a crackle of musket and rifle fire, the two

sets of skirmishers attempting to drive the other backwards. The French had the advantage of numbers, but Sharpe's men had enough rifles to kill the *voltigeur* officers and Sergeants. That would slow the French, but not stop them because, in Sharpe's experience, the *voltigeurs* were among the bravest and best trained troops in Napoleon's service.

Those troops were now pressing hard, forcing the defending skirmishers to scramble uphill. 'I should have sent an extra company to skirmish,' Sharpe said ruefully.

'Wouldn't have made a difference, sir,' d'Alembord said.

'Probably not.' Sharpe knew his men could never defeat such a mass of *voltigeurs*, but he also knew it did not matter except in the number of casualties his men were suffering. The aim of the *voltigeurs* was to drive his skirmishers back so that they could open fire on the main battalion and so weaken it before the column arrived to smash it apart. But his battalion was hidden behind and below the crest, yet still close enough that if any *voltigeur* did reach the slope's summit they would be riddled with musket fire.

Sharpe glanced to his left and saw that the 71st's skirmishers were faring no better than his own. They were fewer because Sir Nathaniel had not thickened their numbers with an extra company, but like Sharpe's men, they were making the enemy suffer. Griggs's Riflemen were coolly aiming and firing at any enemy officer they saw or else picking out the bravest and most belligerent of the enemy.

Down by the woods the two howitzers had vanished and in their place the two columns were forming. A caseshot exploded above the column that would advance on Sharpe's troops and there was momentary disorder as dead and wounded men were dragged back towards the trees.

'Remind me to give Sam Anderson a bottle of brandy,' Sharpe said.

'You have one left?'

'Pat Harper will have one.'

'Damn! That was close!' d'Alembord said as a musket ball passed between his head and Sharpe's.

'Buggers have spotted us,' Sharpe said.

'They're getting too close, sir.'

The leading French *voltigeurs* were now roughly where the first range pegs had been driven into the turf, a hundred paces short of the crest, while Sharpe's skirmishers made a loose line at the crest itself. Sharpe was trying to count the fallen redcoats and greenjackets on the long slope and they were too many, but now his remaining skirmishers were laying flat on the crest and taking their revenge. Sharpe was half tempted to stand his men, march them forward, and sweep the slope free of *voltigeurs* with a massive volley, but he resisted the urge. Best not to show the enemy what waited for them, though any experienced French officer would know exactly what the smoke-shrouded crest concealed. 'Bring them in, Tommy,' he muttered.

Lieutenant Kelleher was still urging his men to resist the *voltigeurs*, but Lieutenant Brooke, the Rifleman sent by Griggs, ran to him and gestured uphill, and Kelleher shouted at his men to retire.

'Looks like we lost half the Light Company,' d'Alembord said gloomily.

'The Crapauds lost more,' Sharpe said vengefully as Kelleher's surviving men scrambled over the crest to join the waiting line. The Riflemen stayed on the crest to keep killing the enemy's leaders. Sharpe saw Hagman was there, kneeling to aim his rifle that spurted thick smoke and denoted another enemy dead. 'God, I love the Rifles,' Sharpe said, then cupped his hands. 'Rifles! Back!' The *voltigeurs*, hard hit by Sharpe's skirmishers, were perilously close to the hill's summit. 'Well done, and form line!'

'So here the buggers come,' d'Alembord muttered, 'here the buggers come.'

The French columns were climbing the slope, driven forward by drummers deep in their ranks who rattled out the *pas de charge*, pausing to let the massed ranks bellow, '*Vive l'Empereur!*' The South Essex, knowing the rhythm of the French drums, also bellowed at every pause, substituting their own verb for the '*vive*'. It made Sharpe smile.

The French twelve-pounders, in an effort to support their infantry, had redoubled their efforts and their roundshots were skimming the crest, though with such velocity they were flying harmlessly over the battalion to fall in the pastureland behind. Even so, Sharpe turned back to take himself away from their skyline. He did not need to see what was happening for a while because he had seen it before. The column would climb the slope and he intended to leave them alone until they had almost reached the top, when he would unleash holy hell on them. He walked along his line.

'They're on their way, lads, but coming in column so you'll have no trouble dealing with the bastards. Reload fast, listen to your officers, and aim low! They'll be a few minutes yet, they're in no hurry to die, but die they will!'

He reached the end of the line and saw Sam Anderson slewing a second nine-pounder to fire across the slope. His men were being harried by *voltigeurs*, but Lieutenant Brooke had placed his remaining Riflemen in front of the guns to deter the Frenchmen.

'Any minute now, sir,' Anderson greeted Sharpe, 'I've got canister over roundshot, which should spoil their day.' His howitzer fired and Sharpe saw the trail of the smoking fuse arc through the sky to fall on the rear of the column where the shell exploded.

'You cut your fuses well,' Sharpe said appreciatively. If the shell's fuse was too short the shell would explode in flight, too long and the shell was liable to bury itself in the damp ground that would extinguish the fuse.

'That's Sergeant Milner, sir,' Anderson said, 'he's a wizard. Me? I tend to cut them too short so I leave it to him.'

Anderson's other guns were firing caseshot to the east, harassing the big column climbing the main road, and again his fuses were expertly cut. Caseshot, the invention of an officer called Shrapnel, was hated by the French, who had yet to devise a similar missile. It was an exploding shell, but the gunpowder that crammed the shell's interior was mixed with musket balls, and the shot was designed to explode just above enemy troops, who would be struck by the musket balls and by jagged iron scraps of shattered shell-casing. Anderson's shots were blasting apart a few feet above the column, and each explosion was killing or wounding at least a dozen men. The French twelve-pounders could see Anderson's guns, and two were concentrating their fire on his battery and one at least had struck its target because one wheel of a nine-pounder had been shattered and the gun, now useless until the wheel was replaced, was canted to its left. The bodies of two gunners lay behind the gun next to a spare wheel.

'If we get five minutes' peace,' Anderson said, seeing where Sharpe was looking, 'we'll bring in the crane and put the new wheel on.'

'I can't promise you five minutes' peace for a while,' Sharpe said. He walked a few paces north and saw that the nearest column had passed the furthest range markers. 'You see the wooden pegs?' he asked Anderson.

'I do, sir.'

'They're just past the three-hundred-yard markers.'

'Which will do me very nicely, sir,' Anderson said. He crouched behind one of the two loaded nine-pounders to check its aim. 'Very nicely indeed,' he added wolfishly, patting the gun's breech.

A *voltigeur*'s musket ball struck the gun's barrel with a clang and ricocheted into the sky. 'That was aimed at you, Sam,' Sharpe said. He took the rifle from his shoulder, checked that it was primed and looked down the slope. A big Frenchman with a lavish moustache was reloading his musket and Sharpe aimed at the man and pulled the trigger.

'Nice shooting, sir,' Anderson said enthusiastically.

'At fifty yards I shouldn't miss,' Sharpe said. He waited for the rifle's smoke to clear and saw that the *voltigeur* was on his back, arms outspread. The other *voltigeurs*, decimated by rifle fire, had pulled back.

'Stand back, sir,' Anderson said. The leading ranks of the French column had just trampled down the three-hundred-yard range pegs. Sharpe moved back a dozen paces and reloaded his rifle and was just ramming the ball down the barrel when both of the nine-pounders fired. The gunners immediately leaped to reload the big guns, while Sharpe, blinded by the powder smoke, heard screams from down the slope. He did not need to see to know what had happened. Two cannon balls had slammed through the column, killing and dismembering men all the way through, and that carnage had been doubled by the spray of canister, which would have slashed a wedge of bloody ruin through the packed ranks. The French officers and Sergeants would be desperately closing the ranks so that the column would strike the hilltop as a solid mass; a human battering ram to break their enemy.

'Ready!' a Gunner Corporal shouted. The nine-pounder fired again and the roundshot with its attendant canister flayed the French again, yet still the drummers beat their instruments and still the shout of '*Vive l'Empereur*' rose above the noise of cannons.

Sharpe moved back along the line, knowing that the climax of the French charge was close. He went back to the crest to see that the column, still reforming its front ranks after being clawed by canister, was two hundred paces away.

'South Essex!' he shouted, using the battalion's older name. 'Stand!'

The redcoats stood. Sharpe waited. He glanced left and saw

that the 71st were also on their feet, which meant that two long lines of redcoats waited for the two French columns, and he knew he had to time his first volley with exquisite care. He heard hoofbeats to the rear of his battalion and guessed that General Barnes or one of his aides had come to witness the clash, but they could wait. He was watching the French. The front rank was some sixty men wide and some of the men in that rank looked pitifully young, confirming his suspicion that they were newly conscripted. They would be terrified, he thought, but even a frightened youngster with a musket could be a killer.

Then a voice hailed him from behind, 'Major Sharpe!'

He ignored it, still watching the French. 'Major Sharpe!' The shout was louder, and Sharpe turned.

Rear Admiral Sir Joel Chase was back. He had dismounted from his horse and now unceremoniously pushed through the two ranks to join Sharpe.

'Good Christ!' the Admiral was gazing at the enemy. 'Hell is empty and all the devils are here!'

'Get the hell out of my way,' Sharpe snarled. 'South Essex! Advance!'

He brought them to the crest and the sight of them on the sudden skyline made the leading ranks of the column halt. Sharpe had taken a place in the front rank of Number Four Company, unceremoniously pushing Sir Joel behind the second rank. 'Present!' Sharpe bellowed, bringing his own rifle to his shoulder, 'Aim low!' then, 'Fire!'

The battalion fired, the blistering crackle of over six hundred muskets deafening, and the screams down the slope were the sound of hell's torments.

'Reload!' Sharpe shouted unnecessarily, then pushed his way through the ranks to stand behind them.

And the company volleys started from the right of the line, rippling down the battalion in stabs of flame, thick smoke and leaden death.

'Sorry I swore at you, sir,' Sharpe said to the Admiral, 'but what the hell are you doing here?'

'Lord Wellington said we could come. He's following with another bloody army. I didn't want to miss this!'

Sharpe saw that Captain Crittenden and Petty Officer Clouter had accompanied Chase, along with a Dragoon officer. 'Are you their guardian?' Sharpe asked the officer.

'I am, sir, Captain Carragher, sir.'

'Then keep them behind the line,' Sharpe insisted, 'and all of you dismount! The Crapauds see horsemen and they suddenly become accurate. And you, sir,' he turned to Chase, 'stay here! And hat off!'

He pushed back through the ranks and, beyond the thinning smoke, saw that his opening volleys had turned the green slope red. The column, its front ranks half destroyed by volleys, had come to a halt, but he could hear officers and Sergeants shouting at the men to keep moving, and they were stepping over their own dead and wounded as they struggled to obey.

Sharpe could also hear his own officers giving fire commands as each company fired a volley in turn. As he had expected, his line far out-lapped the French column and the volleys struck the French from their left, their centre and their right, while Sam Anderson was also flensing the column with canister.

It was slaughter, yet the French were determined to fight back. Men who had thought themselves safe a half-dozen ranks from the front were being pushed into the front rank where, standing in the blood of their comrades, they shot back, and Sharpe heard Patrick Harper bellowing at the redcoats to close up the files, which proved some French musket balls were hitting home.

Sharpe glanced to his left and saw the 71st were also firing company volleys into the other column, which had also halted under the welter of musketry. Most of Griggs's Riflemen had formed up to the right of the 71st and were firing their volleys, though much slower because of the time needed to reload their weapons. Sharpe's own Riflemen, still spread along his line, were seeking out officers among the enemy ranks. He turned back, satisfied with his men's performance, and pushed through the two ranks and hurried eastwards. He wanted a vantage point between the two battalions so he could judge the point where he could turn from defence to offence.

Joel Chase saw him and hurried to catch up. 'You're winning, Sharpe!'

'We're not losing, sir,' Sharpe said, 'the winning will come.'

'Why don't they spread out?'

It was a good question. The mathematics of battle were almost always favourable to the British line, a fact the French knew well, yet still they insisted on attacking in column. A column was a fearsome sight, designed to overawe the enemy by its sheer size, and it was a far more efficient way of moving a mass of troops than advancing them in a slender, wavering line. Yet the drawback of a column was that only the men in the front two ranks, and those at the edges of the column, could fire their muskets, while every British soldier could shoot. A thousand men in column could muster far fewer shots than half their number in line, and it was that grim fact that was holding the two columns down the slope.

'They sometimes try to spread,' Sharpe said, 'but we overlap them, so our flank companies drive them back.'

'It's murderous work!' Chase had to shout because the nearest company had just fired a volley. 'Do the French ever win?'

'Against lesser troops,' Sharpe said, 'they used to win all the time! Their problem is they haven't thought to change, and I hope they never do!' His battalion had started the day with just over six hundred and thirty men and they were holding off at least three times their number, and he reckoned the 71st was even bigger, maybe seven hundred and fifty men, and they were raking a column of maybe fifteen hundred men with murderous volleys. Sir Nathaniel Peacock, still mounted on his fine black stallion, was galloping behind the two ranks screaming commands that Sharpe assumed the Scotsmen were ignoring. They knew their business a lot better than Sir Nathaniel.

So did an officer in the French column opposing the 71st, for he was shouting at the surviving men at the front of the column and his commands were being echoed by other officers and Sergeants. The column itself had halted behind a barricade of dead and wounded men, though the drummers were still pounding their instruments to drive them forward, then suddenly whole groups of men ran from the column to spread into a line equal to the width of the Scottish line that opposed them.

'French Light Infantry,' Sharpe said, 'among their best troops.' Yet even so the 71st could bring more muskets to bear, though not before the new men on the flanks of the column poured a volley at the Scotsmen.

'Seventy-first!' Sir Nathaniel shouted as loud as he could. 'Right about turn!'

'What the . . .' Sharpe began.

'Right about turn and retreat!' Sir Nathaniel screamed. 'Retreat!' Suiting action to his words, he turned his horse and spurred it away from the fight.

The 71st, confused and bewildered, started after him, though most of the men stayed put, but all glanced anxiously behind them to where their commanding officer was rowelling his horse, which was flinging up gouts of turf from its hooves as its rider fled in panic.

'He's running away!' Sir Joel said in amazement.

'Which means the bloody French win,' Sharpe said.

And that he and his battalion were on their own.

CHAPTER EIGHT

Astonishment and confusion had struck the 71st. Many of the men had obeyed their commanding officer and were walking away from the enemy. A few were even running, while Sir Nathaniel had checked his horse and was standing in his stirrups. 'Seventy-first!!' It was almost a screech. 'Right about! And retreat!'

The shrill commands made those obeying hurry, yet at least half of the battalion had stayed in line, though few were now watching the enemy, instead they looked uncertainly at their comrades or towards their confused officers. 'Hurry!' Sir Nathaniel shouted.

Sharpe took a pace forward. 'Seventy-first! Halt! Face front!'

Major Mackenzie, perhaps the most able of the 71st's officers, held up his hands and echoed Sharpe's command, 'Halt! Face front!'

A French musket ball hit John Mackenzie in the head, blasting off his shako in sudden and misted ribbons of blood.

'Retreat!' Peacock screeched even louder.

At that moment Sharpe saw a small Scottish soldier run four or five paces towards Peacock, go to one knee, and aim his musket. The man's shako had either fallen off or been struck from his head, revealing a mass of tangled red hair. He pulled his trigger and the ball must have gone close to Peacock, who almost fell from his horse before shouting one last frantic command, 'Retreat!' then spurring away to the rear as fast as his horse could carry him.

'Seventy-first!' Sharpe bellowed again. 'Stand fast and face front!' He had been a Sergeant once and had a voice that could carry across half a battlefield, and scores of the fugitives, hearing him, stopped and turned fearfully back towards the French.

The French column, seeing the confusion and fear in the battalion, started hurrying. About half of the Scotsmen had not moved and those men fired a ragged volley which threw down much of the column's front rank. Officers and Sergeants were bellowing at men to get into line and to fire. 'Scotsmen don't run!' a Sergeant shouted. 'Fight, you bastards, fight!'

Sharpe turned back to see that the second French column, the one facing his men, had evidently thought the chaos engulfing the 71st was proof that the battle was won and were coming at a run, stumbling over bodies, but sure that the hated redcoats would now be easy meat, and those redcoats, Sharpe's men, had seen the 71st waver, and feared what was about to happen. If the French managed to batter their way through the 71st's tremulous line, then hundreds of enemy infantry would be loose in the rear of Sharpe's battalion. More French would follow; with horse-drawn artillery and cavalry coming to widen the hole torn in the British defence and slash their way through to the supply depots. The slaughter would be horrific and the loss so crippling that Wellington would probably be forced to retreat into the high Pyrenees simply to save what was left of his army from destruction.

Sharpe crossed a few paces to join Sir Joel. 'You said that Nosey is bringing reinforcements over the bridge?'

'They were crossing as we left.'

'Thank God. They may have to stop these bastards. And, please, sir, get back behind my centre companies. You're a target for the bastards in your cocked hat.' He took Sir Joel's arm and rather unceremoniously led him back behind the line. He could hear the French cheering now, not because they had won, but because they thought victory was possible. At the same time he could hear his volleys firing regularly, while to his left the 71st, or as much of it as had kept their heads and stayed in line, was firing, though more raggedly. Casualties were piling behind Sharpe's battalion, the dead sprawled on the wet grass, most of the wounded laying with them, while a few were being helped back to the surgeons in the farm's barn. He glanced over the line and saw a sudden spray of blood as a roundshot sliced through the front of the column. Then a blast of canister flayed the enemy's left flank and the French cheers faded away, though the drummers were still driving them on. Fifty yards away now, maybe less.

'Sergeant-Major!' Sharpe shouted.

He was not sure what he must do, only that he was witnessing a British line as near defeat from a French column as he had ever seen, and he had to stop it.

'Sergeant Major!'

Pat Harper ran back from the line. 'Sir?'

'You're wounded, Pat?' The right side of Harper's green jacket was thick with blood.

'That's Pearce's blood. Poor man got shot in the neck.'

'We're fixing swords and going for the bastards.'

'Swords?' Sir Joel asked.

'Rifle talk for bayonets, sir,' Sharpe explained curtly, then took a deep breath. 'South Essex! Fix swords!'

'Fix bayonets!' Harper bellowed.

Once the bayonets were attached to the muskets it would slow the volley fire, but that was a price which Sharpe reckoned must be paid.

He looked at Sir Joel. 'For God's sake, sir, stay back. If we lose, get on your horse and ride hard.' He did not wait for a response, but pushed between Number Four and Five companies to stand just ahead of the battalion. He heard the clicks as the bayonets were pushed over the muzzles and as the longer sword-bayonets were clipped onto rifles, then he drew his sword. Harper had the seven-volley gun in his big hands. 'That thing's loaded?'

'Double loaded, sir. Like that black fellow suggested.'

'Then let's push them off this bloody hill.'

Sharpe wondered if he was mad to use the bayonet before his muskets had killed even more enemy, then saw that most of the French in the column's front rank had ramrods in their hands. They must have just fired, which meant they could not fire again till their weapons were charged and primed, a difficult thing when marching.

223

'South Essex!' he shouted, 'charge!'

'Murder the bastards!' Harper bellowed, and, as Sharpe ran towards the enemy, he heard his men shouting their new name, 'Murderers! Murderers!'

The French stopped. Some wanted to reload, most just saw the blades coming at them and hurried to draw their own bayonets. They might outnumber Sharpe's battalion by three or four to one, but the sight of a bayonet was terrifying, let alone a line of the weapons. Another roundshot slashed through the column, ploughing three files of men, slinging their muskets and their blood into the still-falling rain.

Sharpe was frightened, only a fool would not be frightened when leading a bayonet charge into a mass of enemy troops, but he was also aware of an exultation. This was his world, the one thing he knew he was good at. He understood that there was a dangerous anger in him, an anger that reckoned it was Richard Sharpe against the whole bloody world. And he could fight, by God he could fight, and no bloody Frenchman could resist him. His heart pounded, he knew he was screaming, but what he screamed he neither knew nor cared. His job now was to kill and he was good at it.

The damned French thought they were winning, but Sharpe would bloody well prove the bastards wrong.

Sharpe tried to remember the last time he had drawn the sword in anger. The big blade had a wooden hilt that had become slippery with blood and he had purchased a slip of fish-skin that he had glued around the hilt and bound with wire. His hand was wet from rain, but the sword felt firm in his hand. He was a pace ahead of his shouting men and he was looking for an enemy and saw an officer holding a slim infantry sword, and behind the officer the Frenchmen looked frozen, not sure whether to finish loading their muskets or draw their bayonets.

'They're dead men!' Sharpe shouted.

'Murder them!' Harper called, and pulled the trigger of the volley gun.

The seven barrels gouted smoke and death. The French officer was hurled backwards and three or four men fell with him, opening a hole in the front rank. Sharpe leaped through it, stabbing the sword forward so it lanced into a man's belly. He ripped the blade free and knocked a musket aside and cut up with the sword to slice into a man's arm. Harper had hurled the empty volley gun behind him where it could lie until the battle was won or lost and had drawn his sword-bayonet. The blade was only twenty-three inches long, but it was wielded by a huge Irishman who had the strength of at least two other men. Harper rammed the blade into a man's belly, lifted him up, then, using the sword-bayonet to carry his victim, he slammed the dying man into the next file, throwing down two men before pulling the blade free and slashing it into a man's neck. He was shouting in his native Gaelic. Sharpe had once asked him what that war shout meant and Harper had shrugged the question away. 'Just the usual, sir, telling them their mothers should have married their fathers.'

'Bastard!' Harper shouted, reverting to English. A young Frenchman had thrust a musket into his belly, luckily without a bayonet attached, and Harper seized him by his long hair, pulled him forward and sliced his throat with his sword-bayonet, soaking the green jacket with yet more blood.

Sharpe was treading on his victims' bodies now, but somehow keeping his balance. He used the sword as a lance, stabbing hard and viciously, for the press of men was too tight to allow savage swings of the long blade. The sword clanged off musket barrels, or shaved long strips of wood from their stocks, but again and again it pierced bellies or chests so that the long blade ran with blood. He mostly stayed silent, choosing his next enemy as the one before died. He felt the strange calm of battle shroud him, the silence despite shots and screams, and the sensation of time slowing. He knew the chances of his own death or severe injury were high, yet he felt invulnerable, twice as fast as his enemies. He was death in a green jacket, a Rifleman. A small part of him worried that his men would be outfought and that he should be behind them, ready to support any threatened part of his line, but nor could he let his men go into the close embrace of a bayonet charge and not lead them.

A bayonet came from Sharpe's left. It caught in his jacket's sleeve, ripped through, and he felt it slide along his ribs. He punched a man in front with the hilt of his sword, then turned left to see Sergeant Henderson pulverise the man who had thrust the bayonet. Henderson had somehow equipped himself with a pioneer's axe and was reducing the Frenchman's skull to bone fragments, blood and crushed brain.

'Bastard!' Henderson grunted. 'Sorry, sir, should have got him sooner.'

'Thanks, Joe!'

Two roundshots tore through the packed French ranks as two loads of canister turned the easternmost files into bloody ruin. Sam Anderson, Sharpe realised, must have turned another nine-pounder to help him. He turned a bayonet thrust aside and rammed the sword forward to drive a Frenchman to his knees. Beyond the man was a rank of drummers, all of them boys and none more than twelve or thirteen years old. Most of them were still trying to beat their drums in the same rhythm as the drummers further back in the column, but a handful just gazed in terror as Sharpe and Harper appeared blood-drenched in front of them.

'Don't kill the boys!' Sharpe bellowed.

'Little bastards,' Harper snarled, and picked a child up by the jacket and threw him, drum and all, over his shoulder. One of the boys, braver or more foolish than the rest, had drawn his *sabre briquet*, a short sword no longer than a rifle bayonet and issued as a token weapon to drummers. The boy was screaming in terror, '*C'est l'enfer, Maman!*', yet he retained the courage to stab his pathetic sword towards Harper, who just hit him on the head with the brass hilt of the sword bayonet, a blow that must have dented the lad's skull, then stepped on the boy's belly as he eviscerated a soldier in the rank beyond.

'Not too fast, Pat!' Sharpe said. He worried that their progress was making his assault like a wedge, with him and Harper at the point. 'Let the others catch up.'

Harper was in his own private fury. Sharpe had seen the big Irishman in many fights, either on battlefields or in taverns, and knew what delight he took from combat. Every fight,

Sharpe guessed, was a revenge on the fate that had driven a proud Irishman into Britain's army, and now French infantry was suffering the consequences.

And still Harper forged ahead, slaughtering the men to his front and forcing Sharpe to keep up to protect the Irishman's left side. Joe Henderson had vanished, but Sharpe was suddenly aware of two Portuguese infantryman to his left, evidence that someone was feeding reinforcements into the fight.

'I want the bloody cuckoo!' Harper suddenly shouted, and Sharpe saw a glint of golden metal ahead and recognised an eagle, perhaps ten ranks deeper in the French column. The eagle was atop a staff from which hung a golden-fringed tricolour flag that drooped, rain-sodden and heavy.

'The flag!' Sharpe bellowed and used both hands to slam his heavy sword into a French Sergeant's chest. He felt the ribs break as the blade broke through, then he twisted the sword and slid it free. A musket fired nearby and the ball struck the stock of Sharpe's rifle, driving a splinter of wood into his right thigh. He staggered to his left, colliding with one of the Portuguese, but the sudden lurch saved him from a bayonet thrust and he stabbed the sword again, cutting into the enemy soldier's neck.

'The flag!' he shouted again. 'It's ours!

'It's mine!' Harper bellowed. His sword-bayonet had bent grotesquely and he was now using a French musket as a club to beat down enemies. Sharpe wished he could find the pioneer's axe that Joe Henderson had been using, but he suspected that was some paces behind, lost in the welter of corpses and dying men, when suddenly it appeared again as a man shrieked defiance at the French and, pushing the smaller Portuguese out of his way, ploughed into the French ranks swinging the axe in dangerous blows, one of which almost struck Sharpe.

It was Clouter, who was shrieking in a language Sharpe did not recognise and who was hacking a gory path towards the eagle, which suddenly vanished in a welter of blood, broken muskets and screams. It was another nine-pounder roundshot slashing through the column, and as the commotion subsided Sharpe heard his men shouting, 'The flag! The flag!'

The eagle rose again, the rain-soaked flag looking torn and ragged. Rumour said that Napoleon himself handed the flags to his battalions, and to defend one was the supreme task of every French soldier. The drummers deep in the column seemed to beat faster and, when they paused, the enemy shouted their war cry, '*Vive l'Empereur!*', but Sharpe sensed the shout was not as enthusiastic as before. The rain, the slope of the hill, the deadly cannon fire and the death being inflicted by bayonets was sapping French resolve.

Whoever held the eagle now swayed it left and right, trying to spread out the wet tricolour, and the sight seemed to energise Sharpe's men and their Portuguese helpers. Harper was beating men to death, while Clouter was hewing them with the axe, and as the two huge men surged forward so they made a path for redcoats, who crowded in behind them. Another roundshot cut through the French ranks and Sharpe hoped Sam Anderson could see how deep inside the column his men now were. A different sound caught Sharpe's senses and he glanced left to see a caseshot explode above the French attacking the 71st. That battalion had somehow been rallied and, like Sharpe's men, was thrusting the French back down the long slope, helped by the same Portuguese reinforcements who were fighting with Sharpe's men. Sam Anderson, bless him, was using the howitzer as well as at least two long nine-pounders to spread death through the columns.

The enticing eagle was closer now, only about five ranks away, and Clouter and Harper were fighting like men possessed. Harper had picked up a discarded sword-bayonet and was using it to support a French corpse that he rammed at his enemies, while Clouter disembowelled men with massive swings of the axe. Both men were drenched in blood that was slowly being diluted by the rain, and both were shouting in their own languages as they cut their way towards the glittering eagle.

Sharpe moved to protect Clouter's left side, where a small Portuguese soldier had just been killed by a stolid-looking Frenchman who was drawing his musket back for another thrust with his bayonet. He never stood a chance as Clouter's axe struck him on the side of his head and shattered his skull. Sharpe stepped over the dead Portuguese and hacked his sword down to split another skull. The dead man's shako stayed stuck on the sword blade that Sharpe rammed forward into a young man's belly. The youngster cried out for his mother, then sank down, and Clouter used the space to swing the axe in another savage blow, but the axe handle was now so soaked in blood that it slipped from Clouter's grasp. Sharpe sliced his sword down to deflect a bayonet thrust, then Clouter drew his own heavy cavalry sword that Sharpe had given him and slammed it sideways with such force that Sharpe thought the enemy's body would be cut in two. 'Nice cutlass, sir,' Clouter grunted.

Sharpe stepped over the mess of intestines that Clouter had loosed with the sword and stabbed another man in the belly, twisted the blade and dragged it free. Four ranks to the eagle!

'I want that bloody eagle!' he shouted, and saw a French officer seize the standard-bearer's elbow and drag him backwards. The standard-bearer must have stumbled because the flag fell again and the relentless drumming faltered. Another roundshot whipped through the blue-coated ranks, throwing up its cockscomb spray of blood and shattered muskets.

'Come on!' Sharpe shouted, trying to slash and stab his way through the four ranks that separated him from the trophy.

Then, quite suddenly, there were no ranks. No eagle either. The French were running! The column's ranks had split apart and were now sprinting downhill to escape the savagery that had greeted them on the hill's top.

'South Essex!' Sharpe shouted, his voice hoarse and his throat dry. 'Halt! Reload!'

Sergeants echoed his orders along the line. To his left the Light Company was firing at the fleeing French, the Riflemen aiming to pick off surviving officers, and beyond them the column assaulting the 71st wavered. They had seen the defeat of their neighbouring column and were facing a battalion of bitter Scotsmen who were stubbornly refusing to yield ground.

'Light Company!' Sharpe shouted. 'Fire left!'

An howitzer shell exploded above the Frenchmen as Sharpe's Light Company began firing into the remaining column, and the panic that had seized the first now spread to the second and the blue-coated men began retreating. They were pursued by musket and rifle shots, and by the jeers of the defenders. A handful of French officers tried to rally their men, but the Riflemen were merciless and those officers fell as the column broke and streamed downhill in panic.

A bagpiper was playing, the sound shrill above the jeers and musket shots. Where the hell had the piper come from, Sharpe wondered. Peacock had sworn never to allow a piper in his battalion, but nevertheless the sole piper was playing and the Scotsmen were cheering.

'Dear sweet God,' Sharpe said and started to laugh. He felt weak suddenly and he put a hand on Harper's shoulder. 'We bloody did it, Pat.'

'That bastard with the eagle got away,' Harper grumbled.

'That was madness, Pat.'

'It was a grand fight, sir. Back to the hilltop?'

'Back to the hilltop. Take them beyond the crest.' The French twelve-pounders, their aim no longer obscured by their own infantry, had opened fire again, their roundshot thumping onto the upper slope. 'Dear God, that was a fight,' Sharpe limped uphill, stopping once to wipe his sword blade with a handful of rain-soaked grass, then drying it on a dead Frenchman's jacket before slamming it into the metal scabbard. 'I have to say thank you to Sam Anderson,' he said to Harper.

'You're wounded, sir.'

The thick splinter sheared from his rifle's stock protruded from his thigh.

'Pull it out, Pat.'

'Better let the surgeon do it, sir.'

'Bugger the surgeon, pull it.'

The splinter came out easily enough and was not followed by a gush of blood, so Sharpe reckoned the wound was trivial.

Once at the hilltop he glanced left and right and saw that the redcoat and Portuguese line had held along the whole line of hills. The French were back on the low ground, leaving behind them slopes vile with wounded and dying men. Sharpe walked on until he was out of sight of the twelve-pounders. His battalion was back in line, but it was a sadly truncated line and he flinched at the thought of how many casualties would be reported.

'Let's hope the buggers don't come again,' he said to Harper. 'A column of choirboys could cut us to shreds.'

'They lost men too, sir. More than us.'

'We must get the wounded back to the farm.' Sharpe was trying to think straight about what needed to be done, when all he wanted to do was to lie on the wet grass and sleep. He looked to the Light Company and saw, to his relief, that Dan Hagman was alive. 'Dan!'

Hagman looked worried as he approached. 'Are you wounded, Mister Sharpe?'

'A scratch, Dan.'

'That was some fight, sir.'

'It was. Just position yourself on the crest and keep your head down and watch the buggers for us. Sing out if they look as if they want more.'

'They'll not be back, Mister Sharpe, not after what we did to them.'

'I hope you're right, Dan. Now off with you.'

Hagman lay on the crest, hidden there by a pair of redcoated corpses, and Sharpe limped on towards a group of officers behind the battalion.

'We'll be digging graves tonight, Pat.'

'Better than being in one, sir.'

Peter d'Alembord broke away from the assembled officers and hurried towards Sharpe. He grimaced when he saw the blood that soaked Sharpe.

'We've done a hurried count, sir.'

'God help us,' Sharpe said, 'tell me.'

Instead d'Alembord held out a scrap of paper on which the number 434 was scrawled in pencil. 'Those are effectives, sir, best as I can tell.'

'Good Christ,' Sharpe said. He tried to remember how many men he had started with and reckoned they must have lost at least a hundred dead or wounded.

'Some of the wounded will recover, sir,' d'Alembord said.

'Let's hope they all do,' Sharpe said, knowing he would be lucky if even half the wounded recovered enough to rejoin the ranks. He stuffed the piece of paper into his cartridge pouch. 'You did well, Peter.'

'I did nothing, sir.'

'You fed in reinforcements, didn't you? Where did the Portuguese come from?'

'Daddy Hill sent them. They were the last reserve.'

'Thank God for them. Did we lose any company commanders?'

'Carline and Peters, sir, and Harry Price is wounded.'

Sharpe flinched. 'Badly?'

'Broken arm, sir, he'll live.'

'Then you'd best reorganise us into eight companies again.'

'I thought as much, sir.'

'I'm sorry about Carline,' Sharpe said, 'he was promising well.' He patted d'Alembord's shoulder. 'I want to thank Sam Anderson and then visit the wounded, so you're in command till I'm back. If the bastards come again just kill them again.'

'Thy will be done, sir,' d'Alembord said.

Sharpe spotted Charlie Weller in the ranks. 'Charlie!'

Weller ran to him and, like d'Alembord before him, looked aghast at the blood which soaked Sharpe from top to toe. 'Sir?'

'Run back to the farm, Charlie, and fetch my horse. Not Sycorax, but the one Lord Wellington loaned me.'

'Yes, sir!' Weller, a farm boy, loved to deal with horses and relished any chance to ride one.

'Quick as you can, Charlie.'

Sharpe turned back to d'Alembord. 'I doubt the bastards will try again, Peter, and if they do there are reinforcements.' He could see two fresh battalions marching towards the hilltop. 'But the lads did well, bloody well.'

'You did, sir.'

'We did our duty, Peter, all of us, God bloody help us.'

'So did the Admiral, sir.' D'Alembord sounded amused.

'Sir Joel?' Sharpe had momentarily forgotten about the Admiral. 'What did he do?'

'Rallied the 71st, sir. He even fetched them a piper, then Auld Grog Willie arrived and took over.'

'Auld Grog was here?'

'Breathing fire,' d'Alembord said, sounding amused. Auld Grog

Willie was properly Lieutenant General Sir William Stewart, a belligerent Scotsman whom Sharpe remembered from his first days as a Rifleman. Stewart had been a founder of the new Rifle regiments and a supporter of recruiting Irishmen like Harper because, he claimed, they had a native ferocity that was invaluable in battle. He also believed that his men needed fortifying with frequent issues of rum. He was popular.

'Auld Grog took them forward, sir,' d'Alembord went on, 'and they fought like tigers.'

'They were always a good regiment,' Sharpe said, 'until that fool Peacock arrived.' He glanced across at the 71st, which looked to have suffered as much as the South Essex, if not worse, and a red-headed soldier caught his eye. 'I'll be back in a minute,' he said to d'Alembord, then strode towards the Scotsmen. 'You!' he shouted towards the man he had spotted. A dozen soldiers turned towards him, but he pointed at the red-headed man. 'You! Come here!'

The man, much shorter than Sharpe, reluctantly crossed to Sharpe who was standing some twenty paces behind the battered battalion. 'Your name?' Sharpe demanded harshly.

The man had to repeat his name three times before Sharpe could decipher it from the thick Scottish accent. 'Hamish McNulty, right?'

'Sir,' McNulty acknowledged surlily.

A Sergeant, seeing one of his men accosted by an officer from a different battalion, came to confront Sharpe. He saluted smartly. 'Is there something wrong, sir?' he demanded.

'You are?'

'Sergeant Bailey, sir.'

'Then tell me, Sergeant, what the penalty is for attempting to kill an officer from your own battalion?'

Bailey looked uncomfortable, McNulty just gazed down at the turf.

'I suspect, sir,' Bailey answered slowly, 'that it would be a flogging. But,' he paused.

'But?' Sharpe demanded.

'Hamish is a good soldier, sir,' he paused again, 'most of the time.'

'I suspect,' Sharpe said harshly, 'that the penalty would be death.' He waited a heartbeat, then sounded more reasonable. 'Lord Wellington might commute the sentence to acknowledge how well your battalion fought, but there again, he might not.'

McNulty suddenly found his voice and appealed to Sharpe, or at least Sharpe thought it was an appeal, but it was hard to distinguish words from the thicket of the Scottish accent.

'What he says, sir,' Bailey sensed Sharpe's difficulty and attempted a translation, 'is that he merely was trying to clean his musket when it just went off.'

'I witnessed what he did,' Sharpe said sternly, 'and Private McNulty must understand that actions have consequences! Do you understand that, McNulty?'

McNulty hesitated, then muttered, 'Aye.'

'Sir,' Bailey protested, 'I'll report the wee bugger to Major Cotter. Best left to us, sir?'

'Private McNulty,' Sharpe went on, still stern, 'did something very wrong. Very wrong indeed! Do you know what you did, McNulty?'

McNulty shrugged, still sullen, and muttered something that Sharpe found entirely unintelligible, but suspected was no adequate explanation of McNulty's attempt to murder Sir Nathaniel Peacock.

'What you did wrong, McNulty,' Sharpe interrupted, 'was to miss! You should have hit the bastard in the spine!' He had fished in his cartridge pouch as he spoke and now brought out a thick silver coin that he held out to the small Scotsman. 'If you had killed the bugger I'd have given you two of those, but that's for trying. Well done, McNulty.'

Sergeant Bailey had seen the size of the coin, which had vanished into the recesses of McNulty's uniform with magical swiftness.

'Sir?' he asked in disbelief, then seemed lost for words.

'Actions have consequences, Sergeant,' Sharpe said, 'and Private McNulty is a credit to his regiment, look after him.'

Bailey saluted Sharpe, then dug a hard elbow into McNulty. 'Salute, you wee bastard. You're in no trouble.'

McNulty gave Sharpe a grin and a vague wave that was supposed to be a salute, and Sharpe grinned back, then turned away to see Charlie Weller waiting nearby with the horse.

Weller slid from the saddle. 'He's a beauty, sir!'

'Wasted on me, Charlie. A leg up?'

Weller heaved Sharpe into the saddle, then lengthened the stirrup leathers to suit Sharpe, who nodded his thanks before kicking the stallion towards d'Alembord.

'I'm off to see Sam Anderson, but I'll be back if the bloody Frogs get lively again.'

'They're beaten, sir,' d'Alembord said confidently.

Sharpe rode eastwards, clumsily guiding the horse to avoid knots of wounded men. A few guns on the crest were still firing northwards, using case- and roundshot to harass the French who had retreated into the woodland at the foot of the hill.

The mood on the hilltop was jubilant, despite the large number of casualties, because the British and Portuguese infantry knew they had won a bitter and blood-soaked victory against a much larger French force.

Sharpe saw a group of officers close to Sam Anderson's battery. General Hill was there, as was Major General Barnes and, to Sharpe's surprise, he recognised Lord Wellington in a long blue cloak. He steered his horse away from them, not wanting to be accosted, and dismounted close to the guns. A Gunner Corporal took his horse and tied the reins to one of the massive gun wheels.

Three of the guns were disabled, all having lost a wheel, and Sharpe found Sam Anderson sitting next to an undamaged nine-pounder. He was leaning back on a wheel and his right arm was in a blood-soaked sling. He was plainly in a lot of pain.

'Shouldn't you be back with the surgeons, Sam?' Sharpe asked, squatting beside him.

'Buggers will only want to take the arm off.' He flinched as he tried to move the arm. 'Bloody twelve-pounder sent a felloe into it. Shattered it.'

'A fellow?' Sharpe asked.

'A felloe, sir. Part of a wheel rim. Bloody thing broke a rib too. But Sergeant Clark strapped me up.'

Sergeant Clark was growling at men who were lifting one of the stricken guns with a small crane so that a new wheel could be attached to its axletree. He was keeping his voice down so as not to attract the attention of the Generals gathered a few paces away.

'A good surgeon might be better, Sam,' Sharpe said.

'They're all bloody butchers.'

'There's a Doctor Amman with the KGL who is a miracle worker. Good man, too.'

'He'll need to be a miracle worker,' Anderson said bitterly. 'I know I've got to see a butcher, but the bloody thing isn't just broken, it's shattered.'

'This'll help,' Sharpe offered his canteen. 'Brandy, fresh from the enemy. Keep it, Sam. I came here to thank you. Your guns did marvels.'

'We couldn't miss at that range,' Anderson sounded bitter, 'I almost felt sorry for the buggers.'

'Then they shouldn't have come out to play,' Sharpe said. 'But really, Sam, thank you.'

'Sharpe!' a peremptory voice called. 'A word, please!'

'I have to go,' Sharpe patted Anderson's unwounded arm and stood.

Lord Wellington had summoned him.

'That's one of mine, isn't it?' Wellington nodded towards the tethered stallion.

'He is, my lord.'

'You like your stirrups long,' Wellington said disapprovingly.

'I'm not a horseman, my lord.'

Wellington had moved his horse a few paces from the other officers and now looked down from the saddle at Sharpe. 'I hope that's not your blood?'

'All French blood, my lord.'

That earned a grunt, then, 'Sir Edward tells me you did well, very well.' He was talking of Sir Edward Barnes, Sharpe's brigade commander.

'My battalion,' Sharpe slightly stressed the 'my', 'fought like tigers, my lord.'

'So did they all, Sharpe! Finest infantry in the world, and the Portuguese are just as good. What are your casualties?'

'Too many, sir. We're more or less cut in half.'

'Five hundred?'

'Just over four, my lord.'

'And you still have that unorthodox Light Company? Half Riflemen?'

'I do, my lord.' What's left of them, Sharpe thought.

Wellington grunted, casting a wary glance at the slope where a tideline of blue-coated bodies lay to mark the furthest extent of the French assault.

'Did the Admiral find you?'

'He did, my lord.'

'And he's alive?'

'He is.'

'I suppose we should be grateful for that.' He paused to bat away an annoying fly. 'Then I want you to take your Light Company to Saint-Jean-de-Luz, Sharpe. Start at dawn tomorrow and report to me by sunset.'

'Yes, my lord.' Sharpe felt a pulse of excitement. His wife,

Jane, was in Saint-Jean-de-Luz, the French seaport almost on the Spanish border where many officers' wives had taken residence until the army marched further north.

His sudden excitement was interrupted by Wellington's sternest voice. 'And another thing, you are the Prince of Wales's Own Volunteers, you are not the Murderers.'

Sharpe was taken aback, but managed a courteous response. 'Of course, my lord.'

'I don't want the Paris press claiming that my army contains self-confessed murderers. They print quite enough rubbish as it is, so keep to your proper name!'

'I will, my lord.'

Wellington turned his horse half away. 'Saint-Jean-de-Luz by tomorrow evening, Sharpe. I have a job for you. The Town Major in Saint-Jean will find your fellows quarters. You can return the horse to me tomorrow, and for God's sake shorten the leathers.' He spurred away from Sharpe, who was left astonished. A job? Evidently one that needed Light Infantry, which suggested it was skirmishing.

Sam Anderson must have overheard at least part of the conversation because he chuckled. 'The devil's work is never done, sir!'

Maybe, Sharpe thought, he should call his men the Devil's Own.

'Go find a surgeon, Sam, before that wound festers.'

A Gunner heaved him up into the saddle and Sharpe rode back to his battalion.

*

The would-be Murderers went back to their billets around the farm where Sharpe ordered his Light Company to prepare a day's rations and to rest before the next morning's march. They grumbled, which Sharpe took as a sign of good morale, then, abandoning the horse to Charlie Weller's enthusiastic care, he went into the barn where his casualties and the wounded of the 71st were under the surgeons' care. A number of local women were there, cutting up sheets for bandages or spooning water into wounded men's mouths. The foul noise of a bone-saw grinding at a man's leg was blessedly short, and Sharpe supposed poor Sam Anderson would soon have to endure the same pain. Then a man beckoned to him urgently and Sharpe saw it was Father Mikel, the parish priest for the nearby village of Saint-Pierre. Was that, Sharpe wondered, what the bloodbath on the line of hills would be called? The battle of Saint Peter?

He stepped between the men laying on beds of straw and crouched beside the priest.

'What is it, Father?'

'He needs your help, Major,' Mikel replied. He was a short, plump man who usefully spoke the local Basque language, as well as French, English and Spanish. 'I have given him God's help, but God cannot do everything.'

It took Sharpe a heartbeat to realise it was Private Gallardo, one of the many Spaniards who had been encouraged to join the British army that was forever short of men. The Spanish government, such as it was, had reluctantly agreed to the arrangement, and the recruits had proven to be useful soldiers, animated by a hatred of the French and eager to revenge themselves. Gallardo was so pale that Sharpe at first did not recognise him, then he took Gallardo's hand.

'What is it, Luis?'

'I have a wife and children,' Gallardo whispered hoarsely.

'I know you do,' Sharpe said, and tried to remember the paperwork he had done when the Spaniards had made their attestations to join his ranks. 'Three children, yes?'

'*Sí, señor.*'

'And you want to know they'll be looked after.'

'*Sí, señor. Por favor.*'

Sharpe squeezed Gallardo's hand. 'They'll get all your back pay and more, Luis, I promise. All of it.' He wondered how he was to keep that promise, then decided it was a problem for another day. 'They'll get you back too! The doctor will look after you.'

Gallardo said nothing to that, but Father Mikel caught Sharpe's eye and gave a minute shake of his head. 'Stomach wound,' he said in a whisper, 'bad.'

'You joined us after Salamanca, right?' Sharpe asked Gallardo, who nodded his head. 'I had a wound just like yours and here I am, still walking! You'll be fine, Luis! You'll march through Paris with us.'

'Bugger Paris,' Gallardo said. Like the other score of Spaniards who had joined Sharpe's ranks, he had quickly mastered the lower ranks of English words.

'We'll do it together, Luis,' Sharpe said, 'and don't you worry about your family. I'll look after them.'

'I don't want to be buried here in France,' Gallardo whispered.

'Wherever you are buried, my son,' Father Mikel answered, 'the ground will be Spanish soil for ever. And God will know where to find you.'

A sudden altercation exploded at the far end of the barn and Sharpe glanced up to see a redcoated officer upbraiding a surgeon who wore an apron turned bright red with blood. 'I insist!' the officer shouted.

The surgeon shook his head, which only triggered another diatribe from the officer, who, Sharpe saw, was Sir Nathaniel Peacock.

'Bloody hell,' Sharpe said, standing. He paused long enough to look down at the dying Gallardo. 'You're a very good soldier, Luis. As good as any in the battalion!' That was true and he could see the words pleased Gallardo. 'And I'll make sure your family knows it.' Sharpe headed towards the altercation.

'You will obey me!' Sir Nathaniel screeched. 'I order you!'

'I will not,' the surgeon answered stubbornly, and then Sharpe joined the pair.

'What's going on?' Sharpe demanded.

'You are not required here,' Peacock snarled at Sharpe. 'This is none of your business!'

'There are good men dying in here,' Sharpe said softly, 'and they deserve quiet.'

'You impudent cullion—' Peacock shouted, then stopped abruptly because Sharpe had punched him hard in the solar plexus. Peacock half bent over, gasping for breath as a number of wounded Scotsmen gave a painful cheer.

'What's the problem?' Sharpe asked the surgeon.

'He wants me to add his name to the list of wounded,' the

doctor answered in a Scottish accent, 'but he's no more wounded than I am.'

'I was struck by a musket ball,' Sir Nathaniel insisted in a strained voice.

'Your coat tail was struck,' the doctor replied scornfully. He was a tall, grey-haired man, his apron rigid with congealed blood. 'And you need a tailor to repair that wound, not a surgeon.'

'Just put me on the list!' Sir Nathaniel was pleading now.

Sharpe understood exactly what Peacock was doing. If he could show his name on the list of wounded then he had a perfect excuse to leave the battlefield, albeit shouting 'Retreat!' at the top of his voice would be harder to justify.

'Put me on the list!' Sir Nathaniel shouted the demand this time, and Sharpe gripped him by his arm.

'You're disturbing wounded men,' Sharpe said, and dragged Peacock towards the door.

'Take your hands off me!'

'Shut up!' Sharpe dragged the man out of the barn, then shoved him so hard that Peacock tripped and sat in a puddle. 'If I see you in that barn again,' Sharpe said, 'I'll bloody kill you.'

'You'll be court-martialled for this,' Peacock snarled.

'I'll welcome that,' Sharpe said, and just then a voice called across the farmyard.

'There he is! Take him!'

It was Sir Edward Barnes, whose bandaged left arm showed that he had himself been attended by surgeons, and who now pointed at Peacock. Two Hussars in their tall brown bearskins

246

walked across the yard and unceremoniously dragged Peacock away.

'Good riddance,' a voice said, and Sharpe turned to see the surgeon who had refused to list Sir Nathaniel. The surgeon took a deep breath of air and stretched his arms wide. He inspected Sharpe. 'I have to thank you,' he said, 'you're Major Sharpe, yes?'

'Yes. And no thanks needed.'

'Hugh McNeil,' the surgeon introduced himself, then nodded at Sharpe's green jacket, 'and is any of that blood yours?'

'A scratch on the leg, nothing else.'

McNeil flexed his fingers, then took another deep breath. The rain was dripping from the lower hem of his apron, each drop stained red. 'Back to butchery,' he said, then shook his head. 'God help us, Major, and I pray He keeps you out of my hands!' He walked back into the barn.

Sir Edward kicked his horse across the yard.

'I hear I'm losing you, Sharpe.'

'I'm afraid so, sir,' Sharpe paused, 'you were wounded, sir?'

'Musket ball broke my arm,' Barnes said patting the sling, 'nothing much, and I'm sorry about that bloody idiot. Your lads did good work today, Sharpe, unlike that poltroon.' Barnes glanced at Sir Nathaniel who was being hauled swiftly away. 'He was discovered in the ammunition park, whipping the Portuguese and claiming he'd gone to fetch cartridges.'

'He bolted, sir.'

'So I hear, and tried to take a damned fine regiment with him! Well, he's finished. God-damned bloody fool!' Sir Edward leaned to pat his horse's neck. 'You know where you're going?'

'Saint-Jean-de-Luz is all I know, sir.'

'Doubtless his lordship will keep you busy, but hurry back to us if you can.' He leaned from the saddle to offer Sharpe his free hand. 'And good luck, Major!'

Sharpe shook the offered hand, but reckoned he had already received his stroke of luck because Jane was in Saint-Jean-de-Luz, and he was going there.

CHAPTER NINE

It was a long march south to Saint-Jean-de-Luz, but the Light Company of the South Essex was glad to be leaving the rain-soaked, blood-slicked hill and, because Sharpe had not told them why they were being separated from the battalion, they conjured for themselves the idea that they were merely going to establish winter quarters. And so they marched willingly, anticipating a town of fine taverns, pliant women, and small danger.

Sharpe walked, like his men, allowing Charlie Weller to ride Lord Wellington's horse, while Sir Joel, riding another of Wellington's horses, kept Sharpe company.

'By God, that was a good day yesterday!'

'I'm glad you enjoyed it,' Sharpe responded sourly, then more enthusiastically, 'what did you do with the 71st, sir?'

'Told them to face front, of course. I heard you shout that command so I galloped along their line and bellowed the same words. They were good lads. They seemed very cheered up by seeing a sailor join them.'

'Captain d'Alembord told me you fetched them a piper, sir?'

'Nonsense! I just found a Sergeant of the 71st and asked him if he knew where we could find some bagpipes. Turned out there was a set hidden in the battalion luggage! Could he play them, I asked, yes, says he, so I give him my horse and tell him to bugger off under full sail! Ten minutes later he's back and up he pipes! Frankly, Sharpe, I wasn't sure that the men left in line would hold on, but once they heard those pipes they began to fight like fiends! Magnificent!'

'He played "Johnnie Cope", Sharpe said, recalling the tune he had heard over the battle din.

'"Johnnie Cope"?' Sir Joel asked.

'A song celebrating a Scottish victory over the English,' Sharpe said.

'Well, by God, it put wind in their sails! Then Sir William Stewart arrived and he told them to attack and off they went. If he hadn't called them back they'd be in Paris by now!'

'Petty Officer Clouter fought like a fiend too, sir,' Sharpe said quietly enough that Clouter, riding behind, could not hear him.

'Oh, he's a savage in battle! Ain't that true, Clouter?' he called.

Clouter muttered a reply and Sir Joel grinned. 'I wish I had another dozen like him!'

'You know why Lord Wellington wants my company in Saint-Jean, sir?' Sharpe asked.

'I thought you might enjoy a reconnaissance, Sharpe.'

'A reconnaissance, sir?'

'Best let him tell you, Sharpe, it won't take long, no more than a week.'

They had crossed the repaired pontoon bridge, which still swarmed with Engineers tightening lines on the rescued boats that supported the plank roadway. The river was still running high and the bridge shuddered, but it was holding and, after a pause to drink tea, they rode on south and west, arriving in Saint-Jean-de-Luz by the middle of the afternoon. Sir Joel, Captain Crittenden and Clouter rode on to Wellington's headquarters while Sharpe found the Town Major, a harassed, nervous Captain, who complained that he had not been forewarned of their arrival, but found them quarters in a warehouse close to the fishing harbour.

'You'll be wanting new uniforms?' he asked, eyeing the bedraggled ranks.

'Uniforms?' Sharpe asked.

'We have new uniforms for the whole army, sir.'

'I'll wait till the whole battalion can have them issued,' Sharpe said, reckoning he and his men would be more comfortable in their old, battle-stained jackets, 'but we will need rations.'

'It'll be fish, more fish, then fish again, sir,' the Captain said, 'even the bloody bread here tastes like fish. And will you be finding your own personal quarters?'

'I will,' Sharpe said, reckoning he would steal time with Jane, and so he left Lieutenant Kelleher to finish the paperwork with the harassed Captain as he walked into Saint-Jean-de-Luz.

There was still an hour or more before the sun set over the Atlantic, so Sharpe wandered the narrow streets with their half-timbered houses. He liked the town, liked the smell of the sea and the sound of the breakers pounding the long beach. He planned to report to Lord Wellington at sunset, then find his way back to Jane's lodgings and the prospect of sleeping in a proper bed with Jane beside him. He had her address from her infrequent letters, which were headed Etxe Lavalt, Rue Chibeau in her round, childish handwriting. Father Mikel had explained it meant the Lavalt dwelling in Chibeau Street, and Sharpe had to ask a half-dozen people for directions before a well-dressed man wearing a white cockade in his hat to denote that he was a Royalist and definitely not a Bonapartist, pointed him towards a tangle of small streets, one of which had a crude charcoal-written sign saying Chibeau. It was a blessedly small street with a café, a bakery, and a fishmongers, and next door to the fishmongers was a red-painted door on which someone had chalked the name Lavalt. The house was narrow, with a frontage of the door and one window, but four storeys high, and looked to be in good condition.

Sharpe knocked on the door.

There was no answer so he knocked again, harder and louder, then knocked a third time, so hard that he rattled the door in its frame. He heard a window open above him and a woman's voice called, 'What is it?' The question sounded irritated and was in English.

Sharpe stepped back to look up and saw a young dark-haired woman peering down at him. 'I'm looking for Jane Sharpe!' he called up.

'And you are?'

'Her husband.'

'Oh good Lord Almighty,' she said, 'wait there!' She vanished, the window slammed shut and a moment later Sharpe heard footsteps on a staircase inside and the door opened. 'I'm Susan

Lassiter,' the young woman introduced herself brusquely, 'and they make good coffee there.' She pointed to the café.

'Jane's not here?' Sharpe asked.

'Lord, no,' Susan said, her tone implying that Sharpe should have known that. 'Coffee first, Colonel, and a slice of cake?'

'It's Major Sharpe,' Sharpe said.

'It is? Jane said you were Lieutenant Colonel Sharpe.'

'Just a Major.' Somehow Sharpe was not surprised that Jane had elevated his rank; being the wife of a Colonel would give her more status among the community of army wives in the small town.

'My husband's Captain Lassiter of the 57th,' Susan said, plucking at Sharpe's elbow to draw him towards the café that had small tables beneath a sailcloth awning on which the ceaseless rain pattered. 'We heard the gunfire yesterday,' she said, 'was there a fight?'

'There was.'

'And you beat the French?'

'We walloped them,' Sharpe said grimly. 'Do you know when Jane will be back?'

Susan paused to give an order to a small girl who scurried back indoors. 'Not till March, I should think.' She looked back to Sharpe. 'But she told me she'd written to you.'

'March!' Sharpe exclaimed.

'She went back to England,' Susan said nervously.

'Christ!' Sharpe snarled, then apologised. 'Sorry, ma'am, but I never received her letter. Why did she go home?'

'Her mother is dying.'

'Her mother died a decade ago, more.'

Susan Lassiter, who had so far impressed Sharpe with her robust confidence, stared down at the table. She was plainly embarrassed. 'Well that's what she said, and she said she'd be back.'

'When did she leave?' Sharpe asked.

She frowned, thinking. 'It was quite a few days ago,' she said uncertainly, 'maybe the Friday before last?'

'Christ!' Sharpe said again, this time not bothering with an apology.

A legless beggar, wearing a tattered blue French infantry-man's jacket and supported by cut-down crutches and with wooden blocks strapped onto the stumps of his severed legs, stopped and made an appeal to Sharpe, who dropped a coin into the man's tin cup. The man grunted something that might have expressed gratitude or might have been a curse, then swung on down the short street.

'Her mother?' Sharpe asked, trying to arrange the thoughts swirling in his confused mind.

'That's what she said.' By now Susan Lassiter was plainly wishing she was anywhere but at this small café table. The small girl had come back with a tray on which were two cups of coffee and two small cakes decorated with almonds. Sharpe had no appetite.

'Maybe she meant her stepmother,' he said, knowing full well that Jane had no such relative.

'I'm sure she meant that,' Susan said, relieved. 'Would you know how the 57th fared yesterday, Major?'

'I don't know, ma'am, I'm sorry.'

'There was such a lot of gunfire,' she said quietly.

Sharpe reckoned it was about fifteen miles as a crow might fly from the site of the battle to Saint-Jean-de-Luz, and the cannon fire must have sounded like unending thunder to the town's inhabitants. 'There was, ma'am,' he said, 'but the 57th did well, very well.' He added the last few words as an attempt to comfort her.

'But suffered losses?'

'We all did, ma'am. I imagine you can get official news from headquarters today or tomorrow?'

'I'm sure you're right,' she said, sounding anything but sure.

'Did Jane leave her belongings here?'

'Oh yes. We share a room and it's full of her things. Do you want something?'

'No, I just wondered.'

'She just left clothes,' Susan said. 'She has a lot, but the navy won't allow too much baggage.'

'The navy?'

'There are ships always coming and going and we're allowed free passage. Well, almost free. She sailed on a ship called the *Pelican*, bound for Portsmouth.'

'You saw her leave?'

'I walked her down to the harbour.'

Sharpe drained his coffee, then put a handful of small coins on the table. 'I'm sorry to have troubled you, ma'am, but allow me to pay for the coffee.'

'Of course, Major, and thank you.'

'Thank you, ma'am, and I'm sure you'll receive good news of your husband very soon.'

She smiled her uncertain thanks and Sharpe stood, gave

her a small bow, and walked on. He was in a daze, oblivious of the streets he walked, torn between anger and hurt, but also, he was honest enough to admit to himself, some relief. It was true he had wanted to see Jane, but that was as much because he knew he had to want that, as it was a genuine desire. He found her difficult, and remembered what Major Hogan had told him at their last meeting. Marry in haste and repent at leisure. He snarled, frightening a poor woman carrying a baby and he half bowed in apology. Other townsfolk were staring at him, shocked by his grim expression and the battle stains on his uniform. He walked on, noting that the shadows were lengthening, then stepped out of the street's centre because of hoofbeats behind him.

'Sir!' a cheerful voice called and he turned to see it was Charlie Weller riding Wellington's horse that Sharpe had promised to return. Weller had ridden the horse with the Light Company, but had insisted he should groom the horse before returning it. 'I washed him down, sir,' Weller said happily, 'gave him a good brushing, and polished his hooves! He got a good feed too.'

'Thanks, Charlie, you know where you're going?'

'To the beach, sir, and look for a bloody great yellow house. Stables are at the back.'

'You shortened the stirrup leathers, I see.'

'I don't want to look like a ploughman going to market, sir. Do you want to ride him, sir?'

'I'm happier walking, Charlie. You go ahead. And the horse looks smart!'

'He's a good 'un, sir, good as I've ever ridden. Oh, and

Johnny Rush cleaned up the saddle and the rest of the tack. Put a right shine on it!'

'I won't forget, Charlie. On you go!'

Weller touched a finger to his shako and, still grinning, kicked the horse on. Sharpe envied him, remembering his own days in the ranks; no responsibilities, few decisions, and the companionship of good fellows. There were things he had forgotten too, but they were best left forgotten.

He turned a corner and saw the wide beach that was being pummelled by waves. The sun was hidden by a bank of Atlantic cloud, but it was near setting and Sharpe looked for the big yellow house that he remembered from his previous visit. It was close by, and was somewhat larger than a house; more a bloody great palace. He pulled his jacket straight and headed for the wide front steps that were guarded by a pair of redcoats who looked surprised by the state of his uniform, but seeing the red sash and sword, one of them courteously saluted and opened the door.

'You have an appointment, sir?'

Sharpe glanced back to see the sky reddening above the bank of cloud. 'About now.'

He found himself in a great entrance hall, its high walls pillared with marble, though one long wall was obscured by scaffolding where a half-dozen labourers mixed plaster that was being spread across a damaged section. In front of the opposite wall were four long wooden benches on which at least a dozen officers were sitting, obviously waiting. There was no obvious place to report and so he joined the waiting officers, leaned back against the wall and closed his eyes.

What the hell was Jane doing? He feared he knew and felt a pulse of anger shake him. They hadn't even been married a year! The unfaithful bitch! His right hand instinctively sought the hilt of his sword. I'll kill the bitch, he thought, slice her from her crotch to her tits, then was immediately ashamed of himself.

'It's just water damage,' an officer sitting a few feet away said.

Sharpe realised the man had spoken to him. 'What?' he asked.

'The wall. They're plastering over water damage and I'll guarantee they haven't stopped the bloody leaks. The roof is probably two hundred years old and rotten. Waste of time. In another month that new plaster will have scabbed and turned black.' He leaned towards Sharpe and held out a hand. 'Captain John Leeson, Royal Engineers.'

Sharpe reluctantly took his hand from the sword's hilt and shook. 'Major Sharpe, South Essex.'

'Ah, I've heard of you,' Leeson said, 'you have an appointment, sir?'

'I was told to be here.'

'By Lord Wellington?'

'Yes.'

'He's not here. He sent word he's gone to see General Hope at his headquarters in Biarritz and won't be back till tomorrow.'

'You're waiting for him too?' Sharpe asked.

'Good Lord, no! I don't move in those circles.' Leeson gave a small laugh. 'I'm here to see Major Whiting, the fellow who arranges passage home.'

'You're off home?' Sharpe asked, surprised. Lord Wellington was famously reluctant to offer leave to officers, claiming their duty was to stay and fight, not run to the comforts of home.

'No choice, sir.' Leeson bent over and rapped his right leg. 'All made of Portuguese cork now,' he said, 'the bloody French shot it away on the Bidassoa. The Peer don't need a one-legged Engineer. If I'm damn lucky I'll be home just in time for Christmas!'

There was a stir in the hallway as the front door opened. A tall naval officer entered and, because his arrival meant nothing to the waiting men, the momentary excitement faded as the naval officer strode across the tiled floor and climbed the stairs.

'Probably not Christmas,' Leeson went on gloomily, 'word is that if you want a swift passage home you have to cross Whiting's greedy palm with silver.'

'And you have none?'

'Not a bent penny.'

'Will silver do?' Sharpe asked. He stood up, convinced there was small point in waiting in this gloomy hallway for Wellington to arrive. Better to find himself some quarters in the town, have a meal and come back next morning. He dropped a five-franc coin into Leeson's lap. 'That should be enough,' he said.

'Silver?' Leeson asked, puzzled.

Sharpe tossed another five-franc coin into the Engineer's lap. 'Merry Christmas, Captain.'

'Sir! I didn't mean to—'

'I took the coins from a dead Frog,' Sharpe said, 'so it's free money.' He stood. 'Go home, Captain, and good luck.'

He reached the door just as it was thrust open, almost

hitting him. He stepped back and bowed as a tall woman laden with bags came from the dying sunlight.

'Major Sharpe!' the woman said.

It was Candelaria, the Portuguese woman who had somehow become attached to Lord Wellington's staff.

'Ma'am,' Sharpe said, now holding the door open for her.

'You are here for his lordship?'

'Yes, ma'am.'

'And look at you! Is that the jacket I washed?'

'Yes, ma'am.'

'Then come with me,' she said sternly. 'His lordship is delayed till tomorrow, which is a good thing.'

'It is?' Sharpe asked, releasing the door which swung ponderously shut.

'You cannot see his lordship dressed like that! You look as if you've been playing games in a butcher's shop.'

'That's more or less what I have been doing, ma'am.'

'My name is Candelaria,' she said, 'didn't I tell you that?'

'You did, M . . .' Sharpe checked himself just in time.

'And yours is Richard, yes?'

'Yes,' Sharpe said. She pronounced his name with the stress on the second syllable which Sharpe found oddly attractive. 'Can I carry something for you?'

'This,' she said, thrusting the heaviest of her bags at him, 'turnips, which his lordship does not like to eat, but I do.'

'I'm not fond of them either,' Sharpe said, now walking beside her.

'You're limping, Major,' she said in an accusatory tone.

'Just a scratch,' Sharpe said, though where the splinter of

wood had pierced his thigh was now a dull ache that intensi-
fied when he put his weight on his right foot. 'It's nothing.'

'So you are a physician as well as a soldier?' she asked.

'I've had worse,' Sharpe said.

'You can climb stairs?'

'Of course, ma'am.'

'Only one floor,' Candelaria said, and watched suspiciously
as he began the ascent. Every eye in the hallway was on him
now, no doubt wondering what his business was in the headquarters. He reached the landing, turned and climbed the next
flight, the ache in his thigh now a dull throb, then followed
Candelaria down a long gloomy passage. 'I hate this house,'
she said, 'too big. Now we go downstairs again.'

She led him down a back stairway, which Sharpe supposed
was there to allow the servants to reach the upper floors without
using the grand central stairway, but it still seemed odd to go
up and down stairs to reach a room on the ground floor. 'Too
many people down the stairs,' Candelaria seemed to intuit his
question, 'I go that way and they ask questions.'

'Questions?'

'About his lordship, and I do not answer. It is not their
business. Here we are!' She had led him into the same big
kitchen in which he had first met her. A small fire burned
in an iron grate at the centre of the enormous hearth. She
placed her purchases on a big table, then gestured to the
feeble flames. 'Make that fire better, Richard,' she said, 'and
I will be back.'

Sharpe riddled the fire with a poker, then heaped more
wood on the flames so that by the time Candelaria returned

261

there was a good blaze flickering shadows about the high-ceilinged kitchen.

'Good!' she said and warmed herself in front of the fire. Just as she had when he first met her she was carrying a heavy robe. 'Now,' she said, 'undress and put that on.' She tossed the robe to him. 'That is all French blood?'

'Almost all.'

'Then take everything off. No rifle this time?'

'I left it with my men.'

'I pull your boots,' she said, and tugged the muddy boots free and tossed them into a corner. 'Your battalion is here?'

'One company is,' Sharpe said as he stood.

'So you rest with them tonight?'

'Either that or find quarters in a tavern.' He had hoped to spend it with Jane, but that dream had curdled.

'The taverns are full,' she said brusquely, 'and not cheap! Their girls are dirty too. Filthy! You are here with the Admiral?'

'You know about him?'

'His name is Sir Joel, his wife is Florence, he has a son called Horatio, and he was the one who told me the tavern girls are dirty. Yes, I know him.' She grinned, 'So yes, I know about him.'

'I'm with him,' Sharpe said, 'at least I think I am.'

'The Admiral is staying here, so you will have a room here too. His lordship would want that.'

'You're sure?'

'I am his lordship's housekeeper. What I decide, he likes. Now undress.'

'Yes ma'am,' Sharpe said, amused. He felt oddly embarrassed

to strip himself naked in front of her, but Candelaria busied herself unpacking her purchases, and only looked at him again when he was swathed in the big dark blue robe.

'Now show me your scratch,' she commanded. Sharpe sat in front of the fire and bared his right thigh. 'Scratch!' she said mockingly, and Sharpe saw that the splinter had gouged a considerable hole in his thigh which now oozed blood past the congealed scab. 'You cleaned it?'

'Just pulled the wood out.'

She cleaned the wound with a wet cloth, then poured brandy into the gash before binding his thigh with clean linen. 'If it doesn't repair soon you see a doctor.'

'Yes, ma'am.'

'He will have to open it and see if there is still something inside.'

'The wood came out clean,' Sharpe said.

'Now the girls make you a bath,' she said.

'A bath?' Sharpe asked in alarm. 'Girls?'

'Maids. They were in the house. They were the Emperor's maids, ha! Now they clean your uniform and I tell them if they do not do it right I will beat them!'

'And would you?'

'No, they are good girls. Now come with me. You don't need your sword, Major!'

'It goes with me,' Sharpe insisted.

She prised it from his grip. 'And you will clean it? Sharpen it? Grease it? I will do that.' She laid it on the table and led him back upstairs to a room which overlooked the sea. 'You will rest here, Richard,' she said sternly.

'I need to visit the stables first,' he said.

'Dressed like that?'

'Oh damn.' He went back downstairs and retrieved his over-alls and jacket from the grisly pile of laundry, pulled on his boots and, guided by Candelaria, went to the big stables where, as he expected, he found Charlie Weller brushing down the horse he had returned. He gave Charlie a coin. 'You can find your way back to where the company is billeted, Charlie?'

'By the harbour, sir, I know where it is.'

'Then tell Lieutenant Kelleher that I'm detained,' he said, 'and I can't rejoin until tomorrow. And say the lads can rest till the morning, and that includes you, Charlie.'

'I'll tell him, sir.' Weller glanced curiously at Candelaria, but had enough sense to resist asking about her.

'And resting,' Sharpe went on, 'doesn't mean the boys can't find a tavern, but remember it's a Crapaud town and not everyone loves us. Don't wander the streets alone at night, and if anyone picks a fight, back off.'

'Or clobber them, sir.'

'Or clobber them bloody hard, Charlie. No! Back off.'

'Got it, sir.' Weller was grinning.

'They're to behave,' Sharpe said sternly, 'and tell Pat Harper I mean him.'

And those were wasted words, Sharpe thought as he followed Candelaria back to the house. Pat Harper had no great hatred of the French any more than he had any love for the English, but he did have a huge affection for a good fight, and Sharpe knew there would be provosts roaming the streets ready to arrest any man found mistreating the town's inhabitants.

'Not my problem,' he muttered as he followed Candelaria upstairs again.

'Major?'

'Nothing, ma'am, just thinking.'

'Worrying?' she asked.

'Just thinking,' Sharpe insisted.

Once back in the pleasant bedroom he found a tin bath in front of the fireplace. A fire was laid in the hearth, though not yet lit, and the bath was half filled with steaming water. 'Get in,' Candelaria commanded and saw him hesitate. 'Don't worry about the wound,' she said, 'you are supposed to keep bandages wet. It hurries the healing.'

'A bowl and a washcloth will do me,' Sharpe said.

'In!'

Sharpe flinched at the water's heat, but lowered himself gingerly into the bath. He could not remember the last time he had bathed, though he was certain it had been at a woman's behest, and he reckoned the two or three freezing dips he had taken in high Pyrenean lakes did not count.

Candelaria lit the fire with a flint and steel, then handed him a lump of soap. 'They make good soap in France,' she said grudgingly, 'not much else, but good soap. I am told there is no soap in England?'

'I'm sure there is.'

'Then they should use it.' She went to the door. 'I will be back soon. Use the cloths,' she indicated a pile on the bed, 'to dry yourself.'

When she returned Sharpe was sitting in a chair by the window, swathed in the thick robe which he suspected was from Wellington's wardrobe. Candelaria was carrying a small bowl which she placed on the window-seat, then took a razor from a pocket.

'Head up, Major!'

'I can shave myself,' Sharpe protested.

'Then you should! But now I shave you!'

She shaved him delicately, the steel razor gliding over his chin and neck, and then she rinsed his face with water infused with lemon juice. She dried his skin, then gestured at the bed. 'Now rest, I will wake you for supper.'

'Candelaria,' Sharpe said as forcefully as he could, 'I can find my own supper.'

She snorted derision at that claim. 'And where? All you will find is fish soup and hard bread in a bad tavern.' She folded the razor. 'Besides, I have your clothes. They are being washed and darned. You go to a tavern like that?'

Sharpe half smiled. 'You win.'

'Of course I win, I am woman! Now rest. Try and sleep.'

After the warm bath and the luxury of a shave Sharpe thought he would sleep, but he just lay wakeful on the bed, his thoughts in a turmoil. Jane, of course, filled his mind with loathing for her apparent betrayal, and though he tried to persuade himself that she must have had good reason to return home, he could only suspect bad reason and that tortured him. He tried to think of his badly shrunken Light Company and what Wellington would demand of it, but the only clues lay in his lordship's brusque demand that they were trained as Light Infantry, and Sir Joel's remark about a reconnaissance, and those clues led nowhere, and then he contemplated the thought that this war was nearly done. The Emperor, true, was still leading armies, but France was ringed with enemies and Wellington's forces were on French soil and threatening to rip northwards like a dagger thrust into France's underbelly. And when peace came? What then?

Sharpe had no trade and, thanks to Jane, no capital either. He had given her the authority to draw funds from his agents in London, and he did not doubt that she had exhausted that small account. So what would he do? He might be able to remain in the army, but he suspected that a peacetime army would have little use for an uneducated officer who had risen from the ranks. No, the army would be filled with the privileged and the well-connected, and Sharpe would be lucky to get a posting in a coastal fort as a Quartermaster. The truth, and he knew it, was that he had no future. Half-pay would keep him in drink and some shabby lodging, and his career, of which he was proud, would peter out in resentment and poverty, while Jane, the foul bitch, floated ever upwards in luxury. And that thought returned his mind to the misery of Jane's behaviour.

He reprimanded himself, trying to persuade himself that his self-pity and hopelessness were unwarranted, but he could not escape their claws. He groped on the table beside the bed and found a small book, presumably left by a previous occupant of the room. The book was called *Childe Harold's Pilgrimage* by someone called Lord Byron. The date on the title page showed it was a new book, scarce more than a year old, and he thought it might distract him and so he tried to read. It was poetry, which was a bad start, but he persevered.

Oh, thou, in Hellas deemed of heavenly birth,
Muse, formed or fabled at the minstrel's will!
Since shamed full oft by later lyres on earth,
Mine dares not call thee from thy sacred hill:

He got that far and the words were just a meaningless blur.
They made no sense, except that the mention of the sacred
hill made him think of the battle, of the close escape from a
bayonet thrust, of a young Frenchman's face as he realised he
was dying, of the smell of shit, blood, and powder smoke, of
the men calling for their mothers as they writhed in agony.
He thought of Captain Carline dead, of Luis Gallardo dying,
and his eyes filled with tears as he dropped the book onto the
floor. God damn it, he thought, but he was wasting his time
in this bedroom. He should be with his battalion where there
was always work to be done. And that made him realise that
the work would soon end in peace and he would have no
future, none. He swore, and saw that the sun had long set and
it was night-time. A sliver of moon was glinting silver reflections from the endless waves rolling towards the beach.

The door opened and Candelaria came in. 'Come downstairs,' she said, 'there is supper and your uniform waiting.' She
placed two unlit candles, both set in tall silver sticks, beside
the bed. 'Put on the robe and come!' she ordered.

The kitchen was well lit by its fire and by a dozen candles
set in mirrored sconces. His uniform, newly washed and neatly
folded, lay on a chair beside his long boots and sword, all now
gleaming.

Candelaria scooped them all up. 'I put these in your room,'

she said decisively. 'If I let you wear them tonight you will go into the town and kill Frenchmen, then I must clean them all again. Sit and eat. The wine is French, but there was no other to be had.'

She went through the door and Sharpe sat to find his supper was bread, butter, cold meats and cheese. He had been feeling hungry, but now discovered he had no appetite.

He poured himself wine and drank it as if it was water, then he toyed with the ham, cold mutton and bread. He could hear the murmur of men's voices deeper in the building and he supposed Sir Joel was dining with the headquarter officers, but Sharpe had no wish to join them, and blessedly no one came to the kitchen to disturb him.

Candelaria returned soon enough and sat opposite him, pouring herself wine. 'You look sad, Major.'

'I do?'

'And you sound sad. Did you sleep?'

'I rested.'

Candelaria sipped her wine. 'War makes us sad.'

'It does.' It was not war, he thought, but Jane.

'If my son had lived,' she said, 'he would have been nineteen last week.'

'Oh God,' Sharpe said, 'I'm sorry.'

'My only child,' she said. 'The French stood him against the church wall and shot him.'

'I'm sorry,' Sharpe said again, not knowing what else to say.

'Two French soldiers were shot near our village, so they took all the young men and shot them.' Tears made her eyes glisten and trickled down her cheeks. 'Alexandre was only fifteen.' She looked at him fiercely, her eyes gleaming in the candlelight. 'How many French have you killed, Richard?'

'God knows,' he paused, 'hundreds.'

'Then you have done God's work.' She paused and, when Sharpe said nothing, used her apron to wipe her eyes. 'When I go home I will look at the damage in the church wall and say a prayer for you.'

Sharpe felt awkward. 'Not sure God cares about me,' he said uncertainly. 'I've never much cared for Him.'

'His lordship says you are a good man,' Candelaria said, 'so God cares for you.'

'He has a strange way of showing it,' Sharpe said. He stood. 'Thank you for everything, ma'am, and if you don't mind I'll get some sleep. I have Lord Wellington to face in the morning, and that's much like seeing God.' He picked up his sword in its shining scabbard, too shiny he thought and made a resolve to paint the scabbard with black paint. 'Thank you for cleaning this too,' he said, 'and goodnight, ma'am.' He offered a bow.

'Goodnight, Richard.' She gave a rueful smile. 'There will be breakfast here in the morning.'

'Thank you, ma'am,' he said, and let himself out of the kitchen.

The passageway and back stairs were unlit, dark, and he climbed slowly, aided by a wash of faint moonlight coming through a window at the stair's landing. Once in his room he revived the fire and used a page torn from *Childe Harold's Pilgrimage* to light a candle. Was there a God? He wondered about that as he took off the thick robe and folded it on top of his newly washed clothes, then he climbed into bed and blew the candle out. Jane came back to torment his thoughts, and he squeezed his eyes shut as if he could evict her from his head, along with his fears for the future. He tried to divert his mind, anticipating what Wellington would demand of him, but there was no answer to that and he sank back into the pain of Jane's betrayal and the small pleasure of imagining a revenge. Somewhere in the huge house a clock chimed eleven, and he turned over, his face to the wall, desperate for the release of sleep that did not come.

He did not even turn back when he heard the door open and close. He lay silent, not even moving when Candelaria slid into the bed beside him. She was crying softly, she said something in such a low voice that the only thing Sharpe recognised was her son's name, and he turned and took her in his arms and felt his own tears come.

They held each other, companions in misery.

War makes us sad, he thought, but the warmth of her body persuaded him that perhaps there was a God after all.

CHAPTER TEN

Sharpe woke with the sun, or at least as bright daylight streamed through the unshuttered window. He was alone, but he could hear voices elsewhere in the house and the clatter of dishes downstairs.

He dressed, revelling in the luxurious feel of clean mended clothes, buckled his sword belt and went downstairs to the kitchen.

'Good morning, Major Sharpe,' Candelaria greeted him.

Four officers were already seated at the table which was spread with coffee, toast, cheese and more cold meats.

'Good morning, ma'am.'

'You slept well?'

'Indeed, ma'am, thank you.'

'Then breakfast, Major,' she said sternly, pointing to a vacant chair.

The four officers were all aides to Lord Wellington and Sharpe nodded a greeting to the two he recognised. 'His lordship has returned?' he asked.

'And is eager to see you, sir,' a Captain in the gaudy uniform of a Hussar replied.

Sharpe grunted at that and busied himself with toast, butter and cheese. He poured himself coffee and half listened to the conversation that was marvelling at the dawning of a sunny day.

'The roads will dry out,' one man observed, 'and the Frogs will march again.'

'They're well thrashed,' another, a redcoated Major, said, 'they won't come near us. What do you think, Sharpe?'

Sharpe, startled at the question, hurriedly swallowed a mouthful of coffee. 'I'm not paid to think,' his reply was surly, 'I'm paid to fight.'

The door had opened behind him and suddenly all the officers were scrambling to their feet with a scrape of chairs.

'Sit down,' Lord Wellington's voice was harsh. 'Ah, Sharpe! Glad you're here.'

Sharpe, who had not moved, turned towards Wellington. 'My lord,' he said in bleak acknowledgement.

'Finish your breakfast, Sharpe. Candelaria? Would you be kind enough to show Major Sharpe to my room when he's done?'

'Of course, my lord.' She gave a curtsey.

'And perhaps you can bring me another pot of tea? And two more cups.'

'Of course, my lord.'

Candelaria busied herself with boiling water, tea leaves and a tray, and, when she was ready, looked enquiringly at Sharpe.

He stood. 'Ready ma'am.'

'He does like his tea,' she said when they had left the kitchen, then looked up at him. 'You won't . . .' she stopped, suddenly nervous.

'Of course I won't,' Sharpe said.

'*Obrigada*,' she said, and hurried on with her tray. Once at the right door she knocked by kicking it with her foot and, when the command to enter sounded, Sharpe opened the door and stepped aside for Candelaria to enter. Wellington was standing beside a large round table on which was a big map, and next to him was Sir Joel Chase's flag captain, Crittenden, who gave Sharpe a nod of recognition.

'So, Sharpe,' Wellington said sternly when Candelaria was gone, 'you're not paid to think? Only to fight?'

'Usually the safest way in the army, my lord.'

That seemed to amuse his lordship, who looked at Captain Crittenden, 'once a Sergeant, always a Sergeant.' Was there a sting in those words, however lightly spoken? Sharpe was not sure and had no time to consider the question because Wellington looked at him. 'Your Light Company is here?'

'What's left of it, my lord.'

'How many?'

'Just twenty-eight men, my lord.'

'That should be sufficient, look here.'

Wellington pointed at the big map which covered most of the table. It took Sharpe a moment to recognise the map, which was on a large scale, showing much of south-western France, from the Atlantic coast well inland. The map was dotted with chess pieces, black for the French and white for Wellington's forces, and Sharpe noted that there were marginally more white than black pieces. There was a large dark mass of black pawns in and around Bayonne, then a string of bishops, rooks and knights dotted along the right bank of the River Adour. The majority of the white pieces were close up to the southern defences of Bayonne, small groups marked the bridges over the Nive, and there was another clump at Saint-Jean-de-Luz. Pawns were strung loosely along the Adour's left bank, presumably watching the French forces across the river, but one single white pawn was far to the east, all alone and far behind the French lines. 'If you were Marshal Soult, Sharpe,' Wellington demanded, 'what would you do?'

'I wouldn't give your lordship a moment's peace,' Sharpe said.

'How?'

'I'd attack these fellows relentlessly.' Sharpe touched a finger to a white queen just south of Bayonne.

'Which he won't do,' Wellington said scornfully. 'He's tried that twice and was rewarded with a bloody nose both times. He's on the defensive now. We have more men, and the Emperor keeps taking more of his troops to defend northern France, so Marshal Soult is dug in behind those massive fortifications. He wants me to assault them so he can destroy enough of my men in his ditches, but I'm of no mind to satisfy that wish.'

And thank God for that, Sharpe thought. Fighting across ditches which were under the cannons of the defenders was a quick way to find a grave. He had done it before and, even if the assault was under the cover of darkness, the French would light the ditches with great burning carcasses of tarred wood, and the cannons would lace the ditch with canister and shell, and the attackers would still have to climb the wall beyond under a hail of musketry.

'So what do I do?' Wellington demanded peremptorily.

Sharpe knew his lordship was not asking advice, but was putting him to the test. And Sharpe knew the answer because Sir Joel had revealed it, but Sharpe could not betray that indiscretion so, instead of looking at the estuary of the Adour, he pointed at the lone white pawn which lay isolated to the east.

'I'm curious, my lord, what those fellows are doing so far off.'

'Not fellows,' Wellington said brusquely, 'just the one. Your friend Major Hogan.'

'He's an exploring officer now?' Sharpe asked.

'He always was,' Wellington said curtly. Exploring officers were brave men who rode on superb horses to reconnoitre territory far behind the enemy lines. They depended on their horsemanship and the quality of their mounts to escape enemy pursuit and to bring Wellington details of rivers, hills, valleys and enemy dispositions.

'And where the exploring officers go, my lord,' Sharpe said, 'your army follows.'

'So?'

'I assume Marshal Soult's orders are to stop us getting farther into France, my lord,' Sharpe went on, 'and if you go east he has to follow you if he has a hope of checking us.'

'But that still leaves Bayonne with a sizeable garrison that could attack any troops I leave here. They could even seize this town.' Wellington stabbed a finger down on Saint-Jean-de-Luz.

'But I assume you'll leave troops here to invest Bayonne, my lord?'

'How?' Wellington snapped the question. Sharpe hesitated, and Wellington complicated the abrupt query. 'I'm confident I can cross the Adour's upper reaches, but to invest Bayonne I need to cross somewhere here,' he swept a finger along the river just to the east of the city, 'and these fellows,' he tapped two or three of the black chess pieces, 'will make that damned difficult.'

Sharpe still hesitated. He knew the answer, but how to deliver it without betraying Sir Joel Chase's indiscretion? Then he realised that Captain Crittenden's silent presence was a godsend. 'I assume that Captain Crittenden is offering you a solution, my lord.'

'Which is?'

'The estuary,' Sharpe said. 'You're planning to cross the Adour on Bayonne's seaward side, my lord, and that probably needs the navy's help.'

'And yours,' Wellington said. 'So you *can* think, Major!' He sounded disgruntled, as though he was disappointed in Sharpe, but Sharpe knew he had passed the test and did his best not to look too pleased with himself. 'The Admiral and Captain Crittenden assure me the navy can build a bridge of boats across the Adour estuary,' Wellington went on, 'but it won't be quick or easy! Tell him, Crittenden.'

Crittenden moved to the map, his sword scabbard rapping against one of the table's legs. 'It won't be easy, my lord, but we are confident it can be done.' He used a pencil to indicate the estuary. 'This is all tidal water and the range is three fathoms at the neaps.' A slight growl from Wellington made him hastily translate. 'So at the smallest tides it rises and falls, say, twelve feet, and at the springs it can be five or six feet more. That provokes strong currents, so any bridge must cope with the strong currents and a tidal rise and fall of fifteen feet or more. The mouth of the estuary,' the pencil moved to the Atlantic shore, 'is protected by a sandbar which is impassable except for a narrow channel which seems to shift north and south, and the enemy has removed the markers that guide mariners. In any onshore wind, which we'll need, that bar is pounded by high surf, so any ship that misses the channel will likely be reduced to wreckage on the shoals. Once past the bar our men will be faced by a dozen French gunboats and one brig, the *Sappho*, which carries sixteen guns in two broadsides, almost certainly twelve-pounders. So far as we can determine there are no shore batteries, but our reconnaissance has seen solitary soldiers evidently posted as coast watchers, all of them on the northern bank.'

'No shore batteries,' Wellington said dubiously. 'They must know we have a navy?'

'I'm certain they are not unaware of that, my lord,' Crittenden said drily, 'but I would venture to suggest that the enemy believe any incursion into the river will fail given the danger of the bar, the surf, and the strength of the tides.'

'But no one interfered with your reconnaissance?'

'We used local fishing boats, my lord, and they raised no apparent suspicion.'

Wellington grunted, evidently in disapproval of French inefficiency. 'The plan,' he was looking at Sharpe now, 'is to put thirty or more fishing boats into the estuary, line them up across the river and lay ropes across them from bank to bank, then place planks on the ropes to make the bridge. It won't be easy.' He looked at Crittenden. 'This *Sappho* could blow it apart before we've begun!'

'I doubt we could get our own gun-brigs into the estuary, my lord. The sandbar will prevent that, but if we construct our own shore batteries on the southern bank? Your artillery will be more than enough to settle the *Sappho*. Even nine-pounders will suffice. Those brigs aren't of heavy construction.'

'I'm sending some eighteens too,' Wellington said.

'They'll reduce the *Sappho* to kindling!' Crittenden said vengefully.

'And the gunboats?' Sharpe asked.

'One shot will sink each,' Crittenden said scornfully. 'They're nothing but launches or cutters with a single cannon mounted amidships pointing forrard. Half the time they spring their planking by just firing the cannon. We're making a handful of our own to protect the bridge upstream of the river, but God knows how long they'll last.'

'If the bridge is feasible at all!' Wellington spoke curtly. 'Your fellow,' he glared at Crittenden, 'says it's impossible!'

'Captain Bampfylde,' Crittenden replied icily, meaning the officer who was next in superiority to Sir Joel, 'is given to pessimism.'

'But suppose he's right?' Wellington demanded.

'And to determine that is why we're here, my lord,' Crittenden said firmly.

'Or why you're here, Sharpe,' Wellington said. 'The problem, as I understand it, is that the bridge will mainly be supported by cables. That's right, is it not?'

'Thirteen-inch cables, my lord,' Crittenden said, 'at least three of them, anchored on both banks.'

'We know the southern bank is solid enough to hold cables,' Wellington said, glancing at Crittenden, 'you plan to put windlasses there?'

'To tension the cables, yes, my lord.'

'The problem, Sharpe, is the northern bank. We already hold the southern bank, but we've not explored the northern, and Captain Bampfylde, who has taken his ship close inshore and inspected the land from his masthead, claims the ground is waterlogged. Nothing but bog! And if he's right then the cables won't be anchored and the bridge won't work.'

'Sir Joel and I disagree, my lord,' Crittenden said quietly.

'But if you're wrong then you'll start to tension the cables and pull their anchoring posts clear out of the quagmire and we'll have no bridge.' Wellington stared down at the map as if it could provide some reassurance.

Crittenden leaned over the map and, using a pencil, drew a thick line which ran the whole length of the estuary's northern bank. 'The ground is saturated, my lord, but the whole northern bank is edged with an embanked road. I judge it to be some twelve- or fourteen-foot high, and our opinion is that the embankment will provide the means to anchor the cables.'

'If the embankment isn't waterlogged,' Wellington said dubiously.

'The fishermen we've questioned claim it's been there many years, my lord.'

'I don't rest the fate of His Majesty's forces on the opinion of fishermen,' Wellington said caustically. 'Sharpe! We're going to land a pair of Engineers on the northern bank and they will determine the feasibility of the ground to hold the cables firmly. We know there are scattered sentries on that bank, and by daylight we've observed a handful of patrols on that embanked road, but we dare not betray too much interest in the ground. The French will see us assembling pontoons here,' he stabbed a finger on the river inland of Bayonne, 'and we hope that will mislead them into thinking we plan to cross there. If our Engineers are captured here,' he pointed to the estuary, 'then the cat will be out of the bag and we're the ones who will be clawed. Which is where you come in, Sharpe.'

Wellington paused, prompting Sharpe to acknowledge the last words. 'My lord?'

'I need you to take your Light Company ashore and make damned sure our Engineers are not captured.'

Sharpe thought for a heartbeat. 'This would be at night, my lord?'

'At night,' Wellington confirmed curtly, 'and without making any noise.' He looked into Sharpe's eyes. 'Cut-throat work, Sharpe, which sounds like an appropriate task for poachers and murderers?'

Sharpe resisted a smile. 'It does, my lord.'

'It has to be silent work,' Wellington went on. 'Even a handful of musket shots will alert the enemy to our interest.'

'So will corpses with slit throats?' Sharp suggested uneasily.

'The picquets are scattered,' Wellington said confidently. 'If you're efficient you should only need to kill a couple, and you can take their bodies back to sea and drop them overboard.'

Sharpe nodded, suspecting that the task would be a deal more difficult than Wellington presumed. He was staring down at the map, which showed a scatter of buildings close to the northern shore, and Sharpe pointed to one. 'Are those farms, my lord?' he asked. 'Or fishermen's cottages?'

'Both probably,' Crittenden answered. 'Does it matter?'

'If the French have picquets along the bank,' Sharpe said, 'then they're likely to have posted at least a company in one of those buildings. I would have.'

'You would?' Crittenden sounded surprised.

'Suppose I had a dozen men posted on the shore,' Sharpe said, 'and they all have to be relieved at least twice in the night. I don't want to march the replacements out from the city, I want them close by.'

'So one of those houses could hold a small garrison,' Crittenden said with a note of alarm.

'Which is why you make no noise.' Wellington put an end to the speculation. 'If there is a small garrison, you let it sleep.'

'Of course, my lord,' Sharpe said, wondering how he was to defend the landing without making noise. 'About how long will it take the Engineers to make a decision?' he asked.

Crittenden answered, 'It depends on what we find. If we have to dig into the ground, it could take an hour, but I expect to make a determination in much less time.'

'You?' Sharpe asked, surprised.

'I am an Engineer as well as a Mariner,' Crittenden responded, looking amused at Sharpe's surprise. 'My father is an Engineer,

Major, and quite famous. He builds wharves, harbours and breakwaters, and working with him introduced me to the sea.'

'And I'm sending one of our own Engineers,' Wellington interrupted, then looked at Crittenden. 'You met Captain Bisby?'

'I had the pleasure last night,' Crittenden said, making it sound anything but a pleasure.

'And he's qualified?'

'A very practical man, my lord,' Crittenden said in faint praise.

'I like practical men,' Wellington said firmly, 'so the only question is when.'

'Tomorrow night would be ideal, my lord,' the naval Captain answered. 'The high tide is a few minutes after nine, so we can go in on the flood, make our exploration, and leave on the ebb. How many men will you bring, Sharpe?'

'Twenty-eight, sir,'

'So two local fishing boats,' Crittenden said.

'And pray the French stay asleep.' Wellington began folding the map. 'Where are your fellows billeted, Sharpe?'

'At the inner harbour, my lord.'

'Perfect,' Crittenden said. 'We'll meet you there at midday tomorrow, Sharpe.'

'Yes, sir.'

'And I do believe that tea is getting cold.' Wellington made the final fold in the map. 'Will you pour, Sharpe?'

Sharpe hesitated, not because he was nervous of pouring tea, but because he remembered something he needed to raise with the army's commander.

'My lord?'

'What?' Wellington sounded impatient.

'In the last fight, my lord, I lost a Spaniard who volunteered into our ranks. A good man! But he was worried his family wouldn't receive his back pay, my lord.'

Wellington grunted. 'You have his attestation?'

'I do, my lord.'

'And that gives his family's address?'

'It lists his home village, my lord.'

'Then write a note on it giving his date of death, sign it, and send it here, addressed to Major Hay. All such men's families will receive what's owed them. Now tea, I think?'

Sharpe poured.

Sharpe felt no compunction to return to his battalion immediately, so instead he took a walk along the beach, his thoughts as complicated and ragged as the big breakers that rolled in from the west to break in crashing foam on the long pale sand.

Jane, he was thinking, Jane, presumably close to England by now, and what had drawn her back? Certainly not a dead or dying relative. In all the time he had known her she had expressed no fondness for any family, but only a desire to escape from her relatives. He tried to convince himself that she had an innocent reason to return, but in his heart he knew her motive was anything but innocent, and that knowledge hurt. It was his pride that had been wounded and the injury felt deep and incapable of repair.

He tried to divert his thoughts by contemplating his new duties; to protect a pair of Engineers from being captured, and to do it without alerting the enemy to British interest in the Adour estuary. Yet the French were already taking precautions against a landing on the estuary's northern bank, the presence of picquets and patrols proved that, and the big map in Wellington's headquarters had revealed a scattering of isolated houses and at least one village along the northern bank of the Adour's estuary, and Sharpe reckoned he was correct in assuming that the picquets were part of a larger force quartered in those buildings. Which meant that if his remnant of a Light Company made any untoward noise then he could be facing a whole battalion of enemy infantry and there would be no chance of keeping the clash silent. There would just be a desperate and noisy retreat to the boats in hope that he left neither corpses nor prisoners behind and the whole reconnaissance would fail. And if it failed then Marshal Soult would doubtless place a formidable force on the estuary's northern bank where the embanked road would make a perfect rampart to shelter the defenders. The more he thought about it, the more hopeless the plan seemed, but he still wanted to execute it. It was a challenge and a challenge to Sharpe was a cause to fight, and if he fought, he won. He would damn well keep it silent, kill the enemy and bring the Engineers safe home and afterwards, he decided, he would ask Wellington for leave to go to England and there make Jane wish she had never been born.

He had thought himself alone on the beach, but then a voice disturbed him. 'Do you believe in heaven, Richard?'

'Eh?' He checked, turned and saw Candelaria. She was cloaked against the cold winter wind.

'Heaven,' she asked lightly, 'is it real for you?'

'I never think about it,' he said. A wave broke and ran up the sand to swirl about his boots.

'I like to walk here,' she said, and pointed out to sea, 'and dream of finding a ship and sailing out there and so home.'

'Is that heaven?'

She nodded and, once the wave had been sucked back into the ocean, she took his arm and walked on. 'Heaven is home, yes?'

'Not sure I have a home,' Sharpe said.

'In England?'

'I did have one,' he said, and thought of Lady Grace and immediately felt tears at his eyes, 'but it's gone. Got nowhere now.'

'So where will you go?'

'When the war ends?' He thought for a few seconds. 'Back to London, I suppose. It's the only place I know well.'

'And what will you do there?'

'I don't know,' he said, thinking that he would probably drink, lie, steal and cheat, just as he had before he joined the army. 'Find a room, I suppose.' In his mind that room would be close to where his mother had been a whore in the east end of the city. He smiled. 'But it won't be heaven, I can promise you that.'

'I will find heaven,' Candelaria said, 'and my son will be there, and Demônio!'

'That was your husband?'

She laughed. 'Demônio was my dog. He was a wonderful dog, so loving and so fearless. The French killed him because he growled at them. But I know he waits for me, and when I enter heaven he will run and leap into my arms.'

Sharpe saw the tears glistening in her eyes.

'I rather think I'll be going to the other place.'

'Oh no!'

'I'm not much about religion. Makes no sense to me.'

'It's not supposed to make sense,' she said sternly, 'it is about love and belief and hope.'

'I've hardly ever been to church,' Sharpe said. 'I've fought inside a few of them, and made a right bloody mess of them, but I never had much time for prayer and such.'

'Church!' she said scornfully. 'Religion is not about church. It is about being alone and talking to God.'

'And you do that?'

'Every day,' she said. 'I give God my sadness and He gives me peace.'

'Then you're lucky.'

'He will listen to you too, Richard.'

God might listen, Sharpe thought, but He won't bring Jane back, and He won't stop the French sending a massive sortie from the city to crush the impudent few soldiers stranded on the northern shore of the Adour's estuary.

'And what will you do at the war's end?' he asked.

'Go home. Find a dog that needs loving. Pick olives, grow vines, maybe marry again?'

'You have land?' Sharpe reckoned vines and olives needed land.

'His lordship will look after me.'

'Him and God, eh?'

'And they will look after you too.'

Sharpe laughed at that. 'I have to get through the war first, love.'

'His lordship says you fight best when you are angry.'

'Then God help the goddamned French,' Sharpe said, 'because I'm angry now.'

'God will never help the French,' she said bitterly. 'They are a disgrace to His creation. Hell will be filled with Frenchmen.'

'I'll not lack for company then.'

She rapped his arm, surprisingly sharply. 'Do not say that, Richard! You do God's work.'

And he would do it on the northern bank of the Adour, that was protected by sand, tides, churning surf, and enemy picquets. Then rain came on the west wind and they turned back to the city.

'We'll be on picquet duty,' Sharpe told Lieutenant Kelleher, the acting commander of the Light Company. Sharpe had wanted to bring Peter d'Alembord, but it made more sense to leave d'Alembord to command what was left of the Prince of Wales's Own Volunteers. Sharpe knew he should have left Pat Harper behind too, because Harper was the best man to keep the battalion's discipline tight, but Sharpe could not imagine going into action without Harper, and so had brought the Sergeant Major along.

'Picquet duty? Sounds easy, sir,' Kelleher said.

'It won't be. We'll likely confront a few Frenchmen, but they have to be killed or captured silently. No rifle or musket shots.'

Kelleher looked dubious. 'Where do we do this, sir?'

'Close to Bayonne, too close.' Judging from his glimpse of the map he reckoned the Engineers would be reconnoitring the embankment about four or five miles west of Bayonne. 'And we leave tomorrow,' he told Kelleher, 'and I expect to be back the next day. Then we go back to the battalion.'

'Bad luck, sir.'

'Bad luck?' Sharpe asked.

'Captain d'Alembord said your wife was here, sir? I thought you'd get a few days with her.'

'Jane's gone home, something to do with a sick mother.' The lie sounded very unconvincing to Sharpe.

'Rotten timing, sir.'

'It is, but we'll all be home soon. We just have a war to win first.'

Sharpe slept in the Light Company's quarters, but slept badly, tormented by his own thoughts and by noise from the fishing harbour. When he finally dragged himself from the straw bed and had scrounged a cup of tea from the duty men standing guard at the warehouse entrance, he walked to the harbour's edge and saw, in the dim fading night, a fleet of fishing vessels lashed together. Labourers were carrying baulks of timber from boat to boat.

'God knows what that's about, sir,' Pat Harper's voice came from behind him.

'Couldn't sleep, Pat?'

'Just woke early, sir. And those bastards are making enough noise to wake the devil.' He nodded towards the men carrying the heavy baulks of timber from one fishing boat to another. The timber was being used to strengthen the gunwales of the boats, each of which was about thirty or forty feet long and had three masts. 'They're called *chass marries*,' Harper said. 'I was talking to an Engineer yesterday, nice fellow, and he reckons they're handy little ships. He tells me they're making them into gunboats, but it's bleeding obvious what they're for.'

'Obvious?'

Harper spat into the harbour. 'Nosey isn't going to attack Bayonne head on, sir. He'll lose too many men and, God bless him, he doesn't like losing men. So he's fetching all these wee *chass marries* to cross the river and attack them from the north. And the Crapauds ain't fools. Marshal Soult will know they're here and be waiting for them.'

Sharpe glanced along the quay and saw a dozen or more French civilians watching the activity below. Any one of them, he thought, could be a spy who knew how to smuggle messages across Bayonne's formidable defences and the heavy slabs of timber that were being used to strengthen the gunwales were surely being placed where the bridge's massive cables would rest. 'Perhaps they're gunboats, Pat?'

'They are making some gunboats,' Harper said, 'but God spare us being on one.'

'We won't be, Pat.'

'Thank God for that. Flimsy bloody things! I'll show you.' He led Sharpe along the quay to where three large rowing boats were moored by a flight of stone steps. Each boat was twenty feet or more long and two of them were armed with massive eighteen-pounder siege guns. They were captured French guns and evidently old because they were made of iron that had rusted. Artificers were building a vast carriage in the heart of the third boat for the last barrel, which lay on the quayside. Two men were sawing a heavy piece of timber while a third was chipping a hollow into another, plainly designed to hold a trunnel of the massive gun. 'Fire one of those bloody things,' Harper said scornfully, 'and the boat will shake to scrap!'

'Not if those bleeding monkeys do their work proper,' a voice spoke from behind Sharpe, who turned to see a man in shirtsleeves. 'Captain Bisby,' he introduced himself, and Sharpe realised Bisby was the engineer who was to accompany Crittenden on the exploration of the estuary, 'nice to see you again, Paddy,' Bisby continued, nodding companionably to Harper, and Sharpe held his breath. The last man who had called Harper 'Paddy' had ended up under the surgeon's care, but to Sharpe's astonishment Harper just grinned and nodded back.

'Major Sharpe,' Sharpe introduced himself.

'Stone the bleeding crows,' Bisby said, 'you're the fellow who nicked an eagle off the Frogs.'

'Sergeant Major Harper helped,' Sharpe said.

'He looks useful,' Bisby said, 'not like those bleeding monkeys. Use a saw on that socket!' he bellowed. 'That bloody chisel will take all week! Bloody hell fire, a squirrel could chew it out quicker! *Más rápido*, you bloody monkey, *más rápido*!'

Sharpe looked down into the nearest boat and saw that the artificers were all dressed in ragged sun-faded uniforms that had started as yellow and now were almost white. 'Spanish cavalry?' he asked, surprised.

'We're short of artificers,' Bisby said, 'so they give me these bleeding monkeys. It's a punishment detail, they're deserters and were caught ransacking a farmhouse, so now they're mine until they're shipped home to their old regiment, whereupon,' he slowed his voice and spoke the next words very clearly, 'they will be bleeding shot or bloody well hanged! Ain't that right, Lieutenant Carey?'

Sharpe turned to see a sullen, redcoated Lieutenant standing nearby with two Privates armed with muskets.

'Bleeding Provost,' Bisby said quietly and savagely. The Provosts were the army's police and Bisby, like most soldiers, was suspicious of them.

'You're guarding these men?' Sharpe asked the Lieutenant.

Carey gazed at Sharpe, evidently unsure whether he was an officer or not. He saw a man in ragged uniform with unkempt hair, but he did have a sword and what had once been a lavish red sash. Then he saw Sharpe's scarred face and straightened. 'Yes, sir.'

'They're deserters?

'Their regiment is up-country with General Hill, sir. These bastards were found a mile from here.'

'Robbing a farmhouse?'

'Thieving, killing and raping, sir.'

'Why not just hang them here?' Sharpe asked.

'That would upset the Spaniards, sir,' Carey said, making his opinion of Spaniards plain with the sour tone of his voice. 'As soon as they finish with Captain Bisby, sir, we march them back to their regiment and let them make an example of them.'

Sharpe drew Bisby back to the edge of the quay. 'You're from London?' he asked, already knowing the answer from Bisby's accent.

'Spitalfields.'

'Not so far from me,' Sharpe said. 'Limehouse,' he said, shaking Bisby's hand.

'You've come a long way, Major,' Bisby said.

'You too.'

'It's in the blood, innit? You want a halfway proper job done then fetch a cockney. Or an Irishman,' he added the last three words hurriedly, 'but not a dozen dozy Spaniards. And look at that bleeding lump!' He waved towards the eighteen-pounder barrel waiting on the quayside. 'Over two tons! Then we got to carry powder and shot. Thank Christ I won't be on board. You gonna be part of this circus, Major?'

'Circus?' Sharpe asked, flicking his gaze towards a pair of civilians who were plainly listening to the conversation.

'Harbour defence.' Bisby had caught the glance. 'These babies lurk just inside the entrance here and if the bloody Frogs come, it's bang and bye-bye, Monsewer. And why they don't just mount them on the bloody quayside, I do not know. But the bloody navy wanted gunboats, so gunboats we will have.'

The gunboats, Sharpe suspected, were for the Adour, not to defend Saint-Jean-de-Luz's harbour, but Bisby was plainly aware of the town's inhabitants overhearing and betraying information. Sharpe also reckoned Harper was right, and that the boats were too fragile for the massive guns they would carry.

'Pablo, you idiot!' Captain Bisby roared. He was looking down into the nearest boat. 'Leave room for the capsquare, you bloody mooncalf! I marked it up! Or did you think I was drawing pretty pictures for you? Christ!' He turned back to Sharpe. 'No wonder they joined the bloody army! No one else would want them.'

'That's why I joined,' Sharpe said, 'no one else wanted me.'

'Really?' Bisby asked.

'Well, a judge gave me a choice.'

'Me too,' Bisby laughed. 'And you, Paddy?'

'I was just bloody hungry, sir.'

'*Thornside* coming alongside!' a voice bellowed from the harbour, and Sharpe turned to see a smartly varnished launch propelled by eight oarsmen gliding into the stone steps. 'Can you move that lump out of the way?' the voice continued. It was the helmsman of the launch, a big and confident man who was sitting beside a naval officer.

'Move it!' Bisby yelled down to the men fashioning the mount for the eighteen-pounder gun. It took the men in the boat time to unmoor the craft and clumsily move it a few feet into the harbour where they tossed an anchor overboard and thus made space for the launch. The oarsmen raised their painted blades and the helmsman brought the boat alongside the steps as the officer stood up. The officer was thin, very tall, and his face was obscured by his battered cocked hat worn fore and aft. He leaped with surprising nimbleness onto the slippery stone steps and ran up to the quay, stopped, and grinned.

'Captain Sharpe!'

'Major now,' Harper said disapprovingly.

'By the blessed Lord God, of course! Wonderful to see you, sir!'

Sharpe could not resist smiling. 'Harry Collier!' He shook Collier's hand. 'I heard you have your own ship now?'

'His Majesty's ship *Thornside*,' Collier said proudly, 'a mere brig, but still the finest ship in the king's navy, sir! Fourteen guns and a thorn in the side of the Frogs! Except tonight my fellows are reduced to sailing *David* and *Goliath*.'

'*David* and *Goliath*?' Sharpe asked.

'A pair of *chasse-marées*,' Collier said, sounding disappointed. 'Local fishing boats, French-built, of course, but remarkably seaworthy despite that. *David* is thirty-six feet overall and *Goliath* four feet longer. Sir Joel named them.'

'You're taking them to the Adour estuary?' Sharpe asked in a very low voice.

'I am,' Collier said quietly, 'only no one's to know that, sir.'

'Then I believe I'm coming with you,' Sharpe said.

'Oh, that's capital, sir, just capital!' Lieutenant Collier actually danced two or three steps in his delight. Sharpe had met Midshipman Collier on board Chase's ship and remembered him as an eager, enthusiastic midshipman of thirteen or fourteen, and even now, though Collier was nine years older and had grown at least two or three inches taller than Sharpe, he still had a face of remarkable freshness and youth. 'Oh it will be capital, sir!' Collier exclaimed and took Sharpe's hand to shake it again. 'And I see you've met Captain Bisby! He's coming too! Only the best will sail to Corunna tonight!' The last few words were spoken loudly.

'Corunna?' Harper muttered to Sharpe.

'That's what he said.'

'I thought we'd done with Spain!' Harper sounded indignant.

'Evidently not,' Sharpe said. He did not believe for a moment that Corunna was their destination, but Collier had spoken loudly enough for any bystander to hear the name, and doubt-less Marshal Soult would hear it by the evening. Meanwhile Sharpe's task, he thought grimly, was to do the impossible; to make sure Marshal Soult never suspected that the British were interested in the northern bank of the Adour estuary, and he was to do it silently. And that, he thought, was the almost impossible demand; he had no doubt his men could protect the two Engineers to do whatever they were sent to do, but silently? For the night to be silent the enemy must agree not to make a noise too, and Sharpe reckoned that was an impos-sibility, then his thoughts were interrupted as Lieutenant Collier snapped to attention and saluted, and Sharpe turned to see Captain Crittenden approaching. Crittenden returned Collier's salute, then beckoned to Sharpe.

'A word, Major?'

'Of course, sir,' Sharpe said, and followed Crittenden a few paces down the quay to a spot where they could not be over-heard.

'This night's endeavours,' Crittenden spoke in a low voice, 'promise to be a waste of time.'

'Sorry to hear that, sir,' Sharpe said.

'Lord Wellington tells me there's a shortage of artificers.'

'I heard the same, sir.'

'Half of them have gone north to Sir John Hope, where they'll be needed to construct the necessary works on the Adour's southern bank, and the rest are still finishing the work on those wretched bridges across the Nive that gave us so much trouble. No time to get any of them here by midday.'

Sharpe glanced down into the boat where the Spanish

prisoners were working. It still seemed ridiculous to him to mount such a heavy cannon in so small a boat, but that was not his problem. 'Do we need artificers, sir?' he asked.

'We need to dig pits, Major,' Crittenden said stiffly. 'It's not enough to walk the ground, we have to explore it. We need to dig deep pits, and then fill them in again so the French don't suspect our intentions.' He hesitated. 'Can your men dig pits?'

Sharpe bridled at the question. 'My men will be busy keeping you safe, sir. I could probably spare a couple of them, but if there's trouble I'll need them. What about your sailors?'

Crittenden shook his head. 'If we need a quick departure, Major, we need them ready to push the boats off the beach. And the pits will have to be deep, at least three or four feet?' He turned towards the harbour's mouth as if seeking inspiration from the wind-fretted sea beyond.

'You need men,' Sharpe said slowly, an idea tantalising him, 'do you have a slip of paper, sir? And a pencil?'

'I do.' Crittenden pulled a scrap of paper from a pocket and gave it with a stub of pencil to Sharpe.

Sharpe, aware that his handwriting was no better than a child's, rested the paper on the breech of the huge eighteen-pounder gun and wrote carefully before giving the paper back to Crittenden who frowned as he read it. 'Lieutenant Carey of the Provosts? How can he help?'

'Ask Lord Wellington to put Lieutenant Carey's prisoners under my command, sir.' Sharpe gestured towards the Spaniards working in the boat. 'Just the prisoners, sir, we won't need Lieutenant Carey or his redcoats.'

297

'Those fellows in the yellow coats?' Crittenden asked dubiously. 'They have tools? Spades?'

'They do, sir! They're Spanish artificers, best pit-diggers in the world. Famous for it!' Sharpe said, sounding enthusiastic because he had just realised how he could do the impossible. His handful of poachers and murderers just needed the help of some thieves, killers, and deserters.

'I hope you know what you're doing, Sharpe,' Crittenden said, then set off towards the headquarters.

Sharpe beckoned to Harper. 'Pat, I need you on the scrounge. I want six shovels and a dozen sword-bayonets. Do it official if you can, otherwise steal them.'

'Are we digging or killing, sir?'

'We're doing the impossible, Pat, the bleeding goddamned bloody impossible.'

'So nothing special then?'

'Nothing special, Pat.'

We are Riflemen, Sharpe thought, and we do the impossible.

CHAPTER ELEVEN

'It's a lugger,' Lieutenant Collier said happily.

Sharpe, crammed in the stern of the boat called *David*, grunted, 'I thought it was a shass-marry,' he said unhappily.

'It is, but she's rigged as a lugger. Three lugsails and a jib!' The boat, despite her small size, boasted three masts, each of which was hung with a sail attached to a slanted yard. 'They're handy little boats,' Collier continued enthusiastically, 'can sail surprisingly close to the wind!'

'Bloody cold wind,' Sharpe grumbled.

'We'll turn away from it when we get far enough offshore,' Collier, who had insisted on being the helmsman, adjusted the tiller. 'It won't be so bad when we run northwards.'

'When will that be?'

'Probably dusk,' Collier said. 'We keep going westwards till we're out of sight of the land, which means Boney's spies will think we're set for Spain, then we'll fly north! And in this sou'westerly it will be a treat!'

A wet treat, Sharpe thought sourly.

The two boats, *David* and *Goliath*, had still not cleared Saint-Jean-de-Luz's harbour, but were beating across the outer harbour through short, cold waves that threw up bucketloads of spray that rattled down on her crowded decks. Half of the Light Company were in the boat, along with the dozen Spanish deserters who had been put under Sharpe's command for the night and who were now armed with sword-bayonets. A half-dozen seamen from Collier's ship were the official crew to man the halliards and sheets, while next to Sharpe on the stern thwart was Captain Bisby. The *Goliath* had experienced trouble hoisting her mainsail and was following *David*. She had the rest of Sharpe's men and a scowling Captain Crittenden in her stern.

'I hate bloody ships,' Bisby snarled, 'unnatural bloody things. How much further?'

'We haven't left the harbour yet, sir,' Collier said cheerfully, 'but taking into account the inshore shoals, we probably have thirty nautical miles to go?'

'Inshore shoals?' Bisby asked suspiciously.

'It's the devil's own coast here,' Collier still sounded cheerful, 'lots of underwater ledges and obstructions; good for fishermen, I'm told, but for us they'd be a quick passage to Fiddler's Green.'

Bisby muttered a curse on Fiddler's Green, the imagined heaven for dead soldiers and sailors where ale, food and women were in ample supply, then glanced forward and looked alarmed. 'We're going to hit that bugger!'

A naval ship was bearing down on them in the narrow entrance channel. She had shortened sail in readiness for entering the harbour, but was still coming fast on the brisk south-westerly wind. Water broke white around her cutwater, and the afternoon sun shone on her white-banded hull with its closed gunports.

'We'll miss the bugger,' Collier said confidently, 'she's only a brig sloop, but doesn't she look grand?'

'Looks big enough to splinter us,' Bisby replied.

'Johnny Tarrant knows his business,' Collier said, evidently talking about the Captain of the looming vessel, 'and he knows we'll leave him to starboard to keep the wind in our sails. See! He's making room for us. Only two masts, but fast as hell! A fine ship, the *Pelican*!'

For a heartbeat Sharpe did not respond, then remembered *Pelican* was the ship Jane had taken to Britain. 'Back from England already?' he asked excitedly.

'England?' Collier laughed. 'Good God, sir, no. She's back from Corunna! She had to ferry some silly Spanish bitch who'd run away from her family to be with some damned Frog. We said she was going to England because there are bloody privateers in Biscay and we didn't want them hearing of *Pelican*'s voyage and pouncing on her. Brig sloops don't carry many guns, and it wouldn't do to return the silly girl's corpse to her dad, would it?'

Sharpe said nothing. Until Collier talked of Corunna he had been supposing that it was too much to hope that Jane would return immediately, but now he understood that she must have been one of the chaperones who had accompanied the Spanish girl home. Jane's lie about her mother dying was just to protect the secrecy of the mission. He laughed, not because there was anything amusing in the situation, but simply from the relief that all his agonising over Jane had been misplaced. He gazed up at the brig sloop as it slid past, hearing the rush of water down her flank, seeing the gleam of copper where she leaned from the wind to reveal her lower hull, then seeing a fair-haired woman leaning over the stern rail.

'Jane!' he bellowed, his voice lost in the welter of water and wind, and then the *David* hit the wash of the *Pelican* and bucked violently, sending gallons of cold water spraying down her length.

'Did you say something, sir?' Collier asked, wrenching the tiller to put the *David* back on course.

'A sneeze,' Sharpe said.

'Then God bless you, sir.'

And just maybe, Sharpe thought, God had blessed him. If he survived this night he would be back in Saint-Jean-de-Luz by midday tomorrow and in bed with Jane by dusk. 'How long will it take us to get home tomorrow?' he asked Collier.

'In this wind, sir? It will be a bugger, we might have to beat westwards a fair ways to make it home. Might not make harbour till evening, and can I prevail on you to take supper with me on board *Thornside*? It would be a pleasure, sir.'

'I rather think Lord Wellington will want to speak with me,' Sharpe said, thinking nothing of the sort and feeling churlish for turning down a generous offer but anticipating pleasures of a different kind. 'Maybe another evening?'

'We'll make it happen!' Collier said enthusiastically, then called to one of the six sailors who crewed the boat, 'Lucas! Give Captain Bisby a bucket!'

Bisby was already violently sick. Sharpe offered his canteen so the poor man could swill out his mouth. 'Bloody boats,' Bisby muttered as he handed the canteen back.

'Only one cure for seasickness,' Collier said happily, 'sit under a tree!'

'Bloody sailors,' Bisby still muttered. 'We're wasting our time, sir,' he added in a lower voice.

'Wasting it?' Sharpe asked.

Bisby hesitated, looked as if he was about to throw up again, then managed to resist the impulse. 'That bloody Crittenden,' he growled.

'What of him?'

'Digging pits! He thinks he can dig deep enough and anchor five posts by filling the pits with soil and stones, but once the cables are tensioned those posts will drag out of the ground like pips from a rotten apple.' He spat overboard as the *David* struck a large wave and bucked like a startled horse.

'Five?' Sharpe asked. 'I thought there were to be three cables.'

'Five now. Trying to spread the bloody load.'

Collier pulled the tiller. 'A bit lively,' he said apologetically as the boat lurched.

Bisby groaned. 'Pits and posts,' he muttered, 'nonsense. The ground is bloody sodden! Put twenty bloody posts there and they'll just rip out like rotten teeth.'

'So how would you do it?' Sharpe asked, hoping to keep Bisby's mind off his rebellious stomach.

'There's an embankment there, right sir?'

'That's what they tell me,' Sharpe agreed.

'So the inside of the embankment is probably sloped at

about forty-five bloody degrees. We lead the cable ends over the embankment and anchor them, of course.'

'With posts?'

'Bugger the posts, they won't hold. You saw those bleeding great French eighteen-pounders I was fitting into launches. That was just make-work, 'cos those lousy launches will split apart if you fire a three-pounder, let alone an eighteen. I want the guns for the bloody bridge. Loop each cable around one of those and just drop it at the bottom of the embankment. Then you tighten the cables, and each rope will be trying to drag over two tons of useless Crapaud metal up a steep sodden slope! They'll never manage it! Those guns will dig in and anchor the bloody cables. The only point of going to the bloody place is to check how steep the inland slope is. I need two more barrels now they've decided on five instead of three cables, but we've captured a score of the bloody things. Oh God.' He turned away and vomited over the boat's stern. 'I'm right,' he said when he had recovered, 'but they won't listen to me. Bloody Crittenden is a gentleman, ain't he? Went to school and passed exams, didn't he? But he can't piss straight even if you hold it for him.' He groaned and leaned over the transom again.

Sharpe cupped his hands. 'Pat!'

'Sir?'

'Canteen!'

Harper looked stubborn for a moment, then decided he could help after all and his canteen was passed back to Sharpe who offered it to Bisby. 'That's brandy,' he said, 'it should settle your stomach.'

'A corner table in the Pig and Whistle would do a better job.' Bisby groaned.

'I've drunk in that pub,' Sharpe said, 'good ale.'

'The Goat and Fiddle sells better,' Bisby said. He took a swig of the brandy and handed the canteen back to Sharpe. 'Kill or cure,' he said, then nodded at Harper who was sitting by the mizzenmast. 'Thanks Paddy!'

'Welcome, Biz!'

'Biz?' Sharpe asked.

'That's what my friends call me, and any man who can supply brandy in the middle of a bloody storm is a friend.'

Collier insisted it was not a storm, merely a lively 'blow', but both small boats were making heavy weather of the seas, slamming their bows into steepening waves as they struggled west towards the setting sun. It seemed to Sharpe, in the cold gloom, that it took forever before Collier reckoned they were well clear of the coast's underwater dangers and turned the *David* north, whereupon the boat's pitching motion lessened and, as the sheets were loosened and the sails caught the following wind, their speed increased. *Goliath* followed and Sharpe marvelled that Captain Crittenden, the senior naval officer in the two boats, was content to let young Collier set the course.

'He trusts me, sir,' Collier explained when Sharpe asked. 'He knows I know this coast a damn sight better than he does. I've already taken *Thornside* into the estuary once, and damned exciting it was too. Captain Crittenden's ship wouldn't dare go within two miles of the Adour's bar!'

'And you can find the entrance in the darkness?'

'Find it and cross it, sir!' Collier sounded utterly confident.

Sharpe had no idea where that confidence came from. The light was fading fast, the sky obscured by clouds, and though an occasional glimpse of land showed to the east, he could not imagine how those glimpses could be helpful for navigation. It would be full dark when they reached the estuary and somehow they must find the narrow gap in the shoals and hope to survive the tumultuous water.

Bisby was silent with his misery and Collier was standing at the tiller, his eyes searching the eastern horizon. Sharpe settled back as comfortably as he could and thought about the night ahead. Bloody madness, he thought, as it began to rain, the drops swamped by the spray being thrown back from the boat's bows. He was to lead his company onto a shore guarded by picquets who, he was certain, would have at least a full company of infantry, if not a whole battalion, sheltering in a nearby village or farm, and French companies and battalions were larger than British, while Sharpe's company was at less than half strength. Madness. Of course if his men could silence the French sentries without alerting the men resting in their nearby billets, then success was possible, but all it would take was one panicked shout or a musket shot and the shore would suddenly be swarming with infantry.

He tried to persuade himself that the picquets would not be reinforced by more men billeted close by, that instead they were marched out of Bayonne and marched back when it was time to be relieved, but that made no sense. Why march men several miles each way when there were houses and farms nearby? No, he reckoned, the French would have at least a company of infantry permanently billeted on the north bank, and if those men were alerted to a British force they would be woken and ordered to the beach. Then all the French would need for the night's purpose to be discovered was one prisoner and within two days the whole northern bank of the estuary would be hardened with batteries of twelve-pounder cannons and battalions of infantry lining the embanked roadway, and Wellington's hope of bridging the estuary would be dead.

So how to defeat the company of infantrymen Sharpe suspected would be waiting at the estuary? The only answer he could conjure in the wet darkness was surprise and savagery, but he knew he needed more, and it was then he recalled a dinner he had attended at which the guest of honour had been Sir John Moore. The dinner had been at the barracks in Shorncliffe, where Moore had trained soldiers to be Light Infantrymen and where the 95th Rifles had honed their lethal skills. 'Knife and fork!' Moore had said to a young officer, and at first Sharpe had thought the General was chiding the young man for his table manners, but Moore had another lesson in mind. 'It's just like eating with a knife and fork,' he had continued, 'the fork holds the meat steady and the knife cuts it. Use half your men to hold the enemy's attention, that's the fork, and send the other half round their flank to kill them! They'll have all their attention on the fork and won't even see the knife.'

'We'll knife and fork the bastards,' Sharpe said aloud.

'Sir?' Collier asked.

'Never mind, just thinking aloud.' Then Sharpe wondered if he was thinking to any purpose. He reckoned he could fork and knife the bastards, but at the end of the night he would still have drawn Marshal Soult's attention to the estuary's northern bank. He needed to have his fight, which he thought inevitable, win it, which seemed possible, and deceive Marshal Soult to its purpose, which was impossible, unless the idea he had conjured on the quayside in Saint-Jean-de-Luz succeeded, and now, in the cold night, that idea seemed fanciful. 'Bugger,' he said aloud.

'It's not all bad news,' Collier said cheerfully, pointing north-eastwards. 'We're making good passage! That's Biarritz!'

'How do you know?'

'See the glow in the sky?' Collier still pointed and Sharpe saw the low clouds were reflecting a faint red glow. 'That's our troops in their encampment,' Collier said confidently. 'Sir John Hope's men!'

Sharpe had seen such glows before. Light enough campfires and the flames reflected from clouds and Sir John Hope's men were concentrated around the odd-named village of Biarritz where they faced the south-western corner of the French garrison in Bayonne. 'Not far now?' he asked.

'A couple of hours,' Collier said, 'and we'll start closing the coast now and pray for a sliver of moonlight.'

It seemed unlikely that the prayer would be answered. The rain clouds were thick and Sharpe had seen neither moon nor starlight, but young Collier still exuded a confidence Sharpe could not understand, but then he supposed that he would have needed a lifetime at sea to comprehend the skill needed to take ships through rough, dark seas and survive. Sharpe's skill was to win fights, and he touched the hilt of his big sword.

Knife and fork, he thought, though how that would help him once he was ashore he did not know. 'It's going to be noisy,' he said.

'Noisy, sir?' Collier asked.

'The fight ashore,' Sharpe said. 'Lord Wellington wants it to be silent, but the French will have other ideas.'

'And you don't think you'll need more than an hour ashore, sir?'

'I hope not.'

'Captain Crittenden reckoned on two hours,' Collier said.

Sharpe twisted on the thwart and saw the dim lantern hoisted on *Goliath*'s mainmast. *David* had a similar storm lantern glimmering from her mizzenmast. 'Captain Crittenden,' he said, 'will leave when I tell him to leave.'

'Because you command ashore, sir?' Collier asked.

'I do,' Sharpe said. Crittenden, as a Post-captain in the navy, was the equivalent of a full Colonel in the army, yet he had sensibly agreed to defer to Sharpe once they were ashore, and Sharpe just hoped Crittenden kept to the agreement. He surreptitiously tapped the wooden thwart with his left hand, 'and if I'm killed, Harry, listen to Pat Harper. He knows what he's doing.'

'You're indestructible, sir,' Collier said encouragingly.

'Everyone is until they're not,' Sharpe said gloomily, then cupped his hands, 'Lieutenant Harris!'

'Sir?' Harris shouted back from the bows of the boat.

'All well?'

'Half of them are sick as dogs, sir, but they'll hunt!'

Rifleman Harris was now the officer commanding the Spanish thieves, killers and deserters. Harris was the best

Spanish speaker in the Light Company, so Sharpe had unofficially, and to the amusement of every other member of the company, made him a Lieutenant, an appointment that would only have to last through this night. He had lent Harris his red officer's sash, equipped him with a straight-bladed infantry officer's sword captured from the enemy, and then put him in charge of the dozen Spanish deserters who were persuaded that Harris was indeed *un oficial inglés*. Sharpe had then given Harris strict orders; that the Spaniards were to fight like devils, kill the hated French ruthlessly, and loot whatever they wanted, but there was to be no rape. Those were more or less Sharpe's standing orders anyway.

The yellow-jacketed twelve were equipped with sword-bayonets and had demanded muskets, but while Sharpe had been confident of Pat Harper's ability to lift a dozen blades from the stores, he had doubted that muskets would be so easy. 'They can take muskets and ammunition from the enemy,' he had promised. Now, fearing that they might be facing a full battalion instead of a company of French troops, he wished he had given them muskets, but at least the twelve cavalrymen were eager to fight and, if they did fight well, Sharpe was sure Wellington would arrange for their death sentences to be commuted.

If any needed to be commuted because, if the night went wrong, Sharpe's men would be nothing but corpses on a wet shore and the French would divine what Wellington planned.

Sharpe looked again for the glow of Sir John Hope's fires and saw, to his surprise, that it seemed behind the boat now. 'We're getting near?' he asked Collier.

'Near enough, sir. The current's with us, sir, which helps. But it'll be a right bastard coming back, especially if the wind veers more to the west.'

'Will it?'

'Only God knows, sir, and he's not telling me. But it could back off and then we'll know He's truly an Englishman.'

Sharpe thought of Candelaria's assertion that God hated Frenchmen and hoped she was right, and thinking of her made him remember Jane and what waited for him in another twenty-four hours, and that thought kept him silent as the boat hammered on into the waves, though their impact was lessened as the seas were now angling in from behind the *David*'s stern. He fell into an uncomfortable doze, wondering if he had ever been this cold and wet.

He was jarred into full alertness when Collier ordered the sails shortened. The lugsail on the mizzenmast was lowered completely while the other two sails were slightly lowered, leaving only the jib fully filled with wind. The *David* slowed to a crawl while Collier searched the sea to the east. The *Goliath*, following the smaller ship's example, had also shortened her sails and came close alongside.

'You see something, Lieutenant?' Crittenden bellowed.

'Very soon, sir! I can hear the bar, can't see it!'

'Lead on when you're sure!'

Collier muttered something that Sharpe was certain was uncomplimentary, then looked east and saw another glow of reflected fires and wondered if they had somehow been driven backwards. 'Biarritz?' he asked.

'Bayonne,' Collier said absently, and Sharpe saw that this

glow was much wider and fainter than the earlier one. He knew that Marshal Soult's army was camped about the southern margin of the city where they were defended by their formidable line of earthworks and batteries, and the fires must have been spread over much more land than Sir John Hope's troops occupied around Biarritz. 'I want to be a little north of the city,' Collier said, 'not much, but the river runs north-west out of Bayonne before running to the sea.'

The boat, underpowered by its sails, pitched and rolled in the short waves, but still crept northwards until Sharpe could hear the pounding of surf and half glimpse a line of white churning foam off to the east.

'The bar!' Collier said, then shouted, 'Bosun! All sails up!' The small crew struggled through the supine men on deck and ran up the sails, and the *David* gained speed again as Collier steered her closer to the turmoil to the east. 'Best sit down, sir,' Collier said to Sharpe who had hardly been aware of standing.

Sharpe had been worried about the French on the Adour's northern bank, but he also knew the night's biggest enemy was the river's bar, a shallow obstacle stretched like a wall at the Adour's mouth. There was one small gap in the bar, and even that was a dangerous place because the depth in the gap was still shallow enough to encourage a maelstrom of water above it.

'Bosun!' Collier shouted again. 'Ready to wear ship!'

'Aye aye, sir! Hands to sheets!' the Bosun roared.

'Dear sweet Christ,' Bisby moaned, 'what's happening?'

'We're almost there,' Sharpe said.

'Dry land?'

'That's what we're here to discover, Biz.'

'Very funny.' Bisby groaned, then clung to the gunwale as Collier barked an order and the boat turned eastwards with a mighty lurch as the sails hammered across the hull and boomed like small cannons as they caught the wind again.

'Keep bailing!' Collier called, and Sharpe's wet and cold men obediently scooped water from the boat's bilges and hurled it overboard with their shakoes. 'Pray I got this right,' Collier said as he sat again next to Sharpe. 'Usually there are a pair of tall leading marks,' Collier said, 'but ever since I brought *Thornside* through the gap the bloody French have chopped them down.'

'Leading marks?' Sharpe asked.

'One tall pole on the southern bank, sir, and another on a hill a mile or so inland. Line the two up and you're headed for the centre of the gap. But even with the marks they lose ships every week.'

'You're worried?'

'Terrified,' Collier said, sounding anything but concerned. 'Get this wrong and we'll be turned over on the bar and pounded to matchwood. Here we go! Hold tight, everyone!'

To Sharpe it seemed as if the boat gathered speed and then plunged into a wave that shuddered every plank in the hull. There was no white foam ahead, but plenty on either side, and Sharpe closed his eyes as what seemed like a ton of spray shattered down the boat's length. The *David* rocked violently, pitched her bows up and the wet sails boomed again as the hull crashed back into the water. Then, suddenly, there was peace, or rather no rocking and no pitching, and the boat was gliding on small unthreatening waves.

'By God, I'm a genius,' Collier said happily.

'We're through?' Sharpe asked.

'Through and alive,' Collier said, turning to see the dim shape of the *Goliath* emerging from the entrance, 'and so are they,' he added.

'So we can go ashore?' Bisby asked.

'One and a half nautical miles upriver,' Collier said, 'just about where the river turns towards the sea.'

The glow in the sky was brighter now and Sharpe could even see lights on both banks. Not a lot of lights, but evidence that there were houses on either side of the estuary, though those to the north were dimmer and farther apart, and some, he reckoned, must be hidden by the embanked road. Sharpe looked back and saw that the lantern was still hoisted on *Goliath*'s foremast. 'Won't they think it's strange for ships to be coming into the river now?'

'No, bless their squalid little Frog hearts, sir, they'll think we're fishermen late home from the sea.' Collier glanced left and right. 'Tide's still flooding, sir, but it'll be slack water any time now. When you go ashore, I'll stay with the boat and keep it from being stranded by the ebb.'

'We'll be as quick as we can,' Sharpe said, knowing that men had to dig pits to Crittenden's satisfaction before he could leave. 'But if the French come for you then push off and wait till I've killed the buggers.'

'I'm sure it won't come to that, sir,' Collier said with his usual confidence.

Sharpe faced forward. 'Lieutenant Harris!'

'*Si señor?*'

'You and your squad land first, once on the beach wait for my orders. Sergeant Major?'

'Sir?'

'Wait with your men till I'm ashore. Hagman?'

'Mister Sharpe?'

'Don't wait for me, just take your boys to the right. Come back when you're done.'

'Sir!' Hagman acknowledged.

'Keep it as silent as possible,' Sharpe called to the whole boat, 'but if things go to buggery, shoot!' He was damned if he would lose any men for want of noise.

Sharpe turned. 'Biz? Stick with me.'

'Like cement,' Bisby muttered.

It seemed oddly lighter now they were in the wide river, and Sharpe could make out the dark banks on either side. Stranger still, he could see small fires dotted along the northern beach and reckoned those must mark the positions of the French sentries. He counted five before the river vanished to the south, but guessed there must be more on the next stretch of the Adour. What fools, he thought, to mark their positions! But he supposed the picquets were wet and cold, and their officers had no suspicion that Wellington was interested in this estuary. The river here was far wider than any pontoon bridge Sharpe could remember, indeed he estimated the Adour was near to half a mile across from bank to bank. 'Bloody long bridge,' he muttered to Captain Bisby.

'Think of it as four or five short bridges stitched together,'

Bisby said, then stood to gaze ahead. 'Are we there yet?' he croaked.

'Bosun!' Collier called. 'We'll wear ship in a moment!'

'Wear ship, aye aye, sir,' the Bosun replied and sailors moved to the leeward sheets.

'Hold on, everybody!' Collier called, then thrust the tiller to windward. The boat lurched, the sails slammed across the hull and the *David* was suddenly creaming northwards to the bank. Collier had sensibly decided to land them between two of the small fires. Sharpe could dimly see three or four other *chasse-marées* on the beach. The *Goliath* followed. For a few heartbeats all Sharpe could hear was the hiss of water seething past the hull, then the *David* struck the shelving beach, everyone lurched forward, the keel grated on sand or shingle and the boat jarred to a stop.

'Welcome to France,' Collier said.

And they went ashore.

Sharpe jumped from the *David*'s bows onto the beach, which was neither sand nor shingle, but glutinous mud. Hagman and his five men had already darted to the right to find and kill the sentries who all seemed to have lit small driftwood fires to offer some comfort during the long, boring hours of keeping watch. Sharpe had no doubts about Hagman. The old poacher could slip through darkness with the stealth and savagery of a weasel, and the mud would make their approach silent. Not that any of the nearer sentries could have missed the noise of two *chasse-marées* beaching themselves, but Sharpe hoped that Collier was right and that the picquets would think them local fishing boats.

'Lieutenant Harris?'

'Sir?'

'Take your fellows to the embankment. Take the shovels! Keep them on this side of it, but go to the top yourself and see what's on the other side. I'll be back with you soon.'

'Sir,' Harris said and called out orders in Spanish. The yellow-coated Dragoons moved to the embankment and crouched.

'Captain Crittenden's in charge till I get back here,' Sharpe said to Harris, 'and if he orders your fellows to dig, then dig. But I really want your fellows for something else, so keep them near here so I can find you.'

'We'll be here, Mister Sharpe,' Harris promised.

'Mind if I cross the embankment?' Bisby asked Sharpe. The Engineer already seemed more cheerful now that he was out of the boat.

'I'd rather you waited for me to get back,' Sharpe said, but he could see that Captain Crittenden was already hurrying towards the embankment, while another dozen of Sharpe's company had jumped ashore from the *Goliath* and now stood on the beach.

'Lieutenant Kelleher!'

'Sir?' The lanky Kelleher tripped on a stone as he hurried towards Sharpe.

Sharpe steadied him. 'Take your dozen men to join Harris's Spaniards. Stay this side of the embankment till I get back.'

'Sir,' Kelleher acknowledged, then turned. 'Sergeant Henderson! To me!'

'Not too loud,' Sharpe said, 'and Harris knows what he's doing so let him do it.'

'Yes, sir,' Kelleher said, plainly disgruntled that he had no authority over 'Lieutenant' Harris and his yellow-jacketed Spaniards.

Crittenden had already disappeared across the embankment, and Sharpe turned back to Bisby. 'You can cross, Biz,' he said, 'but come back if muskets start firing over there. I don't want to lose you.'

'I'm like a flea on a dog, sir, hard to lose.'

'Go,' Sharpe said, smiling. 'Pat! With me!'

Harper led four men, all of them Irish. None of them might possess Hagman's extraordinary stealth, but all were savage in a fight and brave to a fault. 'We'll try to do this silently,' Sharpe said as he led them seawards along the beach, 'but if it's live or die you can use muskets or rifles.' He had slung his own rifle on his shoulder and drawn the long-bladed cavalry sword. He could see six of the small fires strung along the shore, so at most he probably had to deal with just twelve picquets.

The nearest fire was scarce twenty paces away and Sharpe could see one man sitting by the flames while another was standing and staring towards the newly arrived boats. He must have seen Sharpe's men approaching because he advanced a few paces and levelled his musket.

'*Qui est là?*'

'*Vive l'Empereur,*' Harper growled in answer and, astonishingly, the sentry lowered his musket and muttered a quick sentence that meant nothing to Sharpe. The man even turned away, eager to return to the fire's warmth, and Harper simply caught up with the man and clouted him on the side of the head with the brass butt of the volley gun. The man went down into the mud. 'Slit the bastard's throat, Sean,' Harper said, and moved to the man by the fire who was too terrified to make a sound or pick up his musket. He flinched as Harper drew back the volley gun, then made a small sighing noise as he collapsed from the skull-shattering blow. 'Jimmy? This one's yours. Search the eejit first.'

Sharpe caught up with Harper. '*Vive l'Empereur*, Pat?'

'Those lads back at Saint-Pierre told me to say that, sir. They said if you don't know the countersign then that usually works. And it did!'

Sharpe gazed at the next fire, some seventy or eighty yards away. Had the men there seen the brief violence? He could see two men beside the fire, their faces reflecting the flames' light, but neither seemed alarmed.

'I'm reckoning these are local militia, sir,' Harper went on. He had picked up one of the dead men's shakos and peered at it in the small flame light. 'No buggering number on his hat.'

'Makes sense,' Sharpe said. 'Boney wants every man he can get to save France, so he's putting poor militia buggers on coast-watching.'

'Old men and young boys,' Harper said.

Sharpe ignored the pity in Harper's voice. 'The bastards have muskets,' he said, 'and we can't leave them where they are.'

'Lullaby them, sir? Tie them up and sling their guns into the water?'

'Do it,' Sharpe said, 'but bring their guns and pouches back for the Spaniards. You'll find me on the embankment. Try and keep it quiet, Pat, but if you need to, shoot. Even the militia will have some veterans who know their business, so be careful.'

'I promised my ma I'd be home one day, sir, and not in a box. I'll be careful.'

The Irishmen set off towards the next pair of picquets and Sharpe scrambled up the steep side of the embankment. The top was about fifteen feet wide and the road was made of rough stones that had been hammered into a gravel base. Sharpe slid his sword back into its scabbard and wondered if Harper was right and that the enemy here was from the local militia. In one sense that would be good news, they were part-time soldiers who almost certainly lacked the discipline and pride of a line battalion, but on the other hand they were men defending their own homes and all of them could fire a musket. He turned towards the place where he had left Captain Crittenden and Harris and could hear the distant mutter of voices and the louder sound of shovels clashing into the stones of the embankment's roadway.

But at least that, with the wind and rain, was all he could hear. There had been no shots in the night, and no sound of a bugle summoning the enemy, and on the beach the dull lanterns hoisted to the mastheads of *David* and *Goliath* still glimmered undisturbed. He turned and gazed north and could see a long, flat stretch of what he assumed was pastureland, with a single large farmstead perhaps half a mile away. There were lights showing in the house's windows, while off to his right he could see the eerie glow of the French campfires surrounding Bayonne, but he doubted the troops there would bother him. The city was too far away and it would take troops at least two hours to reach this shore. But the farm? If he was in command of the troops watching the estuary's northern bank then that was where he would billet his men. Either there or in the other few farms he could see to east and west. Yet only the one big farm had lit windows, suggesting that someone there was awake. Just to the east of the big house was a large barn with more than enough room for half a battalion to shelter. Christ, he thought, let the enemy have no more than a company! Even a company of competently led militia would be a handful for his own shrunken company to deal with.

He edged gingerly down the steep slope of the embankment's landward face, scrambling the last few paces to land in a waterlogged pasture. The rain beat on his back as he walked towards the sound of the shovels. 'Who goes there?' a voice summoned him from the darkness ahead.

Sharpe recognised the voice. 'It's Major Sharpe, Corporal.'

'And right welcome you are, sir.'

'You know where Captain Crittenden is?'

'He's up on the road, sir. He reckons you can't dig a pit in this bloody marsh.'

'I reckon he's right. Keep watching and well done.' Sharpe turned and laboriously clambered up the embankment again, his feet slipping in the wet grass, but he used his rifle as a crutch and at last reached the roadway where Captain Crittenden was watching three Spaniards hacking at the road.

'I thought you said these fellows were expert artificers,' Crittenden greeted Sharpe.

'They seem to be doing all right, sir,' Sharpe countered. The three men had scraped a hole maybe a foot deep. 'We should have brought pickaxes.'

Crittenden grunted. 'I've at least established we can't sink posts in the lower ground. It's sodden!' He made it sound as if the waterlogged soil was Sharpe's fault. 'But this roadway might suffice.'

'Glad to hear it, sir.'

'The embankment isn't waterlogged,' Crittenden said, 'and if we can go down five or six feet the posts might hold if they're packed with stone from the roadway.'

'Sounds good, sir. So you might be finished soon?'

'I want to get down further,' Crittenden said, 'at least four feet. Another hour at this rate?' he said angrily.

'I'm sure they're doing their best,' Sharpe said placatingly and he patted one yellow-jacketed shoulder and walked on to join Captain Bisby a dozen yards down the roadway. 'Well, Biz?'

'That stupid bugger is making ponds,' Bisby said, nodding towards Crittenden, 'but this embankment will hold the cables. No need for posts, just put junk guns as anchors on the inland side.'

'And the guns weigh two tons each?'

'A bit more.'

'Then how the hell do you get them over the embankment?' Sharpe asked.

'Sheer legs,' Bisby said, 'put timber slabs to stop the poles sinking into the beach, two poles for each crane, bunch of pulleys at the top and a few stout lads to haul on the ropes.

Up the gun goes, swing it over the road and bloody drop it. The bloody things will half bury themselves from the drop alone. Only problem here, sir, is this bleeding road. The friction against those stones will chew into the cables, and even a thirteen-inch cable will fray eventually, and quicker than you think.'

Sharpe looked inland. 'There are cattle out there.'

'Smells like it.'

'Slaughter half a dozen cows,' Sharpe suggested, 'and skin the buggers. Lay the cables on the hides and no friction.'

Bisby suddenly looked cheerful. 'Paddy said you were a clever bugger, sir! That's the answer!'

'You want to tell Captain Crittenden he's wasting his time?'

'I already have, and he told me to piss off.'

'Ah! Army–navy cooperation,' Sharpe said, 'I love it.' He walked back to where Crittenden was snarling at the three Spaniards, who might have delved another six inches. 'When you're satisfied, sir,' he said, 'you will make them fill in the pit?

'Of course I will!' Crittenden bristled. Filling the pit would take more time, but it could not be left open lest the French divined its purpose. 'I'm beginning to think,' Crittenden went on, 'that we don't need to dig further. We're not encountering water.'

Crittenden did not sound entirely certain, but it was, Sharpe supposed, good news. 'How long before you're satisfied, sir?'

'Maybe half an hour?' Crittenden said. 'Maybe an hour? But the sooner we're off this ground and back to sea, the better.'

'Indeed, sir,' Sharpe said. He looked up and down the shore in search of Hagman's and Harper's men. It seemed they were still silencing the picquets so he cupped his hands and raised his voice. 'Lieutenant Kelleher?' he called, 'Harris! To me!'

The two men joined Sharpe who led them a few paces eastward, far enough to be out of Crittenden's earshot. 'I reckon these picquets are billeted in that farm.' He pointed at the dimly lit windows that showed through the incessant rain. 'And the place is big enough to shelter a whole battalion of the bastards.'

'Makes sense,' Harris said.

'I want your men up on this embankment, Lieutenant,' he said to Kelleher. 'If they discover us they'll send reinforcements straight towards us and you stop them. Rifles can fire at any range, but hold your muskets till they're within a hundred paces.'

'You won't be with us, sir?' Kelleher asked nervously.

'No,' Sharpe said, 'but you'll be fine. Just shoot the bastards, and Lieutenant?'

'Sir?'

'It will happen. I'm going to make sure of it.'

'Sir?' Kelleher sounded confused.

'It's all quiet now, Lieutenant, but I intend to kill more than the picquets. You'll probably be outnumbered, but we shoot faster than the Crapauds. I'll leave Dan Hagman and his lads with you. Listen to Dan, he knows how to fight. Now you, Harris.'

'Yes, Mister Sharpe?' Harris sounded eager.

'Bring your Spaniards here,' Sharpe said, kicking the embankment's stones. 'Leave the lads who are digging for Crittenden, but bring all the others. Hagman and Harper will supply your boys with French muskets.'

'They'll like that,' Harris said wolfishly.

'Your Spaniards,' Sharpe said to Harris, 'will go there,' he pointed to the west of the farm, 'and assault the house. I'll be with you and so will Pat's men. Our job is to assault the farm, Harris, and there's three rules.'

'No rape, Mister Sharpe?' Harris offered.

'No rape, no dead civilians and no British corpses or prisoners left behind.'

Harris thought for a heartbeat. 'But the Spaniards . . .' he began.

'Can die for England,' Sharpe said harshly. 'Tell them they're free to plunder the farmhouse, but if any of them die we leave them there, understand?'

'I understand, Mister Sharpe,' Harris said, but sounded confused.

'There's got to be no evidence that this was a British raid,' Sharpe said firmly, 'so we take our own dead with us and pray there'll be none. Lieutenant Kelleher?'

'Sir?' a very nervous Kelleher answered.

'If everything goes wrong at the farm then you'll retreat to the boats with Captains Crittenden and Bisby.' Damn it, Sharpe thought, he should have brought a bugler, because if it came to a retreat then all his men needed to know immediately. But he had no bugler, so they must react to the sound of his whistle. 'The signal for the retreat will be three whistle blasts from me.' Sharpe instinctively checked that his whistle was still on its lanyard. It was.

'Three whistle blasts, sir, yes, sir,' Kelleher sounded as if he deeply wished that signal would sound now.

A click of hobnailed boots on stones sounded and Hagman appeared in the darkness. 'A dozen dead Frogs, Mister Sharpe,' he said happily, 'and we're all safe.'

'Well done, Dan! Now you and your men stay here with Lieutenant Kelleher. I hope you can just rest, but if the Frogs do attack us your job is to keep them looking at this embankment, while the rest of us attack that house.'

'Understood, Mister Sharpe,' Hagman said.

'And if you hear three whistle blasts, Dan, you go to the boats. Tell Lieutenant Collier to wait for me as long as possible.'

'I'll tell him to wait till you're aboard, Mister Sharpe.'

'Not if you've got a company of angry Crapauds firing at you from the shore.'

'They'll be firing high, Mister Sharpe, they always do.'

'You don't wait, Dan,' Sharpe said curtly, 'you go and take the Engineers with you.'

And if that happened, Sharpe thought, then he would be trapped on this bleak shore and by morning Marshal Soult would know that an audacious British reconnaissance had been thwarted on the Adour estuary's northern bank, and within two days that bank would be garrisoned with good troops and batteries of guns. He felt a temptation to leave now, the reconnaissance was as good as done, but the French would naturally assume it had been a British force that slaughtered the picquets and that would defeat Sharpe's purpose as surely as if he left a handful of British corpses. By God, he thought, there were too many 'ifs' in his thinking and if all did go wrong he was not sure how he could get all his men safely off the shore less the couple of corpses he had always planned on leaving behind.

'Get your lads into position along the embankment,' he ordered Kelleher, 'and Dan, well done! Really well done.' He walked back to Captain Crittenden who was testing the depth of his pit with his naval sword. 'Going well?' Sharpe asked.

'Almost done,' Crittenden said, 'the soil's damp, but not nearly as waterlogged as down below.'

'How long do you need, sir?'

'Twenty minutes?' Crittenden said, straightening, 'and the French seem fast asleep.'

Not for long, Sharpe thought, but said nothing and then was startled by a flash of light coming from the sentry fire nearest the sea. The light was large, sudden and red, and in its fading glow Sharpe saw a cloud of smoke, and a heartbeat later came the massive boom of Harper's volley gun. A crackle of rifle and musket shots followed, then silence.

Sharpe turned. 'Lieutenant Harris!'

'Sir?'

'To me! And all of your men, now!'

The silent night had ended and, as if to accentuate the change, a bugle sounded from the house where Sharpe suspected the main French force was billeted.

He gazed at the far house, waiting to see if his conjecture was right and, at the same time, felt a fierce exaltation. He had the noisy fight he had planned, he had wanted, and now must bloody well win.

CHAPTER TWELVE

The first reaction to the noise came from Captain Crittenden who turned on Sharpe. 'You fool! Who started that?'

'Pat Harper, I suspect.'

'You goddamn idiot! The whole point—'

'Shut up!' Sharpe interrupted the irate Crittenden. 'We have a fight to win.' He was still gazing at the far house and saw what he expected to see, the flicker of shadowy figures outlined against the dim lights in the downstairs windows. 'Dan!' he shouted.

'We have to leave!' Crittenden bellowed at Sharpe.

As a Post-captain in the navy Crittenden far outranked Sharpe, but Sharpe had endured his fill of the man. 'I told you to shut up,' he snarled, 'we have a fight to win. Dan!'

'Mister Sharpe?' the reply came.

'See those men at the farm?'

'I see them!'

'Kill some!'

Crittenden turned. 'Do not open fire!' he shouted. 'And that is an order!'

Sharpe knelt, pulled the cork from the muzzle of his rifle, and put the weapon to his shoulder. The gun had been loaded in Saint-Jean-de-Luz and he knew he should have recharged the pan. He doubted any water had found its way into the plugged barrel, but the lock was far more exposed, and he suspected it would misfire, but he pulled the doghead back two clicks.

'What are you doing?' Crittenden demanded angrily.

'My duty,' Sharpe said and pulled the trigger. He thought it unlikely that he would hit any men at the far farm, but his aim was to draw their attention to the embankment. This was the fork, the knife would come.

The flint struck the frizzen, the sparks leaped and the powder in the pan hissed before, to Sharpe's surprise, the rifle fired and the stock struck back into his shoulder. He stood, already taking another cartridge from his pouch.

'Fill your bloody hole,' he told Crittenden, 'then wait at the boats.'

'Damn you, Sharpe! This is a catastrophe! And all your damned fault, you oaf!'

Sharpe was still gazing north and was rewarded by a ragged volley from the distant French, whose range gave them even less chance of hitting a target than Sharpe with his rifle. His glimpse of the volley being fired gave him a crude estimate of the numbers he faced, though counting muzzle flames at that distance in the night was crude indeed, but he suspected there was at least one company of French militia at the farm. Say forty or fifty men? He spat the ball into the muzzle and slid the ramrod out. To his surprise Crittenden said nothing more.

He was on his belly now, evidently sheltering from the erratic and ill-aimed fire from the French. That surprised Sharpe because Crittenden had shown conspicuous courage over the last days, but he said nothing, just turned back, cupped his hands and shouted, 'Lieutenant Kelleher!'

'Sir?' came a nervous reply.

'Rifles can keep firing, save the muskets till the enemy are one hundred paces away!'

'Yes, sir!'

Sharpe turned seawards as boots pounded on the road's stones. 'Is that you, Pat?'

'It is and all in one piece, sir!'

'What happened?'

'The sentries were being relieved, so they were, and their officer didn't like us.'

'So you shot.'

'I did!' Harper sounded pleased with himself. 'What's the matter with that fellow?' He was staring at Crittenden. 'Is he dead?'

'I hope not, he's just taking shelter.'

'Looks dead to me,' Harper said and nudged Crittenden with a boot. The naval officer did not move.

Sharpe knelt and pulled at Crittenden's shoulder hard enough to dislodge the Captain's cocked hat and Sharpe saw blood.

'Bloody hell!'

'They got him?' Harper asked.

'At this range? A musket ball should be spent!'

'That one wasn't,' Harper said, kneeling beside Sharpe.

A musket ball had struck Crittenden on the side of his head and presumably pierced his brain.

'A damned lucky shot,' Sharpe said. Lucky for me, he thought vengefully. 'Connolly?'

'Mister Sharpe?' the Rifleman responded.

'Carry his body to the boats, and make sure you take his hat too. Then come back.'

Connolly scooped up the body and hat and clambered down the seawards side of the embankment. Sharpe dared not leave a dead man in the uniform of the Royal Navy on this shore because that would be the equivalent of leaving a letter saying the British were coming here.

Another ragged volley sounded from the direction of the farm and Sharpe heard the balls passing overhead, while his own Riflemen were responding with measured shots. Someone, Sharpe thought, should extinguish the candles in the farmhouse, but no one had put *deux* and *deux* together to make *quatre*. More fools them, he thought. 'With me, Pat.'

Harris and his Spaniards were waiting on the embankment and Sharpe led them down to the waterlogged pasture, then shouted up to Lieutenant Kelleher. 'Lieutenant? Two men to fill the pit in the roadway!'

'Fill . . .' Kelleher sounded confused.

'Fill the bloody pit, and quickly! And hold those buggers off!'

'Yes, sir.' Kelleher still sounded confused, but he had a couple of Sergeants who would make certain the orders were heard, understood and obeyed.

'If we didn't have Sergeants in this bloody army,' Sharpe grumbled, 'we'd still be back in Lisbon.'

'Very true, sir,' Harper said.

More French musket balls fluttered overhead, some thumping into the embankment.

'Are those buggers getting closer?' Sharpe asked.

'They are,' Harper had superb eyesight. 'There's a tangle of them coming this way,' he paused, 'I think they're trying to be real soldiers! Like making a wee column!'

'Good,' Sharpe said. Kelleher's men on the elevated road were the fork, now it was time to unsheath the knife. 'Let's go!' Sharpe called, just as a man scrambled up the embankment, 'Who's that?'

'Pat Connolly, Mister Sharpe.' Connolly was now wearing Crittenden's cocked hat. 'And that naval fellow isn't dead, Mister Sharpe! He was moaning.'

'He's in the boat?'

'Yes, Mister Sharpe.'

'Then let's go! Lieutenant Harris!'

'Mister Sharpe?'

'We're going, come on!'

Sharpe now led twenty-four men northwards across the soggy pasture. To his right the French were advancing noisily towards the embankment where Sharpe's remaining Riflemen were spitting rifle fire at the dark shapes. Sharpe was leaving those militia men well to his right, planning to make a wide seawards loop before assaulting the farm.

That, at least, was what he had planned. Like any soldier he had tried to anticipate the coming fight and had known it could never be silent. Men died noisily, and he had always known that taking out a whole picquet line in silence was next to impossible. Hagman had succeeded, but Hagman had always been a silent night-killer. Pat Harper had almost succeeded, but the enemy had detected him and the night had been riven by shots, which was precisely what Sharpe had anticipated. It would have been better, he admitted to himself, if the French had never suspected their presence and the Engineers could have completed their work and sailed home, but now that the French were aware of the incursion, Sharpe's aim was to mislead them about the real purpose of the night's work.

It was a pity about Captain Crittenden's death. Evidently the man still lived, but a musket ball in the skull would kill him eventually and Sharpe just hoped there was a seaman in the *Goliath* who could bring the boat back to Saint-Jean-de-Luz, but that was a problem for the future. For now he had to take the farm.

'Harris?'

'Mister Sharpe?'

'Your lads have muskets?'

'Ten of them do.'

'You'll take them into the farmhouse. Noisy as you like, and tell the buggers to plunder it.'

'Oh they'll love that.'

'If anyone resists you can kill them, but not the women.'

'My boys are nasty buggers,' Harris said in warning, 'they all deserve the rope.'

'I'll send Pat in with you, he'll keep them in line.'

'And you, Mister Sharpe?'

'I've a mind to start a fire. Barns usually burn well.'

'And the house too?'

'If you get the women and children out, yes.' Sharpe thought for a second. 'But if any of your men get killed don't leave them to be burned, drag them outside. And Harris.'

'Mister Sharpe?'

'I want a couple of bodies left behind.'

'So I should make sure—'

'That a couple of Spanish-uniformed bodies are left there.' Sharpe glanced behind and saw the musket flames of the advancing French were now well behind him. The militiamen were advancing painfully slowly now, struggling through the soggy ground and, with their numbers being thinned by Riflemen, they were taking every chance to pause, reload and fire. He could hear an officer or Sergeant shouting them forward, but they were reluctant to get closer and that reluctance was more than doubled when Lieutenant Kelleher ordered his musket-armed men to fire, and the embankment's edge was suddenly brilliant with flame that was instantly obscured with powder smoke. Sharpe reckoned Kelleher had fired early, too nervous to allow the enemy closer, but he was doing his job of pinning the French attention on the embankment while Sharpe led his men towards the farmhouse. A wooden fence marked the barrier between pasture and kitchen garden, and Sharpe paused there to tell Harper to accompany Harris's Spaniards. 'I assume there are still soldiers in the house, Pat,' he said, 'and they could well kill a couple of the Spaniards. Make sure their bodies are left in the yard and don't get burned to nothing.'

'Burned, sir?'

'You can burn the house when Harris's lads have looted it.'

'And you don't want the Dagoes burned, sir? They're going to hell anyway, so they are!'

'I do not want them burned. And make sure any women and children are safe before you fire the bloody place.'

'I'll rescue the wains, sir.'

'And when we retreat, we go fast! The same way we came.' By looping to the west they would avoid the retreating militiamen. 'Let's go!'

There would be twenty minutes of chaos, Sharpe thought, but so far the battle, if it could be called a battle, had gone exactly as he had planned. That was satisfying, but he was still outnumbered, and a smart enemy officer could still ruin the night's work. Why weren't they trying to outflank the men defending the embankment? That would have been Sharpe's first move and, done quickly enough, could have captured both boats and all the men, but from the evidence of the musket flames stabbing the night, the fight for the embankment had deteriorated into a duel between the confused French in the pasture and the green-jackets and redcoats on the road. Now Sharpe planned to make the French even more confused.

The wooden fence was demolished by kicking its rotten posts out of the soil. Harris led his men around the northern side of the house and Sharpe heard a door being kicked in and a musket firing followed by cheers, presumably as the Spaniards stormed into the building. Two more muskets sounded, but Sharpe was now past the house, heading for the barn. More muskets sounded in the house and Sharpe supposed that the Frenchmen attacking the embankment would hear those shots and be wondering what new horror was behind them. But it would be ten minutes, Sharpe thought, before any of those men could be back at the farm.

'Connolly!'

'Mister Sharpe?'

'You and I. Let's start making the night worse for those bastards.' He pointed at the distant militiamen who were firing at the embankment from the pasture. Sharpe rested his rifle on the fence that faced southwards and drew back the doghead. He could only see the brief lurid silhouettes of the militiamen outlined by the muzzle flames of their muskets, but they had huddled together, making themselves a larger and more vulnerable target. Sharpe aimed and pulled the trigger. The rifle thumped into his shoulder and he fished out a new cartridge.

'Keane?'

'Mister Sharpe?'

'Take my place and fire at those buggers in the field and don't fire high.'

It would take a few moments before the distant French realised they were under fire from their rear, but eventually they would see the muzzle flashes of the rifles and that would only increase their problems. He heard hoofbeats behind him and turned to see Dromgoole leading two horses from the barn.

'Keep firing,' Sharpe told his two Riflemen, 'and be ready to withdraw when you hear my whistle.'

Sharpe went to the barn to find Flaherty and Rourke driving a dozen sheep out into the night. A lantern, evidently left burning, hung from a rafter and Sharpe could see that one side of the barn was lined with straw palliasses where the militiamen slept. He did a quick, rough count and estimated there were about a hundred mattresses, which suggested the militia had two companies billeted here. He used his sword to cut one palliasse open, then knelt and ripped open a cartridge to spread its powder on the dry straw. He primed the rifle, cocked it, then held the lock against the powder and straw and pulled the trigger. There was a fizzing sound, then small flames started running along the straws. He stood and stepped back, confident that the fire would spread.

'The animals are all safe, Mister Sharpe,' Rourke said.

'Feeling sentimental?' Sharpe asked.

'They're not to blame for the war, Mister Sharpe. And burning is a horrible death for an animal.'

'You're right. So go and join Liam and Tommy at the fence and give some militiamen a horrible death.'

'A pleasure, Mister Sharpe.'

Sharpe kicked a half-dozen palliasses onto the growing flames. In a moment, he knew, that fire would be an inferno that would outline the militiamen struggling across the pasture, making them even easier targets for his Riflemen. He felt an irritation at his enemy's mistakes. Spread your men out, he wanted to shout, send some to the flank! Fight, you bastard! Do something! Don't just stand there and get killed!

But Sharpe now had to get Harris's men out of the house. He ran to its northern side and found two men, two elderly women, and three children standing in a distraught huddle where they were guarded by two Riflemen. One of the men, white-haired, who Sharpe assumed was the farm's owner,

337

nervously tried to intercept Sharpe. *'Buenas noches!'* Sharpe said cheerfully, then pushed past the old man towards the open door of the house, but before he could reach it he heard a woman scream from the top floor. The scream was followed by a musket shot and a body crashed backwards out of the window, splintering the shutters to fall on the farmyard's cobbles. The dead man, his faded yellow jacket splashed with blood, twitched and went still. His breeches were around his ankles. His fellow Spaniards, standing together on the yard's further side, growled in protest, but Pat Harper barked at them to be silent and the volley gun in his hands persuaded them that obedience was the better part of valour.

'All well, Pat?'

'Never better, sir! I've two legs of mutton for breakfast!'

'Good man,' Sharpe answered, then pushed through the door to find himself in a ransacked kitchen, the stone-flagged floor covered in broken dishes and splintered furniture. Three dead French soldiers lay in the wreckage that was illuminated by a blazing fire in the big open hearth. To the right of the hearth a ladder climbed to the upper floor and Sharpe, hearing the girl upstairs sobbing, climbed.

'Quién es?' Harris's voice snarled.

'Sharpe!'

'Oh, hello, Mister Sharpe,' Harris said as Sharpe emerged into a candlelit room where Harris was standing with a musket in one hand. His other hand was stroking the blonde hair of a naked girl who was kneeling at his feet and embracing his legs. 'This is Éloïse, sir,' Harris said, then introduced Sharpe in French. The girl shot Sharpe a look, seemed terrified of his scarred, powder-stained face, and clung tighter to Harris's legs. 'I didn't undress her,' Harris added.

'I assume the bastard who went through the window stripped her?'

'Yes, sir.'

'Tell her she's safe and can get dressed.'

'What happens to her, sir?'

'What do you think? She stays here and gets on with her damned life. What was she? A shepherdess?'

'Probably,' Harris said, 'only I was thinking, sir.'

'You think too much, Harris.'

'I know, sir, but you want the Crapauds to believe this was a raid to plunder a fat farm, isn't that right, sir?'

'More or less.' Sharpe kicked at the pile of clothes that had been pulled from a cupboard.

'Only if we were raiders, sir,' Harris went on, 'we wouldn't leave girls like Éloïse behind, would we?'

Sharpe glanced through the shattered window to see that the barn was burning fiercely.

'You want to take her?' he growled.

'Just look at her, sir.'

Sharpe looked. Éloïse was thin, pale, with a sun-darkened face, and undeniably attractive. 'We can settle her in Saint-Jean-de-Luz,' he said reluctantly, conceding that Harris was right and that no brigand pillaging a farm like this would abandon such a treasure. 'Get her dressed, get her downstairs, and you're responsible for making sure she comes with us.'

'Yes, Mister Sharpe!' Harris said enthusiastically.

'And be quick, I plan to burn this building.'

'Yes, sir! And there's still a dead Spaniard in the front room downstairs, sir. Shot by the French.'

'Be quick, Harris!'

Sharpe dropped down the ladder, found a door to the other downstairs room and seized the dead Spaniard by the ankles and dragged him to the yard.

'Pat!'

'Sir?'

'All your Riflemen here?'

'Every last one, sir.'

'Then back to the boats. Try to avoid the firefight.'

'I always do, sir,' Harper said. The crackle of muskets still sounded in the pasture leading to the embankment, but Sharpe could see that Kelleher's men were still on that embankment and the muzzle flashes of the French militia were no closer than they had been the last time he looked, only now they were illuminated by the burning barn that was giving Sharpe's Riflemen such easy targets. 'I'll stay with you, sir,' Harper said.

'No need, Pat, just get everyone to the boats.'

'My boys will do that, so they will.' Harper's Irish Riflemen were shepherding the remaining Spaniards north towards the estuary. 'They've stolen anything of value,' Harper said, 'knives, forks, ladles, pokers, coats, boots, wine, candlesticks, and cooking pots.'

'And two legs of mutton,' Sharpe added for him.

'Pity to waste them,' Harper said. 'Mutton in vinegar! Delicious. Where in Christ's name is Harris?'

'He's coming,' Sharpe said, and just then Harris appeared at the door with the girl who was now swathed in a thick coat. 'To the boats, Harris!'

'Yes, sir!' He took Éloïse by the arm and hurried her away. She gave a glance towards what Sharpe assumed was her family, but went willingly enough.

Sharpe looked at the two Riflemen guarding the family. 'Keep them there for a minute,' he said, then led Harper into the house. There was a rake beside the door and Sharpe used it to drag the burning wood from the hearth into the kitchen where he tossed the broken chairs and table onto the flames. 'Let's go, Pat.'

Three blasts on his whistle, and they went.

Sharpe was tired, too tired to realise how tired he was, yet duty had insisted he put on what passed for his best uniform, and now he sat in the Admiral's cabin of the *Pucelle*, Sir Joel's old flagship and the same ship in which Sharpe had sailed into the horrors of Trafalgar. The same ship, indeed, in which he had shared his first nights with Lady Grace, and those memories were both sharp and painful.

Sir Joel was the host of this dinner and the guest of honour was Lord Wellington who had been seated beside a young woman in a pale-blue dress cut shamelessly low on her generous breasts and about whose neck hung a diamond-encrusted necklace which, Sharpe reflected sourly, had doubtless come from the dwindling funds he kept with his army agents in London. 'You're a lucky man, Major Sharpe!' Wellington had said earlier, to which Sharpe could only respond tiredly by agreeing with his lordship.

Sir Joel, ebullient as ever, had insisted on retelling the tale of how he had captured the *Revenant* at Trafalgar, outrageously exaggerating Sharpe's role in the battle. Jane had loved every moment of the story. 'Richard only said he had followed you, Sir Joel,' she said, 'and that you were the first to leap on board the enemy!'

'And that was a damned, forgive me ma'am, a very stupid thing to do.'

'A damned brave thing, sir,' Sharpe put in, a verdict that Lieutenant Harry Collier, seated to Sharpe's right, supported by slapping his hand on the polished dinner table.

'We all had to be brave that day,' Sir Joel said. 'Boarding an enemy ship is not unlike your battle at, where was it? Saint-Pierre? You know your boarding party will be outnumbered so you rely on ferocity. I wish you could have seen it, my lord.' He turned to Wellington who appeared to be appraising Jane's necklace. 'Major Sharpe led his rogues down from the crest, bayonets against a horde!'

'I have seen it, Sir Joel,' Wellington said drily. 'I always regret it when necessity demands the use of bayonets, but cannot deny their efficacy.'

'Well I was glad to see it!' Sir Joel said enthusiastically, 'Damned glad! Oh,' he leaned over the diamond-sparkling breasts, 'forgive me ma'am.'

'I am married to a soldier,' Jane said, 'and have heard the word, Sir Joel.' Her remark was followed by laughter from about the table. Apart from Wellington, Sharpe, Jane and one of his lordships's aides, the diners were all naval officers.

'Speaking of which,' Wellington said, 'I was told that General

Hill was heard to use the word at Saint-Pierre. Only the second time he has allowed himself a vulgarity!'

'Really, my lord?' Sharpe asked, 'he swore again?'

'He did! It was that damn fool Peacock,' Wellington explained, 'and Hill could not believe his behaviour! Nor I! But the damned fool is on his way back to England and disgrace.'

'Before long we'll all be home to good old England,' Sir Joel said, 'Boney can't endure much longer?'

'He's a clever man,' Wellington said gloomily, 'and the latest reports show that he's dancing rings about the Prussians and Russians, but let's pray we have peace next year.'

Men slapped the table in agreement and Sharpe leaned back in his chair to watch the red-tinged ripples chasing themselves across the white-painted beams and deckhead, reflections from the harbour water that was coloured by the sunset. The first course, which Sir Joel had announced in French, and which to Sharpe had tasted like fish paste served on burnt toast, had been cleared away and Sir Joel proudly revealed that the main course would be mutton in a vinegar sauce. 'In your lordship's honour,' he had said.

Sharpe was gazing at the ripples and praying there would be no peace, because peace would mean the end of his career. The army would not vanish, of course, there was a war going on in America and India was not entirely pacified, but the army's numbers would be savagely shrunken and Sharpe had no illusions about his chance of being retained. So he would have to scrabble for his living again and do it with an expensive wife. He looked at Jane who was clearly being charmed by both Lord Wellington and Sir Joel.

Wellington's appraisal of Jane's necklace was interrupted by a Midshipman who had requested entrance to the huge stern cabin and now explained that a message had arrived for his lordship. The Midshipman, his errand completed, left and a silence fell on the assembly as Wellington tore open the paper. 'Forgive me, Sir Joel, I was waiting for this. The first reports from inside Bayonne.'

Sir Joel looked surprised. 'You have people there?'

'We have monarchists there who can't wait to see Boney gone,' Wellington said as he read the message. Once read he folded the paper. 'You'll like this, Major Sharpe,' he announced.

'My Lord?'

Wellington was smiling. 'It is reported inside Bayonne that an atrocity was committed last night in the commune of Boucau on the Adour's northern bank. It's being blamed on Spanish soldiery.'

Sharpe could not help smiling. 'I do like it, my lord.'

'A clever ruse, Sharpe, but somewhat ruthless. What would you have done if your Spaniards had somehow stayed alive?'

'Whatever was necessary, my lord.'

'No wonder your men call themselves murderers,' Wellington's tone was sourer, 'and it is a pity that it cost Sir Joel his Flag-captain.' Crittenden had died on the homeward voyage and his body was now somewhere aboard the *Revenant* awaiting burial at sea.

'It is a pity,' Sharpe agreed, 'but at least he lived long enough to give me his opinion.'

'Poor David,' Sir Joel said, 'brave as a lion! And his opinion was?'

Sir Joel had not been in Wellington's headquarters when Sharpe had reported that morning.

Sharpe looked at Sir Joel. 'He told me that the soil of the embankment was too soaked to support his proposed posts, Sir Joel,' he lied, 'and that he concurred with Captain Bisby's notion of using captured eighteen-pounders as anchors instead.'

'A much easier solution!' Sir Joel said, 'and quicker too! That was damned,' he hesitated, then decided he did not need to apologise to Jane, 'damned generous of David! He rather doubted your fellow's expertise.'

'He expressed his admiration for Captain Bisby,' Sharpe continued the lie.

'And you're using five cables?' Wellington asked Sir Joel.

'Five are necessary, my lord.'

'So Bisby needs two more cannon,' Wellington said, 'I'll arrange it. Bayonne is worth two lumps of French iron!'

Most of the officers round the table looked puzzled, but the lumps of iron were not explained and the conversation became general as the lamb was consumed and the first candles lit as the sun sank beneath the western hills.

Sharpe's mood sank with the sun, a gloom centred on his prospects once Napoleon was defeated and the British army would not need Sharpe's skills. He knew those skills, and sensed that he was close to perfecting them, but they had no value in peacetime. He knew he should celebrate peace, but he could not find any happiness for himself in the prospect.

The meal ended after the king was toasted and Sharpe and Jane waited on the quarterdeck as the launch was summoned to take them back to the quay. Jane had her arm through

Sharpe's arm as he gazed at the stern rail where he and Lady Grace had exchanged their first kiss in an Indian Ocean night. Jane withdrew her arm as Lord Wellington approached.

'A word Sharpe?'

His lordship led Sharpe towards the mizzenmast. 'You did damned well, Sharpe.'

'Thank you, my lord.'

'And you brought the other Spaniards home?'

'I did, my lord. They fought well and are back under the Provost's care.'

'I'll recommend their sentences are commuted and that they be sent home.'

'Thank you, my lord.'

A bump sounded as the launch arrived at the *Pucelle*'s side. Wellington crammed on his cocked hat. 'I promised to look after you, Sharpe, and I will. Give my compliments to your lady.'

'Thank you, my lord.'

'We'll be in Paris within a year! Now to our boat.'

The launch carried them across the night-dark harbour. Paris soon, Sharpe thought, and then what? He had no answer.

HISTORICAL NOTE

Sharpe's Storm is set during the final winter of the Peninsular War. Wellington has evicted the French from the Spanish–Portuguese peninsula, crossed the Pyrenees and is now advancing into France itself where, in that final winter, he is fighting a campaign constricted by rivers that provide the French defenders with convenient obstacles.

The opening skirmish in the novel is a fictional account of how most of those rivers were crossed, but once crossed they needed to be bridged, and those bridges were supplied by the Royal Engineers using pontoon bridges. The pontoons were flat-bottomed barges held in place by tensioned cables and their own anchors, and a roadway could be constructed of planks laid athwart the cables. Those bridges were astonishingly durable, but not indestructible, and the description of the storm-riven collapse of the bridge at Villefranque, which was constructed using the heavier river boats, is taken from history.

The destruction of that bridge, even though it was replaced within twenty-four hours, presented Marshal Soult with an opportunity because, just as the novel describes, Wellington's army was divided in half with Sir John Hope's corps on the western bank of the River Nive and Sir Rowland Hill's on the eastern. Soult's army, encamped around Bayonne, outnumbered each of those corps, and Soult's best hope of victory lay in destroying either of the British corps.

His first attempt preceded the loss of the bridge, and those actions at Sir John Hope's headquarters at Barrouillet (near Biarritz) and at the village of Arcangues happened much as described in the novel. That was an attempt to decimate the half of Wellington's forces west of the Nive and failed partly because of the stout defence offered by the British and Portuguese forces and because Wellington was able to bring swift reinforcements from Saint-Jean-de-Luz.

Soult's second attempt followed the destruction of the pontoon bridge at Villefranque and is now known as the Battle of Saint-Pierre which, after the war's conclusion, was described by some British soldiers as the worst of the whole war. It was surely a dreadful slaughter, but ended in a victory for General Hill whose troops repelled an attack by at least three times their own number. I have allowed Sharpe and his fictional battalion to take the place of the 50th Regiment of Foot who defended their hill gallantly and whose left flank was put in serious jeopardy by the behaviour of Sir Nathaniel Peacock who had been placed in command of the 71st, a Scottish regiment that had a fine record in the war.

Sir Nathaniel Peacock, alas, is not a figure of fiction. He existed, and, at the Battle of Saint-Pierre, lost his nerve and ran away, trying to take his battalion with him. Most of that battalion stayed and succeeded in defeating the French column opposed to them, but Sir Nathaniel himself fled as far as the ammunition park where he was discovered flogging Portuguese soldiers and blaming them, quite unjustly, for not supplying his battalion with adequate ammunition. He then claimed to be wounded, though the only injury he suffered was a musket ball through the tails of his coat, which, as one of his officers remarked, did not need a doctor's attention, but a tailor's.

That was the end of Sir Nathaniel's career. He was cashiered from the army, as was Colonel Bunbury, who had retreated with his battalion, the Buffs, from his isolated position far in advance of the British defensive line. I have yet to find any justification for his ill fortune. Indeed, if he had stayed where he had been posted he would surely have been destroyed, and his withdrawal saved a fine battalion, but cost him his career.

The battles on the two banks of the River Nive were desperate affairs in which Wellington's forces were outnumbered, yet fought through to victory, prompting Wellington's comment, 'I will tell you the difference between Soult and me: when he gets into a difficulty, his troops don't get him out of it; mine always do.'

I had always intended the novel to end with a description of the building of the bridge across the estuary of the Adour, and then realised Sharpe could not possibly have witnessed that triumph because he was too busy in *Sharpe's Siege*. So I invented a beach reconnaissance instead, and that fictional foray serves to illustrate the extraordinary difficulties faced by the Royal Navy and Wellington's Engineers when the ambitious plan was put into action. Crossing the bar at the mouth of the river caused boats to be upturned and shattered and too many men drowned, yet enough *chasse-marées* reached the river where they were lined abreast and crossed by five thirteen-inch cables that spanned a river about three hundred yards wide. On the northern bank the cables were 'anchored' by captured French eighteen-pounder siege guns, which were dropped over the embankment and proved more than heavy enough to take the immense strain exerted by five windlasses mounted on a wooden platform on the southern bank. The bridge took less than twenty-four hours to construct and enabled Wellington to despatch troops who would encircle Bayonne. It was an extraordinary achievement, mainly by the Royal Navy, to make such a substantial bridge that turned the left flank of Soult's forces guarding the River Adour. Soult would eventually be driven eastwards to defeat at Orthez, and then, at the war's very end, at Toulouse.

Sharpe's ploy of making his fictional reconnaissance appear to be a raid by vengeful Spanish troops has its roots in truth. Wellington had crossed into France with about thirty-six thousand British troops, twenty-three thousand Portuguese and four thousand five hundred Spaniards, but he was soon forced to send those Spaniards home because they could not be trusted to treat French civilians with respect. That was, perhaps, unsurprising. French behaviour in Spain had been rapacious and bestial towards civilians, and the Spanish were eager and ready to repay them in kind. Yet Wellington understood that such a revenge would probably rouse the French to a guerrilla war as destructive and cruel as the war they had in turn provoked in Spain. The last thing Wellington needed was a hostile population threatening his supply lines or ambushing his troops, and so he gave strict orders that the civilian population was to be treated fairly. The French army had not treated their own civilians well, stealing what food they needed, and that population was pleasantly surprised when Wellington's army paid them for food and forage, though they might have been surprised that the coins with which they were paid were forgeries made by the British army. Wellington had gathered every forger from his ranks, supplied them with silver, and set them to manufacturing French coinage, and the result was that there was no popular uprising by the French population who, on the whole, welcomed the British army. Sadly the Spanish could not be kept in France, simply because their actions were liable to make enemies from civilians, and so they were sent home. Sharpe secures just enough of them to disguise his foray as a raid.

I usually end Sharpe's stories by promising that Sharpe and Harper will march again. I hope they do, but can make no promises. Finally, regrettably, I must note that Sharpe lost a great supporter last year with the death of Susan Watt, who edited all his adventures and continually urged me to reveal more of Sharpe's emotions. He would be devastated by Susan's untimely death, but always remember her as a great editor and a dear friend.

The SHARPE Series

Short stories

THE STARBUCK CHRONICLES

REBEL

COPPERHEAD

BATTLE FLAG

THE BLOODY GROUND

THE WARLORD CHRONICLES

THE WINTER KING

THE ENEMY OF GOD

EXCALIBUR

FOOLS AND MORTALS

GALLOWS THIEF

A CROWNING MERCY

FALLEN ANGELS
(Originally published under the name Susannah Kells,
the pseudonym of Bernard Cornwell and his wife, Judy.)

Non-Fiction

WATERLOO: THE HISTORY OF FOUR DAYS,
THREE ARMIES AND THREE BATTLES